THE SHADOW OF MALABRON

THE SHADOW OF MALABRON

THE PERILOUS REALM
× BOOK ONE ×

THOMAS WHARTON

CANDLEWICK PRESS

Copyright © 2008 by Thomas Wharton

First U.S. edition 2009

Library of Congress Cataloging-in-Publication Data
Wharton, Thomas, date.
The shadow of Malabron / by Thomas Wharton. —1st ed.
p.   cm. —(The perilous realm ; bk. 1)
Summary: When Will, a rebellious teen, stumbles from
the present into the realm where stories come from,
he learns he has a mission concerning the evil Malabron and,
aided by some of the story folk, he faces a host of perils
while seeking the gateless gate that will take him home.
ISBN 978-0-7636-3911-2
[1. Fantasy.]   I. Title. II. Series.
PZ7.W54812Sh 2009
[Fic]—dc22   2009007768

2 4 6 8 10 9 7 5 3 1

Printed in the United States of America

This book was typeset in Palatino and Integrity Lining.

Candlewick Press
99 Dover Street
Somerville, Massachusetts 02144

visit us at www.candlewick.com

For Ronan

You will journey to strange storylands. . . .

— The Book of Errantry

IN A CHAMBER HIGH IN A TOWER, a young woman sits at a loom, weaving threads of many colors into a tapestry so large that it pools around her feet, half covering the chamber's marble floor. When her people first went to war, years ago now, she began to weave the story of their struggle against the enemy that threatened all the world. Everyone who has come to see the tapestry take shape has marveled at the young woman's skill. When you gaze at the intricately woven threads, they seem to move, and change, and reveal more than you had thought was there. The more you gaze, the more there is to see, until you feel you have been drawn into the tapestry yourself and have become part of its weave.

The long work is almost finished. At one end of the tapestry rise the dark clouds, like billowing towers of shadow, from which the hosts of the enemy first marched, spreading fear and death across the land. From there the images sweep across the weave like a rushing tide of story, a story of blood and battle, of bravery and death, of hope lost and found again. And at the end of the tapestry the young woman is still working on, a city rises into the bright morning sky. A city of gleaming towers and crystal fountains upon a mighty rock in the sea. It is the city where the young woman lives with her brother. While she is famed for her weaving, he is known far and wide for his wondrous craft at metalworking. In years past, he made beautiful cups and candlesticks for his people, but for a long time now he has forged only blades and armor. From his smithy at the base of the tower, the sound of his hammer rings day and night.

They are there in the tapestry as well. She has woven her brother working in his smithy and herself in the tower room, where she can be seen pausing for a moment from her work and gazing out through the window, across the waves to the dark wooded shore of the mainland, not yet touched by the light of morning. She has worked all through the night, but she will not finish the tapestry today. The story it tells is not over.

Years ago, on the eve of war, she promised her hand to a brave and noble young man, a prince of the realm. When her betrothed rode away to battle, he swore he would not return until victory was at hand. And now reports have been coming from the distant battlefields that this day is not far off. Her betrothed is said to be riding home even now with a band of heralds, bringing joyous news of the war's end. The young woman gazes long at the causeway that links the island city to the shore. It is empty: no troupe of gladly singing knights crosses it yet today. As she watches sea and shore, her hand strays to the tapestry. Her fingers feel their way across the warp and weft. She has worked on these threads for so long that she knows them by touch.

The causeway in her tapestry is the same as the one outside her window: untraveled, but with space left to weave an army of victory with her betrothed at its head.

Then she sees something that makes her heart beat faster. From the trees on the shore, a great flock of birds rises and wheels in the sky. Something passing through the forest has disturbed them.

She rises eagerly from the loom and descends the tower in haste to meet her brother at his forge. He sees the look on her face, and his eyes widen with hope.

"Is it finished?" he asks.

"Soon," she says, and hurries out. The streets are mostly deserted at this early hour. At the stables she takes a horse and gallops across the great causeway as the bells of the city ring to greet the morning. On the mainland she plunges down a pathway lined with tall white standing stones into the forest.

As she slips under the shadows of the trees, she senses that something is wrong. She can hear no birds, and the air is icy, much colder than it should be at this season. The hoofbeats of her mount on the hard earth are the only sounds to be heard. She rides on until the white stones give out and she is deep within the forest's shade.

There horror meets her eyes. From the branches of a dead tree hang blackened, lifeless bodies. From the remnants of their armor, she knows these are her own people, the knights who had been guarding the forest paths.

The horse shies, and she forces it on, her heart cold with dread. All at once she feels herself pass with a shiver through an invisible web of enchantment. Still she keeps on, until she comes to a clearing and beholds a sight that freezes her blood.

The horse bolts in fear, and she is thrown to the ground.

Picking herself up, she flees back through the deathly silent woods to the causeway, her one thought to warn her people. When she is halfway across the water, she hears a slow clop of hoofbeats behind her, and she whirls, prepared to fight for her life. Riding slowly toward her on a horse armored for war is a man she does not at first recognize. Then her heart leaps.

It is him. He has returned.

His eyes meet hers, and she shudders with a strange foreboding. Her betrothed wears a cloak as sleek and black as a raven's wing, not the bright cloak she wove for him when he rode out to battle so long ago. He is not that young man anymore.

She runs to him. He lifts her into the saddle before him and holds her tightly.

"In the forest," she gasps. "An army of the enemy, hidden by spellcraft. We must warn the city."

"I know of the army," he says. "You are cold. Here."

He unclasps his black cloak and throws it over her shoulders.

"We must ride faster," she says. "There is no time to lose."

"But haste will raise alarm among the sentries," he replies, and his voice chills her. His smile is thin and mocking. "I do not want them alarmed. That would spoil the joyous moment of my return, when all the city will open its doors to welcome me."

Turning to look into his eyes, she sees the truth of what he has become.

She tries to tear herself away, but he holds her in an iron grip. As she struggles against him, she catches a glimpse of the sea far below. The waves are slowing, their crests going hoary white and still. The waves are turning to ice. The sea itself will soon become a passage for the enemy.

A cry of terror and despair wells up in her then, but no sound comes from her throat.

"You will not speak again," he says, his voice as hard as his arms about her.

To her horror she feels her body changing form. Her very bones scream with pain as they shrink and twist into inhuman shapes. She tears at the cloak, but it is no longer something separate from her. Its black feathers are her feathers, their roots embedded in her flesh. She holds her arms before her and sees that they have become wings.

She gives a rasping shriek of horror and turns against her betrothed, her beak stabbing at his eye. He cries out and his grip loosens. Breaking free, she beats her wings frantically and rises, out of his reach. She is flying, higher and higher above the waves. The feeling of freedom that wells up in her is almost enough to overcome her terror. Then she sees the glaze of ice spreading across the water, the black clouds massing over the forest, driven on a sudden icy gale, and she speeds toward the city.

Reaching the walls at last, she alights on the battlements. Somehow she must warn the sentries not to let the traitor through the gates. When she tries to speak, the only sounds that come from her throat are shrill croaks. The sentries have no idea what to make of this strange black bird and its frenzied cries. They shoo her away, and then there is a glad shout. *The prince is returning.* He is on the causeway. The call goes out to open the gates. The trumpets of welcome sound above the roar of the wind.

Her last hope is her brother. She soars down through the city to the tower and through her own window. Her brother is there, admiring the unfinished tapestry. He turns in surprise at the sight of a raven perched on the back of his sister's chair. He does not recognize her. With soothing words he approaches the trembling bird, thinking that it lost its way in the fierce gale that has suddenly sprung up.

Desperate for a way to warn him, she flaps over to the tapestry, alights on it, and with her beak and talons tears at the gleaming city woven there. He cries out and hurries to stop her, then pauses and watches as the bird rends only the walls and towers of the city. As the weaving falls in tatters, he understands, without knowing how it could be, that this creature is his sister. And he sees what she is trying to show him.

"The city," he says in a horrified whisper. "The enemy is here. . . ."

The raven croaks frantically and hops onto his shoulder. He strokes her black wing.

"How?"

She cannot answer, and there is no time. They leave their house together to spread the alarm, but it is already too late. The streets are crowded with people milling in fear and confusion. Somewhere close by a child is screaming for its mother. As they push through the throng, they hear the clash of swords growing louder, the roars and cries of battle drawing nearer. The earth shudders and groans beneath them, as if the very stones of the city have been struck a mortal blow. The streets crack open, and the crystal fountains run red. When they gaze up into the blackening sky, they see that the city's gleaming towers have begun to burn.

They understand then that the story they have always known is over and that a new one is about to begin. Where it will take them, and how it might end, there is no telling.

1

*It is when you have already gone too far
that your journey truly begins.*

— *The Quips and Quiddities of Sir Dagonet*

WILL HAD TAKEN THE MOTORCYCLE. He couldn't believe
he had done it, but here he was, zooming down the highway with the wind buffeting him in the face and the bike
humming powerfully beneath him. He scanned the road
ahead for any sign of the brightly colored tents he had seen
earlier. The late afternoon sky was darkening with thick
clouds. It looked like rain.

Will hunkered down over the handlebars. He was in a lot
of trouble, but there was no turning back now.

He hadn't expected the day to turn out like this. The
Lightfoot family had been on the road since early morning.
It was the third day of their cross-country trip to a new
home. On the first day Will had played Goblin Fortress on
his gamebook until he was sick of it. On the second day he'd
played I-Spy and other kiddie car games with his little sister,

Jess, and wondered if he'd ever been so bored in his entire life. On the third afternoon they passed the hundredth field with cows in it, and he knew for certain he had never been so bored in his entire life. He was staring out the window of the camper at nothing in particular, dazed with boredom and half asleep, when he glimpsed something up ahead that woke him right up.

On the left side of the highway, behind a stand of trees, rose the colorful pennants and pavilions of what looked to be some sort of fair or amusement park.

He nudged Jess. She looked up, and her eyes widened.

"Dad, look at that!" Will shouted.

"Look at what?" Dad said without a glimmer of interest. After three days behind the wheel, he had become a robot, Will thought. A cranky, unshaven robot. And there was another day of driving still to go.

They were getting closer to the amusement park. Will could see tents, flags, the towers of what looked like a real castle. And the snowy top of a huge pavilion painted to look like a mountain. He thought he could hear music, the happy shrieks of kids having fun, and could even smell the mouth-watering scents of popcorn and cotton candy.

Then he saw the sign. A long banner strung between two spindly trees, inviting him in thin, spidery letters to visit

THE PERILOUS REALM
Enter if you dare.
Explore the
HAUNTED FOREST
THE SCARY-GO-ROUND
THE DRAGON'S LAIR
And much, much more!
Something Is Always Happening Here.

The turnoff was coming up fast. Will could see a narrow dirt road snaking into the trees. The sun was going down, and lanterns had already been lit among the branches as if to show the way.

"Let's stop here," he said. "This place looks amazing."

"It's just some flea-bitten old tourist trap," Dad said with a snort.

He wasn't slowing down.

"You don't know that," Will shot back. "Let's just have a look."

"Let's just find a campsite," Dad grumbled. "Maybe we can come back later."

They flew past the turnoff. The tents and flags quickly dwindled to bright specks in the distance, then vanished around the next bend in the road. Will kept talking about what he had seen, in the swiftly fading hope that he could wear Dad down. He tried to get Jess worked up, too, thinking that her voice added to his would tip the scales, but once the amusement park was out of sight, she quickly lost interest. Will wasn't really surprised. Since Mum had died, Jess had become very quiet. She rarely smiled and never laughed. She followed Will around all the time, and whenever he and Dad had one of their arguments, she would hold Will's hand without saying a word. Sometimes he would forget she was there at all.

They drove on and on, and then Dad suddenly pulled off into a big campsite for recreational vehicles. There weren't many other campers in the place, and they soon found a site to park in. Dad shut off the rattling engine of their old rust bucket of a camper and stretched.

"So let's go," Will said eagerly.

"Go where?" Dad asked, clearly having forgotten.

"To the Perilous Realm."

Dad laughed.

"You've got to be kidding," he said. "I've had a long day's drive, and now I've got to make dinner. The place is probably closed for the day anyhow. I bet they've already pulled up stakes and moved on. With money from a lot of suckers."

"It's not late," Will snapped. "There's still lots of time if we go now."

Dad gave him a black look, and then his eyes softened. He glanced at Jess, who was standing nearby, wide-eyed and silent as usual. Then he turned to Will again.

"Will, I really need you to . . ." he began, then he lowered his head and sighed. "Just give it a rest, OK?" he finished, and climbed into the back of the camper to start unloading the camping gear.

Jess tugged Will's sleeve. He knew what that meant, so he walked with her to the toilets up the winding campground road. As usual she tried to take his hand, but he shook her off.

There were spiderwebs in the windows of the building, and a trash can overflowing with discarded food and drink containers near the door. While he waited for Jess outside, Will pictured the tents, the bright flags, the beckoning lights. *Something Is Always Happening Here,* the sign had promised.

Will looked around. Smoke from campfires wafted through the air. From nearby came the sound of country music playing on a tinny radio. Farther away a dog was barking its stupid head off.

"Nothing is always happening here," Will muttered.

A big truck roared by him in the other lane and brought Will's attention back to what he was doing. He could feel the bike wobbling under him as he was buffeted by the truck's wake. For an instant he and the driver had exchanged glances. *A kid on a bike in this weather?* the driver's look had said. Will knew he should slow down, but he had to get off the highway and into the fairground before the rain got worse. He needed to finish this.

The road ahead looked just the same as the road behind. He had been riding long enough, he thought, to have returned by now to the spot where he'd seen the amusement park. There was no way they could have already packed up the tents and moved on. But there was no sign of the lanterns among the trees.

"I won't go back!" he shouted above the roar of the bike and the wind.

He had been angry ever since the day Mum told them she was going into the hospital. He had guessed from the way she and Dad talked that she might not get well again, but even so, he never really thought the worst would happen. And so fast. One day she was there; the next she was gone.

He couldn't believe it was . . . almost three years ago. Jess could hardly remember her. Will thought of her every day. And then a month ago, Dad had announced at dinner that he'd found a new job, as a welder on a big construction project out west, and that they would be moving. Leaving the house where Will and Jess had grown up. The house that Will had come home to every afternoon for the last three years with the hope that he might open the door and find her there, baking something in the kitchen or sitting in a wicker chair on the back porch reading a book. She would dry her hands on her apron, or put down the book and call him to come in and tell her what had happened at school that day.

It was a good job and a great opportunity, Dad had said. For all of them. But Will didn't see it. It was as if his dad was trying to forget. Trying to make them all forget. He'd told himself he wasn't going to let that happen. And so he'd tried to act as if they weren't really moving. He shut himself in his room or stayed out late with his friends, and refused to pack up his things. In the end, though, he'd had no choice. He couldn't win.

When Will and Jess had gotten back to the van, Dad had taken his beloved antique motorcycle down from the rack on the rear of the camper. He'd had to bring the bike along with them, even though almost everything else they owned was coming later in a moving van.

"The old girl's pretty dusty," he said to Will, and held out a plastic bucket. "Why don't you clean her up while I make dinner, and later I'll let you take her for a spin around the campground."

Will took the bucket, held it at arm's length for a moment, then let it drop. It hit the ground with a hollow thunk and rolled to Jess's feet. She bent and picked it up. Dad looked at Will for a long moment without speaking. Then he rubbed his forehead and turned away.

"Grow up, Will," he said over his shoulder.

He climbed back into the camper and soon could be heard banging around in the cupboards. Will turned and saw Jess, still standing there holding the bucket.

"What are you looking at?" Will snapped. She stared wide-eyed at him without speaking.

As Will turned away angrily, he caught sight of Dad's keys on the picnic table next to his jacket. He picked them up and opened the locket that Dad kept on the key ring. In the photograph inside, Mum was smiling, holding a sun hat on her head to keep the wind from blowing it away. Will remembered that the picture had been taken at the lake, the summer before she died. He remembered how he and Dad had come back to the log cabin from their canoe trip, joking about something or other, and Dad had snapped the picture just after Mum said, *What are the pair of you laughing about?* She was already sick then, but she hadn't told Will or Jess. She'd wanted them all to have one last happy time together.

He snapped the locket shut and slid the motorcycle key off the ring.

"I'm going," he said quietly.

"Where?" Jess asked.

"Nowhere. Don't worry about it."

"Don't go, Will," she said.

He ignored her and went over to the motorcycle. He took hold of the handlebars and lifted the kickstand, then began to push the bike out of the campsite. When he was on the road, he looked back at Jess. She was watching him, the bucket still in her hand. She lifted her other hand and waved.

Will frowned and gave her a quick wave back. Then he turned, broke into a trot, and hopped onto the bike. He'd only ever been allowed to ride it up and down the street in front of their house, under Dad's supervision, but he had learned enough to start the engine and ride on his own.

A moment later he was roaring away from the camp. He heard his father shouting his name, but he didn't look back.

As Will rounded a long curve, he saw another vehicle approaching in the opposite lane, and with a jolt he realized it was a police car. At that moment it occurred to him that he wasn't wearing a helmet and that he had no license. He tried to think of a story that might get him out of this mess, but his frantic thoughts wouldn't latch on to anything. All he could do was keep riding as if nothing were wrong, and a few moments later the police car shot past him. He started to relax a little, thinking he'd been lucky, and then glanced in the rearview mirror.

The police car was slowing down to make a turn, and its red and blue lights were flashing.

At the back of his mind a voice told him that his little adventure was over. He should pull over, stop, and face what was coming to him. But he kept on riding, as if his hands were frozen to the handlebars.

Then, out of the rain, there were lights by the side of the road. And there was the huge banner, shining eerily in the twilight. Will squinted into the rain and saw it just ahead, the narrow dirt track leading off from the highway down an embankment.

There was no time to think. He leaned into the turn and dived down the track, his one thought that maybe he could reach the parking lot, ditch the bike, and hide among all the other people who were sure to be at the fairground. As he passed under the banner, he saw that it was badly tattered, the inscription on it faded and almost unreadable. It hadn't looked like that when he first saw it. He ignored that and peered into the gloom, hoping to see lights ahead, but the dirt track had plunged into dark woods and only grew bumpier and narrower, so that he had to slow right down to avoid crashing into the trees. There were no lanterns. The trees and tall undergrowth on either side leaned in like the walls of a dimly lit cave.

Will tried to remember where the switch was to turn on the headlight, but he was too busy keeping his eyes on the path to search for it. Then all of a sudden he slammed on the brakes.

There was no more road.

Ahead of him loomed a wall of leaves and branches. The bike skidded on the wet ground, and with a sickening sense of the inevitable, Will felt it slide underneath him. Then the front wheel struck something, and the bike flipped violently. Will felt himself lifted from the seat and tossed head over heels through the air. He had time to wonder how much this was going to hurt, and then he was crashing into a green darkness that swallowed everything.

2

If you ever get lost, remember:
either your map is wrong
or the world is.

— The Book of Errantry

WILL CLIMBED TO HIS FEET. He felt dazed, and slightly sick, as if he had just been woken suddenly from a deep sleep. He touched his arms, his head. Nothing hurt. There was no blood. Nothing was broken.

It was dark here under the trees, darker than it should have been, he thought. The rain had stopped, and the air was full of the pungent scent of wet earth. Apart from the wind in the trees and the distant chirping of birds, all was quiet. There was no sign of the motorcycle, but around him were scattered what looked like the remains of an amusement park: wooden stakes in the ground, and bits of rope and shreds of canvas hanging in the trees. Other than that, there was nothing to tell him that he hadn't landed right in the middle of nowhere. He turned in a circle, not sure which way he had come from or which way to go.

Then he saw the red and blue lights flickering through the leaves.

Will turned and ran the other way as fast as he could. It was not easy. The undergrowth grew thick and tangled around him. He was scratched and clawed at by thorns and branches. After struggling for as long as he could, he had no choice but to stop and catch his breath. At least the lights of the police car had vanished, but there was still no sign of the fairground. Where were the lights, the tents, the noise, and the crowds of people?

As he stood there, breathing heavily, he became aware of a faint, far-off sound, a delicate musical ringing like that made by bells or wind chimes. The wind rose and stirred the leaves, drowning out the sound, and Will waited, straining to hear. As the wind fell, the sound returned. It was louder now, and it had a tune, Will realized. A slow, enticing melody that rang softly in his ears like a vague memory.

It had to be the Perilous Realm. He was close. He was almost there.

He plunged on in what he thought was the right direction, eagerly pushing tall stems and twining branches out of his path. And then in front of his reaching hands there was nothing but empty air. He stumbled forward, nearly falling.

A wide clearing lay before him, dotted with white flowers that glowed in the light of the setting sun and gave off a sweet, familiar scent. Like the ringing sounds, he knew this scent from somewhere just out of reach of his memory.

In the middle of the clearing, on a rise, stood a huge tree.

The tree was cloven almost in two down the middle, as if it had once been struck by lightning. One half was dead, its bare black limbs tangled and twined together like a withered nest. The other half was topped by a vast canopy of bright green leaves stirred by a faint cool breeze and winking in the last golden light of the vanishing sun. Only the lower trunk was whole, its bark thickly gnarled and cloaked in moss.

Will approached the great tree and stood beneath it. He had found the source of the mysterious chimes. Small shards of glass or metal hung by silver threads from the branches, like some weird kind of fruit. As they stirred in the evening wind, they jostled one another and were set ringing.

The world seemed half asleep, as dazed as he felt.

"I'm dead," Will said out loud. He wasn't sure why he said it, or even if he believed it, but the thought gave him a strange feeling of calm.

As the shards bobbed and turned, he saw his own reflection flit brokenly across their surfaces.

Mirrors, he realized. There were dozens of them, hanging high and low all over the tree. Some of the pieces of mirror were large and jagged, some slender and delicate, others dark and smoky like volcanic glass.

He reached out and nudged the three nearest mirror shards in front of him, setting them softly ringing again. The sound they made was beautiful, even more so than he had thought before, but still he felt an uneasy prickling along the back of his neck. Who had hung the mirrors here, and why? He had the urge to turn around and find his way back to the bike, if he could, even if that meant facing up to what he had done. But then he would be leaving the mirrors and their music behind. All at once the temptation came to slip one of the shards off the branch and take it with him.

He stepped closer and peered at the shards as they turned upon their threads, catching glimpses of his own face. In each shard what he saw was blurred or distorted, like the images in a funhouse. In one, his face was long and thin, as though he had been stretched like a rubber band. In another his image was blurred and indistinct, as though he were looking at it underwater. The third mirror made him recoil and then laugh: in it his face had been squashed and warped almost beyond recognition as a face. He looked like some sort of misshapen goblin out of a book of fairy tales.

Eagerly Will moved away from the first group of mirrors toward the others. He went from shard to shard with the same result, always hazy or ridiculous, until he came to the largest one yet, revolving slowly by itself on its string, untouched by any of the others. Will reached up and took this mirror shard in his hand. This time he did not laugh.

The face in the mirror was his own, but it had changed in a way unlike in the other shards. The hair was longer and wilder than his, the skin was deeply tanned, the mouth set and determined. It was him, but not him. It was a Will Lightfoot who had seen more than he had. More of the world. He had the odd thought that he would like to know this Will Lightfoot.

The mirror caught a beam of sunlight slanting through the leaves. For an instant Will was blinded by the flash, and when he could see again, what he beheld in the mirror froze him in horror.

The eyes in his reflected face were someone else's eyes. Lightless, unwavering eyes that peered at him through the mask that his own face had become. Someone was watching him through his own reflection. And with a terrible certainty he knew that the mind behind the eyes was cold and pitiless, that it had read his thoughts and learned his name and where he had come from, and knew where he was right now.

Will struggled to look away, but found himself unable to move, or even shut his eyes. He felt the grip of an iron will that sought to hold him for its own purpose. And yet, even as he fought with it, he was also aware of what was happening around him in the clearing. The sunlight had dimmed, and there were more sounds now, faint murmurings and whisperings not made by the wind in the trees.

With a last desperate effort, Will tore his gaze away from the shard and stumbled backward. He regained his balance, his breath coming in gasps. When he looked around, he was startled to see that while he had been standing in front of the mirror—hadn't it only been a few moments?—twilight had fallen. The clearing was cloaked in blue shadows.

Will turned in circles, no longer knowing which way he had come. In every direction, the woods were dark and uninviting.

Then he saw the lights. Cold white beams were bobbing and weaving through the trees. It had to be the police, searching for him in the woods with flashights. He had no thought of running from them now.

"I'm here!" he shouted, and started toward them, but halted when he noticed that the lights were acting strangely. They seemed to be moving together, merging, into larger, glowing shapes.

Will stood transfixed. The lights had merged into three pale figures moving among the trees, slowly approaching the clearing. He stared harder, unsure of what he was seeing. They were people, as far as he could tell, but there was something strange about the way they moved, as if their feet were not touching the earth but flowing over it, like water or smoke. As they approached, they became clearer to him, their outlines sharper.

One was a tall, stern-looking man in a long coat. Another was a girl about Jess's age, wearing a white dress, her long flowing hair streaming slowly about her, as though she were walking underwater.

A glad shout of recognition died in his throat. It must be them, but it couldn't be. . . . He shuddered, without knowing why.

The third shape remained hazy and difficult to see. It seemed to be a woman in a long cloak or nightgown, but it lingered farther away from him than the other two, and he could not make out its features. He was suddenly the most afraid of this figure and turned away from it.

There was little doubt now about the other two. Will blinked and stared.

"Dad?" he said, stepping forward. "Jess?"

They kept approaching slowly, never taking their eyes off him, though they did not speak. He called their names again with growing unease. As the man and the girl drew closer, he saw that their eyes were fixed on him not with love or even recognition, but with cold watchfulness, like the eyes he had seen in the mirror.

"Who are you?" he shouted, and fear slid through him like icy water. All at once he knew that these things were not like him, that they were not even beings of flesh and blood. His one thought now was escape, but a strange feeling, like a cold electric charge, was flooding through his limbs. When he tried to move, he felt something hindering him, holding him rooted where he was, just as it had been when the eyes had watched him from the mirror shard. He felt a numb paralysis rising through his limbs, and he cried out.

The pale shapes came to a halt. At first Will thought his cry had stopped them, but then he heard another sound, faint but growing louder. A chorus of many voices, high and low, raised in an eerie, ululating shriek.

The three figures turned in search of the source of the sound, and as they did their bodies and faces seemed to waver, quivering like reflections on water. Swiftly all three began to retreat as one, receding until once more they became dim, smoky shadows and then vanished altogether.

Whatever power had held Will now let him go, and he sank to his knees, trembling. The unearthly chorus grew louder and seemed to be coming from all directions at once. Will stared wildly around. There was no telling what was about to appear out of the trees. He climbed shakily to his feet, turned and ran heedlessly, thinking only to get away from the tree, the clearing, and the impossible things he had seen there. He stumbled headlong through the undergrowth, slapping blindly at the clutching branches in his path.

When he came out into a more open space, he bolted forward, tripped over an exposed tree root, and fell heavily to the earth. He lay stunned for a moment, and then, as he scrambled to his feet, a hand gripped his arm.

"No!" he shouted, pulling away violently. He twisted around and saw that it was a girl, about his age, in a long, dark red cloak. Under the shade of her hood, her eyes glittered like pale green stones. Her hand gripped the handle of a knife that hung in a leather sheath from her belt.

"Follow me," she whispered. "Now."

"I have to get out of here," Will said. "I have to—"

The girl began to speak and then broke off. She raised her head, and her eyes darted around, as though she saw or heard something that Will could not. When she turned to him again, there was fear in her voice.

"If you want to live, follow me."

With that she turned and started off at a run through the trees. Will hesitated, his thoughts whirling madly, and then he followed.

3

Here's a house with good eating,
No beating, no meeting
With enemy's blade.
Daylight conceals it; midnight reveals it.
If you've been there, you wish you had stayed.

— *The Quips and Quiddities of Sir Dagonet*

THE GIRL RAN SO SWIFTLY through the shadows that Will began to wonder if she could see like a cat in the dark. He followed, but it was all he could do just to keep her in sight. The wind strengthened and the air grew sharper. When the clouds parted, stars appeared, more numerous and much brigher than Will had ever seen them at home. After a time he felt a cool breeze on his face and looked up to see that they had come out of the trees into a wide glade of tall reeds that bowed and whispered in the wind. He could hear the sound of water nearby, and soon they came to the bank of a narrow stream that shimmered like a vein of silver in the moonlight.

The girl found a track beside the water, and they followed it to a narrow stone bridge. Once on the other side, they plunged again into deep woods. Here the ground was bare, but rockier, so that Will stumbled several times on protruding stones.

Finally he could go no farther and sagged against a mossy boulder. The girl stopped and came back to him.

"I just need to catch my breath," he said sheepishly.

The girl tossed back her hood and gazed out into the shadows. She stood motionless for a long moment, and Will noticed that her clothes looked like the sort of thing people wore in the *old* olden days. Her long red hair was tied back and held with a silver ring. She took a bulging leather bag from inside her red cloak and handed it to him. He examined it, then glanced questioningly at her.

"It's water," she said. "That's all."

Will pulled out the cork plug, tilted the bag, and drank. The water was ice-cold and delicious. He took a longer, gulping swig and then handed the bag back. The girl took a brief sip, wiped her mouth, then looked warily around them.

"Can you go on?" she asked Will.

He nodded. "I'm fine."

From the weathered pack slung over her shoulder, the girl produced an object wrapped in a black cloth. She unwound the cloth, revealing a small lantern with diamond-shaped glass panes. She held the lantern up, unlit, and started off again. Will waited a moment and then followed.

"That might be more useful," he said, "if you actually lit it."

"It will light on its own," the girl answered, "when we find the place I'm looking for."

Will pondered that for a moment.

"Heaven?" he finally said.

The girl darted him a puzzled look.

"A snug," she said.

Will gave her a puzzled look in return.

"A shelter for travelers," she explained, "with fire and food and beds. We can hide there for a while. Without the waylight, we won't find it."

It was, and was not, an answer. All it led to, for Will, were other questions.

"Where am I?" he asked, more to himself than to the girl.

"This is the Wood," the girl said, "in a land called the Bourne. I think you've come from . . . somewhere else. Somewhere very far away."

He had no idea what she was talking about, and he was tired of mysterious answers.

"So who are you?" he shot back. "Red Riding Hood?"

The girl shook her head. "She doesn't live here," she said flatly.

"Do you?" he asked.

"Not in the Wood, if that's what you mean. I heard the ringing of the mirrors as I was on my way home. I stopped to find out what it was. It's just luck I was nearby."

"This isn't happening," Will said, shaking his head.

"It is," the girl said. "So you'd better come with me. This is no night to be out here alone."

As much as he wanted to, Will could not argue with that.

In the dark of the Wood, the keeper of the mirror shards came to collect his master's trinkets. Silently he plucked them one by one off the branches of the cloven tree and slipped them into his cloak. Near him three pale figures hovered indistinctly, bereft of purpose, like fading dreams. With a thought he sent them on their way. They had failed him, but the boy who had looked into the shards still had to be found. There would be time later for their punishment. A fetch had no solid form, but it possessed enough awareness of its existence that it could be threatened with extinction. With nothingness. How desperately these shades still clung to the dying echo of their being, even if that echo was little more than a cry of fear.

When there was time, he would remind them who they served. He would drag them to the edge of the void and make them gaze into it, as had been done to him. But that would have to wait. There was a trail to follow, and it was already going cold.

Somewhere in the dark, an owl hooted. The keeper of the shards paused and looked about the clearing. For the briefest instant, there was the sense of a presence nearby, a shiver of recognition, and then it was gone.

He had been in this borrowed shape for many long years, and his memory of the life he once knew was cold and insubstantial, like the creatures that served him. But it returned to him now, that other life. A memory that flared brightly and swiftly faded. The faint tang of sea air. The gleam of sunrise on the highest turret of a white tower. The carefree laughter of a girl.

The heart of the keeper of the shards had burned to ash in another age. But the body he wore now was still capable of faint shadows of feeling. Enough that his flesh could still crawl with foreboding when his memories were stirred. That long-abandoned story was not over. His master had not yet devoured it. And with that troubling thought, as always, came rage, and hatred, and beneath them the emptiness he carried within like a gaping mouth. These goads were enough to move him to greater urgency.

The disturbing new thread in the weave of things had eluded him, for now. But he would find it again. He was a hunter of the Shadow Realm. There were other paths open to him than those of the daylight world. Other ways to lure his prey. He could walk in the dreams of those who had looked into the shards. He could search for them within their own desires and fears.

In moments the cloven tree was free of the mirror shards

and stood alone in the clearing, gazed upon only by the stars.

The girl hurried on, and Will struggled to keep up with her. The wind had risen and branches whipped into his face as he plodded on. Finally, to his immense relief, the girl stopped. She still held the lantern before her, but now it had begun to glow, giving off a pale blue light.

Will turned in a circle. The woods looked the same as they did everywhere else, shadowy and cheerless.

"There's nothing here," he said, close to her ear. And then, as soon as he said it, he turned once more and peered into the darkness. A faint blue light glimmered in the dark, so faintly that he wasn't sure it was really there.

Will nudged the girl and pointed.

"That's it," she nodded. "Every snug has its own way-light. It glows only when another one draws near. Come on. There will be shelter, and food."

She started off in the direction of the light. The word *food* made Will aware how hungry he was. Despite the strange things the girl was saying, the thought of a roof over his head and a meal was enough to spur him on.

They hurried as quickly as they could, and the light grew stronger and flickered less, until at last they came to a sort of bower formed by many intertwined branches, like a huge bare wreath. In the midst of this cavelike hollow, almost invisible in the shadows, stood what appeared to be the gnarled trunk of a tree, until Will saw a polished wooden handle and realized it was a door. A small wicker lantern hung above it, and as Will and the girl approached, its light shone out even brighter, then dimmed to a faint pulsing glimmer and went out.

The girl turned the handle and pushed the door gently,

opening it only a little way. Warm yellow firelight spilled out through the gap. She ducked her head inside and back out again.

"Come on," she said to Will, and he followed quickly, not wanting to be left outside alone even for a moment. He slipped sideways through the door as she had and stepped into the snug.

Inside there was no one to be seen, but everything looked as though it had just been prepared for their arrival. Burning logs snapped and crackled invitingly in the stone fireplace at the far side of the small round room, and a large iron pot of something that smelled delicious bubbled and steamed on the hearth. A ladder against the wall rose through an open trapdoor to a loft where Will guessed there would be beds. Everything was polished and tidy and, true to the name, looked snug. Even the keening of the wind outside seemed pleasing from inside this warm, cozy space.

The girl quickly shut the door behind them. She set the waylight on a chair by the door, took off her cloak, slid the ring from her long red hair, and shook it out.

"What if those . . . things find this place?" Will asked.

"Let's hope they don't," the girl said, glancing at the door. "But anyhow it's better being in here than out there."

He wanted to ask what the pale figures were, and why they looked like his family, but he had the feeling he wouldn't like the answer any more than her other explanations.

"Something drove them away," he said. "It sounded like people singing. Sort of."

The girl grinned. From a pouch at her side, she drew a small wooden object on a string. It looked something like a narrow spinning top. The girl spun it swiftly around on the string, and the eerie voices started up, like a warning siren beginning to wail. The girl caught the thing with her hand, and the voices stopped.

"My grandfather made this," she said. "It mimics the sound of something even ghosts are afraid of. I wasn't sure if it would trick those things, but it seems to work. I'll have to tell Grandfather when we get home."

She tucked the top away again, and together she and Will approached the fire, drawn by its light and warmth. The girl took a ladle that hung by the pot, spooned up some of the steaming broth, and blew on it.

"Don't we have to ask?" Will whispered.

"Ask who?" The girl shrugged. She sipped the broth, smacked her lips, and smiled to herself. Will took a good look at her. Her face was thin and pale, but something in the way she stood, and the steadiness of her slender hand, gave him the feeling that she was stronger than she looked. Under her dark brows, her green eyes glittered in the firelight.

There were clay bowls and spoons on the mantel above the fire. The girl reached for two of the bowls and filled them with broth. She handed one to Will. He took it hesitantly, raised a spoonful to his lips, and tried the briefest of sips. It was tasty. Very tasty. He looked up at the girl, trying not to smile.

"I'm Rowen," she said. "Rowen of Blue Hill."

Caught off guard, Will stammered his name. Hungrily he took a bigger mouthful of the broth and dipped the spoon for another, then paused.

"You're right: I am from far away," he said. "Before I crashed the motorcycle, we were—"

He stopped when he saw the girl's brow wrinkle.

"Motorcycle," she echoed. "That sounds like one of the Steam Guild's inventions. What does it do?"

"It . . . well, it carries you," Will said. "From one place

to another. I was trying to get to the Perilous Realm but then—"

"You did."

"What?"

"You did get to the Perilous Realm. You're in it."

"No, that's not right. It can't be. I saw the sign by the road. But when I came back it was . . . different, and then I crashed the bike, and when I woke up, there wasn't—"

He broke off, overwhelmed by all the strange things that had happened to him since he had taken off on the motorcycle. Could all of this really be the amusement park? If this girl was acting a part, she was doing it very well.

She studied him intently, as if he might be the one playing a role.

"When we get home, we'll talk to my grandfather," she said. "He'll explain things better than I can."

She began to eat, and so did Will. After hours without food, he thought he had never tasted anything so delicious. The soup was made of potatoes and carrots and grains, as far as Will could tell, but the hot, peppery broth went a long way toward warming the chill and even some of the fear out of him. He finished quickly and reached for the ladle to pour himself another bowlful. Then he stopped and looked around the room.

"So we just . . . take whatever we want."

"Yes."

"But there must be a lot of people using these snugs."

"Only those who know how to find them."

"What happens if someone else comes here tonight?"

"In that case," said a voice behind them, "you'll have to fill another bowl."

Will and Rowen whirled around. There in the doorway stood a tall figure in black.

"Moth?" Rowen said.

✦ 4 ✦

In one of the forsaken realms stands a forest of bones. In this forest of bones is a lake. In the middle of this lake is a hollow stone. Within this hollow stone lives a creature that guards a shadow. And this shadow hides a secret that the creature has forgotten: that the stone is a palace, and the lake is gold, and the forest of bones is a garden.

— The Kantar

THE FIGURE STEPPED FROM THE SHADOWS into the flickering firelight. Will saw that it was a man, dressed all in worn-looking garments, his long hair as sleek and dark as a crow's wing. He carried a short, curving bow and a leather quiver of gray-feathered arrows over his shoulder. His eyes glittered in his dusky face. Will's first thought was that he was a performer from the amusement park, but he quickly banished that idea. There was something unusual about the man's look and manner, something that held Will's attention. There was a sense of purpose about this stranger, as if now that he was here, he was *meant* to be here. He belonged here, in some way that Will, and even Rowen, did not.

"How did you find the snug?" Rowen asked warily, moving closer to Will. "You don't have a light."

"I have eyes, ears, and a nose," the stranger said. "And this wood is my home. I should know it pretty well, don't you think?"

His voice had a cold, ringing quality that reminded Will of the sound of the mirrors. He stood on his guard, ready to make a break for the door should Rowen give any sign, but she merely stared at the man as if undecided what to do.

"Why are you here?" she said at last.

The man named Moth turned and shut the door before answering.

"I might ask the same thing of you, Rowen. I doubt your grandfather knows you're out here tonight."

"I was just . . ."

"Looking for adventure, perhaps? Well, you found some. More than you wanted, I think."

Rowen appeared to be about to reply, but under Moth's icy gaze she kept silent and lowered her head.

"As for me, I came looking for foolish travelers with no idea what danger they are in," Moth went on, a darker tone in his voice now. "And here you are, tucking in to a pleasant supper. Fetches have come to the Wood, Rowen. Hasn't your grandfather told you about them?"

"Fetches," Rowen said in a shocked whisper. "So that's what they were. You saw them, too?"

"I did," Moth said, and his arresting eyes fell upon Will. "And there are other strangers in the Wood tonight, I see."

"This is Will," Rowen said. "The fetches were after him."

Moth made Will a slight bow.

"Pleased to make your acquaintance," he said with a cold smile. "I am, as you have probably already gathered, the unwelcome Moth. Will, is it?"

Will looked at Rowen, who gave the slightest, almost imperceptible nod. There was something in Moth's manner, a warning edge even to his smile, that kept him on his guard.

"Will Lightfoot," he said finally.

"I met a Will once," Moth said. "A fine wordweaver. Will Break Spear, or Shake Spear. . . . It was a long time ago."

"Oh, him," Will said dubiously. "We had to read one of his plays in school."

"Perhaps you and he are kindred."

"I don't think so."

Moth's way of speaking was strange. Old-fashioned, like Rowen's clothing. And now he was telling them he had met someone who had lived hundreds of years ago, even though he looked no older than Will's father.

Will noticed then that Moth carried two swords. One was long and slender and sheathed in a scabbard of finely worked leather, but it was the other sword that held Will's gaze. The scabbard and the hilt were pitch-black, and both appeared to be made of some darkly lustrous stone.

"We must warn the Errantry about this," Rowen said.

"I have already done so," Moth said. "And as pleasant as it is to chatter here by the fire, we had best leave. Someone or something set the mirror shards as a snare, and it wasn't the fetches. I will take you as far as the main road, and from there you will go straight home, Rowen, or I cannot answer for the consequences."

Rowen kept silent and nodded her head.

Moth went to the door, opened it, and looked out. Lifting his arm, he whistled, two strong, shrill notes.

"What's he doing?" Will whispered, but Rowen did not answer. She looked up, and he followed her gaze, then jumped back in alarm as a large black bird swooped out of the darkness. The bird alighted on Moth's outstretched arm. Its feathers fluttered a moment as it settled, and then it peered with its shining black eye into the snug.

"Morrigan, you know Rowen," Moth said to the bird. "And this is Will Lightfoot. Will, this is Morrigan."

"Hello," Will said, and then felt foolish, for the bird only blinked and tilted its head inquisitively, as any bird might. It was a raven, Will guessed, that Moth had caught and trained. Then, to his surprise, the raven climbed Moth's arm to his shoulder and uttered a series of soft croaks, purrs, and clicks in his ear.

"She has spoken with the king of the owls," Moth said. "The fetches are nowhere to be seen. We should go now, without more delay."

Rowen took a dappled green cloak from a peg on the back of the door and handed it to Will.

"Whose is that?" Will asked.

"Yours, now," Rowen said.

It was all Will could do to keep up with Rowen and Moth, who both moved sure-footed in the dark. At times they followed a path, but often Moth led them away from it into the trackless woods. Several times he whispered for them to stop. Rowen and Will would crouch and wait while he went on ahead and then returned to say it was safe to continue. After a while Will noticed that the archer never came too close to him or Rowen. He always kept himself at a slight distance, even when they were halted together. Watching him, Will was strangely reminded of the cloven tree.

Once when Will and Rowen were crouched together, waiting for Moth, Will whispered, "What is he? I mean, he's not . . . like us."

To his surprise, Rowen laughed.

"In this realm we're the odd ones, not Moth," she said. "He is one of the storyfolk."

"What does that mean?"

"It means this is his home. He's not from elsewhere, like you. If I'm right about where you come from."

"Where I come from?"

"We call it Elsewhere," Rowen said, and Will realized she meant the word as a name. "Or sometimes it's called the Untold. Grandfather says people from there are always trying to find the Perilous Realm. The lands of story. Not many ever do."

"So . . . you're one of these storyfolk, too?"

"Yes, but I'm also a Wayfarer like you."

Will opened his mouth and then closed it again. Every question he asked here only led to more questions.

"Some people say Moth was once a warrior of the Shee n'ashoon," Rowen went on quietly. "The Hidden Folk. He served the Lady of the Green Court, I heard. And then something happened. I don't know what. But Moth left the Court and never returned."

"You didn't seem very happy that he found us in the snug," Will said.

"I've only met him and Morrigan once before," Rowen said, "when I was very young. After what I saw in the clearing, I wasn't sure it was really him."

Will pondered this, and then a new thought occurred to him.

"He told you to go straight home. Where's that?"

"I live in the city of Fable, with my grandfather. He can help you, if anyone can."

Suddenly Moth was there in front of them. He held a finger to his lips and beckoned them to follow.

He led them mostly downhill now, past large moss-cloaked boulders and over fallen logs. As they descended, thin wisps of fog curled about their feet. A fine drizzle began to fall. The thick woods had been left behind, and now they were walking down a rolling meadowland dotted with clumps of fir trees.

Moth halted and crouched. He gestured for Will and Rowen to do the same. "What is it?" Will said.

"*Silence*," Moth hissed. "Stay behind me and do not move."

He slid his bow off his shoulder and notched an arrow in the string.

Will peered into the dimness, and after watching tensely for a while, he thought he could see something moving. At first it was little more than a faint disturbance in the gloom, but slowly it grew and took form as a pale, shifting shadow. At one moment it had a manlike shape, with arms that groped through the murk, then it twisted and shrank, and then, as Will watched, it transformed again into something to which he could give no name: a wispy, churning form-lessness that seemed to be little more than fog taking greater substance. Rowen gripped Will's arm, and he realized that she was as frightened as he was.

A shrill cry went up from somewhere nearby. It sounded to Will like the terrified shriek of a child. The shape-changing form halted, and for the first time it made a sound, a kind of hollow, whistling moan that, if it had come from farther away, Will might have mistaken for the noise the wind makes through a slightly open window. The shadowy shape turned slowly, swaying from side to side. The child's cry sounded again, and the thing melted into the shadows.

Rowen's grip on Will's arm relaxed. She let out a long breath.

"What is it?" Will whispered.

"That is a fetch," Moth said. "We call them *annai*, hungry ghosts, with no story of their own. They are moved only by the will of the one that drives them."

"When I first saw them," Will said, "they looked like . . . They reminded me of my family."

"They can take any shape, to fool the eye and the heart," Moth said. "They can even inhabit the dead, and animate them. If a fetch took hold of you, its deadly chill would seep in, like black water, and your spirit would grow cold and easily led. That sound is something they can send out to help them find their quarry."

"The child. Shouldn't we help it, or—?"

"That was no child. It was Morrigan, leading the hunt away from us."

Again Will's gaze was drawn to the strange black sword that swung at Moth's hip. Moth noticed his look this time, and with a frown he gathered his cloak tighter around himself.

As they set off again, there was a squawk from high above, and the raven came swooping down out of the mist to light on Moth's arm. Morrigan spoke softly in her strange, guttural tongue, and then, with another loud squawk, she flew off again.

"We are almost there," Moth said. "Morrigan thinks we can risk the road."

He led them onto a narrow path, which wound through the meadowland and then dipped down sharply, curved around a rocky bend, and came out into a rolling plain, where it joined a wider road paved with flagstones.

"Here I take my leave," Moth said. "I will search for the mirrors, and drive off the fetches if I can. Morrigan will keep watch on you from above until you reach the city. Good luck, Will Lightfoot."

At a word from Moth, the raven soared into the hazy air. Will watched her go. When he lowered his gaze, Moth was no longer with them.

5

As we have now surveyed the geography and history of the city, it is fitting that we investigate the chief craft of its people, which is stories.

— *Wodden's History of Fable*, Volume Three

ROWEN AND WILL HURRIED ALONG THE ROAD, passing stone farmhouses with pale smoke already rising from their chimneys into the air. The rain began to fall in earnest. Once, a small dog darted out from an open gate in a hedge and trotted along with them a short distance before dashing back the way it had come. Such a familiar sight, like something he might have seen on his own street, cheered Will a little. Then he thought about his father and Jess. It had been hours since he took off on the motorcycle. They would have no idea what had happened to him. They would be searching everywhere. That would pay Dad back for taking them on this move in the first place, Will thought angrily. Then he thought about the cloven tree, and the mirror shards, and the fetches. Dad and Jess might be out there right now, where those things were. . . .

They passed a few other travelers approaching the city. Most plodded along wearily with bundles on their backs. There were also a couple of lone riders who seemed lost in their own thoughts. Most of the people heading to the city wore the same antiquated clothing as Rowen and Moth, but some were dressed in even more outlandish garb. And a few, Will noticed with a shock, might not be called quite human. He caught glimpses of a goatish face on one traveler, and eerie catlike eyes gleamed out at him from under the hood of another.

"Who are these people?" he whispered.

"Most are farmers bringing their wares to market. But some are storyfolk from other lands. That's not unusual, but still, the main road is never this busy so late at night."

She sounded concerned, Will thought.

After a time the walls and spires of a city on a hill appeared dimly through the rain. The gently rising approach to Fable led across a lamp-lit bridge over a swift, narrow stream. The outer wall of the city was not particularly high, and it seemed to have been repaired many times with stones of differing size, shape, and color, so that it resembled a mosaic more than a wall. Above its battlements rose steeply peaked roofs and slender spires that looked weatherworn and dismal. Will could imagine that rain had been falling on them ever since they were first built.

They came at last to the city's main gatehouse, which looked like a small castle, with turrets and many-colored flags, and two arched windows of stained glass. The window on the left depicted a star-shaped flower with five white petals on a field of blue. The window on the right held an image of a gushing fountain of water in the shape of a tree.

Will and Rowen passed through the gate, which was wide open and seemed to be unguarded.

"Doesn't anyone watch to see who enters?" Will asked.

"Oh, the gate is well protected," Rowen said mysteriously.

Once inside the walls, they entered a wide, tree-lined street of shops and stalls, their brightly painted signs advertising food and drink of every kind. To Will's surprise, the shops were open and doing business. People in cloaks and long coats were hurrying to and fro through the rain. From the open door of what appeared to be a tavern came rollicking music of flute and drum, and from another door wafted the enticing scent of baking.

The street was lined with lamps that cast a pale blue light. Some of the new arrivals seemed to know where they were going, but others stopped and stared about them, clearly as unfamiliar with the city as Will was.

"Fable is a kind of crossroads," Rowen said. "Folk from all over the many realms pass through this city on their way to other places. Some come from very far away."

Despite the strangeness of what he was seeing, Will felt the desire to linger, but Rowen kept on, up along the steep, climbing curve of the street. They crossed a wide square without shops or people. The gray terraced houses they passed looked silent and shut up.

"These are the homes of the Enigmatists," Rowen said. "They don't come out much."

"Why not?" Will asked without much interest. His mind was still on the good smells from the bakeries and shops.

"They're thinkers," Rowen said. "They try to solve the mysteries of the Realm. Mostly they come up with more questions."

"You called this place the Bourne, not the Perilous Realm," Will said. "Which is it?"

"The Bourne is just one small part of the Realm. Most who live here are people like you and me. Storyfolk call us

Wayfarers, even if we've lived in the Bourne all our lives. We're the descendents of travelers who came here from Elsewhere and chose to remain, or couldn't find their way home."

As she spoke the last words, Rowen looked at Will and bit her lip.

"Sorry," she said. "But sometimes it happens. Travelers from the Untold don't always leave the Realm."

"I'm not a *traveler*," Will shot back. "I didn't mean to come here."

Rowen led the way up a narrow side street that climbed, in a series of worn steps, to a bridge over a canal. A tall, narrow building of stone and wooden beams stood over the midpoint of the bridge. Rowen and Will passed beneath, through an arched passageway. There was a staircase on each side, leading up into the building.

"The Inn of the Golden Goose," Rowen said. "Wandering storyfolk meet here to share tales or to hire themselves out for quests and adventures."

On one of the steps two figures stood, talking in low tones. One was a tall man in a patched cloak with a small black velvet bag in his hand. The other was a very short, stocky, long-bearded man in scuffed leather armor, who was shaking his head and laughing.

"You must be mad." He chortled at the tall man. "For that price I'd travel no farther than the front gate of town. You're talking to a dwarf, not some toadstool-hopping gnome."

"Fifty silver crowns, then, and all expenses," the tall man said hoarsely, glancing over his shoulder at Will and Rowen. "It's a matter of life and death."

"Not good enough," the dwarf said with a sneer. "Not for the Caverns of Nethergrim. I wouldn't set foot there again for twice that."

Rowen halted suddenly and turned to the dwarf.

"You should go, Mimling," she said firmly.

The dwarf bristled, and then appeared to recognize Rowen. His face grew serious.

"You're sure, my lady?"

"Yes, I'm sure. It's the right thing."

He grinned, bowed to her, then turned back to the man in the patched cloak.

"You're in luck, my friend," he said. "If the lady of Blue Hill says it's what Mimling should do, there's no more argument."

"Was that true, what you told him?" Will whispered as he followed after Rowen. She looked at him strangely.

"Why would I lie? My grandfather and I go to the Golden Goose almost every night. We hear lots of stories, and sometimes, when we meet someone there, someone on a journey or a quest, I get this . . . feeling about them. It's like I see what's supposed to come next. How their story should go. Even if things don't turn out as they hoped, it's still what *should* happen. And they've always come back to tell me this, so I know I haven't lied to them."

On the far side of the bridge, they passed under a stone archway, up a long, curving flight of steps, and out again into another crowded thoroughfare. Some passersby had bundles of paper or books tucked under their arms and rushed along distractedly, while others strolled leisurely or stood chatting together, as if the rain were no bother at all. Will was so busy taking everything in, he didn't see the horse-drawn carriage that would have knocked him down if Rowen hadn't grabbed his arm and pulled him out of harm's way. The carriage's tall wheels rolled through the gutter and sent up a spray of water that splashed Will's cloak and soaked his shoes.

"Don't they have traffic where you come from?" Rowen asked.

Will scowled. He saw then that they were standing at the meeting point of two streets. In the center of the crossing rose a high pedestal of black marble, and upon it stood a life-size bronze statue of a young man in ragged, patchwork clothes, striding along with a bundle slung on a pole over his shoulder. He had been posed with his eyes raised to the sky, while his feet were about to step unknowingly off the edge of the pedestal, which had been sculpted to resemble the jagged edge of a cliff. A little dog followed at the young man's heels, its front legs raised, and its mouth open as if it were barking a warning.

"Sir Dagonet," Rowen said, noticing where Will's gaze was fixed. "The first Lord Mayor of the city."

Rowen led the way up one of the two main streets, which curved steeply upward around a long bend. On one side she pointed out a dark, many-spired building with no windows. Rowen told him this was the Great Library.

"If there's something you want to know, Grandfather says, the Library is the best place to go looking for it."

A little farther along, the rising street ended at a high wall covered in thick ivy. In the center of the wall stood two massive doors of dark polished wood braced with iron. They were closed, but within one of the two larger doors a smaller door stood open.

"Appleyard," Rowen said. "Home of the Errantry."

"You said that word before," Will said. "Errantry. To Moth, in the snug. Who is he?"

"It's not a *he*," Rowen said. "Errantry is what you learn here, and when you complete your training, you join the Errantry, the Guild of Knights-Errant."

"So it's like a school then. Do you go there?"

"I've started sword practice and scouting training. My mother was a knight-errant, and I'm going to be one, too. Though my grandfather isn't happy about it."

"So they teach you to become a warrior or something?"

Rowen considered this for a moment.

"You've heard of the Knights of the Round Table, haven't you?"

"Yes."

"The Errantry is something like that. In fact, when Arthur Pendragon stayed in Fable for a while, he drew up the code of rules that the Errantry still follows."

"Wait. You mean *King* Arthur?"

"Of course. Who else? After his last battle, he came back to the Realm to be healed. I thought that story was well known where you come from."

"I suppose so, but I didn't think . . . I mean, he's not real."

Rowen stared at him, then turned away and raised her hand.

"Here we are," she said.

Will thought Rowen meant the door in the wall, but then he saw she was pointing to a narrow, curving lane that opened off the main street. They followed it to its end, passing several shops on the way. Will saw signs for a shoemaker, a bookseller, an apothecary (whatever that was), and a tailor. At the end of the lane stood a strange building, a tall terraced house, somewhat like those Will had already seen, but narrower and faced with dark green and gray masonry. Arched, shuttered windows climbed in a curious zigzag pattern to an ornate, turreted roof. The house leaned slightly into the street and was so crooked-looking that it seemed to be standing only thanks to the two stockier buildings that flanked it.

Rowen went up to the front door. She spoke a hushed word, and a moment later, it opened.

"After you," she said.

Inside, Will found himself in a long hall that seemed brilliantly lit after the long walk through the dim streets. Once his eyes had adjusted to the blaze of the overhead lamps, he saw two things that struck him. First was that the house seemed larger on the inside, wider and more spacious, than it had from outside. And second were the toys.

There were toys everywhere. Colorful marionettes and lifelike birds hung from the ceiling. The shelves lining the hall were crowded with miniature animals of every description, including strange creatures Will had never seen before, as well as tops and whirligigs, boats, intricate little dolls' houses and castles, chess sets, hoops and balls, marbles, and various odd, unknown contraptions made of wood, metal, wire, and string.

"This is how Grandfather earns his living," Rowen said, "but he's also a master of lore. He knows more stories than anyone in Fable."

At the far end of the hall rose a winding staircase. When Rowen reached it and bounded up the first few steps, she nearly collided with a tiny, apple-cheeked woman in an apron who was coming down. The woman shrieked, and the stack of folded linen she had been carrying flew up and scattered over the stairs.

"Rowen!" the woman gasped, sitting down on the step and pressing a hand to her bosom. "You'll send me to my deathbed someday, child."

"I didn't think you'd be up, Edweth," Rowen mumbled.

"Waiting for you to get home, as always," Edweth said sternly.

"I'm sorry, but I need to see Grandfather right away."

"Who has been greatly worried about you, young lady, going off by yourself like that."

The woman glanced sideways at Will as she proceeded to gather up the scattered linen. Rowen hurried to help her.

"Filthy!" Edweth gasped, batting Rowen's hand away.

"This is Will Lightfoot," Rowen said. "He needs Grandfather's help."

"Well," the woman said with a curt nod at Will, "the master is not here at the moment, and who knows when he'll be back. He's gone to an emergency meeting of the Council. Something has all the wise and mighty in a flap."

"I must find him," Rowen said. "I have important news. Can Will stay here while I'm gone? He's come from . . . from far away."

Edweth now took a long, hard look at Will. He felt himself turn scarlet.

"I suppose he may stay," she finally said. "I'm sure your grandfather will be happy to see you safe and sound, Rowen, but don't be surprised if you can't hold his attention. I haven't seen him so distracted for a good long while."

"Did he say what . . . ?" Rowen began, and then went silent.

The woman shook her head.

"It's business I don't poke my nose into. But I know you won't get into the council chambers dressed like that. Your clothes, child. You look as if you've been traipsing through the middle of Toadmarsh."

Rowen grinned.

"Maybe I have. But I haven't time to change. This is urgent."

Edweth sighed.

"It always is. But you will take a dry cloak. That much

I insist on. Your grandfather is untidy enough without you following in his footsteps."

Rowen gave an impatient sigh and dashed up the stairs. Edweth finished gathering up the linen, then she studied Will again, and her gaze softened.

"So you come from far away, do you?" she said with a knowing look. "That's a big place, I've been told. As easy to get lost there as it is in these parts."

"I'm not lost," Will said. "I just don't know where I . . ."

He trailed off sheepishly. The housekeeper nodded.

"You're in Pendrake's Toy Shop in Pluvius Lane. That's a good place to be, whether you're lost or not."

"I won't be staying long," Will said. "But thank you."

"You can save your thanks for the master," Edweth said. "But in the meantime, while you are here, you will not be treated poorly."

Rowen came bounding back down the stairs, tying the cord of a new cloak around her neck. At the bottom she paused and sniffed.

"Do I smell oranges?"

"The road to the Sunlands is open again," Edweth said. "There was even chocolate at the market yesterday."

"I hope you bought some," Rowen said. At the door she turned to Will. "Please stay here. You're safe in this house. Edweth used to slay ogres for a living."

"Off with you now," the housekeeper snapped.

Rowen laughed and hurried out the door.

"Come with me, Master Lightfoot," Edweth said. "We shall get you settled in."

She went up the stairs, and Will followed, noting that here, too, the walls were inset with niches crammed with more toys, and also with books. And so it continued as they climbed, more toys and books, up several floors, until they reached a landing with four doors. Edweth took a key from a pocket in her apron, opened one of the doors, and gestured for Will to precede her inside.

He found himself in a small room, with stone walls hung with colorful tapestries depicting odd, intertwining figures of plants, birds, and beasts. There was a four-poster bed against the far wall, a writing desk and chair next to it, a mirror in one corner, and a tall wardrobe in another. Will was reminded a little of the snug in the woods, but this room seemed more polished, less secretive and ancient.

"Here we are," said Edweth. "I hope this will serve. Perhaps you should get some sleep."

"No, I'm fine," Will said. "I'll stay awake. Until Rowen gets back."

"Well, then, I'll make you something to eat. And I will heat some water, too, so you can bathe, if you please."

She spoke these last words with a meaningful arch of her eyebrows, and Will wondered just how bad he looked, and smelled, after his long journey. Edweth pointed to a door that Will had not noticed.

"You'll find the bath in there," she said. "Give me a few minutes, and then pull the cord above the tub, and it will fill with hot water. Pull it again when the bath is full."

She must have noticed the look of surprise on his face, for she added, "This isn't a snug in the Wood, young sir. We do things for ourselves here."

"No, that's not it," Will said. "I just didn't think you'd have running water."

As soon as the words were out, he blushed again. Edweth's smile was more like a wince.

"If you know what a bath is," she said, heading for the door, "then you'll know how to use it. I will bring you some fresh clothes. When you're ready to eat, just follow your nose."

*   *   *

After the housekeeper had gone, Will explored the room. On the desk was a thick book with a clock face set into its front cover, an ink bottle, and a quill pen. He opened the drawers of the table and found a stack of blank writing paper. In the wardrobe were several woven blankets, thick folded cloths that Will supposed were towels, and feather pillows, all neatly arranged on shelves.

Will took a towel, went into the inner room, and undressed. After waiting what he hoped was a long enough time, he pulled the tasseled cord above the bath. A stream of hot water gushed out of a stone pipe overhead and splashed into the tub. When it was half full, he shut off the water and took a very brief bath, feeling uncomfortable at being naked in a strange house.

In the water he examined his various bruises and scratches—the only proof of what he had been through since leaving Dad and Jess.

"Where am I?" he wondered out loud.

When he was done, he went back into the other room and found clean clothes laid out on the bed. He dressed slowly, uncertain about these unfamiliar garments and exactly how they were supposed to be worn. Then he stood before the mirror and inspected himself. He was wearing a white cotton shirt and a green waistcoat, knee-length gray woolen breeches, white stockings, and black buckled half boots. The clothes were strange and didn't quite fit him, but the face that stared back at him was definitely the face of the Will Lightfoot he knew very well. He turned away, afraid he would see those terrible eyes again. When he dared another glance, it was still his own reflection looking back at him.

Will Lightfoot, thief and runaway. Lost in some world

that couldn't be real. Rowen had said his own world was called Elsewhere. To him it felt as if that's where he was now. They had walked a long way from the clearing, where he was sure—pretty sure—the motorcycle was still lying somewhere. He remembered the lost look on Jess's face as he rode away on the bike. What was she doing now? She couldn't go to sleep at night unless Will read to her. Before he left, they were only halfway through that book about horses she loved so much. With a sick feeling he thought about Dad, maybe still out there somewhere looking for him. He had lost his wife, and now his son.

Even if he was in trouble back home, Will knew one thing for sure: this place was far worse. He would just have to hope that this loremaster could help him get back to where he belonged.

As Edweth had suggested, Will followed his nose, and the enticing aromas led him downstairs to the kitchen. From hooks in the walls hung shining pots and kitchen tools, and a tall wooden table with chairs stood in one corner. Edweth brusquely invited Will to sit there. She had cooked sausages and eggs and toast and set a heaping plate before him; he proceeded to wolf down the food hungrily.

While he ate, Edweth sat beside him and asked him questions. To his relief, she asked only about his family.

"Jess," she repeated when he had told her about his sister. "A pretty name."

"She's a good kid," Will said with a pang, remembering her silent wave as he left the campsite. "I shouldn't have left her like that."

He continued eating, but without the same eagerness. When he had finished, Edweth told him he could explore the house.

"Anything that you shouldn't touch will be behind a
locked door," she said. "But there's lots to look at, and plenty
of books to read. Just put them back where you found them.
This is the master's house, and he does not take kindly to
having things rearranged."

"I won't touch anything," Will said firmly.

He left the kitchen then and wandered along the curving passageway to a spacious, high-ceilinged chamber, with
hanging tapestries like those in his room. There was a large
stone fireplace here, although no fire was burning in it. High-
backed chairs were arranged about a large round table of
dark polished wood. On the table was a marble chessboard,
the pieces scattered across it as though someone were in the
middle of a game. Will looked more closely at the large,
painted chess pieces. Some were familiar, like the knights on
horseback, but others were strange to him. One was a tall,
hooded figure in white that troubled him for some reason he
did not understand.

In one corner stood a suit of armor, its metal plates
tarnished to a yellowish gray and much marred with cracks
and dents. As Will inspected it, he remembered what Rowen
had told him about the knights-errant. Dingy and battered,
the armor didn't seem to fit well with anything else in the
room. He wondered why Rowen's grandfather, this man
that Edweth called the master, bothered to keep it, or didn't
have it polished up at least.

Confronted once again with questions rather than answers,
Will wandered out into the corridor, found the staircase, and
began to climb. He passed the shelves without paying them
much attention, but he noticed that many of the books had no
title on the spine. Those that did consisted of strange words he
didn't know.

He lost track of how far he had climbed and found himself

on a floor where all the doors were shut except one, which was wide open and showed him a room exactly like the one he had been given. Then he noticed what was different: the light blue tunic lying across the bed as though it had been casually tossed there; the open books on the writing table and others piled haphazardly beside it on the floor. One of the wardrobe doors was open, and hanging from a hook was Rowen's travel-stained red cloak.

Realizing where he was, and alarmed at the thought that he might be found where he didn't belong, Will turned to leave, then caught a glimpse of something that stopped him: on the wall above the writing table was a small woven tapestry depicting a man and a woman. The woman was dressed much like Rowen, but the man wore clothing that Will recognized as that of his own time and place.

Will backed slowly out of the room, and his foot slid beneath him. He regained his balance and looked down. There was a puddle of water on the floor. He thought at first that Rowen must have tracked the water in with her, and then he heard the sound of steady dripping nearby. He turned, searching, and soon located the source: water was trickling down from the floor above.

Will wasn't sure anymore where his own room was, but his first thought was that he had left the water running in the bath. He remembered pulling the cord to shut off the tap, but perhaps something had gone wrong, and it had started flowing again. His impulse was to run downstairs and tell Edweth, but he thought of the poor impression he was likely to make on Rowen's grandfather, coming into his house uninvited and then promptly flooding it.

He would have to deal with this himself, and hope that nobody else found out about it.

He hurried up the stairs to the next landing. Here the walls were bare stone, without shelves, toys, or books. The corridor was in near darkness, as there were no lamps and no windows. Warily, Will followed a slender rivulet of water on the floor and at the far end of the corridor found it seeping from under a door. A narrow and rough-hewn door, not smoothly polished like those on the floors below. There was no sound from inside.

Will stepped back into the middle of the corridor and looked around.

"Hello," he said as loudly as he dared, which wasn't very loud. "Is anybody there?"

No one answered. Will pushed the door, expecting it to be locked.

The door opened easily. The room within was dark.

And it was raining.

There was no roof that Will could see, and no back wall. Just two side walls and a stone floor that receded into darkness. A chill wind flicked icy droplets of rain into his face.

From somewhere far inside the room, if it was a room, lightning flashed.

Will stumbled back and whirled in panic. He bolted down the corridor and collided with someone who gave a loud grunt. Will fell over. When he sat up with his ears ringing, he was facing an old man in a long, dark green coat who was also sitting on the floor, his spectacles tilted sideways and a stunned look on his bearded face. Between the two of them stood Rowen, her eyes wide with shock.

"Grandfather, are you—"

"Nothing damaged, Rowen," the old man muttered, righting his spectacles, "except perhaps my dignity."

He picked himself up and patted the front of his coat.

"I'm sorry. I was—" Will said, scrambling to his feet.

"Never mind," the old man said gruffly. "I expect we'll both recover."

"This is Will Lightfoot, Grandfather," Rowen quickly said. "Will, this is my grandfather, Nicholas Pendrake."

The old man's bushy eyebrows rose slightly. He looked toward the open door of the room.

"I told Grandfather everything," Rowen said to Will. "He's going to help you."

"If I can, Rowen."

Will looked up into the old man's sharp, steady gaze.

"I don't know what this place is," he said as firmly as he could. "I just want to go back to where I belong."

Pendrake frowned and pulled the door of the strange room shut.

"Now that you are here," he said with quiet certainty, "you cannot go back. At least not the way you came. You can only go on."

6

Their once-upon-a-time is our now.

— The Quips and Quiddities of Sir Dagonet

WILL FOLLOWED NUMBLY as the toy maker led them to
his workshop. The old man's words had stunned him. He
had no idea what to think now, and anger smoldered in him,
though he didn't know who he was angry at.

To his surprise, the toy maker's workshop was, compared
to the other rooms he had seen in the house, a mess. Even
worse, if possible, than his own room back home. Its walls
were lined in an alternating pattern of windows and glass-
fronted cabinets crammed with bottles, jars, shards of bone,
pieces of coral and crystal, and other odd, unidentifiable ar-
tifacts. In addition to the numerous finished and unfinished
toys Will saw about the room, there were fat, leather-bound
books piled everywhere. One thick volume on top of a tall
stack had a sword lying between its pages, apparently as
a bookmark. A writing desk on one side of the room was

almost completely hidden under great untidy drifts of paper
and parchment. A huge workbench on the other side was
likewise buried, but in wood shavings and tools. On the
floor sat various objects that seemed to have been placed
there for lack of anywhere else to put them, including a slab
of marbled reddish stone, a shapeless old hat, and a large
glass ball.

"Everything is in its proper place," Pendrake said when
he noticed Will's look of surprise. "A fact that my housekeeper cannot seem to grasp, since she is always trying to
get in here to tidy up. One day she will succeed, and I will be
utterly lost."

The toy maker took off his coat and draped it over the
back of a chair. Then he shut the nearest window and drew
down the blind. Rowen did the same with the other windows.
The room was lit only by the dim flames from the fireplace.
Pendrake invited Will and Rowen to be seated by the fire.

"The raincabinet was already here when I moved into
this house," the old man said as he settled into his own deep
armchair. "I called it the water closet at first, but nobody else
found that amusing. Especially not my housekeeper. Ah,
well. Now, you should know there is a toll that every visitor
to Fable must pay."

"I don't have any money," said Will anxiously.

"It's not that kind of toll. In Fable, sooner or later, someone is sure to ask you to tell your story."

Will nodded, but didn't speak right away. He had a lot to
tell, but he wasn't thinking so much of the impossible things
that had happened to him since coming here. Instead he
remembered what had brought him here in the first place.
He had stolen his father's motorcycle, and he wasn't looking
forward to admitting that. But that wasn't really the beginning, either. There was the move from their old house, and

all the days before it, when it had seemed he hardly said a word to Jess or his father. When he stayed out late with his friends or shut himself in his room all evening. And before that, the day that what he had most feared had come true. When he returned home and his mother was gone, and he knew, he really understood for the first time, that he would never see her again. It had seemed to him that day that his story had ended and that from then on there was nothing left to tell or say.

He could not tell them all that. Not yet. And so he began with the theft of the motorcycle and how it led to his encounter with the fetches, and all that had happened afterward.

Pendrake sat frowning in his armchair by the fire as Will told his tale. He did not ask questions, nor did he offer any explanations for the strange and terrifying things that had occurred. He simply listened while Will, stumbling over his words and often backtracking to add details that he had forgotten, slowly got the story out. Once or twice Rowen jumped in to give her version of the events she had witnessed. Pendrake neither asked her to keep quiet nor commented on what she had to say.

When Will was finished, the old man continued to sit for a time, his gaze distant and his hands pressed together in front of his lips, as if he were deep in thought over what he had heard. The silence was broken only by the snap of the fire and the ticking of a clock, carved to resemble an owl, that hung on the wall above the desk.

Finally Pendrake stirred. He rose from his chair, took a poker, and stood near the fire.

"As I'm sure you've guessed," he said, "you have strayed very far from home. Luckily you have come to a part of the realms that is not utterly different from the world you know. It could have been far worse."

"How could it?" Will said, close to tears. "You told me I can never go back."

"I said you cannot go back the way you came. You will have to find another way, as everyone does who comes here and wishes to leave. The border between this realm and yours is always shifting. What is a door one moment may be a wall the next."

"But nobody knows where I am. It's been hours since I left. My father, Jess, the police—they'll all be looking for me. I have to get back *now*."

"You cannot," Pendrake said simply. "But I can tell you this. The border between realms shifts in time as well as space. You could spend days here and return home to find that only moments had passed. Or the other way around. Much depends on the way you return."

"Do you know the way?" Will whispered, though he already suspected what the answer would be.

"I know of only one way. To find the path that is yours, not anyone else's."

"But what about the fetches, Grandfather?" Rowen interrupted. "They're probably still out there. It was a lucky thing that Moth found us."

Pendrake turned to her with a smile.

"Yes, thank goodness for the Nightwanderer. Since he and Morrigan make their home in the Wood, I asked them a long time ago to keep an eye on my granddaughter. I have had at least that comfort when she goes off in search of adventure without telling anyone."

Rowen frowned and glanced at Will, her face flushing as red as her hair.

"But I have not forgotten the fetches, Rowen," Pendrake added. "The Council met in emergency session when reports came in about strange ghostly creatures prowling our borders.

Thanks to Moth, we now know they are fetches, and this is of grave concern. Things are stirring in the world beyond the Bourne. More storyfolk driven from their lands by Nightbane arrive here every day. And we must assume the Master of Fetches has seen you, Will, through the mirror shard."

"The Master of Fetches . . ." Will echoed. With a shudder he remembered the eyes in the mirror, the presence prowling in his thoughts.

"The Errantry has kept this land peaceful and safe for many years, and most folk who dwell here scarcely think about the world beyond," Pendrake said. "They have heard of the wars of long ago, of the struggle of the Hidden Folk against their great enemy, of the fiery destruction of the city of Eleel, but they consider these only fantastic tales of a vanished age. Perhaps true, perhaps not. But either way as harmless as any other tale told to pass the time in this city of stories."

"Who is this Master, Grandfather?" Rowen asked, her voice a strained whisper. "Why did he send the fetches after Will?"

"We don't know for certain who their prey was. It may have been only chance that you fell into their clutches, Master Lightfoot. If anything in this world happens by chance. You've given me much to think about. Most people who open the raincabinet find only an empty room, or a puddle and a fleeting scent of storm clouds. You are the only visitor to this house who has ever seen the unseen rain."

"What does that mean?" Will asked. "I don't understand."

Pendrake set the poker back into its stand beside the fireplace, then leaned a hand upon the mantel and seemed to be searching the fire as if within it lay the answer to Will's question.

"The Realm is not just a world with stories in it," he said

at last. "This world *is* Story. It is the place that all of the tales in your world come from. Whatever you might find in a story, you will find here. Adventures, strange encounters, riddles. Elves, witches, ghosts, giants. Heroes and monsters. Bravery, goodness, and terrible evil. And many other things that have yet no name in your world. And *you* are here now, Will, and that means you are in a story, too."

"Wait. You're telling me that people like . . . like Robin Hood live here? Or the Big Bad Wolf? Or Harry Pot—"

"I'm telling you that the stories you know began here. The storytellers in your world have always traveled to the Realm, either in the flesh, as you have, or in their dreams or imaginings. The stories they take back to Elsewhere still go on happening here. The stories weave themselves anew. They change, and yet they remain."

"So none of this is real, then," Will said. "It's what I thought. I'm dreaming this, or I'm—"

"Or you're what? It's all real. As real as the world you come from."

Will looked desperately around the room.

"If this is a story, I don't want to be in it. How do I get out?"

"You will have to see it through to the end. It's your story now, as much as it is anyone's. And that might mean a long and difficult road. Or it might be as easy as opening a door. I cannot say. But you should know that your story is part of a larger tale that began a very long time ago. Some call it the Kantar. It is the Story of all stories. The tale of everything that was, is, and will be."

There was a knock at the door, and the housekeeper came in carrying a tray with tea and biscuits.

"Keeping these children up all night," she muttered as

she laid the tea things out on a small table. "They have to eat something more than stories."

"True enough," Pendrake said, clapping his hands. "I could use some refreshment myself. I don't think any of us will get much sleep tonight."

"You're right about that," Edweth muttered as she went out.

Pendrake poured the tea and served it. He sat back in his chair, twirling a spoon in his cup. Will noticed that his shirt front was spotted with old tea stains.

"Perhaps Moth can help Will, Grandfather," Rowen said after a short silence. "He is one of the Fair Folk after all."

"You know Moth does not travel with the Green Court, Rowen. It is hidden from him. And he seldom leaves the Wood. It is one of the last remnants of the lost Realm of Faerie, and he has guarded it for a very long time."

"I know he left the Green Court," Rowen said, "but I never heard why."

"We will save that story for another night," Pendrake said. "I'm sure Will is feeling overwhelmed with all of this."

They both looked at him.

"This Story of stories you talked about . . ." Will began. He *was* overwhelmed, but there was more he had to know.

"The Kantar."

"Yes. Do you know how it ends? Because if you do, then you can just tell me, can't you, and we can just go to that part. Like skipping pages in a book. Can't we?"

Pendrake smiled and set down his cup.

"I wish it worked that way. I've spent my life learning what I could of the Kantar, but what I know is like a drop of water from a mighty river. The Kantar is boundless, it seems. Everything that happens in the many realms, even our conversation this very moment, becomes part of its weave.

I certainly don't know the ending, if there ever will be an ending. No, like a character in a book, you cannot jump to the ending before its time. You must play out your role. As everyone must."

"Isn't someone *telling* the story?"

To his surprise, Pendrake shrugged.

"That's a question for the Enigmatists, I suppose. It is said that ages ago, in the morning of the world, the Stewards spun the Deep Weaving into twelve great realms of Story that are yet one, the Perilous Realm. An endless, ever-renewing ocean of myths, legends, and tales. The Stewards, the *Innathi*, were ageless beings of wisdom and grace, who taught Moth's people, the Tain Shee, much of their lore and craft. The Stewards are gone now. And yet the stories go on."

"So this . . . Master of Fetches. He was the one in the mirror. . . ."

"That is what I fear."

"Who is he?"

"One who wishes all stories to be his. Even though the Kantar belongs to no one and everyone, he would have it all for himself."

Pendrake rose slowly from his chair and went over again to the fire. His gray locks hung over his face as he gazed into the flames.

"Malabron the Night King, Lord of the Shadow Realm and Master of Fetches. Why is it the very worst have the most names? Where he came from, no one knows. But with him fear and shadow entered the realms. And oblivion. The twelve great realms were engulfed in war and broken, sundered. In those dark days, the Tain Shee armed themselves and came to the aid of the Stewards in their struggle against Malabron. Their alliance was a bright host unlike anything seen in the realms before or since. The fair city of Eleel stood then as a beacon to those under Malabron's shadow, until one of their own, a prince of the Tain named Lotan, betrayed his people. The city was thrown open to its enemies. Its bright towers burned."

As the old man spoke, Will watched the light and shadows dance on the walls, and it seemed to him he could almost see the city in flames, its towers shuddering under the blows of the enemy. In the sound of the fire, he heard the roar of battle, the cries of Moth's people as their beloved city fell.

"Did Moth and Morrigan live there?" Rowen asked, and Will realized that she had never heard most of this story.

"They did, and like their fellow Shee, they fled, into a realm that lay in ruins. In his lust for power, Malabron struck at the Deep Weaving itself. The damage he wrought was like a terrible wound to all the storylands. Much perished; much was changed forever. So many stories consumed, abandoned, forgotten. . . . That time became known as the Great Unweaving. Eleel itself sank beneath the waves. Prince Lotan, who had taken lordship of the city in his master's name, perished in its ruin, or so it was believed. The Tain themselves became exiles in a broken land. The Shee n'ashoon they are called now. The Hidden Folk. Their home is the Green Court, a wandering kingdom of tents and pavilions that never stays in one place for long. In their ceaseless struggle against Malabron, the Shee have become masters of concealment and illusion. They elude the Night King's hunters, they strike against his minions and his armies, then they vanish again into the shadows of the forest."

While the toy maker was speaking, the fire had dimmed to embers. He stirred the blackened wood with the poker, and new flames leaped up.

"The Stewards could not defeat Malabron, but they did halt him for a time, and heal much of what he destroyed. He has striven ever since against their fading power, and now I fear he seeks again to dominate and conquer all."

"But he's not interested in Wayfarers," Rowen said. "You told me that once, Grandfather. Why would he send fetches to the Bourne?"

"You're right, Rowen, that folk from the Untold have never been of interest to him. He believes we have no stories. And so he has never turned his eye on the Bourne before. But it may be that our good fortune is at an end."

"This is all happening now," Will said in a stunned whisper. "He's not just some . . . dark lord from a storybook."

"There are some in the Bourne who would like to believe that. But the story of the war against the Night King is true, and it is not over. It reaches into the here and now, into this very room."

At that moment there was a tapping at one of the windows. Will jumped. Pendrake strode to the window and pulled up the blind. A tiny ball of bright bluish light bobbed in the dark outside, flicking its fiery form at the pane. Pendrake turned the latch and swung the window open. The ball of light darted inside and hovered in the air.

"Ah, Sputter," the old man said. "What do you have for me?"

The ball of light sped to the toy maker's desk, where it danced over the surface of a blank sheet of yellowish paper. As Will watched, lines of flowing script began to appear on the paper.

"What is that thing?" Will whispered to Rowen.

"It's called a wisp," she whispered back. "They carry messages."

When it reached the end of the page, the wisp rose sharply

and then dropped with a hiss into a bottle of ink beside the paper.

Pendrake went over to the desk and quickly scanned the message.

"From the Marshal of the Errantry," he said, looking up from the paper. "He's heard about your arrival, Will, and asks me to report to him."

Pendrake dipped a black-feathered quill pen in the ink bottle into which the wisp had disappeared. He scratched a few lines on another sheet of paper, and then to Will's surprise, crumpled up the paper and tossed it in the fire. Almost instantly there was a crackle and a flash of light, and the messenger wisp, or one just like it, came zinging out of the flames. It buzzed around the room twice, trailing sparks, and bumped into a closed window, then into another. Finally it found the open window and shot out into the air, its hum swiftly fading.

"You must use up a lot of paper that way," Will said, scarcely believing what he had seen.

"It's salamander parchment," Rowen said. "When the fire burns out, it will still be there, and blank, to be used again."

"That wisp seemed a little . . . confused."

"Sputter's fine. An Enigmatist tried to take him apart once, to find out what wisps are made of. Grandfather patched him up as well as he could."

"There is more to tell you." Pendrake sighed, taking off his spectacles and rubbing his eyes. He got up from the desk and took his coat from the back of the chair. "So much more. But enough for now. While there is still some night left, get some rest. I'll tell Edweth not to wake you too early. And, Will, do not fear. You're safer here than anywhere I know."

*   *   *

Rowen escorted Will to his room. He was exhausted, but too shaken by what he had heard to feel sleepy. And he had the nagging feeling that Pendrake had kept things from him. While he was speaking of the Master of Fetches, and the Stewards, and their long-ago war, he'd glanced at Rowen with a troubled look. The same look Will had seen in his father's face before he told Will how sick his mother really was. He wanted to trust the old man, but he couldn't. In a place like this, he wasn't sure he could trust anyone.

At the door, he remembered what Pendrake had told him, that the way home was his to find. Which must mean he was on his own. And this Marshal of the Errantry would probably order him out of the city, once he heard what Pendrake had to say. They would get rid of him before anything else happened, before he brought something worse down on their heads. He would be back *out there*, alone.

"Sleep well," Rowen said, turning to go.

"Wait. You know how to use a sword, right?"

"I've been learning," Rowen said. "Why?"

"How long does it take to learn?"

Rowen gave him a puzzled look, and then understanding came into her eyes.

"They won't send you off on your own," she said firmly. "And if they did, I'd go with you."

7

Travelers who have just arrived from Elsewhere usually have
a very dim understanding of what they will encounter here,
but indeed, we who call these strange lands home must admit
we know little more. How well can you know a story, after all,
when you're still in the middle of it?

— Redquill's *Atlas and Gazetteer of the Perilous Realm*

HE WAS WALKING IN A GRASSY MEADOW. The sun was
shining. The world was bright and green. He could smell
the scent of flowers in the warm air and hear the birds
chattering and singing in the trees. The cloven tree, half in
shadow and half in light, stood alone on its rise. Now that
he had found it, he had no need to hurry. His search was
over.

He walked, gazed around him, and saw that there were
stones in the grass. Small gray stones were scattered everywhere he looked. They were not here when he came to the
clearing the last time, he was sure of that. He stopped and
picked up one of the stones. It was heavy, its surface cold
and smooth. He turned it over in his hand.

The stone opened an eye and looked at him.

He cried out in fear and dropped the stone, backing away

from it. In the grass all the other stones were watching him now with unblinking eyes.

He ran for the tree, but as he came nearer, the leaves on its living half began to fall. As they drifted and spun through the darkening air, they turned gray and then white.

The leaves were becoming huge wet flakes of snow, falling more and more thickly until he could see nothing beyond them. He stopped running and shouted for Dad and Jess, but the wind that had risen with the snow drowned out his voice, even from himself. His panting breath turned to steam in the cold air.

He started forward again cautiously, holding his hands out in front of him and blinking to see through the flurrying snow.

The hairs rose on the back of his neck. He turned.

Through the veils of falling snow came a dim figure. Will's first thought was that the fetches had found him again. Then he saw how the figure moved, with slow, careful steps, and he knew that this was no ghostly shape but a being of flesh with its own will and purpose.

As the figure came closer, Will saw that it was a tall man dressed in a dark crimson robe. His long hair was as white as the snow, though he appeared to be young. As he walked, his eyes searched the snow-covered ground, as if he were looking for . . . footprints.

The man had not seen him yet, but in another moment he would cross the tracks Will had made in the snow. Will's first impulse was to flee, but he didn't move. He watched the tall man draw closer. Something in this stranger's look or bearing reminded him very much of Moth.

Then it was too late.

The man came to Will's tracks, halted suddenly, and looked up. His icy, almost colorless eyes found Will and held him.

The man opened his mouth to speak, but instead of words there was only silence.

The snow fell thicker and faster, and the stranger receded into it, until his red robe became a faint blur and then vanished completely. Will found himself alone again in a nowhere of whirling whiteness, not even sure anymore which way was up or down. The cold was seeping into him now, dulling his thoughts and making his limbs sluggish. He staggered backward and fell, tumbling over and over. The snow was in his eyes, his ears, his mouth. He curled up into a ball.

"It's just a dream," he whispered feverishly. "I have to wake up."

Rowen did not fall asleep for a long time. When she finally did, she dreamed of Will. She saw him riding the machine he called a motorcycle, and in her dream it was a bulky contraption of clanking metal parts and giant wooden wheels, with tall pipes rising from it that sent up hissing jets of steam. And then she was seated on the machine behind him, hanging on desperately as they sped through the streets of Fable.

"Where are we going?" she asked him over the roar and hiss of the machine.

"I have no idea," he shouted back, a wild grin on his face.

The streets of the city had become steep, twisting canyons. They plunged down them at a terrible speed, shuddering over the cobblestones. The shrieking wind stung Rowen's eyes to tears. Her hair whipped in her face. The motorcycle's pipes screamed, and bits and pieces of it began to fly off.

Below them, the street ended in a blank wall of stone.

Will turned to her.

"We're going to crash now," he said calmly.

"Can't you do anything?" she shouted. "Can't you stop it?"

"Not me," he said with a shrug. "I don't have any control over it at all."

Rowen put her hands over her face and peered out between her fingers. Just before they smashed headlong into the wall, she woke up.

Sunlight was streaming through her window. She thought of Will. What was going to happen to him? And what was going to happen to Fable? Why were so many storyfolk coming here these days?

Slipping on a dressing gown, she went to the chest at the end of her bed and opened it. Underneath a stack of blankets lay a pile of old books. This was the one place Edweth never looked. As long as Rowen kept everything neatly tucked away in the chest, there was no reason for the housekeeper to go rooting around in it. And that meant this was the one place in her room she could hide something.

She shoved the books aside and laid bare a bedsheet wrapped around something long and bulky. She lifted the bundle from the chest, set it down on her bed, and unwrapped it. Inside lay a sword. Its silver hilt was inscribed with the seal of the Errantry, a five-petaled white flower within a circle.

Rowen took the sword in both hands and held it in front of her. The blade gleamed in the morning light.

She had found it in the uppermost attic of the house, in a locked trunk, the key to which had cost her many days of searching. The sword was her mother's, there was no doubt of that. Her grandfather had hidden it away from her, but Rowen had found it. She was meant to find it. And with it she would do great things.

A cry came from down the corridor, in the direction of Will's room. Hurriedly Rowen tucked away the sword and went out onto the landing. At Will's door she stopped and listened.

A bird was singing somewhere. There was warm sunlight on his eyelids. But he was still cold and shivering. What had happened to his blankets? He groped for the covers, eyes still closed, wondering what Dad was making for breakfast. Jess would probably be up soon and tugging on his pajama sleeve, wanting him to watch cartoons with her.

Then he remembered.

Will opened his eyes. He was lying, curled up, at the end of his bed. Groggily he raised his head. The blankets were in a heap on the floor.

He was in his room in the toy maker's house. He had been dreaming about the clearing with the cloven tree, and the strange white-haired man, but *this* was no dream. He was really here, in the Perilous Realm. The mirrors in the woods and the fetches, meeting Rowen and Moth . . .

It had all really happened.

"The city of Fable," he said out loud, as if he wouldn't believe it until he heard himself say it. "In a land called the Bourne."

The memory of what the toy maker had said last night returned, and a cold dread settled in his stomach. He was trapped in a story. A dangerous one. With things in it he couldn't even understand. And why him? He was sure the old man hadn't told him everything, but he knew he didn't want to hear anymore. It was time to do something, anything, to get out of here, if he could.

There was a knock at the door.

"Will? Are you all right?"

The girl's voice. Rowen.

"I'm fine," he called out. "Just a dream."

"Well, I'll be downstairs then. I'll ask Edweth to make us something."

Will climbed groggily from the bed. His old clothes were hanging in the wardrobe. He dressed and went down to the kitchen, where he found Rowen and Edweth. For a moment he considered telling them about his disturbing dream but decided against it. The housekeeper had just made breakfast, and Will's stomach growled hungrily as he surveyed the food spread out on the table. There was fresh bread with jam and honey, eggs and ham and sausage, and berries in cream.

As Will dug in, Rowen told him that her grandfather had already gone out.

"And he made it very clear," Edweth said, "that the two of you are to stay here in the house until he comes back."

After breakfast Rowen suggested that they go up to her grandfather's workshop and look at his maps. Will already knew he would not find his own country shown on a chart here, but he had to do something other than sit and wait. From a cabinet she brought out and unrolled a large parchment map of the Bourne and the surrounding storylands, as she called them. Will was dismayed to see that while the Bourne itself was filled in with rivers and roads and place names, the regions beyond its borders were mostly white space. How was he supposed to get home with a map that faded away at the edges?

Rowen told him that nearby, to the east and south of the Bourne, there were friendly lands and kingdoms, but for the most part the north and west were sparsely, and sometimes dangerously, populated. Once there had been many flourishing storylands here, but most of them had been

broken or devoured by the Night King. These lands were
known as Wildernesse, and people from the Bourne avoided
traveling through them if they could.

"Grandfather has traveled all over the Realm, gathering
tales and helping storyfolk," Rowen said. "He says that in
Wildernesse you can't put much trust in a map. You're likely
to find things very different from what you expect."

Will sighed.

"Is this the best map you've got?" he asked.

"The Great Library has lots of maps," Rowen said. "And
books, too, of course. They say there's a book there for everyone in the Realm."

"So there might be a book there for me. A book that could
show me the way home."

"Well, maybe, but—"

"I've got to go there," Will said.

Rowen pursed her lips.

"You heard what Edweth said."

"I'm not going to sit here and do nothing."

"If Grandfather finds out—"

"*You* don't listen to him," Will said. "Why should I?"

Rowen sighed. She went to the door and listened for a
moment. Then she turned to Will.

"We'll have to get past Edweth," she said. "That won't be
easy. Come on."

When they reached the steps of the Great Library, Will saw
that it was an even larger building than it had seemed to him
the night before. Unlike most of the structures he had seen so
far in Fable, its towering walls were not made of many blocks
of hewn stone, but rather seemed carved of one single great
mass of rock that was hoary with moss. Wide steps led up to
a pair of tall narrow doors, and on either side of them stood

a stone statue, in the shape of a strange creature the likes of which Will had never seen. Like a gryphon, it had a lion's body, an eagle's head, and wings, but the wings were oddly shaped. As Will reached the top of the staircase, he was able to see that they were not wings at all, but rather the ragged-edged pages of a book that was spread open upon the creature's back.

Will and Rowen passed without speaking through the doors of the Library's entrance and into a long hall, lit by tall, narrow lamps in deep alcoves. On both sides of the central aisle down which they walked stood large desks at which men and women sat, scratching busily with quill pens or sorting through stacks of books.

"The assistant librarians," Rowen whispered. "A cranky bunch. Worse than Edweth. Try not to make a noise."

Rowen and Will walked quietly and quickly past the people at the desks, none of whom gave them the merest glance. At the far end of the hall, in the center of a semi-circular space from which several corridors branched off, was the tallest desk of all, a massive pulpit of carved oak. From where Will and Rowen stood, only the shiny top of a bald head and the end of a furiously fluttering quill feather could be seen. Rowen cleared her throat.

"Excuse me," she said.

The feather stopped fluttering. The bald head stirred slightly, and a voice mumbled something unintelligible.

"Excuse me," Rowen said again.

There was another grunt, and then the entire head rose into view. It belonged to a very old man with a long, thin face, a large beak of a nose, and a straggly white beard sprouting from his chin. His hands reached over and clutched the edge of the desk, and Will saw that all the nails were trimmed short, save one on the index finger of the right hand that poked out, yellow and curved, like a single claw. The old man glowered down at them in silence.

"We need help, please," Rowen said, her voice raised slightly above a whisper.

"Speak up," the old man said, cocking his head to one side.

"We need help with something important," Rowen said loudly, and her voice echoed in the long hall. The scratching of quills stopped. Most of the assistant librarians had raised their heads and were staring at Will and Rowen.

The old man tapped the desk with his one long nail.

"Consult the catalogs," he said dismissively, in a voice like gravel crunched underfoot.

"I don't think it would help us," Rowen said, and she gestured to Will. "We're looking for something for *him*. And he's not . . ."

The old man frowned and peered down at Will. Now all the assistant librarians were staring openly in his direction.

"He's not *what*?" the old man said, not taking his iron gaze off Will.

"We're looking for a book for him," Rowen said, her voice trailing off weakly. "To help him get home."

"What makes him think there is such a book here?"

"She told me there was," Will blurted out, pointing at Rowen. She opened her mouth, shut it again, and shot Will a look of annoyance. The old man stared coldly at both of them, his yellow talon now tapping the side of his head.

"I suppose you're a new recruit from Appleyard?" he said to Will with a grimace.

Will shook his head.

"I thought you looked a little too puny for an apprentice," the old man said, and pointed his talon like an accusation at the nearest assistant librarian.

"Nymm," he said. A small, sour-faced man with ink-stained fingers popped up from his desk like a jack-in-the-box and hurried over.

"Someone looking for *his* book," the old man said, a thin trickle of amusement leaking into his voice.

The assistant librarian bowed slightly and, without another word, led Will and Rowen down the farthest corridor on their left. At the far end of its long curve they came out into a large circular room. It was lit by hanging glass globes that contained what looked like messenger wisps, glowing dimly.

In the room were more books than Will had ever seen. Far more than his old school library, or even the big public library where Mum used to take him and Jess before she became ill.

Tall cases of books ran round the perimeter, and two other, higher galleries of shelves rose above to a domed glass ceiling. In addition to all the books lining the shelves on three floors, stacks and heaps and ziggurats of books sat everywhere, even piled on top of the large desk that stood in the middle of the room. Here and there people were sitting at tables, absorbed in their reading, or copying from texts and making notes. Between the shelves on the main floor stood tall cabinets with many drawers, and now and then one of the drawers would slide open noiselessly, and something that resembled a large white butterfly would dart out and flutter over to one of the tables, where it would settle, either on the tabletop, or on a book, or on the arm of a reader. When one of the butterflies passed close to Will, he saw that it was in fact a piece of paper folded down the middle to form what looked like a pair of wings.

"You may as well start here, in the catalog room," Nymm

said. He went over to one of the desks, took a quill pen out of
its stand, and handed it to Will.

"I don't know what I'm supposed to do," Will muttered,
and the librarian rolled his eyes.

"Never been in a library before, likely," he said. "Well,
what is it you want your book to do for you?"

"Get me home."

"Well, then, when one of the catalog slips comes to you,
write your request on it, and then follow the slip. A simple
matter, for most."

"It's that easy?"

"I did not say *easy*," Nymm snapped. "I said *simple*, and
I meant the second definition of the word, as found in the
Eleventh Compendium of the Languages of the Realm, volume
seventy-three. *Simple* in the sense of *straightforward*. If the
slip can find your book, it will. If it can't, I suggest you try
elsewhere."

"That's what I'm trying to find," Will muttered.

Grudgingly the librarian handed him a lantern.

"You'll need this. And remember: the Library is very old
and very large, and parts of it haven't been visited by anyone, not even us librarians, for a long time. If you get lost, or
if you encounter . . . things, fold the slip the other way, and
it will return here. If you lose track of the slip, well, someone
will come looking for you. Eventually."

He turned to go, then frowned at Rowen.

"Oh, and one more thing. You must go alone. No chance
of it working otherwise. It confuses the slips if someone else
comes along, which you would know were you a regular
patron of this Library."

With that he rolled his eyes once more and strode back
out the way he had led them. Will turned to Rowen, who
shrugged.

"I suppose I'd better wait here then," she said, and moved away to examine the books on the nearest shelf.

Will pulled out a chair and sat down at the table, pushing aside a stack of books to make some room in front of him. Two other people were sitting at the far end of the long table but had their heads bent over books and paid him no attention. He didn't have long to wait. After a few moments he heard a soft flutter in the air, and a slip landed gently on the back of his hand, its paper wings stirring slightly as it settled on its chosen perch. Carefully Will took the slip by one corner and set it onto the table, where its wings spread open and it lay flat and motionless, like an ordinary scrap of paper.

Will lifted the quill pen and set the nib to the paper, expecting the slip to move. It did not stir. Tentatively he scratched a line. Nothing appeared.

"You need ink," Rowen said.

Will frowned and dipped the pen in the black bottle at his elbow. He held it poised over the slip, and then hesitated.

"Have you ever done this?" he whispered to Rowen.

Without turning to look at him, she whispered back, "No. I use the catalogs. What's the matter?"

"I don't know what to write."

"Just ask for what you want, like he said. Simple, remember?"

Will grimaced and set the nib to the paper again. He thought for a moment, wrote the word *home*, then plonked the pen back into its stand.

An instant later the slip's wings began to rise again, and then to beat rapidly, like the wings of a hummingbird. It fluttered up from the table, sped across the room, and hovered at the arched entrance to one of the dim branching corridors. Will jumped up, grabbed the lantern, and with one quick backward look at Rowen, he followed.

8

It is an old city, and thus it is many cities, the oldest of which may not have had a name or even have been inhabited by beings that walk on two legs.

— Wodden's *History of Fable*, Preface

AFTER A LONG TIME, HE KNEW that he was lost. And worse, he was pretty sure the slip was, too.

He had followed the fluttering scrap of paper through halls and rooms and corridors of bookshelves, up and down stairs, and along winding passageways, until he began to wonder whether there was any end to the Library at all. Every now and then he had passed someone browsing the shelves, or trudging along with an armload of books, or sitting at a desk under one of the dim light globes, poring over some huge, ancient tome. Most of these solitary souls looked as dusty and faded as the books, as though they themselves had not left the Library in years. Will paid them little heed, since most of his attention stayed focused on the slip, which flew along purposefully without slackening its speed, as if it did not care whether Will was keeping up or not.

As he followed, from time to time Will heard strange noises, soft shufflings and mutterings from the shadowy recesses around him. Once, from a narrow aisle, a dim figure in gray rags approached him, silently mouthing words. Its feet were chained to two immense books, and worse, the feet and the books were suspended a foot above the floor. Will fled from the specter, shouting at the slip to wait for him. He felt foolish talking to a piece of paper, but it was better than having no companion at all in such a place.

When the slip had finally begun to slow down, its wings beating less urgently, Will assumed that this meant they were nearing their goal, and he followed with a burst of new energy. Even when the slip had slowed to a stationary hover, and then turned a slow circle and began to fly back the way they had come, Will was not too concerned. This could simply mean that the slip was honing in on its precise destination. But after many minutes of this turning and darting down other aisles and coming back and trying another direction, Will's confidence in the slip's powers began to falter. Especially when he realized that he hadn't seen another living soul for some time and that the light globes were becoming dimmer and spaced farther apart.

With growing unease he followed the slip through a maze of aisles that went on and on, until at last they came to a place where there was no light at all apart from the weak illumination of the lantern. Crooked aisles like tunnels ran off in all directions between shelves that rose to great heights until they were lost in darkness. Scraps of paper littered the floor, which was paved with narrow stones that Will realized with shock were actually the spines of books.

He was not only *in* the Library; he was walking on it.

Here the slip gave in at last. Its wings ceased beating and it spiraled helplessly down toward Will. He lifted his hand

and let the slip drop into his palm. If it hadn't been a piece of paper, he would have sworn the slip was exhausted beyond endurance and trembling with fatigue, or even fear. One thing was clear: the search was over, and they hadn't found his book. The Library could not help him.

"Let's go back now," he said, and folded the tiny piece of paper the other way, as the librarian had told him to. The slip stirred feebly, then lay still.

"Come on," Will said loudly, and heard his voice echo through the endless corridors. "Just do what you're supposed to."

He folded the slip the other way, and back again, but it did not move. Will swallowed hard. What chance was there he could retrace his steps back through the Library on his own?

He lowered his gaze and noticed for the first time that the papers scattered over the floor like fallen snow were slips like the one that had led him here. He tucked his own slip into a pocket and stooped to pick up one of the others. On it someone had written: *The Infinite Book, Abridged Edition.* He let it drop and picked up another: *The New Revised Almanack of True Prophecy.* Both pieces of paper were dry and yellowed, looking as though they had lain here for many years. He tried folding this slip the other way, but nothing happened. He picked up several others and tried them, too. In most cases the seeker, like him, seemed to have no particular book in mind.

Beauty.
Riches.
Love.
Death.

Will dropped the last of these other slips and looked around. He had no idea which way to turn. Every direction looked the same: uninviting. Suddenly he was angry with the librarian, the slip, and himself. By going off on this stupid book hunt, he had just landed himself in more trouble than he was in before. It didn't seem to matter what he did; nothing could make things worse now.

At random he chose one of the aisles and headed down it.

The pavement of ancient books here was uneven and in places heaved up like cracked stone. Will was cheered only by a faint, cool draft, which gave him hope that he would soon reach a way out. He clung to that hope and kept on, until the light of his lantern had dimmed to a feeble red glow that scarcely lit more than the hand that carried it. The scraps of paper that lay underfoot were yellowed and brittle, crackling under his tread like dry leaves.

He stopped, sensing more than seeing that there was an *edge* before him. Here the floor of books dropped steeply into a truly inky blackness. Will looked up and saw what appeared to be faint twinkling stars. He wondered if he had found the way out, but could it be night already outside? And if he was still in the Library, what had happened to the roof?

He took another step, craning his neck to peer down, and felt the floor sag and shift beneath him. He scrambled backward, but it was too late. The ancient volumes under his feet had begun to collapse, and he was pulled helplessly down with them.

Dropping the lantern, he clutched the edge of one huge book and hung on as it slid and tumbled in a roaring avalanche of paper and binding, then finally flipped over and sent him flying through the air.

He landed in a mass of books and paper scraps that felt like a huge pile of dead leaves. A cloud of dust settled all around him, and he went into a spasm of coughing. When it had passed, he looked up and saw nothing but darkness everywhere, lit faintly by some dull gray gleam that seemed to come from nowhere. He saw the lantern nearby. Somehow it had landed upright and was still lit. As Will reached for it, he heard a loud cough.

He went very still. There was no sound other than the faint whistle of the wind, the scratch and skitter of paper, and his own breathing.

The fear that he had managed to fend off by keeping moving now threatened to become panic.

"Is anyone there?" he shouted.

The echo of his shout faded away, and then a voice that seemed to come from very close by said, "Yes."

The flesh on Will's neck rose in goose bumps. He turned wildly, but could see nothing in any direction.

"Who's there?" he said.

"I am," the voice said. It was a voice unlike any he had heard before. It was made, he thought, of many sounds: water trickling over stones, leaves stirring in the wind, the rustle of animals through the grass. It was somehow a comforting voice, like all the sounds of the sunlit world beyond this tomb of books.

"Who are you?"

There was a brief silence, and then the voice spoke again, hesitantly this time, as though surprised at its own words. "Who am I . . . ?"

"Where are you?" Will said. "I can't see you."

Immediately he wished he had not said this. He stood up with the lantern raised, trying to still the trembling in his hand, and then heard the pad of soft, slow footfalls. He turned to the sound, and out of the shadows, as if taking shape from them, came a large silver-gray wolf.

Will's first impulse was to run, but before he could move, the wolf spoke.

"I was told to wait," the wolf said, as if to himself. "I was supposed to wait for . . . someone."

Will could not move. The creature stopped a few paces from him and gazed around searchingly with large yellow-gold eyes. He was larger than Will thought wolves were supposed to be. His head reached the height of Will's chest.

The wolf lifted his snout and sniffed the air.

"I'll . . . um . . . let you wait then," Will finally gasped, taking a step back. "I'll just go, and you can wait."

"Things are not the same," the wolf said, and growled. He turned in a circle and then looked at Will again, his eyes reflecting the red light of the lantern. "The world was not this way when I went to sleep. I don't know this place. I don't know you."

"I'm not actually, you know, from here," Will stammered. "I'm . . . I'm lost."

"Lost," the wolf echoed, and his ears perked up.

"I'm sorry I woke you. It was an accident. Really. I didn't mean to come here."

"Lost," the wolf repeated, and he made a huffing sound that might have been a laugh. "I was supposed to wait, and someone would come. Yes. Someone who was lost."

"It must be someone else," Will said, still backing away. "If I see anybody on the way out, I'll tell them where to find you."

The wolf arched his back and shook himself, just like a dog waking from a long, satisfying nap. Then he sniffed the air again and gazed into the absolute night that surrounded them. Will saw with a shiver that the wolf's large, gleaming eyes were definitely those of a hunting animal.

"I have waited, and someone has come," the wolf finally said, and his gaze fell upon Will again and stayed. "Now I must do as I was bidden."

Rowen was very worried. Will had been gone for hours.

When he first left, she had explored the shelves in the catalog room and had taken down a few interesting-looking volumes to skim through. She distracted herself for a good while with the misadventures of Sir Peridor the Extremely Unlucky and with the imagined history of the unreachable city of Arzareth, which no one has ever actually visited, and then she read about the curious architecture of the palace of Bazeen-Barathrum, where the furniture roamed in herds and if you wanted a bed or a chair, you had to hunt for it with a net and rope. Eventually she grew tired of browsing, but Will was still not back. Then there was a long time during which she paced around the circular room and went some distance into each of the corridors that led from it, hoping to catch sight of Will.

Finally, when there could be little doubt that something had gone wrong, she sat at one of the tables and debated what to do. The right thing was to go and find her grandfather, but she was not looking forward to what he would say.

Twice already, Nymm, the assistant librarian, had come nosing into the catalog room as if for the express purpose of checking up on her. The second time, when he found her still alone, he had nodded his head and grinned, clearly pleased to find that his expectations had been confirmed.

"*Easy,*" he said with a smirk, and strolled away.

Now he came in a third time, and her grandfather was with him. Rowen stifled a cry of relief and stood up to await the stern lecture that was sure to come.

"No sign of the slip, either," Nymm was saying to the toy maker, as he hurried to keep up with the old man's long stride. "That is most unusual. I will to have to notify the head librarian. He is not going to be pleased."

Pendrake came up to Rowen and looked at her without speaking.

"I'm sorry, Grandfather," she said, lowering her eyes. "It's my fault. I brought him here."

"You wanted to help, Rowen," Pendrake said, placing a hand on her shoulder. "That wasn't wrong."

"Will you be searching for him yourselves, then," Nymm asked sweetly, "or would you prefer that we do it for you?"

"Neither, I think," Pendrake said, and he gestured across the room to one of the branching corridors. Rowen turned to where he was pointing and to her great relief saw Will walking toward them out of the shadows. An instant later she saw the large silver-gray wolf that came trotting after him into the light, and the glad shout that she had been about to utter turned into a gasp. All over the room, heads rose from books, and an even more complete silence fell.

The wolf seemed unconcerned about all the eyes turned to him, as if his presence here were an everyday occurrence.

Will himself was a sight: his clothes were covered in dust and grime and there were bits of paper and strands of cobweb in his hair.

"What happened?" Rowen said, stepping forward. Then she halted and watched the wolf, who had stopped and was now standing calmly at Will's side. "Where did you . . . ?"

She faltered. The wolf's startling eyes fixed on her, then roamed about the room.

"This cave is strange to me," the animal said in his mesmerizing voice. "The smell is not right."

By now some of the other Library patrons had jumped out of their chairs and backed away to the far edges of the room. Nymm had taken refuge behind Pendrake. As the toy maker approached Will, the wolf perked up its ears and gave a yip. It bounded forward, then skidded to a stop and blinked at the old man in apparent confusion.

"I thought you were . . ." the wolf began to say, but did not finish.

The toy maker studied the strange creature intently. He took off his spectacles, rubbed them on his sleeve, and put them back on.

"What in all the Realms . . . ?" he said softly.

He turned his gaze on Will.

"It was my idea to come here," Will said. "I couldn't just stay in the toy shop and do nothing."

Pendrake raised a hand.

"We will discuss it later," he said sternly, and then to Will's relief, he looked at the wolf again and laughed softly. "This is a surprise. Or perhaps not."

Nymm now inched his way out cautiously from behind the toy maker.

"Where did this . . . *animal* come from?" he said, wrinkling his nose.

"I found him," Will said. "Well, he found me. Then he found the way out."

"But where in the Library did this happen? I've never heard of such a—"

"I . . . don't know," Will said, handing Nymm the slip, which feebly flapped a wing. "He's been here a long time. Longer than the books, maybe."

"And you intend to just *take* it?"

"I'm not *taking* him," Will said. "He's coming with me."

The wolf padded slowly up to the assistant librarian, sniffed, and wrinkled his nose. Nymm clutched the toy maker's sleeve and stared wide-eyed at the creature.

"But you can't. . . . This is . . ." the librarian sputtered, his eyes blinking rapidly. "Every item removed from the Library has to be properly checked out. We have to find out if it . . . he has even been cataloged."

"You may inform the head librarian," Pendrake said to Nymm, "that I will discuss the matter with him later."

Nymm's bloodless face actually reddened. He turned on his heel and fled the room.

"And now we must hurry," Pendrake said, turning to Will and Rowen again. "Will has been summoned by the Marshal."

Will and Rowen exchanged glances.

"We cannot stay here," the toy maker said to the wolf. "Where will you go?"

"I must go with the one who found me," the wolf said, and then his voice softened, as if he were mimicking the words of another: *"The one who is lost will be a seeker of the gateless gate. Stay with him until it is found."*

"The gateless gate?"

"That is what I was bidden. To stay with the seeker of the gateless gate."

To Will's surprise, the toy maker nodded.

"Very well then," Pendrake said. "You're welcome to come with us. But tell me, do you have a name?"

The wolf lowered his shaggy head as if to ponder this difficult question, and then he lifted his yellow-gold eyes to the old man.

"Shade. That was it. The name I was given is Shade."

9

These are the rules. Learn them so that when the time comes, you will not need them.

— The Book of Errantry

AS THEY MADE THEIR WAY through the streets to the house, Will told Rowen and the toy maker how he and the wolf had encountered each other.

"I went looking for a book and found *him* instead," he said when he had finished his story. He watched Shade, who had trotted on ahead as soon as they left the Library and was sniffing the air eagerly.

"But what is he, Grandfather?" Rowen said. "Where did the wolf come from?"

"I have my hunches, child, but no answers."

Many of those who passed by stopped in their tracks and stared uneasily at the alarmingly large creature padding along the paving stones, but none of them shouted or ran.

When a messenger wisp zinged overhead, the wolf grunted.

"I remember that one," he said, a trace of annoyance in his voice. "That one was always going too fast. Always hurrying, even in the days before the Storyeater came."

"You know that wisp?" Rowen asked.

"Wisp?" the wolf said, as if he'd never heard the word before. "Yes, I know that one. He was with the First Ones." He halted suddenly and raised his head.

"The First Ones," he said. "Have you seen them? Are they . . . ?"

"They are not here, Shade," Pendrake said quietly. "The First Ones no longer walk among us. They have not done so for a very long time."

The wolf paced beside them in silence. After some time, he spoke, and his voice was low and husky.

"My friend said it would be that way. He said we would not see each other again."

Edweth did not betray the slightest surprise when they arrived at the house with Shade. She merely gave the wolf her usual stern, appraising look and then returned to her kitchen, where dinner was under way. Will cleaned himself up and then sat down with the others to a quick meal of stew and bread. He was famished and dug in to his food eagerly. Then he looked up and saw the wolf, who sat calmly watching him from the kitchen doorway.

"I wonder if he's hungry," Rowen said. "I wonder if he even eats at all."

Edweth regarded the wolf with her hands on her hips.

"Now that's the strangest thing I've seen in a good while," she said. "Something four-legged that doesn't hang around the table begging. Maybe that's why he looks a little underfed. You can offer him something, Master Will."

Will took a chunk of bone from Edweth's chopping board

and carried it over to Shade. The wolf cautiously sniffed the offering, then gazed up at Edweth.

"If the fare is not to your liking . . ." the housekeeper began.

"You are kind," Shade said. "Thank you."

He took the bone in his jaws and gnawed at it energetically.

"That answers your question, Rowen," Pendrake said. "Though I would guess it has been a long time since he has *needed* to eat anything."

"But how did he get into the Library?" Rowen asked.

Will darted an apprehensive look at Shade. He felt uncomfortable talking about the wolf as if he were an ordinary animal that could not understand what they were saying. But Shade was busy with his treat and paid them no attention.

"He was a Companion of the Stewards," Pendrake said. "Or as he calls them, the First Ones. He is one of the Speaking Creatures, birds and beasts with the power of speech and understanding. There aren't many left, at least in this part of the Realm. His story, whatever it is, must be one of the oldest in the Kantar. He was here before the rise of Malabron and the destruction of Eleel. The Broken Years after the Great Unweaving are unknown to him. As for his being in the Library, I am as puzzled as you are."

"What is this gateless gate he was talking about?" Will asked. "Is it some way out of here?"

"I have no answers about that either, Will. A few scattered verses in the Kantar speak of such a thing, but in riddles. It is said that there were once gateways, called farholds, made by the Stewards. They were wishing portals. You could use them to transport yourself to any place inside or out of the Realm, just by wishing to go there. It is also said they were all broken or sealed in the time of the Great Unweaving."

"Maybe the Hidden Folk know about these gates," Rowen said eagerly. "People say the Lady of the Green Court knows all the secret paths in the Perilous Realm. She could help Will get home."

"That she could. But no one can find the Green Court unless the Lady wishes it so. Except perhaps you, Will."

Will wanted to ask the toy maker what he meant, but something told him he would not like the answer.

Dusk was falling as Will set out for the home of the Errantry with Pendrake and Shade. Rowen had pleaded to come along, but Pendrake would not let her.

"You've done enough for one day," he said drily. Rowen looked about to protest, but she crossed her arms and said nothing.

There were few people in the street at this hour. Sooner than Will wished it, they came to the ivy-covered wall of Appleyard. One of the larger doors was open, and as they approached, a file of four riders on horseback came out through the gateway. There were three men and one woman, all wearing long gray coats.

Inside the enclosure there were more people in long coats hurrying to and fro across a wide lawn crisscrossed by narrow stone paths. A horn sounded somewhere nearby, and then another. A second group of riders came trotting in through another gateway.

The lawn was dotted with apple trees and sloped gently up toward a building unlike any Will had ever seen. It was more than a house, and not quite a castle. Its peaked roofs, slender turrets, and many arched doorways looked as if they had not been built but had grown from the earth. And in fact four great trees grew right up against the corners, so that it was hard to tell where their massive white trunks ended and the stone began.

"The Gathering House," Pendrake said. "Home of the Errantry."

They followed one of the paths, which took them past a fountain where several men and women were gathered, talking in quiet, serious tones. Some of them nodded to Pendrake as he went by. Farther in the distance Will caught sight of a fenced circular enclosure where a young woman was riding a dappled brown-and-white horse. Mount and rider were trotting in tight circles around the enclosure, watched by a man with a long stick who pointed out the way they should go. From somewhere unseen came a ringing sound that Will guessed must be a hammer striking metal. He wondered if swords or armor were being made, and if all this activity meant that the Errantry was preparing for a possible invasion by the fetches. He doubted that swords would be of much use against them.

Reaching the hall, they climbed a wide staircase to a high, arched entryway. Here at last there were guards, one on each side of the doorway. At least Will thought they were guards. They wore no helmets or armor, but were dressed in the same long gray coats as the other people Will had seen. It came to him that these were knights of the Errantry, as were all of the men and women they had seen so far in Appleyard. They looked nothing like the knights in books and movies. Where was the shiny armor, the chain mail?

At the door Pendrake paused and turned to Shade.

"You'll have to stay here, I'm afraid," he said. "You were not summoned. I will make certain Will is safe until we return."

The wolf scowled, but did not protest. He gave Will a long look, then sat down in front of the doorway, immediately becoming as still and unperturbed as a statue. The guards looked inquiringly at the toy maker, who gave them a nod of reassurance and then beckoned Will to follow him.

They went down a long corridor lit by many candles, and up a flight of stairs to a wide, high-ceilinged hall with pillars down its length. Low wooden benches lined the walls, and tapestries hung from the roof beams. On each tapestry was an image of a man or woman. Many were dressed in long coats, but some wore clothing and armor that made them look more like what Will thought of as a knight, from the pictures he had seen in books back home.

"Renowned knights-errant of the past," Pendrake said. He gestured to the image of a woman with long red hair. "That is Gildred of Blue Hill."

"She has the same last name as . . ." Will began.

"She was my daughter," Pendrake said. "Rowen's mother. Rowen hopes to be just like her someday."

Pendrake had used the word *was*, but Will could not bring himself to ask what had happened.

Will expected to see the Marshal in this great hall, seated on some sort of high throne and frowning down at him. To his surprise the toy maker led him all the way through the hall and across a narrow corridor to a much smaller room. Here the walls were bare except for a large framed map. There was a small fireplace in one corner and a tall cabinet in another, stacked with scrolls and bundles of paper. In the center of the room was a wooden desk where a broad-shouldered man with cropped silver hair sat, studying a sheet of parchment. His high-collared brown cloak made Will think of a monk or priest. On the desk sat a glass of what looked like red wine, a loaf of bread, and a wedge of cheese, nothing of which appeared to have been touched.

"Lord Caliburn, Marshal of the Errantry," Pendrake said.

Will was startled. He had thought the man was the Marshal's assistant or secretary.

Caliburn's steel-gray eyes flicked up and then back down to the paper he was reading.

"Thank you for coming, Loremaster," he said in a low, clipped voice. "And for bringing the boy."

"This is Will Lightfoot," Pendrake said, gesturing for Will to come forward.

"From Elsewhere, yes," the Marshal said, his eyes still on the parchment. "I have the report here. And another that just came in from Arrow Company, which tells of ghostly shapes at night in the fields near Deeve Holm. These fetches, as you call them, are apparently still here in the Bourne."

"I didn't bring those things here," Will blurted out, and then regretted it. The Marshal had not accused him of anything, and now he had made himself sound guilty.

Caliburn set down the document he had been reading and looked at Will.

"You're certain of that, are you?" he said, then turned to the toy maker. "Surely you've told the boy what you suspect."

"Not yet," Pendrake said stiffly. "I didn't want to trouble him needlessly, if it turned out I was mistaken. But recent events make it much more certain that I am not."

"Yes, I've already been informed about the Library," Caliburn said. "And what was discovered there."

"You're talking about Shade," Will said.

"And you," Caliburn said. "A boy from Elsewhere, newly arrived in the Realm, who was able to find something that generations of librarians somehow missed."

"I didn't mean to," Will shot back. The Marshal's suspicious tone angered him. Once again he was being treated like a problem. Everything that happened seemed to draw him further into this strange world and deeper into trouble.

It seemed as though they were blaming him for everything. The fetches weren't his fault. Nothing was. He hadn't asked to come here. "I was looking for a book. These things just seem to happen to me here. I don't want them to."

"Perhaps not," Caliburn said, studying him. "But still they happen. To you."

"Lots of strange things have happened," Will said. "Why does it have anything to do with me? Maybe I just . . . stumbled into the middle of something."

"That's it exactly, I'm afraid," Pendrake said. "Once in a long while a Wayfarer comes along who stumbles upon that which others miss. Who ends up in the middle of things, as you say. In the Bourne we tell comical tales of a boy called Blunder, who was always falling in and out of danger."

"Things turned out well for him in the end, I believe," Caliburn said. "But unfortunately we are not in his *comical* tale. Our own blunders could cost us dearly."

"Someone with such a gift," Pendrake went on, "meets with strange happenings and coincidences wherever he goes. Most would call this chance, some call it fate, but I believe that the heart of such a Wayfarer is open to the perilous paths of this world in a rare way. I am more certain all the time, Will, that you are such a Wayfarer."

At that moment Will remembered the waylight he had seen in the Wood after he first met Rowen. He had known where to look for it before it began to glow. He had seen it before Rowen did.

"This is all wrong," he protested, backing toward the door. "It was just an accident. I'm nobody special."

"Yet you found your way here," Caliburn said, leaning forward suddenly in his chair, as if afraid Will would flee the room. "That's rare in itself. The Perilous Realm is difficult to reach, by all accounts. Many try all their lives and fail.

Spindlefog the printer even publishes misguidebooks for the very purpose of keeping unwary travelers out of these dangerous lands. For their own good. And yet you found your way in, apparently with no intention of doing so."

"All wanderers who come through the borderlands from the Untold must have something of these powers," Pendrake said. "But I suspect that you are greatly gifted with them. It explains Shade, and much else. And if it's true . . ."

He took a deep breath.

"It is a matter of grave consequence," the Marshal said, finishing Pendrake's sentence. "I know little of the tales that Master Pendrake has studied all his life. The ancient legends of the Realm are not my concern. The safety of Bourne and its folk is. And I see great danger here. But I also see what could be an advantage to us in a time of need."

"What Lord Caliburn means," Pendrake said, "is that your powers could be trained and made use of by the Errantry."

"Not *could*, Master Pendrake. *Should*."

Will stood in shocked silence, and then shook his head.

"You want me to stay here. . . ." he began, and a surge of fear took his breath away. "I can't do that. I don't belong here. Why won't you listen? I have to get home. They need me—"

"The loremaster is fond of telling me that very little happens by chance," the Marshal said. "Storyfolk seek refuge here now in greater numbers than ever before, bringing tales of Nightbane and other terrors. We know that creatures out of legend prowl our borders, and all we have is a fog of questions. Questions that a gifted Wayfarer might help us answer. And now it seems one has come among us at a crucial moment. I would not call that chance, but opportunity. Though the loremaster does not agree."

"We have discussed it already at length," Pendrake said

in a strained voice, and it was clear to Will that the discussion had been heated. "But we cannot ask Will to stay in Fable any longer than he wishes."

"We can *ask*," Caliburn said. "Surely we can still do that much."

"I thought, Marshal, we had decided against it."

"I don't think anything was decided for certain, Master Pendrake. Not when we hadn't yet spoken to the boy."

He turned to Will.

"Master Pendrake fears that if you remain in the Realm, you could be the prey of others who wish to make use of your powers, and not with good intent. Has he spoken to you about that?"

"He told me about the Night King," Will said slowly. "He was the one who saw me in the mirror. I don't understand why he's after me. I'm not from here. I don't have anything he could want."

"Yet he, or someone, went to a lot of trouble to snare you. Which, it seems to me, leaves us with a choice of two evils. If you stay here, we could find ourselves besieged. And if you leave Fable in search of your home, you could fall into the wrong hands and perhaps become another weapon turned against us. The wiser course, it seems to me, is to keep you here in Fable, guarded behind strong walls, until we know more."

"A weapon," Will faltered. "How could I—?"

"The Realm is a shifting place that endlessly reshapes itself, like stories in the retelling," Pendrake said. "Nothing here remains where it is, or what it is, for very long. There are a few places where this constant change is slower and less noticeable, like islands in a sea. The Bourne is one of them. That is why folk who have lost their stories come here. This is neutral ground, and all are welcome, provided they lay aside their feuds and grievances. No enchantment holds sway here but that of a tale well told. But out there, in Wildernesse, no road is certain. Very little can be trusted."

"And very few," Caliburn added. "One who can stumble upon dangers and hidden traps, who can find a straight road where others see a maze, would be much sought after. By many powers in this Realm."

"It is possible that Malabron seeks you for his own purposes, Will," Pendrake said. "He could send a Wayfarer like you in search of what he seeks above all."

"What is that?" Will whispered, swallowing hard.

"The Hidden Folk," Pendrake said. "The Night King's greatest desire, beyond the domination of all the realms and the end of stories, is to find the Shee n'ashoon and destroy them. In these days, when so much that might help us has been lost, only the Shee have the wisdom and the power to oppose him. And that is a danger for you, and for them."

"What do you mean? How could I be dangerous to people like Moth? I just want to go home."

"Yes, and the Lady could grant your wish, if anyone can. It would seem, then, that your best choice is to test your gift for . . . stumbling. To search for the Green Court. Just as the Night King himself is doing."

Will was standing near the fire, but it seemed to him that the room had gone cold. All at once he understood what the toy maker was telling him.

"If I go looking for the Hidden Folk," he said slowly, "I might be followed. I could lead their enemies straight to them."

"You are free to leave the city," the Marshal said after a long silence, "though I think such a course is folly. You cannot understand what waits out there, beyond our borders. There is a reason Wayfarers call these lands perilous. This is a world of fear and shadow, where even dreaming is dangerous."

"There must be another way," Will said, turning frantically to the loremaster. "You're telling me that I can't stay in Fable but that it would be crazy to go out *there*. So what am I supposed to do?"

"You *must* leave Fable, Will," Pendrake said. "I see no other way. You must set out on a journey into the unknown. Thus it has always been with Wayfarers in these storylands. But if it's of any comfort, I will be there with you on your road. To help, if I can."

"You'll come with me?"

A smile finally flickered across Pendrake's face.

"And Rowen, as she has been hoping," he said. "It's the only way I'll know for sure what she's up to."

"I would prefer that you stayed in Fable, Master Pendrake," Caliburn said. "Not because I will miss these debates over niceties of conduct while the legions of darkness gather around us. But the Council may need your experience in such matters. And I'm afraid that given the present threat to the Bourne, I cannot spare any of our knights to escort you. There are precious few in the city now as it is."

"The Guild of Knights-Errant has never refused help to those in need," Pendrake said.

"And we're not refusing it now," Caliburn answered gruffly, shuffling through the documents on his desk. "A member of the Errantry will go with you. But it will be a scout or a knight-in-training. I will look over the roster and select someone who—"

Just then came a sound from the doorway, a quiet cough.

Will turned to see a young man with a rolled parchment under his arm. His long ash-blond hair was tied back with a black band. His coat was shorter than those Will had seen before, and light brown rather than gray.

The young man looked directly at the Marshal without seeming to see Will or the toy maker.

"What is it?" the Marshal said without looking up, and the young man quickly entered the room.

"The report from Owl Company, sir," he said in a low voice. "You asked—"

"Yes. Good," the Marshal said curtly. "Leave it on the desk."

The young man did as he was told. As he set down the parchment, Will noticed a silver ring on his finger, with a bright green stone. Then the young man bowed slightly and turned to leave.

"Finn," Pendrake said quietly to him as he passed.

"Wait," Caliburn commanded. The young man stopped and turned again to face the Marshal.

"Madoc, isn't it?"

"Finn Madoc, sir. Knight-candidate in Owl Company."

"How many long patrols have you been on, Madoc?"

The young man hesitated a moment before answering.

"Four, sir," he said.

"How far afield?"

"On our last patrol, we reached the edge of the Screaming Wastes. An unthunk attacked our camp on the first night. We drove it off, but the next—"

"Thank you, Madoc. Yes, you will do." The Marshal dipped a pen in ink and wrote hurriedly on a piece of parchment. "I'm assigning you to escort this boy out of the Bourne. As you are still a candidate, I'm authorizing you to

stay with his party for seven days and then return. Report
to the duty officer and prepare your gear. Master Pendrake
will call for you when it is time."

Caliburn rolled up the parchment and handed it to
Madoc.

"Thank you, sir," the young man said. He still had not
looked at Will or the toy maker, and now he bowed again to
the Marshal and strode swiftly from the room.

Will watched him go, then turned quickly as the Marshal
spoke again.

"Will that do, Master Pendrake?"

"Yes, he will do very well, thank you."

"I wish you a safe and fortunate journey, Will Lightfoot,"
Caliburn said, without a hint of warmth in his frosty voice.
"And I hope that your land, wherever it lies, is never dark-
ened by the shadow that threatens ours."

10

Do not burden yourself with possessions.
Live as though you expect any moment
to set out on a long journey.

— The Book of Errantry

WHEN THEY RETURNED FROM APPLEYARD, Rowen met them in the hall. She wanted to know everything that had been said, and if they had met any of the famous knights-errant, but Will did not feel like talking. He soon said good night and took Shade with him up to his room.

The wolf stretched out on the rug by the bed, and very quickly fell into what seemed a deep, untroubled sleep, though Will had the uncanny sense that Shade was still wide awake. Which would make sense, he supposed, if Pendrake was right and the wolf had been sleeping for hundreds of years. Will himself lay for a long time with his eyes open, gazing at the ceiling. Outside, rain began to fall, pattering loudly at the window as the wind rose. Lightning flashed, and thunder boomed, and Will turned this way and that in the bed, unable to rest. He thought of his father and Jess.

Where were they now? Were they lying awake like him, wondering where he was? Once again he remembered his last sight of Jess, standing alone by the picnic table, her hand raised to wave good-bye. He imagined her still there, alone, waiting for him in the rain. Tears stung his eyes, and he wiped them angrily away.

Then he thought of Rowen and the young man named Finn. Pendrake was taking them all into the wilds beyond Fable, with no destination, no plan. What if the old man was wrong? They were all leaving the safety of Fable for Will's sake, even though it meant they might be walking straight into terrible danger.

Finally he sat up.

"I'll go by myself," he said.

He got out of bed as quietly as he could, opened the door of his room, and peered warily out. He heard a sound behind him and jumped. Shade was standing there, alert and watching him.

"I will not harm you, Will Lightfoot."

"I know. I'm sorry. I'm just not used to being around wolves."

"There are no wolves where you come from?"

"None like you. Listen, Shade, I have to leave. Now."

"Then so do I," Shade said.

Will was about to protest, then noticed the calm way the wolf stood there, as if nothing could frighten or daunt him, and he nodded his agreement. He thought that with Shade beside him, he might actually have the nerve to walk out of the door into the night.

"I'm glad," he said finally.

Will slipped on the cloak he had taken from the snug and went out onto the landing. The house was silent. With Shade at his heels, Will started down the stairs, wondering if he dared sneak into Edweth's kitchen for some bread, and then he stopped. He couldn't just go, not without thanking them all, Edweth, Rowen, and the toy maker, for what they had done for him. He would have to leave them something. After a long hesitation, he turned and tiptoed back up the stairs.

"That's as far as we're going?" Shade asked.

"For now," Will said. "There's something I must do first."

He went back to his room, sat down at the desk, and wrote a short letter, which he folded and tucked into his pocket. He slipped back out into the corridor, then paused, wondering where it would be best to leave the letter so it would be found. In the end he decided that slipping the paper under the door of the toy maker's workshop was the best choice, and so he climbed the stairs to the top floor, trying not to make any noise as he ascended. The wolf's claws clicked on the polished floorboards, and it seemed to Will that even this faint sound must be carrying all over the house. It also occurred to him that he didn't know where the toy maker slept, if indeed he slept at all.

The top floor was dark. The door of the workshop was closed, but a thin bar of light showed at the bottom edge and streamed out into the corridor. Hurriedly Will bent and began to slide the letter under the door, into the light. At the last moment, just when it was almost out of sight, the door began to open.

Will snatched the letter back and stood up.

Pendrake stood in the doorway.

"Will," he said sternly. "I was just thinking about you."

Will remembered that he was dressed in a cloak, but the toy maker didn't seem to notice. Fearing a lecture or worse, he said nothing.

"Come in," the old man said. "It appears we've both had trouble sleeping tonight."

"Sorry to bother you," Will muttered, and could think of nothing else to say. His plan of slipping away in the night was laid bare, and he had revealed it himself, as if his own will was working against him. Reluctantly he followed the old man into the room, and Shade padded in after him. A dying fire was glowing in the hearth, and on the toy maker's desk, under the light of a lamp, lay a small wooden toy in the shape of a wolf.

"Is that me?" Shade asked.

"I suppose it is," Pendrake said. "When I have something to think about or a problem to solve, I make a toy. Sometimes I barely notice what it is I'm making."

Pendrake poured two cups of tea from the pot hanging over the fire and handed one to Will. They sat in chairs by the fire, and Shade sat between them, his calm amber eyes watching both of them in turn.

"I've done much thinking about you, Shade," Pendrake said. "Wondering how you came to be in the Library."

"I remember more now," the wolf said. "More of who I was, before."

"We would like to hear about it, if you'll tell us."

"There was a time," Shade began slowly, "when my mate and I led our pack. We hunted in the forests. We did not speak as I do now. We knew the world with our eyes, ears, and noses. Our life was sweet, and happy, until the *ghool* came who hunted us with fire and iron."

"Nightbane," Pendrake said. "Creatures from the shadow side of Story."

The wolf made a noise of disgust in his throat. When he spoke again, his voice was low and menacing. The change in it sent a shiver through Will.

"They snared us with nets and traps. The wolves they caught they bred to be like them, cruel and wicked. Then those wolves hunted us, too. Their own kind. One day the *ghool* found my mate alone and tried to take her. She was fierce and strong, my mate, and she fought. She fought, but they were too many."

Shade was silent for a long time.

"I followed the tracks they left, to their camp," he said at last. "I tore and killed many, and those that were left ran off, but they had pierced me with their iron in many places. I wandered, a fever burning in me. I could not hunt, could not eat. I came at last to a forest where I smelled a new scent, one that was unknown to me. The scent of folk like you. I did not know if it meant danger or not. I crept up to their dwellings, in a clearing in the woods. There were people there, working, talking, laughing together. I had never heard laughter. It sounded strange to me, and I think I would have liked it, but all I could feel was pain, and hate.

"And then I saw a child. A girl in a red cloak with a hood, going off into the forest by herself. She was carrying a basket covered in a cloth. I followed her. I was hungry, and I wanted to kill. The girl walked quickly, but I ran ahead of her and stood in her path. She was frightened, but she was brave, too. And she did not hate. I could see that in her eyes. She was not like the *ghool*.

"I turned and I ran. I ran without knowing where I was going, and then I came to a house that stood by itself in the forest. Good smells came from that house. Good things to eat. I could not stop myself this time. The door was open, and I went in. There was an old woman there. She screamed and ran away. I let her go, and ate what food I could find. But it was too late. I felt the fever growing in me, from the iron of the *ghool*. I knew that no food would help me now. There was a bed in one corner. I climbed into it.

"I don't know how long I lay there. After some time I heard a sound. The girl in the red cloak was standing in the doorway. She came toward the bed, but in the dark of the house she did not see me. She called out a greeting. She thought I was the old woman. I stood up in the bed, ready to flee. My limbs were shaking, and there was a rasp in my throat. The girl saw me then. She screamed. I leaped over her and bounded out of the door. I ran, with what was left of my strength. And when I could not run, I crawled. I heard the sounds of the girl's folk following me. Their shouts, their anger. They were hunting for me, to kill me."

"I know that story," Will interrupted. "But it's not the same as I heard it."

"Stories never are," Pendrake said. "That is how they live on. How did you escape, Shade?"

"I did not," the wolf said. "Not from the death that was already in me. When I could crawl no farther, I dug a hole in the wet earth to lie in. I waited for sleep, and it came, and I forgot everything. There was no more time. Nothing. Then someone was there. I heard the tread of his feet on the earth and in my bones, waking me, but I knew he would not harm me. He spoke a name, and I knew it was my name. I rose and came to him. He put his hand upon me, and I could run again."

"Who was he?" Will said.

"He gave me a voice, and taught me many things," the wolf said, as if he hadn't heard. "His name was . . . in the sound of the rain, and the light at sunset. We ran together in the moonlight. We rested under the trees when the sun was high. Sometimes we journeyed a great distance to meet the others like him. The First Ones. We would meet them under a tree on a green hill. The tiny annoying ones, the ones you call wisps, would be there, too. And others, like me."

"Other wolves?" Will asked.

"They had been given speech, like me, but they had other shapes of bird and beast. On the hill the First Ones would dance and sing, and tell stories."

"The hill of Tuath Dara," Pendrake said. "The green mount of Peace. That was where the Stewards met every year at midsummer."

"Yes," Shade said. "Until it was . . . changed. By the sickness that came over the land. We marched then in a great company, and all who were friends of the First Ones joined us. We met the hosts of shadow, and we fought. We fought for a long time, and finally we began to drive the enemy back. But then *he* came. The Storyeater. He came as a blinding light that was really darkness inside. Like a sun that gave no heat. He blinded and burned us, and we were scattered far and wide, and many fell. Then my friend told me that there was something else for me to do. He told me to find the grove where he had woken me. He said I should wait there, and someone would come. Someone lost who would need my help to find the gateless gate. My friend told me that we would not see each other again. I did not want to leave him. But in the end . . . I did as he wished."

The wolf nodded his head slowly.

"I did as he wished," he said again, his voice little more than a whisper. "I ran, through forests and over hills, and everywhere was fear, and a shadow falling, but I did not stop. At last I found the place among the trees where he had woken me. There the sickness had not yet come, and I stayed and I waited. I waited a long time, under sun and stars, and at last I could not stay awake any longer, and I slept. Then Will Lightfoot came, and woke me."

"I'm glad he did," Pendrake said with a smile. "And I am very glad you are coming with us on this journey, Shade."

Will had been caught up in Shade's story. Now he remembered why he had come to the toy maker's door.

"But what if Lord Caliburn is right?" he said. "What if I'm captured out there and turned into a . . . a weapon? What will happen to you and Rowen then?"

Pendrake set down his cup.

"Listen to me, Will," he said. "What happens in this world, or in any other, is the result of many actions, both great and small. Nobody, not even Lord Caliburn, can weigh and measure the contribution each of us makes to that. I can tell you that your arrival has stirred up things that have remained quiet for too long, so that it was easy to ignore them. You've reminded me that I have spent far too much time cooped up in this house, when I should be out there, where the stories come from. Otherwise I cannot call myself master of anything but a pile of dusty maps and books."

"But Rowen, and Finn Madoc . . ."

"Rowen, as you may have noticed, can hold her own quite well. And I have known Finn for a long time. He may not have been knighted yet, but anyone trained by the Errantry is a force to be reckoned with, believe me. And like you he has his own story, one that he must be given the freedom to live."

"If I'm in a story, I wish I knew which one it was."

"Perhaps that's why you're here. Some come to this realm because they have no story. Some because they believe in a story so passionately that it becomes their own. And some find themselves here because it is time for a new story, one that can't be told without them. I don't know which of these is your tale, Will. But we will take this road together, and perhaps we'll find out."

"But that's just it," Will said. "I don't know what road to take. I don't know where to start or what direction to go in. Am I just supposed to start walking and see where I end up?"

"Why not?" Pendrake shrugged. "It's what folk in stories have always done." His face softened and he smiled. "From my experience, it's usually better not to set out on journeys like this with too many plans and expectations. Or even much hope. *Do not forget your goal, but let the way to it find you*, as a great knight-errant once said. We can discuss the various roads we might take, but I have a feeling you'll know what to do when the time comes. And it would be prudent, I think, to wait until the last possible moment to make the choice. That way there's less chance of others learning our purpose."

"You mean there might be spies here?"

"In Fable, news spreads like fire in dry grass. Those who pass on such news might not intend harm, but it's better to be cautious. If we don't know where we're going, no one else will, either. "

Will nodded. He was suddenly very tired. The day he had stolen the motorcycle seemed long ago and far away.

"The thing is," he said, "it was running off on my own that started this whole thing."

"Have faith in yourself, Will," Pendrake said. "There is more in you than you know."

Will sighed.

"That's what I'm afraid of," he said.

They did not set out for several days. Pendrake was waiting for the Errantry to report on any further sign of the fetches or others who might be servants of the Night King. Only when all of the scouts had reported that there was no stirring or rumor of danger in the Bourne did he feel it safe to leave Fable.

One morning, with Pendrake's permission, Rowen took
Will on a tour of Appleyard. They visited the lecture hall, and
Will was surprised to see that the classrooms were very much
like those back home, although the long wooden benches
looked a lot less comfortable than the desks he was used to.
On the grounds outside, they met three novices, friends of
Rowen, who had heard about the newcomer and wanted to
see him for themselves. Pendrake had cautioned Will not to
tell anyone that he had come directly from the Untold, but
he hadn't thought to make up a cover story. Now he wished
he had. One of Rowen's friends, a tall boy named Peter,
wanted to know what part of the Bourne he had come from.
Will glanced at Rowen helplessly.

"He's not from here," Rowen said quickly. "He's from a
storyland in the east. The kingdom of . . . the motorcycles."

"Never heard of it," Peter said with a suspicious frown.
He turned to Will. "Is it far away?"

"I think so," Will said cautiously.

"You *think* so?" echoed one of the other novices, a girl
named Maeve. "How can you not know?" Just then the bells
at the Gathering House sounded the hour, and Rowen's
friends hurried off to their lesson, much to Will's relief.

Next they visited the smithy, a cavelike structure of black
stone at the rear of the college, its air acrid and roiling from
the forge fire. Through the smoke they could see a bearded
man in a black apron working at an anvil, hammering at a
red-hot bar of metal. Near him a boy not much older than
Will polished a breastplate. Rowen explained that knights-
in-training were apprenticed for a time to the armorer. In
this way they learned the lore and craft of weapons and
helped to make their own armor and their first sword.

"But they don't wear armor," Will said.

"They do in battle," Rowen said. "The forges have been working day and night lately. It's not a good sign."

They watched as the boy set down the breastplate, took up a mallet, and tapped at the pieces of a gauntlet, smoothing and shaping the thin metal. Then he saw Rowen and called her and Will over. They talked for a while, and again Will was careful not to say too much about himself. The boy's name was Simon Thorn. He was a good friend of Rowen's, and Will learned that he would be leaving soon on his first quest, as a squire to a knight-errant.

"Are you thinking of joining the Errantry?" Simon asked Will.

"I don't think so," Will said quickly, then felt he should say something more friendly. "But it looks like a great time."

Simon laughed and wiped the sweat from his brow. "As you can see," he said.

After they left Simon to his work, Rowen said, "If all goes well, Simon will be riding out on his own in a year or so. I can't wait for my turn."

When they returned to the toy shop for the midday meal, Pendrake was there. He thought it would be a good idea for Will to get some training in defending himself before they left the city. Will agreed, eager to try out a sword.

And so Will and Rowen spent part of each day at Appleyard with Finn. On the first day they waited for him in the sparring ground, a circular field ringed with colorful banners strung from tall poles. When the young man appeared, he bowed slightly to them, his face expressionless. He had brought several wooden practice swords that he called bevins. Much of Will's eagerness vanished when he saw them.

Finn handed Will one of the bevins and showed him how

to stand and hold the weapon. They sparred several times, and while Finn carefully pointed out what Will needed to learn, he never smiled or said anything encouraging. Each time they began again, Finn would repeat his instruction about how to stand and hold the sword. After a while Will grew impatient.

"I understand all about *that* part," he said finally.

In an instant, with a movement too quick for Will to follow, the bevin was out of his hand and in Finn's, the point of the wooden blade at Will's neck.

"How about this part?" Finn said coldly.

Will said nothing. He glanced at Rowen out of the corner of his eye and felt his face redden.

Finn handed back the bevin.

"In combat you always have two weapons," he said. "Yours and your opponent's. Learn to use them both, and you'll never be unarmed. Let's start again."

Will threw down the bevin.

"This is a waste of time," he said. "Where I come from, we have better weapons than this."

Finn picked up the sword.

"My family came from Elsewhere, too," he said. "A long time ago. Here in the Bourne we know about the powerful weapons of the Untold, but we've learned to be careful about what we use to protect ourselves. There are creatures here that cannot be harmed by anything that doesn't belong in their own stories. And we've found that some tools, no matter how helpful they seem at first, always end up serving the Dark Powers."

"Did anyone in your family ever go back to Elsewhere?"

"Not that I know of. When you've lived here a long time, you become more like one of the storyfolk, I think. It's very rare that one of them can cross over into the Untold. Some who try lose their way and are snared by the Night King, or choose to serve him because they believe he alone holds the keys to all doors in and out of Story. That lie has tempted many Wayfarers."

As he spoke these last words, Finn looked searchingly into Will's eyes. *He's wondering if I'll be one of those,* Will thought. He was about to answer Finn's look with angry words, but they died in his throat. He didn't know any better than Finn what was going to happen to him.

Finn held out the bevin.

"Again," he said.

On the evening before their departure, the toy maker met Will, Rowen, and Finn in his workshop. He swept aside the clutter on his work desk and unrolled a large parchment map, placing tea cups and stones at the corners to keep it flat.

"This is the task, and the danger, that lies before us," Pendrake said, his hand on the map. "Will is setting out in search of a way home, and we are pledged to help him. Will's gifts as a Wayfarer may lead him to the Green Court. We will do nothing to hinder this, if it happens, yet at the same time we must go warily, to elude any pursuers."

It was the map that Rowen had shown Will earlier. The travelers gathered around it and discussed the merits of the various roads they might take. It became clear to Will that no matter what direction they set out in, they would eventually come to lands where friendly folk were few and far between and one could never be sure what lay around the next bend. Once, these ungoverned and little-known regions were considered one of the Bourne's best defenses, but over the years, foul and malevolent things had crept slowly into them and made their dwellings there.

They talked about returning to the Wood, which stretched northeast from the city to the River Arrow, the Bourne's eastern boundary. This was the place where Will had crossed into the Realm, and so it seemed the likeliest direction to begin a search for the way back. Moth had reported to Pendrake that there was no longer any sign of the fetches or the mirrors. But as the toy maker reminded everyone, the fetches likely could not have set the trap of the mirrors themselves. They were shadowbeings that moved only under the power of someone or something else sent by the Night King. Going into the Wood might mean walking straight into the greatest danger.

They considered going west, through the great forest of Eldark to the lands beyond. The ancient land of the Hidden Folk, before their exile, was in the west.

Finn looked at the vast forest spreading across most of the western half of the map and shook his head.

"There are scouts and knights-errant who know these woods far better than I do," he said.

"Yes," Pendrake said, "but those who've traveled a place often might not see what is right in front of them."

He cautioned that when it came to the whereabouts of the Green Court, nothing was certain. There were many tales of wanderers encountering the Hidden Folk in unlikely, far-flung regions. And the forest, for that matter, held many dangers.

The other directions were carefully discussed and considered, but in the end, there was no clear answer to the question of the road they were best to take.

Pendrake noticed Will intent upon the map, his gaze traveling hopelessly over the many strange names.

"Tomorrow," he said, placing a hand on Will's shoulder, "we will go to the crossroads, and there a path will be chosen. Until then, let's not worry over what hasn't happened yet. Sleep is more important right now than plans. As the Kantar says, you have to walk a road with your feet."

After Finn had left for Appleyard, the others went back downstairs for bed. Will and Shade said good night to Rowen and the old man at the door of Will's room. At her own door, Rowen paused before going in.

"Thank you, Grandfather," she said. "For letting me come along. I know you don't really want me with you. . . ."

Pendrake took off his spectacles and nervously tapped the earpieces together. Then he slipped the spectacles back on again, sighed, and looked into Rowen's eyes.

"I want you where you'll be safe, child," he said softly. "But I don't know where that is anymore. Maybe there are no safe places. Maybe there never have been. And maybe I've protected you too much. Though you've managed to learn quite a lot about protecting yourself, despite me."

He looked past her into the room, and she saw his eyes fall on the chest at the end of her bed. She blushed and looked down at the floor.

"Do you think that I could be like . . . that I could be a great knight-errant someday?"

Pendrake hesitated.

"You will do wondrous things," he said at last, and there was sadness in his voice. "I've always known that."

Rowen started to say something else, but Pendrake turned and went back up the stairs alone. When he was well away from Rowen, he sighed heavily. As he passed the rain-cabinet, he paused and leaned toward the door. From within came the faint but steady sound of the downpour that had not ceased for a moment since he had first come to live in this house, so many years ago.

His granddaughter had grown up under the same roof

and did not question the rain. It had always been there, just one more unexplained marvel in a house of wonders. She had lived so far without the knowledge that the rain was there for her, to keep her hidden.

And now he was taking her out into the world, perhaps far from home. Deep into the weave of the Kantar, into the next chapter of her own story. With that thought, the toy maker's heart misgave him. She was not ready. But would he ever feel otherwise? This time had been coming since she was born. He knew that she would have to learn of her inheritance, and that it was right, and he could not prevent it, no matter how much he feared for her. Until now he had thought of that day as far in the future, but with the coming of the boy and all that had happened since, he knew it was now rushing toward them and that it would soon be here.

He walked away from the raincabinet, went into his workshop, and closed the door. Light burned in the windows long into the night.

Finn Madoc set out the traveling clothes he would wear in the morning. His small room was almost bare: it held his bed, a washbasin on a wooden stand, a shelf with a few tattered books. A parchment map hung on one wall. Brass pins dotted it in many places. Markers of all the places he had searched, so far in vain. It had been ten years now, and no word had yet come to Fable of the fate of the missing.

As he stood gazing at the map, he turned the ring with the green stone on his finger, as if to confirm that it was still there. Each time he set out on a mission for the Errantry, he went in hope that this time he would stumble across some clue, some trace of those he sought. And each time he returned to Appleyard, his hope had lessened and the Realm seemed an even larger place.

He took up his sword and went out into the dark corridor of the dormitory. The night sentry nodded to him as he passed through the entryway into the great hall, which was empty. Most of the knights he knew had already left on missions. He would be the only member of the Errantry keeping vigil tonight.

Moonlight streamed into the room from the high windows. There were benches underneath each of the tapestries that pictured the legendary knights of the past. Finn did not take his place under any of these. He went instead to the farthest corner of the hall, where there was a space between the pillars with no tapestry. Here he sat on the bench, laid his sword on the cold stone floor in front of him, and set his hands in his lap. He heaved a sigh, and then went so still that he might have been one more silent figure on a tapestry.

Shade the wolf lay on the rug beside Will's bed. His eyes were open. He had slept for so long in the dark of the Library that it may be he no longer had any need for sleep. When the boy stirred, or there was some unidentifiable creak or shuffle from somewhere in the house, his ears would twitch, but other than that, and his slow, steady breathing, he did not move. What thoughts wolves have, they generally keep to themselves. Or perhaps anyone who had seen him then would have said that the wolf *was* his thought and that that thought was watchfulness.

11

Serpent without head or tail,
Arm without flesh or bone,
Running far without motion,
Unwinding ribbon of stone.

— *The Quips and Quiddities of Sir Dagonet*

THEY SET OUT FOR APPLEYARD before dawn the next day.
As they were leaving the house, Pendrake gave Edweth its
keys on a great iron ring.

"While I'm gone," he said to her, "you will not clean my
workshop."

"Of course not, sir," Edweth said, solemnly shaking her
head.

The housekeeper put up a stern front as she bustled
about, making sure that Will and Rowen's packs contained
everything they might need, without being too weighty.
But as they said their farewells, she gave both Rowen and
Will a tight hug and tears brimmed in her eyes. For the first
time, it occurred to Will that if his journey was successful,
he would not be coming back here. He would never see this
house, or Edweth, ever again. He had come to appreciate
the housekeeper's gruff good nature, and her cooking.

Finn met them at the doors of the Gathering House. This time he was wearing a long gray coat like the other knights-errant. As usual he had little to say, and only nodded to Will and Rowen without smiling. Will had seen knights coming and going on horseback, and he wondered out loud if that was how they were going to travel.

"There are few mounts to spare," Finn said. "And on foot we'll blend in better with the other travelers on the road. And we may find paths that would be missed from horseback."

"Walking was how you found your way here, after all," Pendrake told Will. "It's said that the realms of Story are found by those who walk rather than run. Perhaps that's also true for those who wish to leave."

As they were preparing to set out, Lord Caliburn arrived to see them off, though he had little to say. He surveyed their gear with a stern eye and saved an especially dark look for the wolf.

"An unusual company," he said. "You're not likely to pass unremarked. And even in the Bourne that's cause for concern. No road can be considered completely safe, not anymore."

"No road ever was," Pendrake said. "But we're not without friends, even out in Wildernesse."

"May these friends prove trustworthy," Caliburn said.

He suggested that Will and the others take the main road south, which was well traveled by members of the Errantry on their way to the citadel of Stonebow, three days distant, where they would find refuge if need be.

"We have considered the south road, along with all the others," Pendrake said. "But it is Will's choice to make."

Lord Caliburn looked to be about to reply but pursed his lips and said nothing. He gave them all one final wish for a safe journey and strode away.

*   *   *

Will and his companions left Fable by a back gate in the
south wall and followed a narrow, winding path down to
the paved road, which they joined at the bottom of the hill.
The story they had prepared was a simple one, that they were
on a journey to visit friends in other parts, not an uncommon
thing among people in the Bourne. They had all dressed
in inconspicuous garments of green and brown cloth. Will
carried his own clothes in his pack. He hadn't wanted to
leave them behind, as they were the only link he felt he had
left with home.

Finn had a sword at his side, and on his back he carried
a short bow of pale wood and a quiver of snowy-feathered
arrows. Pendrake walked with a long, gently curved staff of
polished wood and a leather bag slung over one shoulder.
He carried no weapon that Will could see. For Will, Finn
brought a long knife that was much like Rowen's. He said
that the hilts were new but that the blades had come from
a storyland where a war was fought over a magic ring that
made its wearer invisible. The knives were crafted to bite
into wraiths that no ordinary weapon could harm.

"I know that story," Will exclaimed. "I read the books.
And I saw the movies."

"Movies?" Rowen asked.

"Another kind of story," Will explained. "With pictures
that move. So these knives come from *that* story? How did
they get here?"

"They've been in the armory a long time," Finn said.
"They were probably brought here by a traveler who bar-
tered them for something else he needed more. A lot of
weapons and magical objects end up in Fable that way."

Finn had also given Will and Rowen each a pack to carry
food and bedding, and supplied them with leather tunics
and sturdy, well-fitting boots for long travel. The tunic was

stiff and felt constraining. When Will first tried it on, he'd complained the the tunic was too small. He said it jokingly, not wanting Finn to know how scared he suddenly felt, now that his journey was really about to begin.

"It's meant for protection, not comfort," the young man had said with his usual coldness.

The knife felt strange on his hip. Will pulled it from its leather sheath once before they left Appleyard. It was heavier in his hand than he expected and had no markings. The steel hilt was wrapped in dark leather, and the blade, burnished to a mirror-smooth luster, tapered to an alarmingly sharp point. He tried to imagine stabbing someone with it and quickly slipped it back into its sheath.

When they reached the road, Shade walked sometimes at Will's side but often trotted ahead eagerly or plunged into the roadside greenery nose-first. Will watched him, both amused and troubled by this fierce yet somehow innocent creature and the way he had come into his life.

"Shade seems glad to be on the road," Rowen observed.

"Fable was his first city, I suspect," Pendrake said. "We're finally in a world that he knows."

"This *is* the world," the wolf growled over his shoulder.

They went southwest toward the crossroads of the Bourne. As they walked the morning chill from their limbs, the sun rose behind a veil of mist. They walked through the quiet valley at an easy pace, past the farms and outlying houses. The same small dog Will had seen the night he arrived darted out of its gate barking, took one look at Shade, and sped back the way it had come. There were fewer people on the road than there had been before, and Will wondered whether this was a good sign or not. He thought of asking Finn or the toy maker, but then he decided he didn't want to risk any more bad news.

"There," Rowen said, taking Will out of his thoughts. She was pointing to a wooded rise. "That's where we came out of the Wood."

Will looked at the faint track winding into the trees and wondered where Moth and Morrigan were now.

Farther along they descended into a dell shaded by drooping willow trees and crossed a wooden bridge over a slow-moving stream. On the far side of the dell, they came out into dazzling sunshine. It promised to be a warm day. Birdsong soon filled the air. The roadsides were bright with summer flowers, and in the distance fields of ripening wheat and corn rippled in the morning breeze. The world seemed so peaceful that Will could not prevent a surge of hope from rising in him. He could almost believe that his pursuers had gone far away, or forgotten him. Or that it had all been a mistake: the stories of darkness and evil were just that, only stories, and no one was hunting for him after all.

When the sun was well up in the sky, they reached a slight rise, shaded by a ring of tall elms, where roads from five directions met. In addition to the road from Fable, here the wide stone main road of the Bourne ran north and south, and crossed the narrower but well-tended east–west way.

"Here is where you make your first choice, Will," Pendrake said.

Will nodded tersely. He was annoyed but hoped it didn't show. Why did it have to be his choice? He didn't know what he was doing or where he was going. Pendrake knew much more than he did about this world. And he was the one who had insisted that Will go on this journey in the first place.

Will sighed and looked about him, thinking over what he had learned from studying the toy maker's maps. He knew that directly south on the main road lay the town of Goodfare, a day's walk distant. To the east were Stook

and Owlet, two tiny villages less than a mile away, the pale
wood smoke of their chimneys visible above the trees. Other
larger towns lay that way, too, and beyond them, the River
Arrow and the eastern borderlands. To the north the main
road wound up through a range of hills called the Brades
and so to the citadel of Annen Bawn upon the Bourne's
stony northern marches. The road west led to several farm-
ing villages and other branching ways, then ended at the
vast forest that had been spoken of with unease and concern the night before.

Yet he was here now, without the map, and in every
direction he saw only trees, and flowering hedges, and green
fields. There was no way to tell the roads apart, nothing
to hint at what dangers each might have in store. He went
still and waited for something inside to speak to him, but
nothing came, or at least nothing certain. One moment a
particular road seemed to beckon him, but the next moment
it was another. While he stood and waited for some kind
of revelation, and wondered how he would know if it *was*
one, a wagon pulled by two stocky horses and loaded with
barrels came up slowly from the south, then at the crossroads
turned onto the road to Fable. The thickset man driving the
wagon glowered at them as he passed.

"Quests," they heard him mutter sourly. "Why can't folk
just stay at home?"

Will found himself wondering the same thing. He turned
in a circle, still undecided. Rowen sat down by the wayside,
on a large flat stone that looked as if it had been carved as
a seat for just that purpose. It occurred to Will that many
travelers over the years must have sat here, like him, with
a choice to make. Finn Madoc stood nearby, gazing into the
distance in each direction in turn. Shade went sniffing down
one of the roads, seemingly unconcerned about the whole

affair. Will avoided looking at the toy maker. Not for the first time, he was sure the old man's faith in him was misplaced.

Then he looked again at Shade, who was still nosing his way along one of the roads. Will called his name, and the wolf halted and came loping back.

"Don't tell me that's it already," he grumbled. "You never get very far in your travels, Will Lightfoot."

In spite of himself, Will smiled. Then he remembered the statue of Sir Dagonet, the Lord Mayor, at the crossing point of the city's main streets. He thought of the dog barking to warn his master of danger, and an idea came to him.

"Shade will decide," he said.

Rowen grinned and stood up. Finn shot a dubious glance at Pendrake, who merely nodded and said, "Very well."

"You wish me to choose our road?" the wolf said, cocking his head to one side.

Will nodded, wondering what on earth he was doing.

"Then I will choose it," Shade said. Without hesitation he trotted back the way he had just come, stopping once to look over his shoulder with a glare of annoyance that the others had not yet followed him.

"This way," he called. "This is the way back to the lands I know."

Shouldering their packs, the others walked along after him without speaking, and Will wondered if he had just made a terrible mistake. Shade had chosen the western road that led to the forest of Eldark.

For the rest of that day, they followed the road through the farmlands in the west of the Bourne. They met many other travelers, most of them country folk going about their business. Almost all were heading the way that Will and his companions had come, toward Fable. Some looked friendly, and smiled or exchanged a greeting, while others eyed them suspiciously, especially when they saw the wolf. Finn said that the nearer one came to the forest, the more wary folk were of strangers.

In the afternoon they halted at a branching where a slender track angled away northwest from the main road. Without hesitation Shade chose the narrower road. This led them for a while between fields of green barley and wheat that in places rose over their heads. Then the countryside grew more rolling, and the road wound down through a pastureland dotted with clumps of trees, where cows grazed. Here and there steep hillocks with sides of naked rock jutted out of the softly rolling landscape.

As evening was falling they came out of the pastures. The road climbed between two steep hillsides and then leveled off. Ahead of them in the distance, Will could see a few lights twinkling in the gloom.

"That would be the village of Hare's Hill," Finn said. "One of our riders passed this way yesterday and reported that all was quiet. There is an inn where we could sleep, and the folk are trustworthy."

"But Lord Caliburn was right: we make a strange company," Pendrake said, eyeing the wolf. "The news of our stopping there would be told to anyone else who came this way."

"I know a place where we can shelter," Shade said. "It's not far."

The others consented, and the wolf led them away from the road, through a grove of stunted, thorny trees. The ground rose steadily, and soon they found themselves at the foot of a grassy hillock. Shade led them around to the far side, and there they came to a small hollow ringed by three huge jagged stones that leaned together as though they were holding a secret conference.

"This will make a fine campsite," said Finn, looking around approvingly. "It's out of the wind and gives some concealment. I think we can risk a fire."

Rowen and her grandfather had been gathering dry sticks as they traveled, and now they set about making a fire, while Finn went off to scout the surrounding area.

As soon as he stopped walking and sat down heavily, Will's feet began to throb and ache even worse than they had all day. He tugged off his boots, certain that he had never walked so much in a single day. Rowen looked tired, too, and even Shade was content to sit quietly near them. The toy maker wandered off a short distance and seemed to be studying one of the stones.

Will rubbed his sore feet.

"I don't think I'll be able to walk again," he groaned.

"Today wasn't too bad," Rowen replied. "Once we leave the Bourne, there won't be any nice smooth roads like this."

Will gaped at her.

"If we don't know where we're going," he said, "why are we hurrying?"

"We weren't hurrying. I suppose people don't walk much where you come from."

Will said nothing. He had to admit it was true. At home, he rarely walked anywhere if he could avoid it.

"Have you met others like me?" he asked finally. "People that your grandfather has helped?"

"The last I know of was my father. He came here when he was a young man, from Elsewhere. He was determined to find his own way home. Until he met my mother." Rowen smiled. "Grandfather says he was a lot like me."

Will remembered the tapestry he had seen in Rowen's bedroom, the man dressed in the clothing of his own world.

"Have you ever been there? To where your father came from, I mean."

Rowen shook her head.

"I'd like to see the Untold. At least I think I would. But it's not easy. And Grandfather says that once you've gone there, it's even harder to find your way back."

An owl hooted nearby, an eerie sound that made Will aware of the unknown countryside surrounding them. He thought of the warmth and comfort of Pendrake's house.

"What happened to them?" he asked. "Your mother and father."

At first Rowen did not answer. She fed a handful of dry twigs into the fire, and then at last she spoke.

"When I was very young, we lived in the Brades, north of Fable. Our farm was called Blue Hill. One winter a large band of mordog came out of the north, looting and burning. Such a thing had not happened for many years."

"What are mordog?"

"A breed of Nightbane. Wicked storyfolk bred by Malabron to serve him. There are many kinds. Goblins. Creech. Yagsha, that suck your blood. Then there's hogmen. They walk like men, but they have pigs' faces. They eat people, but luckily they aren't very clever. Mordog are the worst. They come without warning, take what they want by force, and vanish."

"That's what happened to you?"

Rowen nodded.

"A raiding party attacked our farm one evening. We had no warning. My grandfather came the next day with riders of the Errantry, but it was too late for my mother and father. Moth and Morrigan found me hiding in the woods and brought me to Grandfather. I don't remember anything from before that day. I don't remember what my parents looked like, or the sound of their voices."

"I'm sorry," Will said. He thought about his mother. He wanted to tell Rowen about her, but he held back. He wasn't ready to speak about it to this girl he hardly knew.

Rowen snapped a larger stick in two and tossed it on the flames.

"I wasn't the only one who lost their family," she said stiffly. "Many farms were burned. Finn's older brother Corr set out with a band of riders in pursuit of the mordog, but neither he nor any of his companions ever returned. No one knows what happened to them."

"Do you think that'll happen to us?" Will said dejectedly.

"No, I don't," Rowen said with quiet intensity. "We're with Grandfather, and Finn. And Shade, too. Something is beginning. Something scary, but exciting, too. Can't you feel it? Grandfather calls the Bourne a place where stories are told, not lived. We're leaving it now. We're entering the true Realm. This is a real story we're in."

"I wouldn't know," Will said, still unconvinced. "Where I come from, life isn't like stories. Things happen that don't make any sense. Nothing turns out the way it should."

"Sometimes it's like that in stories, too," Rowen said. "The people in them don't know the ending. If everything always turned out the way you expected, none of it would matter."

Before Will could reply, Finn returned. The toy maker joined him at the lip of the hollow, and they stood together, talking in low voices. Will wondered if what Rowen had told him about the young man was the reason for his aloofness.

"Has he . . . Finn, I mean . . . been in a lot of battles?" Will asked Rowen.

"A few, maybe," she said. "I don't really know. The Guild knights don't boast about what they do. It's part of the code. But in Fable stories get around, of course. They say Finn fought a giant unthunk in the Screaming Wastes and killed it single-handed."

Will remembered the somewhat different story Finn had told Lord Caliburn. He didn't know what a giant unthunk was, and at the moment he didn't care to find out. As long as the Screaming Wastes were far away, that was fine with him.

Pendrake finally sat down near the fire, and after a while Finn joined them. As the firelight illuminated the faces of the three towering stones, Will looked at them more closely. He stood and examined the stone nearest to him. There were faint curving lines carved upon the stone's surface, worn almost invisible by age.

"What are these markings?" he asked Pendrake.

"Words," the toy maker said. "In an ancient language. They tell the story of a boy named Conn the Clever, the hero of the Riverfolk. They lived in this land long before there was a country called the Bourne. The carvings tell how he outwitted an ogre and how the stones got here."

"Tell us the story, Grandfather," Rowen said eagerly.

"It happened once that a groog took up residence in the forest near the home of the Riverfolk. Now, a groog is a large, nasty kind of ogre with metal fangs of varying size and jaggedness, and huge arms that hang down to its scaly feet. A groog is always hungry and moves surprisingly fast for something that looks like a mountain with teeth. This particular groog began to make off with sheep and chickens from the Riverfolk, and even a few dogs went missing. Ogres were known to steal children, too, preferably plump ones.

"*Conn the Clever decided he had to deal with this matter before sheep-stealing led to something worse. So he set off one morning in search of the groog. He had to admit to himself that he was a little bit afraid, but as he walked through the forest, he told himself a story about one of his own adventures, a story of peril and last-minute escape, and that cheered him up somewhat, since the story was mostly true.*

"*Conn had little trouble finding the groog's lair. The biggest clue was the stench. It led him to a cave in a hillside, comfortably furnished with armchairs and lamps and bookshelves and a bearskin rug (no, on second glance it was a whole bear, squashed flat), and also less tastefully strewn with bones and maggot-ridden animal carcasses. The smell of blood and rot was so overpowering that Conn didn't notice the groog sneaking up on him from behind. Before the boy could escape, the evil creature seized him in his claws.*

"*'Lucky day,' the groog chortled, his breath almost enough to finish the boy off right then and there. 'Caught Conn of Riverfolk I have. Eat him I will. Yum, yum.'*

"*'Of course you've caught me,' Conn said, thinking quickly. 'I came here on purpose, looking for you. I told everyone in the village that you and I would simply have to battle it out. For I have heard that you are the strongest ogre in the whole world. Or am I wrong?'*

"*The startled monster hurried to affirm that he was the one that Conn sought. There was, he could personally attest, no ogre stronger. Upon hearing this, Conn feigned great pleasure and presented the groog with a proposal: that the pair of them engage in mortal combat to prove who was the better of the two. 'For I am without doubt the cleverest boy in the world and, as I'm sure you know, when you're the best at something, it's difficult finding opponents worth your time and effort. So why don't we find out whether my wits are any match for your might?'*

"Ogres generally cannot resist challenges of this kind, as Conn well knew, and fortunately this groog was no exception. He quickly agreed, a hungry grin spreading across his hideous face.

" 'And the one who does not win,' he chortled, drool oozing down his chin, 'will be yummy-yum din-din.'

" 'That's fine,' Conn told him, 'but first you will have to prove that you're as powerful as everyone claims. Otherwise I'm just wasting my time challenging you.'

"They went outside, and the groog picked up a huge fallen log and lifted it over his head as if it were a twig.

" 'I've seen my grandmother fling bigger sticks than that out of her path,' Conn said. The groog growled and hurtled the log into the air. Conn stifled a gulp when he heard the distant crash as the log fell in the forest far away. It occurred to him that this groog might really be the strongest in the world. In which case he was in serious trouble.

" 'I also heard you were the swiftest creature on two legs, though looking at you I find that hard to believe,' Conn said. 'Show me how fast you can run to where that stick landed, and back.'

" 'Big dumbskull Conn thinks me,' the groog said with a sneer. 'If to fallen log I run, gone he'll be when back I come.'

"The boy praised the groog's talent for near rhyme and swore that no such trickery was in his mind, but nevertheless the groog picked him up and tucked him under one arm. He then set off at a truly astonishing pace for such a huge, lumbering creature, almost leaping as he bounded through the woods to the log and back to the cave in almost no time at all.

" 'Not bad,' Conn said as the groog set him down, and he swallowed hard, for it was clear to him now that if his plan failed, he was surely doomed. 'However, the last groog I met could pull up the biggest stone in the forest by the roots,' he went on. 'Now, I know that's asking a lot. . . .'

"Brushing Conn aside, the groog, still huffing and puffing from his run, wrapped his arms around a huge chunk of rock that had stood nearby, embedded in the earth, since the very first tale was spun. He heaved and grunted and grew purple in the face, and at last the stone came up out of the ground, dangling thick clods of earth.

" 'Excellent,' Conn said. 'But don't set it down just yet, not if you really want to impress me. I've seen my baby brother twirl a pebble like that on the tip of his finger.'

The groog's limbs began to shake and his breath started coming in gasps. At last with a groan he tossed the stone aside. It fell with an earth-shaking thud, and the groog nearly toppled over with it.

"Conn shrugged and said, 'Very well. If that's your best, it will have to do. Let's not waste any more time. Prepare for battle.'

"The groog, wheezing and panting from his exertions, hoped to buy some time to catch his breath, and so he gasped out that first it was Conn's turn to prove that he was indeed the cleverest boy in the world.

"Conn laughed.

" 'I just did,' he said, and took to his heels.

"The exhausted groog was too worn out to chase after him. And he knew that the tale of his stupidity would soon be general knowledge. He would be the laughingstock of the entire ogre brotherhood. At their yearly gatherings his story would be tossed around like a juicy bone for everyone to gnaw at. In his shame and rage, he butted his head against the stone, and it cracked into three pieces. Then he packed up his belongings and moved far away to another land, where he hoped no one would ever hear of his defeat at the wits of Conn the Clever."

"What happened to the Riverfolk?" Will asked. 'Do they still live around here?"

"When Wayfarers first came to the Bourne, they found no folk living here. Only these ancient, faded writings on stone."

He fell silent and wrapped his cloak around himself.

"I will take the first watch," Finn said, and he rose from the fire and climbed to the rim of the hollow.

After the others had bedded down for the night, Will lay awake for a long while, looking up at the stones, black against the powdery light of the stars. Pendrake's tale had reminded him of the stories he used to tell Jess. She and Dad seemed farther away with every step he took. He was thinking also of what Rowen had told him about her parents, and he wished he could've thought of something comforting to say to her. He felt he understood her better now, and he was glad she had come with them on this journey. If she was hopeful about what lay ahead, then maybe he could be, too.

12

FINN WAS UP LONG BEFORE DAWN and had the fire going again and water boiling before Will had even opened his eyes. He crawled out from under his blanket, groggy and shivering, wondering if he had ever risen this early before. A faint trace of his dreams remained with him: once again he had glimpsed the clearing of the cloven tree through falling snow. And once again the tall white-haired man in the red robe appeared and opened his mouth to speak, but the dream ended before Will could hear any words.

The dream was quickly forgotten when he sat down to breakfast. Finn had fried up a kind of flatbread he called bannog. When Will had eaten his fill, he licked his lips and said it was delicious.

"That's good to hear, since we'll likely be eating a lot of it," Finn said, scraping out the pan. "And by the way, it wasn't a giant unthunk. Just an ordinary-size one."

Will reddened. He tore off a hunk of the bread to give to Shade and then realized that the wolf was not with them.

"Have you seen Shade?" Will asked Rowen. She shook her head.

"He went off on his own, just before dawn," Pendrake said, appearing at the rim of the hollow. "I could tell by the way he was pacing that he wished to leave, so I told him I would watch over you until he returned."

"Should we allow him to come and go like that?" Finn asked as he packed away his gear. "After all, we don't really know much about him."

"And he doesn't know much about us," Pendrake said.

As they were packing their things, Will glimpsed a moving shape above them and looked up eagerly, expecting to see Shade. A man in ragged, patched leather stood at the lip of the hollow. A moment later two other men joined him. All three carried bulging canvas sacks and had hats pulled down low over their brows. Will whispered a warning, and everyone looked up.

"Morning," said the first man. "Fine camping spot."

"It is," the toy maker said. "We're just leaving now, so you're welcome to it."

"Indeed we are, since it's ours."

"We weren't aware of that. Our apologies."

The first man set down his bundle, and the others did likewise. From his belt he drew a long knife with a jagged blade. The other two slid thick wooden cudgels from their coats. All three began to descend slowly into the hollow.

"Apology accepted, old man," the man with the knife said. "However, you've inconvenienced us, and we'll take some recompense. Kindly hand over all your belongings, then you can be on your way."

Finn stepped forward. His sword, Will saw with alarm,

was lying beside his other gear, out of reach. Will looked at Rowen and the toy maker, who made a gesture with his hand that told Will not to move. His heart began to pound, and he wished that Shade would come back.

"We're happy to share our breakfast with you," Finn said, "but we won't give you our things."

"And how are you going to stop us, boy?" the man with the knife said, laughing. "Maybe you should get the old fellow to do your fighting for you. Or the girl."

Without warning the three men lunged at Finn. What happened next was over so quickly that Will barely had time to cry out in surprise. Finn dodged the attack of the man with the knife and with a darting thrust of his leg sent him tumbling head over heels. Close behind came the men with the cudgels. Finn had the weapon out of one man's hand an instant later and brought it down with a crack upon the knuckles of the other, who howled and dropped his own cudgel. Three more lightning-fast blows and all three attackers lay in the grass, groaning.

Calmly, Finn bent, picked the first man's knife out of the grass, and tucked it into his belt. He broke the cudgels against one of the stones and tossed them on the remains of the fire.

"You can have your camping spot back now," he said. "Sorry for the inconvenience."

"There were reports of thieves in this district," Finn said as they left the hollow. "I hope they'll consider taking up a new trade."

As they returned to the road, Shade trotted up. He seemed to be in high spirits and came bounding to meet them.

"Where were you?" Finn asked.

"Running," the wolf said with a wild happiness in his

voice. Finn eyed him uneasily, then shook his head and said nothing more.

The road continued much as it had the day before, through farmlands and wooded stretches, but there were fewer travelers, and soon the companions found themselves alone. In the afternoon the road began to roll up and down across a line of steeper hills, and at each crest the eaves of the forest grew closer. From time to time they would pass a road leading north or south, to other inhabited parts of the Bourne. Still Shade headed west, although it was clear that he had little sense of a straight line. As they walked down the middle of the road, the wolf's path wove from one side to the other. He chased after birds, nosed around in stands of tall grass, and once frightened a rabbit out of its concealment in a willow thicket. He seemed to be having a great deal of fun, which was more than Will could say for himself.

On the second evening they found another hidden spot not far from the road, in a grove of tall pines. Rain fell in the night, but they were sheltered by the trees and were able to keep dry for the most part, despite what turned into a heavy downpour. Will woke up once to find that the rain had stopped. Shade sat beside him, wide awake, his ears cocked as though he were listening to something Will could not hear.

"What is it, Shade?" Will whispered.

"Listen," the wolf said. Will held his breath. He could hear the soft, steady drip of raindrops falling from the needles of the pines.

"I have not heard that song for a very long time," Shade said.

Will listened with him. He wondered if it was raining where Jess and his father were. He wondered if by now they had given up hope and gone on to their new home. That thought became a cold, hollow feeling that settled in his stomach and refused to fade.

"When I told my story," Shade said after a long silence, "you said you already knew it. How can that be?"

"I don't understand it either," Will said. "Master Pendrake says that all the stories in my world come from here. But your story was . . . different when I heard it."

"How was it different?"

"Well, *you* were different. You were . . . well, *bad*. You ate the little girl's grandmother and tried to eat the girl, too. If it *was* you."

"I see. And what happened to me in that story?"

Will looked away from Shade's calm, steady gaze.

"It was not a happy ending. For the wolf. So it couldn't have been you."

Shade nodded slowly.

"Perhaps you're right," he said quietly. "Although my story isn't over yet."

At dawn the next morning, the travelers set out reluctantly into a cold and damp fog that took its time drawing off. Eventually the sun won through and warmed them as they walked. Birds sang and the road wove its way through low hills dotted with sweet-smelling flowers. They passed another road with a signpost that read MOLLY'S ARM, 4 LEAGUES, and Pendrake told a funny tale about the people who lived there. They were exiled storyfolk who had once lived in houseboats on the Eastern Sea, and even now they insisted on living in boats, on dry land. Their village was on a hill overlooking the forest, and the treetops rippling in the wind had become their seascape. When they went hunting in the forest, they called it fishing. Will and Rowen smiled at the story, and even Finn seemed to be enjoying the day. Will had almost forgotten where they were making for when all at once they came around a rocky hillock, and there before them was the forest of Eldark.

Will halted and stared in stunned silence. He had glimpsed the forest from a distance, but hadn't realized how big the trees really were. Their huge trunks, some straight and smooth, others crooked and gnarled, towered far over his head, rising to vast canopies of leaves like green clouds. The fog of early morning seemed to have lingered under the trees after the sun had burned it away everywhere else. The vaults of the forest were hazy and full of shifting shadows.

Will looked to see if there might be a more inviting way in, but the closely gathered trees made a high, dark wall running north and south as far as the eye could see.

He suddenly felt very small.

"*That's* a forest," he said.

The other thing that made him go still was the hush that had fallen over the land. There was no birdsong, only a faint stirring of wind through the leaves and now and then the creak of a tree limb that only served to make the eerie quiet even more unsettling.

"The Deep Dark Forest," Pendrake said. "It holds as many tales as it does trees, they say."

Shade did not hesitate. He loped eagerly onward, and with less enthusiasm they followed him in under the gloom of the mighty trees.

The road they had been on narrowed to a winding track. The paths of the Wood had been enticing and mysterious, but here Will had the feeling that he and his companions were being watched, and not by eyes that wished them well. There was no breeze under the dark green canopy of leaves. It was as if the forest itself was holding its breath. In places the great mossy roots of the trees reached over the path like archways, and overhead their branches seemed almost knotted together, forming a leafy vault through which the sunlight pierced in thin, slanting columns.

After they had gone a short distance, they heard the shrill cry of a bird. Finn halted, put his fingers to his lips, and made an answering sound. Not long after, a man appeared before them out of the shadows. He was cloaked in dappled green, with a deep hood shadowing his face. Will stepped back in alarm, but Finn raised a hand in greeting. He went to the man, and they spoke together in low voices. Then, as quickly as he had appeared, the hooded man turned and melted back into the trees.

"Fox Company reports that the eaves of the forest are quiet," said Finn. "Nothing unusual under their watch."

After a while the path began to wind steadily upward, through stands of towering pine and fir. Squirrels chattered at them as they passed. The sun here was brighter, and the steep climb was hot work. Will sipped often from his water flask and quickly emptied it. Finn saw this and shared his flask with Will.

"You have to be careful with the water," he said. "It could be a while before we find more."

Dad always said the same thing whenever they went hiking, Will remembered with a pang of regret. He'd always thought it was useless advice, since they never went very far on their walks.

At the top of the highest rise, which was open to the sky, they halted briefly to catch their breath. From this height, Will was surprised to see only forest, a great rolling carpet of treetops, stretching away to the horizon in every direction. He had not imagined they had come so far into the forest already.

They descended under the trees, and after another hour's

walk came to a narrow stone bridge over a stream. Here they refilled their flasks and rested. Shade lapped thirstily at the water, then flopped down on the bank with a contented sigh. The surface of the stream was as still and silent as glass, except where it spilled over a rock ledge. Even here the water uttered only the faintest musical trickle.

Will turned from the stream and saw Finn nearby, sitting cross-legged on a flat stone with his sword lying across his legs. The young man was so still that Will was intrigued. He came closer.

"What are you doing?" he asked.

"Sitting," Finn said matter-of-factly, without looking at Will. "It's part of our training."

Will grinned.

"They teach you to just *sit* there?"

"Sitting teaches us to be still and calm, no matter what's happening. Then even in the thick of battle, you can be like this, inside."

He took a deep breath and fell silent. Will stood there a moment longer, then turned abruptly and walked away along the stream. He thought he might be able to like Finn, if the young man wasn't so . . . *If he liked me*, Will said to himself. But Finn didn't seem to like anyone.

Will came to a cool, shady spot where two large willow trees grew side by side. They were bowed so that the space between them, curtained with drooping catkins, looked like the mouth of a small cave. Will drew closer. He felt a sensation in his stomach like the butterflies he always got on a fairground ride. A kind of excitement and fear mixed together, with a disturbing feeling that what he did next mattered, though he didn't know why.

Cautiously he peered into the dim space between the trees. There didn't seem to be any danger. And in fact he could see a leafy flicker of sunlight in the depths of the shadows. A few steps and he would be on the other side of this little cave of branches. It would only take a moment.

He ducked under the twined arms of the willows and down into a damp, dark hollow, brushing thick bunches of drooping leaves out of his way. When he looked back, he could still see the mouth of the cave, although it seemed much farther away than he would have expected. The walls of the hollow grew closer, and as he placed his hands against them to steady himself in the dark, he was surprised to feel not leaves and branches but something cold and smooth.

He had no time to wonder about it, because just then he stepped out into the light.

He was in a meadow of tall grass, dotted with white flowers and alive with the hum of bees. There was a hill just ahead of him, a long, rolling, sandy-colored hill that was somehow very odd, though he couldn't put his finger on what bothered him about it. From somewhere came a deep, low rumbling.

For an instant he had the wild hope that he had found it, the clearing with the cloven tree. The tunnel under the willows must be one of those farholds, the wishing portals that Pendrake had talked about. Then he peered closer at the hill and saw that it looked very much like a gigantic human form, stretched out upon the ground and dressed in tanned, cracked leather. There were things that looked just like feet, far off at one end, with enormous toes, and at the other end, nearer to Will, was a huge bare lump of smooth pink stone, very much like a head, half hidden by a clump of bushes.

Then the hill moved.

Moments later Will was back through the tunnel under the willows and among his friends, gasping out the tale of what he had seen.

"It's just over there, on the other side of those trees," he said breathlessly, gesturing back the way he had come. "It's someone big. Someone sleeping who's big. Very big. Huge."

He would not say the word. No. It could not be true, and saying the word would make it true.

"You mean a giant?" Rowen asked.

"I'll have a look," Finn said.

"I'm coming, too," Rowen said eagerly, but Finn shook his head. Drawing his sword, he walked over to the willows, ducked into the tunnel, and vanished. A very short time later, he was back.

"All that's on the other side of these trees is more trees," he said with a shrug. "I saw nothing bigger than a squirrel."

"I don't understand," Will said. "It was just on the other side."

Pendrake placed a hand on Will's shoulder.

"Show me what you found," he said, and followed Will into the tunnel under the trees. As they neared the far end, Will stopped.

"It's just out *there*," he whispered. "It could be waiting for us."

"Then let's not keep it waiting any longer," Pendrake said, and he led the way out into the meadow, Will trailing behind the toy maker and ready to run.

There it was. A reclining figure the size of a hill, clothed in a hide of wrinkled tan leather, with its bald head under the leafy shade of a stand of trees. The giant's breath was the low rumbling Will had heard.

"We don't need to be afraid," Pendrake said. "I've met him before. A gentle soul. Never squashed a peasant's hut or stole a golden harp that I've heard of. Prefers sleep to just about anything."

"You're sure it's *that* one, not some other . . . ?" Will

whispered, still poised to bolt at the slightest movement other than the slow rise and fall of the giant's breathing.

In answer Pendrake pointed into the distance.

"That sharp-peaked hill over there is called the Targe. It is the northernmost of a range of hills known as the Winden Tors. This is where he lives. This is where his story takes place."

Will nodded, too disappointed about not finding a far-hold to care very much about the name of a hill.

"These hills are three days' journey from where we left Rowen and the others," Pendrake added.

"What do you mean?" Will asked impatiently. "They're just on the other side of those trees."

"They are, and they aren't," Pendrake said. "That tunnel under the willows is a knot-path. Although they may seem very short, knot-paths cross great distances. That is how they get their name. It's like tying a knot in a piece of string. The knot makes the string of your journey shorter. They were once paths between the various storylands, but now most of them simply lead from one part of the wild to another."

"Then where are we?"

"About twenty leagues southwest, as Morrigan would fly, from where our friends are waiting for us. Tell me why you decided to go through the tunnel."

"I felt there was . . . something for me to do here. As if everything was waiting for what I chose next. I don't know how to explain it."

"No need to try. Pay attention to that sense, Will. It will serve you well."

"Why didn't Finn find the knot-path?"

"Because he is not you," Pendrake said, and just then there issued a louder rumble from the sleeping figure, and a thunderous snort, and then the vast form turned over with

a sound like a landslide, and they saw, through a screen
of leaves, his hairy face and his huge eyes blinking, sleepily
regarding them.

Pendrake raised a hand in greeting. The giant's eye widened a moment and then slowly closed.

"Let's go," Pendrake said quietly, and they turned back
to the tunnel, and now Will saw that it was a huge leather
boot.

"I thought I'd found the clearing," Will said as they came
out the other end, where the boot had become a willow
bower again. "The place where I came into the Realm."

"I'm afraid not," Pendrake said, "but you have discovered something important, nonetheless."

When they reappeared, Rowen and the others were there,
waiting. The toy maker quickly explained what Will had
found.

"It's a good thing the path led back to the place you came
from," Finn said. "I've heard it said that not all of them do."

"Where would they take you then?" Rowen asked, but
not even the toy maker had an answer to this question.

They set off again and, as the shadows lengthened in the
evening, the path began to descend into thicker, gloomier
woods, where it seemed to Will that night was suddenly
much closer. Finally Finn led them off the path and in among
the trees, where Pendrake took out his waylight and soon
brought them to a snug.

Will was surprised and relieved. He had thought that
snugs were found only in the Wood. This one looked almost
exactly like the snug he and Rowen had taken refuge in,
right down to the pot bubbling on the hearth. After they
had all eaten, Rowen gave a great yawn that brought tears
to her eyes. She said good night and climbed up to one of

the featherbeds in the loft. After a short time they heard her
soft snoring and smiled at one another. Shade curled up at
Will's feet and seemed to sleep, too, although as always Will
wondered about that. He had the sense the wolf could and
would rouse himself instantly at the slightest disturbance.
Finn, however, did not even take off his boots. He sat down
near the door, took a small book with a dark brown cover out
of his coat pocket, read a few lines, and put the book away
again. Then he wrapped himself in his cloak and sat, slowly
turning the green ring upon his finger.

Will was so glad to be out of the cold and dark that his
weariness had vanished, and he sat for a long time by the
fire and talked with Pendrake. The old man told him tales
of the ancient realms of Story. As he spoke, Will felt himself
falling under a kind of enchantment, but not like that of the
mirrors. Instead it seemed to him that everything in the snug
was listening along with him: the crackling fire, the chairs,
the bobbing shadows on the walls. Everything around them
had become woven into the stories the old man told.

Pendrake spoke of how, in the long struggle of the Stewards against the Night King, the snugs and other secrets of
the Realm first appeared, to give refuge and help to those
who found themselves far from light and home.

"You said the Stewards aren't here anymore," Will said
when Pendrake had finished. "Did Malabron kill them?"

"The sun shines," Pendrake said, raising his hand. "The
rain falls."

Slowly he lowered his hand.

"The trees put forth leaves each spring, and the birds nest
among them. Can you say how this all happens, or why?"

"Well . . . no."

"It is that way with this snug, and the others like it. It is not
magic. There is much magic in this world, to be sure. Many

different kinds, in fact. Much of it works only in some stories and not in others. There are quite a few out-of-work wizards wandering the Realm, looking for somewhere to weave their spells. But the power of the Stewards runs deeper than any spellcraft. If it can be called magic, then everything around us is magic. And so are we."

Pendrake nodded toward Shade.

"If you need proof that the Stewards did not die," Pendrake said, "all you have to do is look around you."

Will took a deep breath.

"You said this world was where all the stories come from. Most of the books I've read had happy endings."

Pendrake smiled.

"Does any story ever really end?" he said. "The story-teller falls silent, or we close the book, but we know there's more that hasn't been told. And when we find ourselves in a story, we try to make it stop at the ending we would like, but it keeps on going. Sometimes we find it's no longer a story about us. Or it is, but we're playing a new role. This is what Malabron, for all his cunning, does not understand. He wants there to be one story only. His own. And he wants it to end as he desires, with all under his dominion. He would destroy the world to bring about his own happy ending."

"But that can't happen, can it?"

The toy maker stood and stretched his arms over his head.

"One thing has certainly ended," he said, taking off his spectacles, "and that is this day. Get some sleep, Will. The story will go on tomorrow."

13

Phoenix and Hedgehog sat in a boxwood tree,
trying their hand at philosophy.
Asked Hedgehog of his friend, when I come to an end,
do I start once more as I was before, or is there nothing more?
Said Phoenix, that must depend on whether you are me
or you, my friend.

— The Not-Poems of Sir Dagonet

FOR THE NEXT FOUR DAYS, they followed a path that wound and rose and fell through the still, green caverns of the wood, on and on, mile after long mile, until Will began to feel that he had never done anything in his life other than trudge through this endless forest. And every night was the same, too. They would find a snug, and when he went to sleep, Will would have the same disturbing dream he'd first had at the toy maker's house. He would find himself in the clearing of the cloven tree, with snow falling, and then the man with the long white hair would appear and open his mouth to speak, but the dream would end before Will could hear what he was saying. Again he considered telling the toy maker about the dream, but once more he decided to keep it to himself. He didn't want to hear anything worse than what he'd already been told.

Each evening before keeping watch, Finn would read briefly from the small leather-bound book he kept in his pocket. Finally Will's curiosity got the better of him, and he asked Finn what he was reading. The young man quickly shut the book and looked at Will coldly. Then his face softened.

"You've heard that there's a book for everyone in the Great Library," Finn said.

"Yes, but I didn't find mine."

"Well, this book is like that for me. A copy of it is given to every knight-in-training. It's a kind of guidebook."

"With maps and landmarks, you mean?"

"You could say that."

"What does it say about where we are now?"

"Pretty much the same thing it says about everywhere else. Keep on your toes."

On the morning of their fifth day in Eldark, they came to a less gloomy part of the forest. The trees were not so large or close set here, and shafts of welcome sunlight streamed down through the branches. When they halted to rest, Finn shared some bannog and then began to pack up his gear. It was time for him to return to the Bourne.

"The forest only gets darker and more dangerous from here on," he said with a frown. "I feel I should stay with you."

"We'd all be happy if you did," Pendrake said, clapping a hand on his shoulder. "But you've seen us safely out of the Bourne, and you have other duties to return to. I hope your journey home will be uneventful."

"That's the one thing a knight-in-training isn't supposed to want. But I hope the same for your journey."

Will thanked Finn. Although he still felt awkward around the serious young man, he wasn't happy to see him go. Finn wished him good luck.

"If all goes as it should," he said, "we won't meet again, Will. I'm sorry for that. You could use more sword practice."

For the first time Will saw a quick smile pass across Finn's face. Then he waved a farewell and slipped away into the shadows of the forest.

As dusk fell, the travelers left the path as before. Pendrake uncovered his waylight, but this time it stayed unlit and no answering glimmer appeared in the gloom. They walked on slowly, and night fell around them like a cloak, until they were only shadows to one another. After a while Will noticed a pale silver light all around him and looked up to see the moon flickering through the treetops. He was cheered by the sight, but Pendrake's waylight still failed to glow.

"Maybe there are no snugs in this part of the woods," Rowen said.

"The waylight calls them forth," Pendrake said. "Sometimes it takes a while for a snug to appear. But this is strange."

They walked on until it grew completely dark. Pendrake continued to hold out his waylight, and finally a tiny blue star appeared in the blackness before them. Will started forward eagerly, but the toy maker held him back.

"Don't move," he whispered, and then Will saw that Pendrake's waylight was still dark.

"What does that mean?" Rowen whispered.

"I'm not sure, but I intend to find out," Pendrake said. "Shade, guard Will and Rowen well. If I do not return by the time the moon touches the top of that dead tree, flee this place. Head for the Bourne. Find a patrol of the Errantry, if you can."

The toy maker tucked the lantern away, took up his staff, and swiftly vanished. The others crouched down and waited. From time to time Will caught the faint gleam of Rowen's drawn blade in the moonlight, but little else. He wanted to speak to her, to relieve the heavy silence, but he didn't know what to say. The sound of her quickened breathing reached him, and he knew she was as frightened as he was. He felt Shade's shoulder against his, and he was grateful for the wolf's nearness. After a long time, when he was about to speak aloud just to break the tension, he felt Shade stiffen and rise from a crouch.

"What is it?" he whispered.

"Other wolves," Shade said excitedly. "Can't you hear them?"

"I can't," Will said. He strained to listen, and he did hear faint sounds, but not the howling of wolves. Instead he heard happy shouts and laughter, as if from a great distance. It sounded very much like his friends at home. Fooling around in the school yard. Teasing each other about girls and shoving one another around. What were they shouting about now? Which game console was the best, probably. Then one voice rose about the others.

Will! Where are you?

It was Jess's voice. She sounded as if she'd been crying.

I don't like this game, Will. Come out. I'm scared.

"Did you hear that?" he asked Rowen. "It's my sister. She's looking for me."

Rowen shook her head.

"I heard horns blowing," she said. "It sounded like a troupe of the Errantry riding this way. But it's gone now."

Just then Shade gave an excited yip and bounded off. Will shouted his name, and the wolf reluctantly pulled up.

"They're singing," he called back to Will. "The First Ones. They're singing the song of gathering. They're calling all of us together. All the Companions. I won't be long. I'll find them and bring them back."

"I can't hear any singing, Shade," Will said. "Don't go, please. Something's not right."

The wolf hesitated, his limbs trembling. Then he lowered his head and came plodding back.

"It's gone now," he said sadly. "There's nothing. How can that be?"

Rowen suddenly stood up.

"It's Grandfather," she cried. "He's calling me. I can hear him calling for me."

Will listened.

"I can't hear it," he said. "I don't think it's really him, Rowen."

Rowen stared at him, then turned away and pointed.

"He's just over there," she said. "He sounds hurt. I have to . . ."

"We've all heard different things," Will said. "It doesn't make sense. I don't think what we're hearing is what we think it is."

She didn't seem to hear him. After another moment, during which she seemed to be straining to hear, she turned to Will with an agonized look.

"He's getting farther away. I *must* go to him. I have to make sure."

An instant later she had plunged into the shadows and was gone.

"Rowen, wait," Will called after her, leaping to his feet. "Come on, Shade, we've got to follow her."

He grabbed hold of the shaggy fur behind Shade's ears, and they started off together into the darkness. Without Shade, Will would have been utterly lost, but he trusted the wolf's sense of smell and direction. The only problem was that he had to keep holding on to Shade so that he wouldn't get left behind, and that meant they had to run at a slower pace.

Will struggled to keep up his courage. Finn was gone. Pendrake seemed to have deserted them. And now Rowen ... He should never have agreed to go on this foolish journey. Look where it had brought them.

It was not long before the wolf halted, and for once he seemed uncertain.

"She came this way," he said. "I am sure of it. But now there's nothing."

Will looked around the glade they had come to and noticed something odd. The trunks of the trees were all smooth and straight, like columns. The floor of the forest was hard, bare earth, almost completely free of leaves and other litter. There was no wind here, no creaking of tree limbs, no sounds of forest creatures. The dim amber light in the glade did not seem to be coming from the moon but from all over and from nowhere. It almost seemed as if they had left the forest without knowing and entered a vast pillared room lit by dim unseen fires.

"Rowen?" Will called, and the echo of his voice seemed to return from all directions at once.

"I'm here!" Rowen shouted, her voice echoing from all sides, as if bouncing like a ball around the glade.

"Where are you?" Will said. "We can't see you."

"I can't see you either," came the answer from many places. "But I'm not hurt. He just wanted someone to talk to."

Will and Shade exchanged a baffled look.

"He?"

Rowen didn't answer.

"Who's . . . there with you?" Will asked warily.

"I don't know, exactly," Rowen said, and then there she was, standing in the middle of the glade, as if she had materialized out of thin air. "I don't know if anyone is."

Did you like the game? asked a strange voice, like a chorus of echoes. It seemed to come from far off and from right by Will's ear, so that he jumped in surprise. Shade growled.

"Who's there?" Will said angrily.

Who is who is who is who . . . the voice echoed, trailing off into silence.

"Answer me!" Will shouted.

"He's all around us—" Rowen began, but she was cut off by a burst of giddy laughter.

Who is all around who? said the voice, but now it was quieter and more urgent. *Answer this true. . . .*

"You're the one who made us hear all those sounds, aren't you?" Will said.

"He did," said Rowen. "I don't think he meant any harm."

There was a sound like a gust of wind sweeping through the glade, though no wind touched their faces. They caught sight of shadowy shapes moving through the trees.

Someone made the sounds; you heard them, the voice said eagerly. *Or maybe you made them, and someone heard them. Someone is never sure about that, but we did it together. That's the game.*

"It's not a game," Will said. "We have to find—"

Lost, the voice interrupted. *That's the game. The game and its name are the same. Shall we play some more? Someone can make many things. Someone can be many things. Because someone's not really here. Isn't that funny? Here, there, anywhere. Someone, somewhat, somewho.*

The sound of wind keened and moaned around them again, and then all the flitting shadows seemed to flock together into one spot, high among the branches of a tree. Something large and shaggy began to take shape. The amber light picked out the sheen of golden fur, wings, a curling tail. Two huge round yellow eyes gazed down at them.

The game is getting lost and found, the voice from every-where went on. *To wit, to woo. To rue. Someone got lost a long time ago, and never found again. Isn't that sad? Sometimes it is. Sometimes it's funny. Sometimes it turns us inside out. But we can make it a game. That's what we're doing, now that we're all not here. We're all not here, together.*

"Whoever you are," Will said, moving to stand beside Rowen, "we need to go now. We're looking for someone. We can't stay and . . . play. I'm sorry."

The creature in the tree seemed to shiver all over. All at once it vanished and immediately reappeared higher up and in another tree, its yellow eyes peering out from a screen of leaves.

There is another one, too, the voice said. *Another someone looking for you.*

"Grandfather!" Rowen exclaimed. "Do you know where he is? An old man with a staff."

Not that one. No, this is another one. He is not old, not young. He is coming this way very quickly. He walks like a man, but he isn't. That one is even more not here than we aren't. Isn't that strange? Or is it funny? Someone doesn't think that one thinks it's very funny. If he comes here, there will be no game. There will be no you, someone thinks. You won't be lost, you'll be gone. You'll be Not. You don't want to be Not. Not with that one.

"You're right about that," Will said. "We don't. So we need to go."

There was a sound like a vast sigh, or many sighs rushing together.

So someone will let you go, the voice said at last, and its tone was no longer lively. *The one who keeps his promises. But first you have to do something that someone wants. First we play another game.*

"Another game," Rowen said, her shoulders drooping.

The game is a riddle; the riddle is a game. Someone will riddle it, and you have to answer. One guess. Only one. One riddle, one answer. Are you ready?

"We're leaving," Will said angrily.

You can't! the voice shouted in a thunder of echoes. The sound of wind rose to a roar. The leaves of the trees hissed and shivered.

Ask that red-haired one, the voice said more softly after a long silence. *She tried. She found out that here is there and there is here, where we aren't. Until the game is done. Until the riddle finds its answer.*

Will turned to Rowen, who nodded.

"This glade is his home," she said. "It's a maze. Only he knows the way out."

"Shade?" Will said.

The wolf shook his head.

"It's as if we're nowhere, to my nose and ears," he muttered. "I don't understand how that can be. . . ."

Will's frustration was greater than his fear. He sighed.

"Is this one of those riddles that no one could guess in a hundred years?" he asked.

The creature in the tree disappeared again without answering. Shadows swooped high and low about the glade. Then the voice spoke again, and this time it came from behind them. They all whirled. Leaves were swirling around and around, like a small cyclone. They spun faster and faster, and drew closely together, until all at once they stopped and settled. A small, pale-skinned boy stood there, dressed in rough garments made of brown, brittle leaves. His eyes were large and seemed to shine with their own light, but there was something eerily familiar about him. Will realized with a shudder that he was looking at his own face.

"This one will ask the riddle," the boy said, and his voice

had lost its echoes and had become one single voice, both Will's and not Will's. "Here it is. Pay attention now.

> *"I have been many, but known to few.*
> *I wear many faces; only one is true.*
> *Speak my true name, and I disappear.*
> *The moment I'm found, I'm no longer here.*
> *I live in the shadows; I die in the light.*
> *The answer you seek lies in plain sight."*

He stopped and gazed at them expectantly.

"So," he said. "What am I?"

Will and Rowen turned to each other with blank looks.

"Do you have an answer?" the boy asked urgently, his wide eyes searching all three of them in turn. "You must have an answer. There has to be an answer."

"We need to think about it," Rowen said. "Just give us a moment."

"It must be answered now!" the boy shouted, stamping his foot. "Before the one with the toys comes. He played the game before. He guessed. He knew."

"The one with the toys," Rowen cried. "Is he coming this way?"

"You don't know the answer," the boy said, ignoring her question. "You could guess another guess. Name another game. Game another name. You could tell someone the answer inside the answer."

"Where is the toy maker?" Rowen tried again. "Can you lead him to us?"

The boy closed his eyes for a moment, then opened them again.

"He's on his way," he finally said. "Wait. No. He's where we're not now."

And there was Pendrake. The toy maker hurried to them, embraced Rowen, then turned to the boy.

"The answer to the riddle," he said, "is *a riddle*. When it's answered, it's not a riddle anymore. The moment it's found, it's no longer here."

The boy gaped at Pendrake with hurt and fear in his eyes. The leafy garments he was covered in began to fly from him as if they were being torn from a tree in a strong gale. Again the wind roared and the trees thrashed. Moments later there was nothing but a swirl of dry leaves blowing across the ground. The boy was nowhere to be seen. Neither was the creature in the trees.

It's not fair, the strange echoing voice wailed from all around them. *You guessed that when you were not here before. Someone let you go then, and now you're not here again. Not fair. You didn't let the others guess. It was their game. It was their turn.*

"The riddle has been answered," the toy maker said. "Those were the terms. You have to let us go now."

But the answer, the voice cried, rising to a wail like the wind. *The answer is a riddle, but what is the answer to that riddle? What is inside the inside? Who is there? Someone needs to know what it is. Someone . . .*

The voice trailed off.

"I'm sorry we can't answer that riddle for you," said Pendrake, "but something is hunting us. A terrible thing. You must know of it. We have to get away before it finds us. Perhaps you can bring it here, into your house. You can play the game. That might keep it from finding us. It would be very kind of you to do that."

The roaring of wind grew even louder and then subsided.

Someone doesn't want to play the game with that one, the

voice announced like a pouting child. *That one is a riddle, too. A riddle that no one wants to answer. Someone is . . . afraid.*

"But remember," Pendrake said, "you're not here. And it's not here either. It can't find you. It can't hurt you."

They waited for a response, but none came. The glade was silent.

"Let's go," Pendrake whispered. They followed him as he strode quickly out of the glade. After a short time the straight, columnlike tree trunks gave way to more familiar shapes, surrounded by thick, leafy undergrowth.

"We must get away from here," Pendrake said as they went along. "Shade, we will need your eyes. Make sure no one strays. Follow me, and not another sound until I give the word."

On they went, moving slowly and cautiously through the thick, clinging undergrowth. Will scarcely dared to breathe. He sensed rather than saw Shade at his side, and whenever the wolf moved farther away, he had to stop himself from reaching out. The wind grew stronger and whispered in the leaves. This helped to conceal the sounds the companions made as they crept along, but it also meant that every creak of a branch in the wind, every moving shadow, brought fear.

Will was suddenly aware that Shade was not beside him. He stopped. He couldn't hear the sounds of the others. Panicking, he started forward again, shoving the clinging branches out of his way, but not daring to call out.

Then his feet slid from beneath him.

Will threw himself backward and grasped for a handhold. He clung to a tangle of branches and pulled himself back up onto level ground.

Breathing heavily, he looked over his shoulder. A stray

beam of moonlight revealed a sheer drop into a stony darkness. He had almost fallen into what looked to be a deep, narrow gorge. As he backed away instinctively from the drop, he saw the gleam of wet stone plunging down into blackness, heard the faint trickle of falling water.

As he picked himself up off the ground, Shade and the others appeared.

"That would have been a nasty fall," Rowen said.

On they went, until at last Pendrake halted them with a word. The canopy of trees was not so thick here, and by the brighter moonlight Will could see that they had come to a sheltering hollow beneath the mossy overhang of a dry stream bank. Wearily they sat down in a huddled group.

"I think we're safe, for now," Pendrake said.

"From what, Grandfather?" Rowen asked.

"It was a true waylight that we saw," Pendrake said. "But the snug had been broken open."

"I thought they were hidden," said Will.

"They have always been safe against most intruders, but as Moth suspected, another power came into the Bourne with the fetches. The secret of the snugs has been found out, and their light can now be used falsely to lure us into a trap."

"Did you see anything?" Rowen said.

"No, but something warned me to keep my distance," Pendrake said. "I felt a presence, like a dark thread in the weave of the Kantar. We are hunted, by someone or something I have never encountered before. A being of great strength and malice, that much is certain. I do not think it was aware of me. If it had been, I doubt I would have escaped to return to you. I don't sense it now. We may have given it the slip, with a little help from our friend in the glade."

"Whoever he is," said Rowen.

"Some call him the Woodwraith. I came this way before and ended up in his house, as he calls it. From what he told me then, I guessed that he had been lost in the forest long ago, in a story that ended without his being found. He doesn't know who or what he is anymore. Or even if he is anything at all. He seeks the answer to that riddle, though there doesn't seem to be one. It has driven him more than a little mad, poor thing. But he is not wicked. He lures the unwary into his game, but always lets them go, eventually. He may even have decided to help us, by distracting our pursuer. Where we go from here, though, is the next question."

Just then Shade raised his head and gave a low growl. Pendrake stood hastily, and the others did the same.

"What is it?" Will whispered.

"I know that scent," the wolf snarled, his voice colder and more frightening than Will had ever heard it. "The enemy is near."

14

As evening fell, she came to a bleak marsh where the wind howled over the dark waters. She was lost and afraid, and said aloud, "What will become of me?"

In the gloom she saw a light and eagerly hurried toward it. When she got closer, she saw that the light came from the window of a cheery little cottage, just sitting there in the middle of nowhere. She was about to knock on the door when she paused and thought, "I'm not sure I like the way this tale is going. But really, what choice do I have?"

— Tales from the Golden Goose

"I WASN'T CAREFUL ENOUGH," Pendrake said in a tense whisper. "The thing that broke into the snug must have sensed my presence and followed me."

"This *ghool* will not harm Will Lightfoot," Shade growled. "I will go to meet it, while you seek safety."

"I don't doubt your courage, Shade," Pendrake said, "but I fear this enemy would outmatch even you. No, we must stay together, and perhaps I can contrive something to throw the hunter off the scent. Follow me."

"No," Will said, the word out of his mouth before he knew why. They all stopped and stared at him. He stood, unable to explain himself yet. *Moonlight on wet stone . . .*

"No," he said again, and now he understood. "We must go back. Back to where I slipped. There's a knot-path there. We can use it to get away."

"Are you sure?" Pendrake asked, studying Will carefully, his eyes uncertain.

Will turned away from the old man's searching gaze. It was clear Pendrake didn't really trust him, even though he had appeared certain of Will's gifts before they left Fable. They were all waiting for him to decide. It was up to him, again.

"It was like before, with the cave under the willows," Will said, "but I was too scared to notice. Yes, I'm sure."

"We can't turn back now," Rowen said. "We'll be heading straight toward whatever's coming after us."

Pendrake bowed his head, then he looked up, and there was no more doubt in his eyes. He took his waylight, swung open one of the diamond-shaped panes, and spoke a few words in a low voice. There was a tiny flash, and a bright blue wisp appeared, pulsing softly in the toy maker's palm.

"We will have to risk a light, in order to move quickly," he said, and then he turned to the wolf. "Shade, can you find the spot where Will stumbled?"

The wolf merely grunted, as if amused that anyone could doubt it, then he bounded off the way they had come. As the others followed, the wisp stayed with Pendrake, hovering just over his head, but its light was strong enough for them to see one another clearly. In that way they were able to stay together as they raced through the forest after the wolf, and in a much shorter time than Will expected, Shade halted, panting.

"This is the place," the wolf said, and he lowered his snout to the earth and turned in a circle, sniffing.

"There's no gorge," Rowen said. "Maybe you're wrong, Shade."

"No, he's right," Will insisted. "I'm sure of it."

Shade stiffened and raised his head.

"Someone is here," he growled.

A figure loomed out of the shadows. Rowen cried out and drew her knife. Will backed into Shade's flank. The figure moved into the light, and they saw that it was Finn Madoc.

"Thank goodness I found you," he said breathlessly, and then searched their faces. "Though I think you already know why I was looking."

Pendrake nodded.

"We are being hunted," he said. "And our pursuer is closing in."

"After I left you, I met another Fox Company scout. He reported they'd encountered something unknown prowling the forest, coming this way. Something that was breaking into the snugs. I had to return, to warn you. But where can we go now for shelter if the snugs are not safe?"

"Will has found a knot-path," Rowen said.

"Have I?" Will muttered, and turned away.

He pushed his way through a tangle of branches and met only more branches, which snagged his cloak and scratched his face. Turning, he tried another direction and met with disappointment there. A sick dread began to well up in him, and he struggled against it. Tears stung his eyes.

"It's no use," he said, his voice shaking. "It was an accident before. I can't make it happen again."

"Stay calm, Will," Pendrake said. "It's here. Just look, and listen."

Will took a deep breath and closed his eyes. His senses brought him a jumble of messages that seemed to grow stronger and more distracting as he struggled to ignore them: the thrash of leafy branches in the wind, the humid scent of moss and earth, the labored breathing of his companions, and his own thudding heartbeat. Then he remembered Finn by the stream, just sitting. What had he said? A knight-errant learned to be still and calm inside, no matter what was happening around him.

Will opened his eyes. He took a deep breath and slowly let it out. His senses were still full of the world, but instead of trying to shut everything out, he stood in the midst of it without moving. He was here, now. There was nowhere else he could be. As he felt his fear drop away, he knew without any doubt that the path he needed was—

Will took three steps forward, and the ground dropped away underneath him.

Strong hands clutched and held him. He turned and saw Pendrake shaking his head.

"I don't think your powers include flight," the old man said with a wink.

Will's boots found a firm footing on rock, and he leaned forward. There was the gorge, a slender throat of mossy stone plunging into a deeper night than the one over their heads. He knew for certain now that he had been right. If they took this path, they would vanish as if they had been swallowed up by the earth. And he knew something else, too.

He disengaged himself from Pendrake's grip and stepped forward over the edge.

"Will!" Rowen cried.

He landed in a springy bed of moss, not much more than his own height below where the others stood. He took a deep breath and felt his legs shaking.

"I'm fine," he called up to the others. "It's an illusion. The gorge isn't deep."

"Are you sure?" Rowen said doubtfully. "We can barely see you."

"It's only a short drop," Will said. "Trust me."

"I'll stay behind," Finn said. "If this hunter finds the knot-path, at least I can try to bar its way."

"And if it can't find the path, you'll be telling it exactly
where to look," Pendrake said. "No, you must come with
us, Finn. For your own sake, too. This is not an opponent for
your sword."

After some hesitation, the others jumped down, first
Shade, and then Finn and Rowen. Pendrake still stood at the
lip of the gorge, the wisp cupped in his hands, illuminating
his face eerily with its dim pulsing light.

"Go, Sputter," Pendrake said softly, and the tiny creature
sped off with a swiftly diminishing hum.

Soon they were standing together between high rock
walls that almost met overhead. It was colder in the gorge,
and the air carried a dank, earthy scent, like mushrooms and
rotting logs.

"Are we safe now?" Rowen whispered.

"We don't know what our pursuer is capable of," Pendrake
said. "We must keep moving."

Without a word they set off together with Will leading
them. After a few steps, the gorge narrowed even farther and
then began to turn in a slow curve. To Will's surprise, it kept
on curving until he was sure they had come full circle and
were about to return to where they had started. But that did
not happen. They continued in a curving path, and Will's
sense of time grew hazy. One moment he felt that they had
only just set out, and the next he was sure they had been
walking through the gorge for hours. No one spoke, and Will
began to wonder if somehow he had fallen asleep and was
walking in a dream.

Then he felt a change in the air. It was moving again, the
slightest of breezes, but it was enough to jolt him awake.
Although the bottom of the gorge was still in deep shadow, Will
knew that dawn was approaching in the world outside. They
were coming to the end of the knot-path. He was sure of it.

As they walked, the walls on either side dropped in height and grew mossier, like crumbling garden walls, until they were swallowed up altogether in thick, tangled undergrowth. Now it was as if they were passing through a tunnel of green, much like the one Will had discovered between the willows.

And there before them was the way out, a narrow space bright with morning light. And at the same time, the twittering and chirping of birds reached their ears.

As he emerged from the knot-path, Will felt certain that they had come a great distance, but he wasn't sure how he knew. Then he realized that the trees were smaller, more stunted and sickly-looking. The smell of the forest was different, too, carrying a faint reek of something unpleasant.

Will looked at Pendrake now, who was intently scanning the horizon. The old man seemed lost, and baffled. Will was suddenly very tired, as if they had been walking in the knot-path for hours. Everything they had done so far had only made things worse.

"Any idea where we are?" Finn asked the toy maker, who slowly shook his head.

"I'm afraid you're much farther than seven days' travel from Appleyard," he said at last. "How much farther I can't say. But you won't be returning on time."

Finn nodded and straightened the knapsack on his shoulders.

"I've already disobeyed my orders by coming back to find you," he said with a shrug, "so I might as well keep going."

He glanced at Will, who was teetering from weariness where he stood, and added, "But first we should find somewhere safe to rest."

Before they set off again, Pendrake dug into his bag and took out a small silver box with a crank handle sticking out of one side. He turned the crank, and the top of the box sprang open. A whirling cloud of gray dust rose from the box and swiftly flew apart on the breeze.

"The dust of many roads, gathered on many journeys," Pendrake said as he shut the box. "With luck it will hide the thread of ours."

Led by Shade, they walked a short distance through the woods and then found some concealment in a stand of squat, crooked pine trees. They shared Finn's bannog and drank from their flasks, and then Will lay down on a bed of fir needles and was soon dropping off to sleep. When Pendrake woke him, after what seemed only moments, the sun was high in the sky. It was time to move on.

After a short march through steadily falling country, they came to a steep bank that looked out over a vast, flat plain of mossy ground, dotted with pools of dark water. Here and there stood a few gaunt, stunted black pines, like ragged spears jabbed into the wet earth. There was a pungent stench in the air of stagnant water and decay. Will realized that this was what he had smelled when they came out of the knot-path. The smell and the bleak sight brought with it a memory, sudden and sharp, that stopped Will in his tracks.

One summer his father had taken him on a duck-hunting trip up north. They had traveled a long way to a marsh in the middle of nowhere. In the morning they were up before dawn, and spent the day crouched in the tall grass or slogging through the marsh. Will had been eager for a chance to shoot his father's gun, but when the duck he finally hit was hanging limp in his hand, he felt the cold and damp of the marsh seep into him. They walked on, but Will's heart wasn't in it anymore. He lagged behind, until suddenly he realized he was alone. Dad had taught him to stay in one place if he got lost, but he panicked and began to run. He fell into the water several times and lost the ducks he had been carrying. Dad finally found him, soaked and nearly frozen, and was angry that he hadn't done as he was told. The next time Dad invited him on a hunting trip, he came up with an excuse not to go.

Shade came up beside Will and sniffed. "This is a strange place," he said. "I don't like the smell."

"This is the Bog of Mool," Pendrake said. "I traveled along its margins once before, years ago. There were more birds and trees then. I do not like the way it has changed. But at least it gives me some idea of how far we've come. I'd guess the knot-path has brought us a four-day march farther west, and a little north."

"Four days," Rowen said, wide-eyed. "Then if whatever's hunting us can't find the knot-path, we're safe."

"A very large *if*," Pendrake said. "We shouldn't let down our guard."

"Let's stay close together, then," Finn said. "We don't want to get separated here."

"Walk carefully," Pendrake said. "The bog is land floating on water. One wrong step and you go straight down."

They started forward without any eagerness, compelled only by the need to keep moving. The sun burned sullenly through shifting veils of mist. The damp spongy earth squelched under their feet. They heard bubbling and hissing, and at times saw clouds of vapor steaming up out of the earth. Shade took the lead, keeping his nose low to the ground. No one spoke. The gloom of their surroundings kept them moving only in the hope of finding somewhere to rest from the cold and damp. They had eaten nothing for hours but a bit of bannog.

As night fell, they found meager shelter beneath the

tangled branches of a low clump of thorn trees and debated
what to do next. Pendrake suggested they make for the city
of Skald, on the far side of the bog.

"That's the city of the Northmen," Finn said with a frown.
"The Errantry is not welcome there."

"Theirs was a great story once, but it was swallowed up
by Malabron long ago," Pendrake said. "Those who sur-
vived fled south in search of refuge. It is true they are wary
of strangers and quick to anger, but they live in a wild land
surrounded by enemies. I have spent some time in Skald. I
know they seldom turn away travelers who seek the shelter
of their walls."

The next day was spent toiling slowly through the seemingly
endless bog. Led by Shade, they moved from one patch of
more or less solid ground to another, but often Will would
take a step that plunged his foot or entire leg deep into the
bog, and then he would pitch forward and fall. The same
happened to the others, with the exception of Shade, who
seemed to have an uncanny sense for finding the most solid
ground.

The sun remained hidden behind the pale shroud of mist.
There was nothing to relieve the eyes from the monotonous
landscape of mossy hummocks, pools of brown water, and
withered trees. To make matters worse, they were accompanied every step of the way by swarms of mosquitoes. Finn
brought out a sharp-smelling ointment, and they all rubbed
it on their faces and arms. All except for Shade, who refused
to have the stuff on his fur. The ointment kept away most but
not all of the whining, relentless insects, and before long Will
was itching from numerous bites. Every now and then he
would stop, ready to topple from weariness and annoyance,
and have to summon every ounce of effort and willpower

to keep going. He even felt as though his very thoughts had become sodden and heavy, so that he was having difficulty thinking of anything other than his next step. There seemed to be nothing in his mind but this unending trudge, as if he had never done anything else. He looked at Rowen toiling near him, and for a frightening moment he couldn't even remember her name.

Finally, when he was ready to give up and sink down in defeat, Shade called out.

In the distance stood an unusual shape. It seemed to be a large upright stone, but when they drew closer, they saw that it was the remains of a tower. They all stared at it as if this forlorn ruin was a beacon of hope, after hours of flat, gray nothingness. There was no roof, and on one side the wall had fallen in completely, so that the stones that remained standing formed a jagged half circle. Shade ran ahead, nosed around the base of the tower, and came trotting back.

"No scent," he said in a disappointed tone. "No life. No one has been here for a long time."

"Who would build a tower out here?" Will said. "There's nothing to see."

"Something's wrong," Rowen said. Her face was pale, and her brow had broken out in beads of sweat.

"Are you all right?" Will asked.

Rowen shook her head. "I don't know. Can't you feel it? This place is strange. Wrong somehow. It's as if everything is closing in on us."

"I don't understand."

"Neither do I. But we shouldn't be here."

A brief inspection of the tower revealed nothing but chunks and fragments of stone that were half buried in the boggy ground. The tower remained a silent mystery.

The travelers kept on, and Will began to lose his sense

that any time was passing at all. The sun still could not be seen through the mist, so there was no telling the time of day from its place in the sky. They had to trust solely in Shade's sense of direction.

A tall shape appeared in the murk, and when they got closer, they saw that it was the remains of a tower. They all stared at it as if this forlorn ruin was a beacon of hope, after hours of flat, gray nothingness. There was no roof, and on one side the wall had fallen in completely, so that the stones that remained standing formed a jagged half circle. Shade ran ahead, nosed around the base of the tower, and came trotting back.

"Still no scent," he said in a disappointed tone. "No life. No one has been here for a long time."

"Who would build a tower out here?" Will said, and his own voice sounded thick and sleepy to him. "There's nothing to see."

"Something's . . . wrong, " Rowen said haltingly, as if she was struggling to speak.

She looked at Will. Her face was pale, and her brow had broken out in beads of sweat.

"Are you all right?" Will asked.

Rowen shook her head. "We saw this already," she said. "And we said the same things the last time."

"Did we? I don't think so. . . ."

"Rowen is right," Pendrake said slowly, his brow knitting. "And it may be worse than that."

"What's happening to us?" Finn asked. He, too, spoke as if he were half asleep and having trouble forming the words.

The toy maker did not answer. Instead he started off again, and after exchanging puzzled looks, the others shook off their weariness and followed.

After some time a tall shape appeared in the murk, and when they got closer, they saw that it was the remains of a tower. They all stared at it as if this forlorn ruin was a beacon of hope, after hours of flat, gray nothingness. There was no roof, and on one side the wall had fallen in completely, so that the stones that remained standing formed a jagged half circle. Shade ran ahead, nosed around the base of the tower, and came trotting back.

"Not again," he grumbled.

"Who would build a tower out here?" Will said drowsily. "There's nothing to see."

"Something's wrong—" Rowen began, and then she broke off and looked at Will.

"I'm about to tell you that we saw this already," she said. "And then you'll ask me if I'm all right. . . ."

"What? What do you . . . ?"

The toy maker took a few slow steps away from the group, gazed around for a long moment, and then came back, stroking his beard. He looked grim, and Will's heart sank.

"What's happening to us?" Finn asked.

"We've stumbled into a storyshard," Pendrake said wearily. "A fragment of a longer story torn loose from its place in the Kantar. The same broken-off bit of story, over and over. I can't even say how many times we've repeated it already. But I know that if we walk away from the tower, we'll return to it again and do everything we did before."

They were all silent.

"We should walk away in another direction," Finn said at last. "Try something different."

"But how will we be sure it's different?" Will asked.

"I'll find the way out," Shade growled, tense and ready to run. He seemed to be the least affected by the lethargy and slowness of speech that had fallen over everyone else.

"You can't, Shade," Pendrake said to him. "Nor will walking a different way make any difference. The storyshard is sealed off from the world surrounding it, like a bubble. When you reach the edge of the bubble, you don't pass through it. You find yourself back where you started, doing it all over again."

"For how long?" Will asked.

Pendrake did not answer. He closed his eyes and appeared to be deep in thought.

"But now we know what's happened," Rowen said with a new trace of life in her voice. "The first time we came here we didn't know. At least I don't think we did. But that means we've changed the story, doesn't it? It's not the same; it's not repeating exactly. So maybe we can get out."

Pendrake shook his head.

"If only it were that easy. We've changed the story, yes. But it is changing us. Haven't you noticed? It's getting harder to remember things."

Rowen nodded.

"I forgot just now why we came here, to the bog," she said. "And where we were before this. It's all getting hazy."

"I fear that the longer we stay here, the more woven into the shard we will be. We'll lose our own stories. Forget we ever did anything other than what happens here. Or knew of any place other than this. It's already happening. If we stay here too long we'll forget our past, our loved ones outside the shard, the purpose of our journey. We won't even know or care about escaping."

"There's nothing we can do?" Finn asked.

"It can't end like this," Rowen said, her eyes blazing. "There must be some way out."

"We still have a chance, perhaps," Pendrake said, turning

in a slow circle, his eyes searching the distance. "There may be others trapped here with us, characters from the story the shard was once part of. Sometimes the broken tales repeat because storyfolk are unable or unwilling to move on. They can no longer see that there might be more to their story. It's their own will, grown hardened and powerful over the years, that has made the shard a trap and a prison."

"If we can find someone like that," Rowen said, "we can tell them what's happened. . . ."

"And set them free," Will finished.

Pendrake nodded. "It may be our only hope."

"How do we find them, if they're here?" Finn said. "If we set off from the tower again, won't we just come back to it?"

Pendrake turned to the wolf.

"Shade, you don't seem to be as tired as the rest of us. That tells me you've been least affected by the shard as yet. I think this has to do with how old your own story is. It's the most resistant to forgetfulness."

"Thank you," Shade said. "But how can that help?"

"The rest of us must stay here, while you go off to search. That may be enough of a change in what we've done before to gain us a little more time."

"I'll do it," Shade said eagerly. "What am I looking for?"

"Anyone," the toy maker said. "Man, woman, or child. Bird or beast. Anything different from what we've seen before. And hurry."

The wolf bounded off without another word. They watched him until he was lost in the mist. For a long time no one spoke. Will was afraid he would say something that he had said before, and he guessed that the others were thinking the same thing.

Then Pendrake spoke, and he seemed to be struggling to form the words.

"Tell us . . . Will . . . about your life before you came to the Realm. Tell us about that. If we tell our own stories, we may be able to . . . slow down the forgetting."

"What story should I tell?" Will said.

"Whatever comes to mind," Pendrake said. "Tell us the happiest thing you can remember."

At that Will's thoughts fled to that summer vacation at the lake. The last one before he found out that his mother was sick. His memories came in bits and pieces that he had to clutch at before they faded away. The log cabin they had stayed in. With a loft and a real fireplace. Toasting marshmallows and telling jokes. Rain drumming on the roof.

On the last night of their stay, he hadn't been able to sleep. He got up and found his mother sitting on the front porch swing. She said she hadn't been able to sleep either. What did they do then? They looked at the stars together. Then she told him something. It was so hard to remember. . . . A story. A story from her childhood. Her family went to a cabin like this when she was a girl. She had wondered what life would be like when she grew up, whether she would have any children of her own. She used to imagine what they would be like, the children she didn't have yet.

What had he asked her then?

He had asked her what they were like. Her imaginary children.

They were perfect, she'd answered. *Always smiling, never fighting, always listening to their parents. The best kids in the whole world.*

You must be disappointed, he'd said.

She'd smiled and held him close. Then she'd said . . . She said . . .

I couldn't be happier, she'd said. *Because I didn't get those imaginary kids. I really did get the best kids in the whole world.*

As Will began the story, he felt the bleakness of the bog sink into him. In this lifeless landscape, what he had lost was that much clearer and more painful. He groped for words and found it hard to keep the memories clear in the fog that clouded his mind. When he came to that last night in the cabin, his voice trailed off.

"I'm sorry," he said. "I can't . . . I don't . . ."

He saw that Rowen had moved away from the others and was gazing up at the tower.

"Who would build a tower out here," he said, and it was no longer even a question moved by the slightest curiosity. "There's nothing to see."

"Something's—" Rowen began, but Pendrake interrupted her with a raised hand.

"We're starting it all over again," he said. "We need . . . another story. I'll tell one this time."

He had begun the first slow, hesitant words of a tale when Shade came loping back.

"I found someone, I think," he said doubtfully. "Follow me."

Will and the others needed no further encouragement. They set off doggedly after Shade, who ran slower than before, to allow them to keep up. After some time they saw the same looming shape before them once more, and Will's renewed hope began to fade, but before the tower was close enough to solidify out of the murk, Shade halted.

At first Will saw nothing, and then he realized that some-one was crouched in front of them. Someone the same gray lifeless color as the bog.

It appeared to be a large, bald, muscular man covered completely in wet clay. His thick arms were plunged into the bog, and he seemed to be straining to pull something out of the muck. He made no sound as he labored and seemed oblivious to the approach of Will and the others. His face was gray and expressionless.

"Who is he?" Rowen whispered.

"He does not speak," Shade said. "He must be deaf. Or very unfriendly."

"I think it must be a golem," Pendrake said. "A man-shape made of clay and brought to life with sorcery."

The creature gave a soundless heave. His arms came up out of the earth with a wet, squelching sound. Between his hands was a huge, dark brown stone. Slowly the golem straightened up, and then, even more slowly, as if he, too, were made of stone, he began to turn in the direction of the tower.

"What's he doing with that?" Rowen said.

"The tower isn't a ruin," Will said, as the truth struck him. "The golem is building it."

"I believe you're right, Will," Pendrake said. "But he can't finish. He moves so slowly that the tower sinks into the bog faster than he can build it up. It's a hopeless, endless task. That's why he's trapped here, and us with him."

The golem began walking now, toward the tower—if his sluggish plod, slower than a snail's creep, could be called walking. It was like watching a mountain come to life and take its first ponderous steps. As the creature moved, there was a sound like gravel grinding between wet stones.

"Can we stop him from doing this?" Finn asked. "He doesn't seem to know we're here."

"I don't think he does," Pendrake said. "Or we simply don't matter to him. He was made for one purpose only. To build this tower. If he could finish it, this part of his story might stop repeating. But we can't wait for that to happen. Let me think. There must be some way. . . ."

He went close to the golem, who towered over him by at least a head, and peered up at his gray, impassive face.

"Just as I thought," he said. "That's it. Someone lend me a knife."

Quickly Rowen handed hers over. The toy maker dug the blade's tip into the golem's forehead as if he were trying to pry something loose. The creature kept on without paying this intrusion the slightest notice. Suddenly something popped from the golem's forehead, and Pendrake caught it in his other hand.

The golem came to a stop and stood frozen, with the stone in his hands.

Pendrake opened his palm to show the others what he had found. It was a small, thick, yellow disk, like a piece of wax about the size of a shirt button. There was a letter or figure carved into its surface that vaguely resembled a bird with a long tail. They all turned to the motionless golem and saw the shallow hole in his forehead where the disk had been.

"Ord," Pendrake said, his eyebrows furrowing. "The letter is Ord."

"That's his name?" Will asked.

"You could say that. The disk is the seal that gave him life, and his purpose. Without it, he does nothing. He is nothing."

"Then his story's over now," Finn said. "So we can leave the shard, right?"

Pendrake looked past Finn and pointed. Everyone turned. The tower was still there.

"No, no, I was wrong," Pendrake growled, shaking his head. "Old fool. Shard dulled my wits. His story isn't over, just stopped. We'll stop, too, probably in a few moments."

He raised the disk to the golem's forehead, but his motions were slow and clumsy, and the disk slipped from his fingers.

"Where is it?" Rowen cried.

"I can't see it," Will said.

With weary urgency they searched the mud at their feet.

"Never mind," Pendrake said. He fished in one of his many pockets and brought out a handful of small objects: beads, buttons, marbles, and other tiny trinkets.

"There must be something. . . ." the toy maker muttered to himself as he sifted through the items in his hand. "Yes. This might do it."

He held up an object that looked to Will like a small checkers piece made of pale wood and pressed it into the hole in the golem's forehead. Everyone else stepped back.

Nothing happened.

Pendrake tried another object, a blue-green marble. Again nothing happened to the golem. Then he popped one of the buttons off his coat and raised it to the golem's forehead. By now his movements had become so agonizingly slow that Will had to suppress an angry shout. The button, like the checkers piece and the marble, had no apparent effect on the golem. And as the toy maker took the button away, his arm slowed until it stopped moving and stayed held out.

"Grandfather?" Rowen said.

"It's already happening," the toy maker said in a faltering voice, and to his horror Will could feel it in himself, too. As in those bad dreams he sometimes had where he could not move, his limbs were stiffening, refusing to obey his will. It was like being plunged into swiftly hardening concrete.

"Hurry . . ." Pendrake said, gasping. "Try another. . . ."

Rowen plucked urgently at the objects in Pendrake's palm, but her sluggish, clumsy attempt sent most of them falling to the ground. They seemed to take a long time getting there.

Rowen gave a choked cry.

"I can't move my legs." She gasped.

Finn struggled forward, holding out the green ring he wore on his right hand. He reached up and pressed it to the hole in the golem's forehead. An instant later came a flash of emerald light from the ring, and the clay giant shuddered from head to foot. There was a cracking sound, and Finn stumbled away from the golem. The ring's band was still around his finger, but the stone was lodged in the golem's forehead and glowed with a dull green fire.

In the next moment everything seemed to speed up. The toy maker suddenly lurched forward. Finn caught him before he fell.

"What did you . . . ?" he said to Finn, who was watching the golem with wide eyes.

"My brother's emerald. He gave it to me before he left home. His memory was all I had left in my mind just now. I was trying to hold on to it, and then I thought of the ring."

The huge lump of stone fell from the golem's hands and hit the ground with a wet thud. The clay giant began walking again, but this time much faster than before.

Will and the others watched him, stunned, and then began to follow. Will breathed deeply, aware that the weariness in his body and fog in his mind were already beginning to vanish. He felt as though he had just woken up from a deep, dreamless slumber that had gone on for years. And even the bog itself seemed to come to a kind of life. The mist thinned, swept by a warmer breeze, and patches of blue appeared in the sky.

"Where's he going?" Rowen asked, watching the golem trudge on.

"Ord seems to know, which will have to be enough for us," Pendrake said.

As they drew closer to the tower, they wondered if the golem would stop, but he passed by the lonely pile of stones without so much as a glance. And as Will and the others followed, they saw to their relief that the tower was sinking visibly. They heard the creaking and groaning of the stones as they shifted and slid.

"There must have been a kingdom here long ago," Pendrake said, "before this land became a bog. For all we know, the tower is only the tallest turret of an entire castle sunk in the earth for hundreds of years."

The golem's pace began to quicken, and although Shade seemed able to keep up with him, the others were still weary from their time in the storyshard and lagged behind. Finally Pendrake called a halt. They gathered together and watched as the golem trudged on without them. Only Finn kept on after the creature, until he sank to his knees in the mire and came plodding slowly back.

"I do not think you will get your green stone back," Shade said to him. The young man shook his head wearily, but there was a light in his eyes Will had not seen before.

"It was not mine," he said. "And I wasn't trying to get it back. Where else would the golem go but to find the one who used to wear the ring? A foolish hope, I suppose."

Already the golem had dwindled to a gray blur. Pendrake put a hand on Finn's shoulder.

"You may meet Ord again someday."

When they looked again, the golem had vanished.

15

Every storyteller has a bag of tricks.

— The Kantar

THEY TRUDGED ON, and when the tower did not reappear, they felt certain that they had escaped, especially when they found themselves in a region of the bog with more trees. Spindly spruce and pines stood in greater numbers here, and even some tall birch grew between the pools. Patches of warm sunlight dappled the earth, and the air smelled fresh and raw.

In the evening they took shelter from the biting wind in a clump of straggly pines. Tattered clouds sped across the sky, hiding and revealing the stars. Shade nosed some fleshy roots from the soil, and Finn lit a fire long enough to cook a thin but warming broth.

The moon rose out of a mass of clouds on the horizon. Pale silver light flooded the bog. Pendrake gazed up at the bright silver orb and made a sound of surprise.

"What is it?" Rowen asked.

"The moon is at its full," Pendrake said. "We were trapped in the storyshard for at least two days."

"That's not possible," said Finn. "It was only a few hours, at most."

"Not even that long," Rowen added.

"If we hadn't escaped," Pendrake said, "for us it would have become eternity, and no time at all. But perhaps we can be thankful. By disappearing for so long, we may have thrown off our pursuer."

After a while Will sat down beside Rowen.

"I guess I shouldn't ask you again if you're all right."

Rowen smirked.

"Funny," she said. "I'm fine now, I think. What happened in the shard, I thought I'd never felt anything like that before. Then I remembered how I'd listen to the stories at the Golden Goose, and sometimes I would know what was going to be told before the storyteller said a word. I could tell what storyfolk should do, even if they didn't know themselves. In the shard I knew we had stumbled into some kind of story, a story that was *wrong* somehow, even before Grandfather knew. I don't understand how I knew that. He's the loremaster, not me."

Will remembered the troubling feeling he'd had when the loremaster first told him about Malabron and the Stewards, a sense that the old man was keeping something back. But he felt now that he shouldn't admit this to Rowen, and suddenly he knew why. Pendrake was keeping something not from him but from Rowen.

"Your grandfather's told you a lot of stories," he suggested halfheartedly. "Maybe you're just learning to see things the way he does."

"I suppose so," Rowen said doubtfully. "I wondered if

someday I would. But I don't feel as if I learned this. It just . . . took hold of me."

"That's like what happens to me, with the knot-paths. I'm from the Untold, and so was your father. Maybe that's why things are different for us. You should ask your grandfather about it."

They both looked across the fire at Pendrake, who was sewing a button back onto his coat.

"I know I should," Rowen said. "But I'm afraid to."

The next morning the companions continued on and soon came to an area of the bog that was less flat and featureless. The land rose to bald hummocks and dropped into gullies, down which water ran in swift streams. The mist thinned long enough to give them a glimpse of blue hills to the west, and beyond them the peaks of high mountains tipped with snow. The air smelled fresher, too, less heavy with the rankness of the bog. Pendrake announced that they must be near the edge of the bog at last.

He was as dismayed as the others when they crested a hill late that afternoon and saw a vast lake lying before them, gleaming a dull red in the setting sun. The air was colder here, too, as the west wind drove a chill off the water.

"This lake was not here when I came this way last," the toy maker said. "We will have to go around. How far, I cannot say. Let's go down to the shore. I want to see how deep the water is."

This was not news that anyone wanted to hear, but there was no choice, so they hoisted their packs and headed downhill. At the bottom they plunged into a field of tall reeds that swayed and whispered in the wind. They pushed through the damp reeds, which soon rose over Will's head, scaring up a few shorebirds along the way. Suddenly they came out into a clearing. A wall of hissing reeds ringed them on all sides, except for a narrow gap that led down a kind of tunnel to the lake. They could hear the lap of waves on the shore. The wind stung Will's eyes and brought tears.

The setting sun blazed a moment through the clouds in the west, then sank below the black wall of the mountains and suddenly winked out.

Will lowered his head and started forward, but was halted by an urgent whisper from Pendrake.

"Listen."

There was a rustling from nearby. A flock of birds rose into the air with shrill cries and a clamor of flapping wings.

"We didn't cause that," Finn said.

Will felt a chill slide down his neck like cold water, a chill that he knew had nothing to do with the wind off the lake. A low, whistling moan whispered through the rushes. Before anyone had a chance to speak or move, three figures rose before them as if out of the ground.

They were tall, and pale as moonlight. Their faces were cold as stone but beautiful, like faces on the ancient tombs of kings and queens. Two were men, and the third, the one closest to them, was a woman with long flowing hair.

"Fetches," Rowen cried. "They found us."

"Keep quiet," Pendrake whispered. "They'll be drawn to our voices."

As he spoke, they heard another eerie moan from behind them. They turned. At the top of the hill they had just come down, there hovered two more fetches, like smoke taking shape from black shadows. These had also assumed the form of tall, kingly figures, though like the others they carried no weapons other than the fear that went before them like a creeping fog.

The companions moved to face out in a tight ring. Shade began to snarl and pace around them in a circle.

"I've fought these shadowshapes before," he said. "Teeth and claws are no use against them."

"Neither are swords," Pendrake said. "And do not look them in the eye, whatever you do."

The fetches on the hill descended swiftly and vanished into the encircling reeds, while the other three stood motionless, blocking the path to the water. Despite the toy maker's warning, Will could not tear his eyes away from the fetch that had taken a woman's shape. She was gazing at him, he was startled to see, with what looked like recognition, and even sadness. And though she did not open her mouth to speak, Will heard a voice speaking softly inside his head.

Do not be afraid, the voice said gently. *You had need of us, and we have come.*

Who are you? he answered, and his own voice seemed to come not from his mouth, but from his thoughts.

You know the answer already. Come with us and find what you seek.

At once a new hope leaped into Will's heart. *The Hidden Folk.* The toy maker had said they were masters of concealment and illusion. Maybe this was how they eluded their enemies, by taking these ghostly shapes.

"Everyone stay together," Pendrake said, and at the sound of his voice, Will felt his mind lurch free, as though he had been drifting toward sleep and had been jolted awake. He turned to the toy maker, who bowed his head briefly and then looked up with a grim face. Pendrake began to sweep the staff slowly through the air over his head, while chanting over and over in a soft voice that grew louder:

"End and beginning
  woven together

as day and night,
in the fathomless fire
ever changing,
ceasing never,
let the shadows
bring forth light."

As Will watched in awe, faint streaks of luminescence, like thin streams of fog, began to form in the wake of the toy maker's staff. It seemed as if by stirring the air he had spun light from the gloom itself. The streaks grew larger and brighter, and began slowly to descend, moving in a ring about Will and his friends like rippling bands of the northern lights.

The two fetches approaching from the hill came out of the reeds into the clearing and suddenly halted. They seemed confused, or distracted, moving toward the swirling streamers of light, then back again.

For a moment Will could see the swaying reeds through the fetches' wavering forms. But as the lights began to fade, they took on shape again, and continued to advance, though more slowly than before.

"They're still closing in," Finn muttered. "What can we do?"

"I will try to draw off the three," Pendrake said. "That should give you a chance to get Will and Rowen to the lake. These creatures usually avoid water. That may be our only defense. Shade, go with them."

"I will, Master Pendrake."

"When I give the word," the toy maker said, "run for the lake and do not look back."

The companions turned again to the three fetches that stood between them and the pathway to the lake. The toy maker clutched his staff with both hands and began to speak in a strange language, his eyes closed and his voice strained as though he were drawing the words up like water from a deep well. Once again Will found himself looking into the eyes of the woman.

Who is she? he wondered, and an answer came to him.

The Lady of the Green Court.

The woman held out her arms. Her eyes were filled with sorrow, and love. She smiled. The urge to flee faded in Will. And then a soft, soothing voice spoke in his thoughts.

You have come so far, Will. You have tried so hard.

He had. She knew what he had been through. She understood.

"I'm . . . lost," he said. "I don't know what to do."

She nodded and stepped closer.

You've been led astray. But at last we've found you.

He was so tired. She understood everything. She would keep him safe. With her beside him there would be . . .

No more running, her gentle voice promised him. *No more fear.*

"I shouldn't listen to you," he said, struggling to think, to remember something urgent that was slipping away from him.

You don't have to listen to anyone anymore. You don't have to do what others tell you to do.

She was telling him the truth. She knew everything. How did he really know that anything the old man had said was true? Just like his father, Pendrake had dragged him on a pointless journey to nowhere. But he didn't have to listen anymore. He didn't have to be lost and afraid.

Will lowered his knife and took a step forward. Now he could see her as she really was. There was no longer any doubt. She was standing at the sink in the kitchen at home.

He could smell baking. Sunlight was streaming in through the window. As he came toward her, she turned and wiped her hands on her apron and smiled at him.

Home at last, she said. *I was wondering where you had got to.*

She opened her arms, and Will walked toward her. As he moved, he heard Rowen cry his name, but her voice seemed to come from very far away. Dimly he was aware that she was warning him of danger, but it no longer mattered. He had found his way to the end of the story.

As his hand touched *hers*, he felt his body go cold, as if he had plunged into icy water. Everything around him grew dark, except for a pale, pulsing light that hovered just beyond his reach. *She* had vanished, and he stumbled forward, desperate to find her again. The light moved farther away as he approached it. He felt no fear. He felt nothing at all, only the need to follow the light.

He heard a shout then, and felt something pulling him backward, away from where *she* had been. Slowly he turned, trying to shrug off whatever was holding him back. A face swam toward him out of the dark. It was Rowen's, he thought, but she was someone he had known long ago, and only for a little while. Why was she here now? What did she want of him? *Will, come on!* she was shouting. *Fight them.* Her voice was distant and muffled, as if it were reaching him from underwater.

He saw that she had her knife drawn and was holding it out in front of her, warding off something he couldn't see. Vaguely he knew what she was telling him; he knew he should listen to her, but he couldn't remember why it mattered.

Then Pendrake was there in front of him. He gave a great shout and raised his staff over his head. Dazzling silver light bloomed in the air.

Will put his hands over his eyes. The light was hurting him, bringing back pain and fear. Bringing back everything that he wanted to forget. He cried out in anguish.

When he opened his eyes, he saw that Pendrake had vanished, and *she* stood before him again. But she was farther away now, and somehow changed. She was still beautiful, but her smile was colder, her eyes watchful. Will's thoughts cleared, and he understood that his friends were trying to save him. He knew that she was not who he wanted her to be. But he no longer cared. She was his only hope.

As he struggled forward, desperate to reach her, there was a shrill screech from above. Will halted. The woman appeared to hear it, too. Her eyes widened, and her pale form wavered. There was a rush of beating wings, and through the woman a ragged black shape suddenly burst, as if through a veil of fog. It shot past Will, coming so close to him that he had to duck his head. It was gone in an instant, but he had glimpsed sleek black wings and a bright eye.

Morrigan.

The woman's form, shredded like smoke in a gust of wind, began to close around the hole that had been torn in it. Will watched in horror as the warmth and recognition faded from her eyes, replaced with a cold, murderous fire. Her form coiled in upon itself, and in the next instant it billowed out again, growing in size and changing shape once more. The slender hands elongated into bony claws. Black, batlike wings plumed from the woman's arching back. Her lovely face contorted into a white mask of fury.

Will stumbled back as the fetch rose over him. Then he heard a shout and saw Moth nearby, his bow drawn, an arrow notched and ready. An instant later, just as the fetch lunged at Will, the archer let fly. With a hiss the shaft sped from the bow and struck.

The fetch thrashed and shuddered, clutching at the arrow in its breast. It began to shudder and twist, and then lose color and form. For an instant the arrow hung as if suspended in nothing but a wisp of fog. Then, with a sound halfway between a shriek and a sigh like a dying breath, the fetch vanished. The arrow dropped harmlessly to the ground.

Will felt himself come awake with a shock, as if cold water had been thrown over him. His heart seemed to begin beating again. It throbbed in his chest like a wound. He stifled a cry of fear and loss, and stared wildly around.

Rowen was at his side, with Finn and Shade. Pendrake stood nearby. And there was Moth, with Morrigan circling above him.

The other two fetches had already begun to draw back. A second arrow from Moth's bow transfixed one of them, and with an unearthly cry it vanished like the first. The third fetch halted, and then, like a rope that had been held taut and suddenly let go, it collapsed into a coil and slithered away through the reeds.

Will staggered forward and then toppled helplessly to the ground. Finn helped him to his feet, and he felt the world heave under him and spin. He would have fallen again, but Finn held him. He watched as the two fetches approaching from the hilltop now moved apart from each other, either to flee or to come at their quarry from two sides. As they advanced they began to sink into the ground as if they were wading into deepening water, and then they were gone.

"This way," Moth said, nodding his head toward the path to the lake. "Quickly, before worse happens."

16

THE COMPANIONS HURRIED AFTER MOTH down the tunnel of reeds. In a few moments they were at the lakeshore. There, a little way from the bank, floated a raft of thickly matted moss and sticks, like a tiny island. Moth urged them on, and everyone quickly leaped across the gap. The raft held them solidly, but there was barely enough room for everyone. When he had joined them, the archer took up one of two thick wooden poles lying across the middle of the raft and shoved away from the shore.

Finn helped Will down onto the soft, mossy surface of the raft, then took up the other pole. The raft drifted slowly out into the lake and then seemed to catch a current that moved it more swiftly into open water. Shade stood at the trailing end of the raft and growled at the receding shore. Rowen and her grandfather crouched beside Will.

"Are you hurt?" Rowen asked anxiously.

Will struggled to answer, but no words would come. His body was cold and lifeless, as if icy slush were flowing sluggishly in his veins. The only thing he could feel was a throb of agony from his heart. His friends had saved him, but they had taken him from *her*.

Tears filled his eyes.

"The power of the fetch is still working in you, Will," Moth said gravely, bending to examine him. "It will take some time to fade. Rest now. You are safe from them here."

Shade ceased growling, padded swiftly across the raft to Will, and sat beside him. Will reached out a shaking hand and stroked the wolf's fur.

Pendrake stood and turned to Moth.

"You saved our lives, old friend," he said. "Thank you."

"The danger is far from over," Moth said. "Your pursuer is the one who set the mirrors in the Wood. Morrigan and I picked up his trail there at last, and we were following him. We knew he was after you."

"The wisp I sent to throw him off . . ." Pendrake began.

"Found me, and led me to the knot-path." Moth reached within his cloak and brought out the wisp, which bobbed and danced on his palm. Pendrake searched for his waylight and opened it. Sputter darted inside, and its light swiftly dimmed and went out.

"You can find the knot-paths?" Rowen asked.

"They are usually invisible to me, but Will had just opened it, and I was able to slip through before it vanished again. I lost your trail in the bog, found it, then lost it again. You were doing a fine job of eluding any pursuers."

"We almost lost ourselves," Pendrake said drily. "But we'll save that tale for later."

"Morrigan and I arrived at the lake not long ago. Morrigan

had seen that the fetches were near and were closing in on you. Since we once lived in this bog for a time, we knew of a way we might escape them."

The raft was moving swiftly now, and Moth stopped poling.

"I have met others like you," Shade said to the archer. "Long ago. They had arrows like yours that could pierce the shadowshapes."

Moth looked closely at the wolf and then spoke a few words in another language. Shade's ears perked up. He replied in the same tongue and bowed his shaggy head.

"Your people were friends to the Speaking Creatures," Shade said. "We were proud to stand alongside you in battle."

"One of the Companions," Moth said, his eyes wide. "There is clearly a tale here. But it will have to wait, too, like Master Pendrake's. Until we decide what is to be done."

They heard a loud cawing overhead and then Morrigan swooped down. She alighted on the tip of the pole that Moth held at arm's length, and folded her wings. The raven and the wolf stared fixedly at each other, and for a moment it seemed to Will that they were two ordinary animals, each uneasy about this other creature close at hand. Then Morrigan cocked her head at Will and the others as if to comment on their strange choice in traveling companions. She hopped onto Moth's arm, leaned toward his ear, and spoke in her odd language of croaks and clicks.

"The fetches are still at the shore," Moth said when the raven had finished. "Waiting for the one that leads them."

"I hope you have more of those arrows," Finn said.

"They will not stop *him*."

"Whoever their master is, he discovered the secret of the snugs," Pendrake said.

"Yes, I found one with blood runes carved into its door,"

Moth said. "Ancient spells of great power. There is no doubt anymore. It is the Angel that hunts you."

"After all this time . . ." Pendrake began.

"He has returned," Moth continued, and his hand went to the hilt of the strange black sword at his hip. "You escaped him through the knot-path, but he must have sent the fetches on ahead, as if he knew or guessed which way you were going. I did not sense his presence in the bog, but I fear he is not far away."

He whispered a word to Morrigan, and with a flap of her black wings the raven lifted from his shoulder and flew off in the direction from which they had come.

"I've heard of this Angel," Finn said, "but always in the oldest stories. I thought he had been destroyed ages ago."

"So it was thought," Moth said. "I knew him once as Lotan, a traitor to his people. After Eleel fell, his own slaves rose against him, returning hate for hate. They feared he might come back even from death, so they cut off his head, burned his body, wrapped it in chains, and threw it into the sea. They were right to fear."

"I've heard about him," Will said, remembering the story Pendrake had told about the city of Eleel. Everyone looked at him. "He was . . ."

"A prince of the Shee," Moth finished, his eyes on Morrigan as she dwindled to a blurry black speck on the horizon. "Now he is a lord of the Shadow Realm, where stories fall into darkness. His body was destroyed, but through sorcery he was able to mold dead flesh over the nothingness that is his spirit. He can see like a cat in darkness, run day and night without tiring, without sleep. Steel shatters on his spell-guarded flesh, and fire does not harm him."

He turned to Will.

"The Angel does not stop until he has found his prey."

*   *   *

They floated across the lake in the dark, and then the moon
came out from a black bank of clouds, a shining white face
that seemed to be watching them. Its pale light turned the
water to silver. As the companions shared what little food
they had, Will told Moth the tale of how he had found Shade
in the Library. Pendrake described the journey from Fable
and their captivity in the storyshard.

"I believe Morrigan and I saw the golem, on our way to
find you," Moth said. "He was heading straight north, and
moving at astonishing speed. We had no idea what he was or
where he was going, and our concern was to find you, so we
didn't bother about him."

"North," Finn said quietly.

"As an arrow flies," Moth said, turning to look at the
young man.

"This is Finn Madoc, of the Errantry," Pendrake said to
him.

The archer bowed.

"I met your brother once," he said. "A brave man. I hope
he finds his way home."

Finn bowed in return but said nothing.

"What's in the north?" Will asked Rowen in a whisper.

"The Night King's fortress was there, in the time of the
Great Unweaving. The Armanath. It's mostly just wasteland
now, Grandfather says. Beyond is Arkland, the wilderness of
ice and snow."

By this time the raft had drifted to a part of the lake that
was broken up into channels between small rocky hillocks
and larger islands thick with trees and undergrowth. Moth
and Finn took up the poles again to keep the raft in the
midst of the current that was tugging them steadily westward. Will noticed again, as he had at the snug that first

night, that the archer kept as far apart as he could from those around him.

Rowen gave Will some water from her flask and sat beside him quietly, a look of tense concentration on her face, as if she were listening for the slightest sound out of the ordinary. Pendrake stood near them, withdrawn into his own thoughts, and from time to time the old man would shake his head or mouth words to himself, as though he were reaching deep into his gathered lore for something half remembered. His grim, weary look had not changed since they had discovered the identity of their pursuer.

"Grandfather," Rowen finally said, and the old man stirred, "what you did, back on the shore, with the light . . ."

"I should not have done," Pendrake said, finishing her sentence. "There was little choice, but it may cost us dearly."

"What *did* you do?" Will asked.

"I reached into the Weaving," Pendrake said. "Something I have not attempted for a long time. All stories wait there, as possibilities, as dreams of what might be. As the flame waits in dry kindling."

"But you helped us escape the fetches," Will said.

"And changed the weave of the Kantar. A dangerous thing to do. The Night King waits in his Shadow Realm, like a spider in its web, for any twitch or quiver in the threads he has woven to catch his prey. I didn't just touch a thread; I gave one a good tug. And that may have made it much easier for Malabron's creatures to find us."

"I didn't know," Rowen said, staring at her grandfather with a look of mingled awe and fear. "I didn't know a lore-master could do these things. I thought only the Stewards had that power."

"Not everything the Stewards taught was lost," said

Pendrake, and then he turned away to gaze out across the water. It was clear that he didn't want to say any more.

In the moonlit dimness ahead of them, they saw a cluster of tiny glimmering lights that seemed to be close to the surface of the water.

"What is that?" Rowen cried.

As they approached, the lights quickly went out. The raft passed the spot where the lights had been, and in the pale light Will could just make out what appeared to be a low mound of earth and twigs, like a tiny island.

"Creelings," Moth said as they left the mound behind. "Smallfolk. That mound is one of their cities. We are floating on another one."

Rowen sat up suddenly and touched the surface of the raft.

"This is a . . . city?"

"It was, once," Moth said. "There is no one in it now. The creelings often move from place to place. They like to keep to themselves, so they use these floating islands as decoys, to mislead anyone who comes this far into the bog. Morrigan and I met the creelings long ago and befriended them. They were kind enough to lend us one of their floating islands for our escape."

Will peered through the gloom at the island as it slid away behind them, but saw nothing. How empty it seemed out here in the wild, and yet how full it might be with creatures that he simply couldn't see or wouldn't notice because he didn't know where to look. Or how.

He felt the world around him brimming with an unseen energy, a tumult of stories just beyond his sight. Was this the Weaving the toy maker had spoken of? Then the sensation passed, and the world was just the world again. Wind and water and darkness.

After a time Morrigan returned and perched on Moth's shoulder. Shade was surprised again and glared at the raven as though he were tempted to lunge at it. Will reached out and hesitantly scratched the wolf behind the ears, more glad than ever of his company. To his relief, Shade did not flinch from the touch but seemed to welcome it. He lifted a huge paw and placed it gently on Will's arm.

"How are you now, Will Lightfoot?" he asked.

"Better," Will said. The numbing chill in his veins was ebbing, but now and then he caught what seemed to be a faint echo of *her* voice, like ghostly whispers in his head. He stirred, restlessly wishing for some way to banish these phantom murmurings.

"I don't understand about the fetches," he finally said to Moth. "If they're ghosts, how can arrows hurt them?"

"No weapon of wood or metal can harm them," the archer said, his eyes still keenly scanning the wooded shore of the large island they were passing. "My arrowheads are engraved with runes to cut the spellstrings that hold the *annai* captive to the Night King's will. Once that bond is broken, the fetch can pass on. It is no longer bound to another's desires."

"So the ones you shot won't come after us anymore?"

"Some fetches linger whether a spell holds them or not, hating the living and doing them harm. But most vanish and are never seen again. Whatever they are, though, they all speak with the same voice, that of their master."

"You could hear them?"

"Could you not?" Moth asked, turning to look at Will at last, his gaze cold and piercing.

Will nodded, but kept silent, afraid to admit to one of the Hidden Folk that the fetches were still whispering in his thoughts. He felt safer now that Moth had joined their company, but the archer's mood was even more grim and aloof than it had been when they first met. He was strung as tightly as his own bowstring, tensed and ready for anything, and for the first time Will glimpsed the fiery spirit brooding within the Tain warrior. He would charge into certain death, Will thought, without hesitation.

The steady lapping of the waves was soothing, and soon Will found that he was having trouble keeping his eyes open. Pendrake saw him drooping and urged him to sleep while he could. Gratefully Will curled up with his head resting on Shade's warm flank.

A shriek from Morrigan brought him back to wakefulness. He opened his eyes to see the raven alight on Moth's arm, squawking frantically. The sky was pale gray. It seemed to Will he had been asleep only a few minutes, but the night had passed and dawn had come.

"Everyone crouch down and do not move," Moth said in a low but commanding voice.

As they obeyed him, the archer turned, scanned the water ahead of them, and pointed.

"Finn, we must find shelter."

While the others stayed low, Moth and Finn poled the raft swiftly and noiselessly to the nearest of the islands and ran it in under the cover of some drooping willow trees.

"What is it?" Rowen whispered, and Moth put a finger to his lips. They waited like this for a few breathless moments, and then they heard a faint sound that swiftly grew louder, a billowing and snapping like a flag fluttering in a strong wind. As whatever it was passed overhead, Will peered up through the canopy of leaves and for an instant saw a ragged white shape, rippling and writhing in the air. In the next instant the thing had passed and the sounds faded. Moth rose from a crouch, and the others did likewise.

"I can answer your question now," he said to Rowen. "Lotan travels on foot, but now he has a watcher in the sky, as we do with Morrigan."

"It looked like a white sheet," Will said.

"It is his cloak," Moth said. "A creature of nightmare called a shrowde. It has bound itself to Lotan and gives him concealment, so that he may go unseen. The cloak also shields him from the sun, whose rays burn his borrowed flesh. But if need be, he will send the shrowde from him, to scout ahead. The creature can see, and hear, although like the fetches its powers are diminished in daylight."

"Then we can't stay on the lake," Rowen said. "That thing might come back this way and spot us."

"I do not think we are far from the western shore," Moth said, and suddenly he turned, as if he had heard or sensed something. He leaped from the raft to the island's stony shingle, which rose steeply from the water to the trees.

The others quickly followed him. On the crest of the slope above them, green trees touched by the light of dawn beckoned like a vision of summer on a dark winter's day. Morrigan circled over their heads, calling with what sounded to Will like joy.

"My people have been here," Moth said, and Will stared at him, startled at the change in the archer's voice. To his surprise, Moth unbuckled his black sword and cast it down on the pebbled shore as if it were a hated thing. With Morrigan on his shoulder, he climbed the slope, gazing straight ahead like someone in a trance, and passed under the leafy shade. After a moment, Will and his friends followed.

In the center of the island, in a hollow of stone ringed by

trees, lay a small still pool of clear water. Moth was already there on one knee. He held his open hand over the surface.

"*Énye Taina thu qantar,*" he whispered. "*El'il . . .*"

He looked up, his gaze far away.

"The Green Court was here. My people rested in the shade of these trees. The Lady of the Starlight sat beside this pool and sang of Eleel."

Small white flowers grew among the thick moss beside the pool, and Moth passed his hand over these as well. Will remembered that he had seen this particular flower before, depicted in glass above the gate into Fable.

"The flower is called *aíne,*" Finn said to him quietly. "They say it grows wherever the Lady has been. That's why it was named for her."

"Can you tell how long ago they were here?" Pendrake asked Moth. For a long time the archer did not answer. Then he rose to his feet, and Will saw that his eyes were shining.

"Days. Or years," Moth said, shaking his head. "Nor could I say which way they went after they left the island. There was a time when I could have followed them, and found them, but no more."

He turned and walked away slowly through the trees.

Rowen had strayed farther than the others and returned with the news that there were wild berries growing nearby.

She turned to lead the way, and Will was about to go with her when he remembered Moth's sword. The archer had left it lying on the shingle and had apparently forgotten it. While the others followed Rowen, Will turned back and climbed down to the shore. The sword lay there, like something cast up by the waves. Will picked it up by the scabbard, which felt ice cold to the touch and perfectly smooth. He had been right: the scabbard was made of a lightweight black stone, or something that felt very much like stone.

Will meant to tuck the weapon under his arm and return it right away to Moth, but something made him hesitate. He touched the hilt, which was as cold as the scabbard, and, like it, shone with a lustrous darkness blacker than night. It seemed as if hilt and scabbard were one single piece, and now Will wondered whether there really was a blade concealed inside.

"Are you not coming, Will Lightfoot?"

Startled, he looked up to see Shade at the edge of the trees, regarding him with curiosity.

"In a moment," Will said with a twinge of anger. Why did everyone have to watch him all the time?

"That is the Nightwanderer's sword."

"I know that. You needn't wait."

Shade seemed about to reply, then he turned and loped back into the trees. When he was gone, Will fixed his attention on the sword. If anything, the wolf's interruption had made him even more eager to solve the mystery of the archer's strange blade. He hesitated a moment longer, holding his breath, and then he drew the sword from the scabbard.

The blade made a sharp ringing sound as it slid out, but unlike the ring Will's knife made, this sound did not fade quickly away. Instead it lingered in his ears, a faint metallic hum that was vaguely troubling. He held the sword before him and was disappointed to see that there was nothing unusual about it, as far as he could tell. The blade looked rough and dull-edged, not polished and reflective like his own knife, as though it were made of some raw, impure ore. Will turned the sword this way and that, trying to catch some kind of gleam on its surface. There was none, but as he peered closely at the blade, he noticed that the sword's eerie hum had become a kind of low vibration, more a warmth in the hand than a sound. He could feel it against his palm, growing to a pulsing heat, and as he continued to stare at the blade, he felt a hot, exhilarating dread grow inside him, as if in answer.

There was great power in this sword. With it he could do . . . wondrous and terrifying things.

From behind him someone spoke his name. Will knew before he turned around who it would be, as if the sword had summoned him.

17

There are fires in the earth, deep beneath the snow.

— Legends of the Northlands

NEAR HIM ON THE SHORE was the white-haired man in red from his dreams. He was sitting on a bleached driftwood log before a small fire. With a long stick he was turning the crackling bits of firewood. When he looked up, Will's first instinct was to run, but the man's eyes, so like Moth's, held him.

"Who are you?" Will said.

"You already know," the man said. His voice was like Moth's as well, musical and haunting. It made Will want to stay and listen. It was a voice that promised to speak of important things, wonders, mysteries. A voice you waited eagerly to hear speak again. "No doubt you have been told stories about me."

"You're the—" Will began, but fear took him by the throat and choked his voice.

"Do you know why some call me the Angel?" Lotan asked.

Will gave no answer. He searched the trees, desperately hoping to see Shade or the others, even though he knew somehow that he was no longer where they were. The Angel set down his stick and rose to his feet. The fire seemed to dim as he stood over it.

"I serve the one true lord of this world," Lotan said. "I am the emissary of Malabron, his right hand and his shadow. I stand at the end of stories, and I bring them all before my master. As I shall bring you."

"No," Will said, shaking his head. "They . . . my friends won't let that happen."

Lotan smiled coldly.

"Your friends fear what they do not understand. They fear you, as well, Will Lightfoot. They fear what you will become. Why do you think the old man brought you out here, into the wild, as far as he could from his quiet little land? He could have found another way, surely. But instead he dragged you on this foolish journey that takes you farther from home with every step."

"That's not true!" Will shouted. "He's trying to help me."

"Is he? Well, now you see where *his* plans have brought you. Perhaps you were better off before you met him. Before you met any of them."

The man's calm, almost gentle voice dulled Will's fear, compelling him to listen. Did the loremaster really know what he was doing? *If this is a dream, I should be able to end it,* he told himself desperately. *I should be able to wake up.*

Something cold stung the back of his neck. Large, hoary flakes of snow were drifting slowly down from the sunless sky. They fell into the water, but instead of vanishing, they began to cover it in a layer of ice, like frost growing across a windowpane.

"The truth is," Lotan went on, "your companions have doomed themselves. The old fool who led you on this aimless quest knows that, if he knows little else. He knows there is really no hope, and yet he carries on. One can admire that. Despite the certain fate that awaits him, and the others."

"What do you mean?"

Lotan came closer, through the snow that was falling faster and thicker now but did not settle on him. There were no flakes in his hair, on his eyelashes, anywhere.

"The Lord of Story will punish them," Lotan said, "for keeping you from him. In the end there is nowhere to hide, no story he cannot enter. Your friends will learn that truth, and then they will die."

Will raised Moth's sword in both hands and held it between him and Lotan. He felt its power burn through him like fire.

"Go away!" he shouted, his voice breaking. "Go away, or I will kill you."

As Lotan's gaze fell upon the sword, his eyes flickered with surprise and even fear. It happened so fast that Will wasn't even sure he had really seen it. An instant later the cold smile had returned to Lotan's face.

"If you wish to destroy me, Will Lightfoot, then come. But know that I am the gate you seek. No one enters or leaves the realms but by my master's will. And I am the way to him."

Will raised the sword, and with a scream, he lunged at the Angel, who stood his ground without moving. Will swung the blade with all his strength and went staggering to one side as the blade passed through empty air.

Lotan had vanished into the swirling snow.

Then Will saw that the lake and the island had also disappeared. Instead he found himself standing in a high place, far above a land of forests and hills. On the distant horizon, the sun was setting in a red bank of clouds. Will craned his neck to look down and saw, through the falling snow, a great cliff that plummeted in a sheer drop for hundreds of feet to a valley filled with black shadows.

He scrambled away from the terrifying drop, and once more snow swirled around him. He groped his way through it, and there was the Angel again, calmly standing before him, a hand held out beckoningly.

"This is already my master's story," he said, with something almost like sadness in his voice. "It can end only one way."

Will raised the sword once more, but then slowly let it fall.

"No," he whispered, hanging his head.

"For the sake of your friends, come with me now."

Will choked back tears. As he stepped forward, a sharp stabbing pain bit into his wrist. With a gasp he tried to pull his arm away but could not. Something he couldn't see was holding him. He struggled and cried out.

He was standing on the shore of the island, Moth's sword in his hand. The Angel was nowhere to be seen. There was no snow falling. At his side stood Shade, regarding him with concern.

"Am I dreaming?" Will muttered groggily.

"I would say no," the wolf replied.

"Did you . . . did you bite me, Shade?" Will asked, rubbing his wrist, which he suddenly noticed was throbbing with a dull pain.

"Only a little," the wolf said. "You were talking to someone who was not there. You were frightened. I tried to speak to you, but you would not listen."

Will placed a hand on the wolf's shaggy ruff.

"I'm glad you're here, Shade," he said.

"So am I, Will Lightfoot. And I am sorry about the bite. I was not going to eat you."

"I know that. Listen, Shade. I have to go now, by myself, before the others come back. If they stay with me, something terrible is coming. For you, too. I don't want that to happen."

"Neither do I," a voice said, and Will looked up to see Moth at the edge of the trees. "Put down the sword *now*."

The archer's voice was cold and commanding. Like a dry twig the power of the blade seemed to snap in two, and Will found he had no choice but to obey. Both sword and scabbard slipped from his hands and clattered on the stones.

"Get away from it," Moth said, advancing down the slope.

"I only wanted to see," Will muttered, stumbling backward. "I didn't know. . . ."

Moth lunged, and with one swift movement, he had the scabbard in his hand and the blade back within it. As he buckled the sword back onto his belt, Will saw him grimace with pain. The color drained from his face as though that terrible blade had been thrust into him.

"I should never have left this," Moth said under his breath, and then he fixed Will with a grave look. "I have been far too careless."

"I was going to bring it to you," Will mumbled, lowering his head. He was sorry for what he had done, but also angry at Moth for taking the sword from him, and the intensity of his anger frightened him.

Moth placed a hand on his shoulder.

"Do not trouble yourself," he said. His face looked aged, and beads of sweat stood out on his forehead. "It is my fault. I should have warned you about the sword when I first saw that you were curious about it."

"What's wrong with it?"

Moth laughed soundlessly.

"Only what is wrong with this world," he said. "The blade is forged of *gaal*. It is deadly to storyfolk, and dangerous to most others."

"How can you carry it around, if—" Will broke off as understanding flooded through him. "It hurts you. All the time."

Moth swept the sword out of sight under his cloak.

"I am able to bear it," he said, "because the hilt and scabbard are made of dragon bone. The one substance that can shield against the power of the *gaal*."

"You've been searching for *him*," Will said. "To use the sword against him."

He heard a sound and saw that the others had joined them on the shore.

"I saw the Angel," Will said.

"He was here?" Rowen asked, her eyes wide with fear.

"I don't know. It must have been a dream, but it was so real."

"When you took the sword, you came closer to the Shadow Realm," Moth said. "Lotan walks there as well as here. He can be many miles away, but all too close."

He handed Will a small leather flask.

"Drink this," he said. "It is called everenth. It will restore some of your strength and help you resist if Lotan appears to you again."

Will took a tentative sip. The drink tasted slightly bitter, like unsweetened tea, but almost immediately he felt a warmth flowing into him. He took another sip and handed back the flask. Then, at Pendrake's bidding, he told them what had happened when he held the sword, and at last admitted the dreams of Lotan he'd been having since he first arrived in the Bourne.

As he described what he had seen, it occurred to him that Lotan hadn't been wearing the shrowde cloak.

"He revealed himself to you as he once was," Moth said. "Morrigan and I knew the Angel long before he took that name. He and I will meet again, Will, but not today. Keeping you out of his clutches is what matters most for the present. But I promise you, until you are safely beyond the reach of these shadows, I will be here, no matter what."

"I should have told you about my dreams before," Will said. "I'm sorry. I've made things worse."

The toy maker had listened in grim silence, and now he asked Will to repeat what he had said about the high cliff.

"There is only one place I know of like that," Pendrake said when Will had finished.

"The Great Rampart," Rowen said eagerly. "I've seen it on Grandfather's maps. It's on the far side of the Shining Mountains. A long wall of rock that falls sheer a thousand feet to the valley of the River Bel."

"Facing the setting sun," Pendrake added.

"What if it's an omen?" Rowen said. "Maybe we shouldn't go there . . . or maybe it means we will. Maybe there's a far-hold there—"

"That's the problem with omens," Pendrake said. "They can be dangerous to interpret. And when you start looking for them, they turn up everywhere. I think it's better to keep on our own path until we know more."

"One thing we know with too much certainty," said Moth, "is that Lotan is still on our trail."

"He's afraid of the sword," Will said, remembering. "I saw it in his eyes. That's why you carry it."

"Among you, I think only Master Pendrake knows the tale," Moth said, glancing at the others.

"Fever iron," the toy maker said, nodding, and then he closed his eyes and recited:

"In the land where hope comes not,
The great wheel turns unceasing,
Clawing out the secret ore
To feed the howling forges."

He opened his eyes.

"It is deep, ancient *innumith*," Pendrake said, "the lifeblood of story, melded with fire and spellcraft into a weapon."

"Sometimes the arrows and knives of the Nightbane are made with it," Finn said. "Though why it doesn't kill *them*—"

"It does kill them, eventually," Moth said. "Anyone wounded by such a weapon falls into a fever and madness. This gives the Nightbane a berserk strength, for a time. The fever began to touch you, Will. It is what made you attack Lotan, which is exactly what he wished. His goal was to draw you ever closer to his master's realm, so that he could find you in this one."

"Why do you keep the sword?" Rowen asked the archer. "Why not bury it or melt it in a forge—"

She broke off, and her eyes widened. Will saw that she had understood. The sword was the only thing that could harm Lotan.

"I will be rid of it when it has served its purpose," Moth said coldly.

Overhead, Morrigan gave a loud caw and swooped down from the branch she had been perched on, to settle on Moth's shoulder. Together they moved away into the dappled shade under the trees.

A soft rain began to fall. Shade had already found shelter, and now he led them across the island to the largest tree, which leaned out at a precipitous angle over the water. There was a bowl-shaped bower among the leaves, its encircling walls formed of woven branches, like a roofed bird's nest. Something had perhaps lived here, but the bower was deserted now. They climbed up the thick sloping trunk to reach it and settled in to share the berries they had gathered.

Will huddled in one corner, cold and miserable. He noticed Pendrake looking at him with concern.

"You've felt the power of the Shadow Realm, Will," the old man said. "That is not easy to bear. Moth and Morrigan have carried it with them for years. Their story and yours have become intertwined, and there are things you deserve to know. Perhaps I should have told you earlier, but I did not wish to burden you any more than necessary."

"You know why they've been searching for the Angel," Will said.

Pendrake nodded.

"I know some of the tale," he said, and closed his eyes for a moment, as if gathering the story from within himself. Then he opened them again and began.

He told them of the shining city of Eleel-upon-the-Sea, and of Seelah, the weaver of wondrous tapestries, and her brother Ethain, the smith. He spoke of Lotan, the noble prince to whom Seelah was betrothed, and how he went away to war against the forces of the Night King, and how Seelah waited for him and wove her greatest work, a tapestry that told the history of the long war. And how at long last Lotan returned, but as a betrayer, leading an army of Nightbane under concealing spellcraft to the unsuspecting city. Seelah rode out to meet him, and she discovered the truth, but before she could warn her people, Lotan changed her into a raven. She escaped from him and flew back to Eleel, but her voice came out in harsh croaks, and no one understood her warnings, except her brother Ethain.

"By then it was too late," Pendrake said.

As the sun rose, Lotan led the enemy through the opened gates. The city's last day began in fear and fire. Where there had been music and light, cries of horror rose to the sky. Blood stained the once-gleaming stones. The city itself was unshaped. The bright towers became jagged black spires of fear. When it was clear that Eleel was lost, Ethain and Seelah fled with the other survivors. And so they became the Shee n'ashoon, the Hidden Folk, and the Green Court began its long wandering. But while she was bound to Lotan by spell-craft, Seelah could not remain with her people. She went into exile. And Ethain went with her."

A shadow filled the entrance to the bower. Moth stood there a moment, looking back, then ducked his head and entered.

"Lotan was once as I am," he said, sitting beside Will. "I knew that a blade of fever iron could tear apart the spells that knit borrowed flesh over his nothingness. And so I forged one and carried it with me wherever we went."

"The two of you went searching for him," Finn said.

"We took new names, darker names to hide our true origin. We searched for many years, but found no trace of Lotan. It was said that he had perished in the fall of Eleel, but we knew he had lived on, because the spell upon Seelah was not broken. Then we began to hear rumors of the Angel, and we wondered if he was Lotan returned, though we could never find him. We searched, and many years went by, and wherever we went, the curse of the *gaal* turned the hearts of good folk against us. At last we sought refuge and peace in the Bourne. I thought we would stay there forever, Will, until you came."

"But you could return to your people," Rowen said. "Just for a short time, I mean. If we find them, maybe Will can get home. . . ." She faltered when she saw the look of bitterness on Moth's face.

"Over the years the *gaal* blinded us to our own people," he said, "as if we, too, have become like Lotan. We cannot pierce the veils of enchantment that the Tain have woven around themselves. Morrigan and I would find the Green Court for you, Will, if we could, but we cannot even find it for ourselves."

18

The burning was seen from afar, and the creatures of forest and mountain grew afraid at the sight and hid themselves in thickets and beneath stones. The sun was veiled in smoke, and men looked at one another with fear, and took up swords and axes.

— Legends of the Northlands

WHEN THE RAIN let up, they set off to finish crossing the lake. Other than the occasional bird or small animal darting through the tussocks, nothing moved except themselves. They kept careful watch for the shrowde but saw no sign of it.

Shortly after noon, they reached dry ground and found a track that wound up through the stony hills they had glimpsed from the other side of the lake. The day was cold and sunless, and the raw air seemed to scrape at their faces.

Before long they caught the scent of a fire. Morrigan investigated and returned to report that a number of people, forty or so men, women, and children, were camped in the woods nearby. Finn went to speak to these other travelers. As a knight-candidate of the Errantry, he was the most likely to be journeying alone in these lands. He was not gone long, and when he returned, he told the others what he had learned. The people camped in the woods were folk who had once lived near Skald, farmers for the most part and their families. They were abandoning their homes and had banded together for protection as they searched for safer lands.

"There is no refuge any longer in Skald, they told me," Finn said. "They would say no more about it. I could tell they wished me gone. Anyone who dares travel alone in this country is suspect."

In the afternoon their path crossed a narrow, rising road. The companions decided to risk taking it, for the greater swiftness it would give their route to Skald. As they climbed, the hills on each side grew steeper, until they became sloping walls of bare rock.

They had not been on the road long when they heard the creak of wheels and the slow clop of hooves approaching from around a bend up ahead.

"I will meet these folk," Pendrake said quickly. "An old man is less of a threat, and we may learn more."

While the others concealed themselves in the undergrowth, Pendrake sat down on a fallen log by the side of the road. A cart piled with all manner of things came into view, pulled by a dispirited-looking horse. An equally glum-looking cow plodded after the cart on a lead. The driver of the cart, a young man with a dusty, careworn face, caught sight of Pendrake and brought the horse to a halt. Beside him sat a young woman with a child on her knee, and from the cart, hidden among chicken crates and furniture, two other small faces peeped out.

"Where are you bound, father?" the driver asked. "We have a little room left. Enough for one more, at least."

"Much thanks for your kindness, but I am going the other way, toward Skald. Is it much farther along this road?"

"Skald?" the man said sharply, and now he eyed the toy maker with mistrust. "Why would you want to go to there?"

"My errand takes me to that city."

"Then it is a fool's errand," the man growled, and flicked the reins. The cart creaked away, raising dust in its wake.

As evening fell, the road led through a steeply descending ravine. On either side lay a deep, shadowy ditch filled with thornbushes. They followed the road around a last rocky outcrop, and before them, at the far end of a long narrow valley, rose the dark walls of Skald. Beyond the city loomed the black shapes of the hills, silhouetted by the setting sun. As the wind streamed across the valley toward them, Will caught a cold, familiar scent and realized it was snow.

Even in the twilight Will could see that this city was not at all like Fable. Its outer wall was high and seemed to have been carved out of the stony hillside. The final approach to its gates was a narrow, arching bridge across a dark chasm. The bridge was made of translucent stone and lined with torches burning yellow, red, green, and blue, so that the stones themselves seemed to glow with a many-colored light. What could be glimpsed of the city was not as welcoming. The battlements and towers looked huddled and lifeless. The only other illumination was a sullen, bluish-green flickering that rose here and there among the spires and rooftops.

"What is that, Grandfather?" Rowen asked. "It looks like fire, but . . ."

Pendrake seemed lost in thought and did not answer.

"This is worse than I imagined," he said finally, his voice weary and grave. "Yes, that is a kind of fire, Rowen, but it gives no warmth. I wonder what has happened to the mages who had the guarding of the city. A dangerous force has been let loose here."

"Then we should stay away," Finn said. "This city is as unsafe as the land that surrounds it."

"The power of the sword has been growing as we neared the city," Moth agreed. "If nightcrawlers and shadow-folk now roam free in these streets, they will be drawn to the *gaal*. And not only that, but the fire obscures my sight, and Morrigan's, too. Evil could be nearby, and we might not sense it in time."

"I have encountered such fire, and such creatures before," Pendrake said. "If it came to a choice between Skald and the thing hunting us, I prefer our chances here. However, it is not my decision to make."

He turned to Will, who gave the eerily glowing rooftops of the city another look. Did it really matter what he chose? So far they had run from one danger straight into another. He felt nothing inside but weariness and doubt.

"Skald," he said, just to end the silence.

"Morrigan and I should remain outside the city, then," Moth said, "at least for now. We came here once before, and we were not welcome. Besides, we will be of better use to you out here. While you are in the city, we can scout out the road ahead and keep watch for any sign of Lotan or his minions."

"Very well," Pendrake said. "Should we choose a place and time to meet?"

"We will find you," Moth said. "We have done it before, after all."

Just then Finn raised a hand in warning, and a moment later from out of the ditches rose a group of cloaked fig-ures. Naked steel flashed in the twilight. The companions quickly gathered into a circle and drew their weapons.

"Who are you?" a low, gruff voice demanded. "Why have you come to Skald? Speak."

"We are travelers stopping here on our way to other parts," Pendrake said in a calm, unhurried tone. "The last time I visited this city, the reception was more welcoming."

Will peered at the shadowy figures surrounding them. In the gloom he could not be sure how many there were, and the terrifying thought struck him that these were not living people but fetches.

"Have you not heard?" the voice said. "No one comes to this city now. No one with good intent, anyhow."

"If we had known—" Finn began.

"Silence," the voice commanded. "Where is the other? The tall one with the bird of the slain. He was here only a moment ago."

Will looked around. Somehow Moth and Morrigan had melted into the evening shadows, although he felt sure they were nearby, ready to strike if it came to that.

"They were companions of ours for a time, but they went their own way," Pendrake said. "You needn't be concerned about them."

"Enough. You will turn around now and go back the way you came, or by the black dog you will regret it."

To Will's astonishment, Pendrake burst into laughter.

"The black dog," he echoed, stepping forward. "Only one man I know swears by that animal. Is this your new occupation, Ragnar Harke, waylaying innocent travelers on the road?"

There was a brief silence, followed by a murmured consultation among several of the shadowy figures. Then a lantern appeared from underneath a cloak and lit the faces around it. One among these faces held Will's gaze: it was half hidden by a bushy beard and so broad and ruddy that it was almost troll-like. The tangled hair that framed this strange face was coal-black but streaked with threads of silver. One of the eyes was murky and apparently sightless, while the other stared hard at the toy maker in apparent disbelief.

"Pendrake?" this man said cautiously, his strange face now going through a swift contortion that took it from deep suspicion to surprise and dawning delight. He drew back his hood and stepped forward. "Nicholas Pendrake of the Bourne, or hang me."

"The first of the two, let us hope," said the toy maker. "I take it hard that you didn't know my voice, Ragnar. Has it been that many years?"

"Too many," the bearded man said, coming forward to grasp the toy maker by the hand. Over his shoulder rested a huge, long-handled ax. His rough face beamed with pleasure, but in the next instant his good eye had taken in the rest of the companions. His gaze lingered on Shade, and a shadow passed over his features.

"What has happened here, Ragnar?" Pendrake asked. "The last time I was in Skald, you were working at your smithy crafting shoes and plowshares, not standing guard outside the walls in the dark."

"What has happened here indeed," the man named Harke said bitterly. "Our own folly has much to do with it."

Will thought Harke was about to say more, but the blacksmith broke off abruptly and seemed to be weighing something in his thoughts. He turned to his companions and in an undertone conversed with them. Will could not hear what was said, but there seemed to be some disagreement between them. Finally Harke turned back to the toy maker.

"For your own good I shouldn't allow you to take another step nearer to this city," he said. "But I know you well enough, Master Nicholas, to guess that it is for someone else's good that you're here at all. I don't know what your errand is, and I don't care to know, but if you wish to stop in Skald for a while, I won't hinder you."

"Is that wise, Ragnar?" one of his companions said in a whisper that was audible to everyone.

"Wiser than most of the choices we've made lately," Harke muttered. "Yes, I will take you into the city myself."

"But not the wolf," said the man who had spoken before.

"The wolf is no threat to Skald," Pendrake said. "He has been our faithful companion on the road."

"It is a creature of darkness," the man said, and there were murmurs of agreement from the others.

Ragnar shot a stern look at his companions, then turned to Pendrake.

"You must understand, such beasts haunt our oldest nightmares. We may have left our homeland ages ago, but we brought our tales with us."

Will had been listening to this exchange with anger growing in him, and now he could not contain himself.

"Shade is my friend," he said hotly, stepping forward. "He saved our lives in the bog. He fought for the Stewards against the Night King."

"Will—" Pendrake began warningly.

"If you don't trust Master Pendrake's word," Will went on, not heeding the toy maker, "then why are you letting any of us into the city?"

Harke's good eye went wide. He studied Will for a moment, then something like a grin creased his weathered face.

"A good question, lad," he said at last. "There is no one's

word I trust more than Nicholas Pendrake's. If the rest of you have come here with him, I will trust you as well. And you will all enter Skald with me." He turned to his companions with a look that silenced the murmuring. "By the black dog, you will."

19

If you wish for a tale,
Then bid the teller welcome.
Light the cheerful lanterns
And open wide the doors.
Sit him by the fire;
Bring honey and sweet ale.
He cannot sing for you
From a dry throat.

— The Kantar

THE BLACKSMITH LED THEM across the translucent, many-colored bridge to the gates of the city. Will noticed that he walked with a limp and sometimes grunted from pain or effort. The gates were shut, but after Harke showed his face by the lantern's light to some unseen watcher and called out a strange singsong password, a rope ladder dropped down the stonework in front of them.

"The doors are barricaded every night," he said. "Not that it does much good. There are things dwelling in Skald now that can slither through wood and stone like it was broken netting."

"I've never climbed one of these before," Shade said, eyeing the ladder askance. Harke started at the unexpected voice.

"I forgot about your werewolf," he mumbled, then put

his fingers to his lips and whistled. After a brief delay, a large wicker basket was lowered down beside the ladder on a rope sling. Shade gave this contraption a disdainful glance, and then, muttering *"werewolf"* under his breath, he began awkwardly but determinedly to climb the rope ladder. Harke gaped at this astonishing sight, then he and the others followed Shade up the ladder. The basket was hauled up empty beside them.

At the top of the wall they were met by several men with pikes and bows, with whom Harke spoke in low tones. He did not introduce Pendrake or the others, but led them on along the battlement until they reached a flight of steps.

As they descended, a cold, wet flurry of sleet began to fall. At the bottom of the stairs, Harke hurried the companions into the shelter of a long, low-roofed wooden building beside the wall, which Will guessed was a guardhouse. There were several men inside, gathered around a small fire burning in a metal drum. They sprang up when Harke and the others entered, but after a word from the blacksmith, they sat back down again. He led the companions into a second room where another, smaller fire of coals was fitfully burning. There was a table here and several benches and chairs, as well as bare shelves that looked as though they might once have been used for stocking provisions.

"We have little to offer guests these days," he said with a rueful shrug. "And what we have is meager fare. Most of the outlying farms have been deserted. Our lakes have been spoiled with the filth of the Nightbane, and there are no fish."

When they were all seated, one of the men from the other room brought in tea in metal mugs. Will and the others accepted the hot drink gratefully and sipped it while the sleet pattered on the windows.

"Even the weather is unnatural these days," Harke muttered. He stirred restlessly, then got up and went out. By the time he returned, shaking the water from his hair, his guests had finished their drinks.

"Seems to be a quiet night out there," he said. "I'll take you up the street to the smithy. Though it's more like an armed camp than a smithy these days. Still, it's as safe as anywhere in Skald, and besides, Ulla and the children will be glad to see you."

"What has happened here, Ragnar?" the toy maker asked.

"You know about the League of Four," the blacksmith growled.

"They had come to Skald not long before my last stay here," Pendrake said. "I had my misgivings back then, but other business took me away, and I heard nothing more about them."

"Well, there is no cursed League anymore," Harke growled, "and the back of our hand to them. When those four so-called mages first came to Skald, they promised to protect the city and bring prosperity. We were so desperate after the last few mordog raids that we believed them, and we welcomed them in."

Will glanced at Rowen, who was staring at the black-smith. Harke saw her look and nodded.

"You've heard of them, I see, child."

"This is my granddaughter, Rowen," Pendrake said.

Harke bowed his head.

"Honored to meet you," he said. "Though I wish for your sake it was anywhere but here."

"Do the mordog still prowl this country?" Finn asked.

"They didn't, after the mages came. The League delivered on its promises at first, I'll grant them that. Nightbane were not seen in these parts for a long time, and there was peace, and crops grew well, and folk were happy. But the cost was higher than we had reckoned. Much higher."

"From what I can already see," Pendrake said, "I would say the League practiced their art poorly, or with wicked purpose."

"Both," Harke muttered. "Maybe they had good intentions, at first. But after a time they thought only of their own power and how to make it grow. Some said they even began to traffic with ambassadors of the Dark Powers. What is certain is that their conjuring brought shadows, not light, and the safety of the city was forgotten. Finally we went to them, a delegation of the townsfolk, and demanded answers, but they would not see us. Instead they barricaded themselves in the keep with their eldritch arts. Then one night, while the city slept, the werefire first blazed out, and it has never stopped burning. And worse, it has acted like a beacon to all the evil for miles around. Foul things have crept here from the bog and every other festering hole they hide in. We were overrun before we knew what was happening."

"Didn't the mages try to stop the fire?" Rowen asked.

"Ah, the brave League," the blacksmith said with a sneer. "They've slithered off and left us to our fate. I suppose it's what we deserve for letting them in to begin with."

The blacksmith lapsed into a string of muttered words Will did not catch.

"What of the keep?" Pendrake asked. "It had the strongest walls in the city. Is it no longer used as a refuge?"

"The keep is a refuge all right, but not for Skaldings," Harke said bitterly. "Even in the daylight, that place is best left alone. It was the home of the League, and few have dared set foot in it since. It seems to be the source of the werefire, and something evil dwells there now. A demon, some say."

"Do *you* say that?" Finn asked.

"I say little about things I haven't seen for myself," Harke said. "A large party of us went there one night to drive this thing out or kill it. We discovered that over the years the League had transformed the keep, turned it into a treacherous maze. The thing that dwells there had no trouble staying one step ahead of us. Since then no one goes near the wretched place. We hear the creature almost every night. The sounds it makes can chill the very blood in your veins."

He wrapped his cloak more tightly around himself and said nothing more. No one else spoke. In the silence Will noticed that the sleet had stopped. Finally Harke stirred, and after a few words with his fellow watchers, he led the way from the guardhouse, across a deserted square, and up the winding curve of a narrow street. The city was uncannily silent. Most of the windows in the houses they passed were shuttered and lightless.

Harke went along at a swift pace and then halted abruptly at an alcove in a wall. Will could just barely make out the shape of a door in the shadows. Harke took a large iron key from his belt, unlocked the door, and opened it. He gestured for the others to enter before him. They did, and found themselves in a walled court. On their left stood a long, low-roofed building that Will guessed was the smithy itself. A wavering reddish light came from its wide doorway, and Will could hear the sound of a hammer ringing from within. On the right was a small, rickety-looking house of stone and timber, three or perhaps four stories high.

"We have guests, Freya," the blacksmith called to someone in the smithy. Will saw a figure silhouetted by the glow of the forge, a figure that turned and came at a jog out into the courtyard. It was a young woman with braided white-blond hair and a streak of soot across her brow. Her face was ruddy and glistened with sweat. In her hands was an iron hammer.

The young woman was far more pleasant to look at than the blacksmith, Will thought, but still there was no doubt she was Harke's daughter.

"You're back early, Father," she said, glancing warily at the strangers. "Will you come and look at the work?"

"Damp the fire, Freya," Harke said. "That'll be all for tonight. Is your mother within?"

"Yes, she's with Thorri."

The girl studied the toy maker's face for a long moment and then broke into a smile. To Will's astonishment she ran up to the old man and hugged him.

"Father Nicholas," she cried, burying her face in his shoulder. "It *is* you."

"Freya," Pendrake said with a laugh. "You've grown, my child."

"Father said you would come back someday," Freya said, stepping back with a wide smile.

"You were hoping I'd bring toys, like last time?"

Now it was the young woman's turn to laugh.

"No, just yourself," she said. "I'll see you inside when I'm finished here."

She gave the rest of Pendrake's party another quick, curious look, then returned to the smithy. Harke led his guests to the house. As they climbed the steps, the door opened and a woman appeared, the warm light from within at her back. Her hair was less threaded with silver than Harke's, but Will could see where Freya's good looks had come from. The woman surveyed Will and his friends with a keen eye, and then, like her husband and daughter, her face beamed with happy surprise when she recognized the toy maker. She hurried forward to embrace him.

"We thought you had forgotten us, Nicholas," she said in a trembling voice.

"Never, Ulla," Pendrake said. "I have been kept busy."

He turned to Rowen. The toy maker introduced her to Harke's wife.

"A lovely girl," Ulla said, and embraced Rowen, who stammered a polite reply.

"And this is Will Lightfoot, and his friend Shade," Pendrake went on. "And Finn Madoc of the Errantry."

Now that she had welcomed the toy maker, Ulla seemed not to notice or care what a strange company the five of them made. Without hesitation she invited them into the house and led them to the kitchen. A boy of three or four was playing on the floor with several wooden toys that had once been brightly painted but had lost most of their color. He looked up at the strangers with startled, haunted eyes. The same look, Will thought with a pang of sadness, that he had seen in Jess's eyes after their mother died. Then the boy saw Ulla and as if nothing had happened, he returned to his play.

"Good to see those toys still getting use," Pendrake said with a smile.

"Children still play," Harke said with a nod. "Despite the dark. We can be thankful for that."

The room had a stout brick oven and a domed ceiling, and was bright with a multitude of metal pots and pans that Will guessed had likely been made by Harke and his daughter. It was a cozy, welcoming room, but a sword hung within easy reach by the door.

Ulla ushered them into the kitchen and invited them to sit on benches around the table. She served them broth and hard bread, with a few thin slices of cheese. She glanced at Shade, who was sitting at Will's feet.

"I'm afraid I don't even have a soup bone, for . . ." she began apologetically.

"I do not need to eat," Shade said, and both Ulla and Freya stared at him in amazement. After that, Ulla seemed unwilling to ask too many questions, but made up for the awkwardness by talking about the way things were in Skald now.

"When the werefire first broke out, Ragnar and I wanted to leave," she said. "For Freya and Thorri. We even began packing, but in the end we stayed. We thought of all those who gave their lives for this city over the years. They never despaired, and neither will we."

"We didn't know about this in Fable," Finn said. "When riders of the Errantry came to Skald, they were . . ."

He hesitated.

"Made unwelcome," Harke said. "The mages didn't want any knights of the Guild interfering with their plans. And fools like me decided it wasn't any of our business and did nothing."

"Ragnar and I have lain awake many a night, listening to the foul things that haunt our streets," Ulla said to Pendrake. "We wondered if our old friend Nicholas would ever return—"

She broke off, and her eyes filled with tears.

"Harke has told me about the dweller in the keep," Pendrake said. "It sounds as if that is the source of the werefire, and most of the trouble."

"You're right, I'm sure," Harke said. "But what can we do about it?"

Pendrake stroked his beard thoughtfully but said nothing. Freya came in to sit with them and share the meal. She was introduced to everyone and soon began asking questions about their journey and why they had come, but when she saw that no one was willing to tell very much, she turned to speaking of other things.

"I help Father make the armor for the Watch," she said when Pendrake asked. "And sometimes I go on watch, too."

"They let you fight?" Rowen asked eagerly.

"She's one of our fiercest," Harke said proudly.

When the companions had finished eating, the blacksmith showed them upstairs to a narrow loft where they could spend the night. There were no beds, but several thick blankets and bolsters were arranged along the walls. A small round window in a deep alcove looked out onto the street.

"We often have guests these days," Harke said. "Folk driven from their houses and farms by the cursed hellthings that prowl ever closer to our gates. The mordog and others can smell the city's dying."

"What *is* the werefire?" Will asked after he had taken a long look out of the window. The blacksmith's good eye fixed upon him. *He knows I'm the reason we're here,* Will thought.

To his surprise, Rowen answered his question.

"It's the Weaving," she said with a startled look, as if she had just realized it herself. "It's what becomes stories."

Pendrake nodded, studying her carefully.

"*Innumith.* The fathomless fire. Mages can draw it out of the Weaving like raw ore, not yet refined into tales. If this is done with care, good can be accomplished, but there are dangers. If done recklessly, the raw storystuff runs wild. It cannot harm you as a real flame would, but it can dazzle the eyes and mislead the mind. The fire desires to become stories, but there is nothing to shape it, so it creates illusions that flicker and change like flames. And worse, blood-hobs and deathdancers and other shadowfolk are attracted to the fire and feed on it. Until it dies down, these creatures are sure to stay."

"How long does it take for the fire to die?" Harke asked the toy maker. "Months? Years?"

"That depends on many things, especially the fire's source."

"There are only vague rumors of what happened," Harke said. "We know that the Four often left the city. They were looking, it was said, for some lost artifact, a thing of spellcraft that would give them even more power. Not long before the werefire broke out, they returned from such a journey, but one of them, the mage Strigon, was not with them, and the other three were very troubled. Then one night the werefire was suddenly everywhere, and soon afterward folk began to speak of the dweller in the keep. We went to demand answers of the League, but by then they had fled the city."

Harke was about to leave them for the night when there was a shriek from the street below, followed by the sound of raised voices and running feet. Will and Rowen hurried to the window and looked out: they were in time to see a group of cloaked figures with torches running up the street.

"Another band of the Watch," Harke said, joining Will and Rowen at the window. "After something that just slithered out of its lair."

Will was about to turn away from the window, but he lingered, looking across the rooftops at the distant battlements of the keep, lit by the eerie green glow of the werefire. The flames were stronger there than anywhere else he looked.

For an instant the small window was filled by a face, white as a ghost's, with huge bloodshot eyes. Even as Will shouted and leaped back, the face was gone.

"Roofcrawler," Harke said. "A kind of large bat. Or something in a bat's shape, with a man's face. They look in windows a lot, but they never try to get in. The only trouble they make is stealing dogs and cats for food. You should keep your . . . friend indoors with you tonight."

He nodded toward Shade, who bristled.

"For their sake," the wolf growled.

"Grandfather," Rowen said, and her voice was so weak they all turned in alarm. She had sat down on one of the makeshift beds. Her face was pale and gleaming with sweat, as it had been in the storyshard. Pendrake hurried to her side.

"I'm just a little dizzy," she said. "Tired."

"It's the werefire," Pendrake said. "It affects some more than others. This happened to me the first time I was exposed to the fire. You need rest."

"And I'll try to see you get it," Harke said, and once again he gave Will a quick, uneasy glance. "I will post sentries from the Watch at my gate."

He bade them good night and went out. Will turned to Rowen and was alarmed to see terror in her eyes.

"What is it?" he asked, sitting beside her.

"I see shapes," Rowen said. "People. Things. At the corners of my eyes. I can't stop them. They're there and then they vanish."

"They can't harm you, Rowen," Pendrake said. "They are only illusions, created by the werefire."

"But why? Why am I seeing them, and no one else?"

"Just let them come and go, Rowen," Pendrake said, running his hand gently over her brow. "Don't try to stop them. They're like dreams. Shadows of stories that haven't come to be."

"Is this what you see, as a loremaster?" Rowen asked, her eyes wide. "Is that what's happening to me?"

Pendrake studied her with concern.

"When I was very young, younger than you," he said, "I stumbled upon an outbreak of werefire. I was foolhardy. I thought I could step unscathed into the Weaving, learn the secrets of the fathomless fire. It almost destroyed me, but it taught me who I am. To be a loremaster is more than a choice, or a duty. It is in my blood. And so it is in yours."

Rowen stared at him, her face white.

"You knew this would happen—"

"I didn't know, not for certain. Your mother never displayed the gift."

"The gift . . ." Rowen said in a hollow voice, then she looked up at Pendrake, her eyes burning. "Why didn't you tell me?"

Pendrake placed a hand on her shoulder.

"I'm sorry, my child. I wished not to burden you, if this day never came."

Rowen's eyes filled with tears.

"Will it . . . will it get worse?"

"I can't say. This outbreak of werefire is the worst I've seen, and that is probably why you have been affected so powerfully. In time, with me here to guide you, you should be able to control the visions."

Rowen wiped her eyes. She stared fixedly in front of her, not looking at anyone. Then she lay down on the bed, shivering, and turned away from them. Will watched her anxiously, wishing there was some way he could help, then he gathered with the others by the window.

"That creature that looked in at us," Finn said. "Another servant of the Angel?"

"I don't believe so," Pendrake said. "It looked as startled as we were. Still, with this city in such a state, it would not be difficult for Lotan to find allies here. We need to be wary, and ready to flee at a moment's notice."

"Then we should leave this house now," Finn said. "Before we bring worse trouble to these good folk. And there's Rowen to think about. What this place is doing to her."

"I've considered all that," Pendrake said, and Will heard anger in his voice. "But I also have faith in Moth and Morrigan. If danger threatens, they will know, and find a way to warn us. We will leave in the morning."

He turned from the window. His eyes met Will's briefly then looked away.

"The best thing for all of us is sleep," he said wearily.

20

Take thee unrefined Brimstone and the skin of the Batrachian worm, ground to powder in a mortar of mulciber marble. Dissolve in unrefined Essence of Story and let stand for one waxing and waning of the Moon. Heat in the alembic to Vulcan's degree and let the concoction seethe well, then cool with thirteen dollops of blood from a black Unicorn. Of the resultant potion take but three drops in a vial of purest crystal. One drop more or less, and all is ruined.

— Greymould's *Sorcery for Dunces*

AFTER HE LAY DOWN, Will deliberately kept himself awake. A suspicion had entered his mind when Pendrake had looked at him, and he wanted to confirm it. He was not sure how long he waited, but after what seemed hours of listening to the steady breathing of the others, he finally heard a sound, opened his eyes, and saw the old man rise, don his coat, and take up his staff. Before he left, he bent over Rowen, gazed at her for a long moment, and stroked her hair. Shade, who was resting beneath the window, raised his head, but made no sound.

Will sat up. Pendrake turned, saw him, and shook his head.

"You should be sleeping," he chided.

"You're going to the keep, aren't you?" Will asked in a whisper.

"To look around, yes. You're safe here with Shade and the Watch. Get some rest, Will. I'll return as soon as I can."

"What about Rowen?" Will asked. "What if something happens to her while you're gone?"

"She is sleeping quietly now, thank goodness. If I can do something about the werefire, perhaps it will help her."

Will looked at the wolf, who was silently watching this exchange with his calm, penetrating gaze.

"You should take Shade with you," he said. "You'll need him . . . out there."

"I go where you go, Will Lightfoot," Shade said quietly.

"And you are *not* going to the keep, Will Lightfoot," Pendrake said emphatically.

"No, Grandfather," Rowen said, and they all turned at the sound of her voice. She was pulling on her cloak. "Will *should* go to the keep."

Pendrake gave her a searching look, his brows knitting.

"Rowen, you're not well. You don't know what you're saying—"

"I do know what I'm saying. You know I do. Will should go to the keep. And so should I."

Her eyes met Will's, and he remembered what she had told him outside the Golden Goose. He took a deep breath.

"Then I'll go," he said.

"And so will I," Shade said.

"Listen to me now, Will," Pendrake said, his face darkening. "This city is dangerous. I cannot let you take that risk."

"I'm coming with you," Rowen said firmly. "If I do have this gift, then you should let me try to use it. Maybe I can help you."

"Rowen, you need to rest—"

"I won't stay here without you."

"We may be going straight to the source of the werefire. It could be too much for you—"

"*Please*, Grandfather. I have to do this."

Pendrake stared at the three of them, his jaw working. At last he sighed and shook his head.

"And I thought I'd slip out of here unnoticed," he muttered. "I've become clumsy in my old age. Soon I'll be huddled in front of the fire, dribbling soup down my chin."

"Not for a while yet, I hope," Finn said. He was standing on the other side of Will, already slipping on his coat. Pendrake laughed softly and shrugged.

"Well, since stealth is now out of the question, we had better wake Ragnar and tell him what we're up to. We don't want to go blundering around his house in the dark."

As it turned out, the blacksmith met them at the bottom of the stairs. He carried a lit candlestick in one hand and a sword in the other.

"I thought it was you, but I had to be sure," he said with an embarrassed sideways look. "Now, Master Nicholas, I want you to know there's no blame at all. This city is best kept away from, I know that, so please don't think twice about leaving—"

He broke off, and Will saw understanding come into his face.

"You're going to the keep—"

"We are," Pendrake growled. "And by the time we get there, clearly the whole town will know about it."

"You would do that for us. . . ." Harke faltered. He coughed loudly and rubbed his good eye. "Well, then, you'll need something to eat before you set out. . . ."

Will and the others followed him to the kitchen and found Ulla there, already cutting bread and setting out bowls.

"You've got a fox's ears, my love," Harke said.

"Of course you're going with them, Ragnar," she said as she dished out porridge.

"No, he's not, Mother," said Freya, standing in the doorway. She wore a tunic of chain mail over her clothes and bands of steel at her wrists. Her hammer, and a long knife, hung at her belt.

"Freya . . ." Ulla began. "Taking watch duty is one thing, but the keep . . ."

"Father, you know I should be the one to go. You're not—" She caught herself, and her ruddy face grew even more crimson.

Harke's hand went to the thigh of his bad leg.

"I know, Freya," he said quietly. "I'm not up to such adventures anymore."

"You should stay with your family, Freya," said Pendrake. "They need you here."

"Let her guide you, old friend," Harke said. "The streets are treacherous, and not only because of the nightcrawlers. The werefire has collapsed pavements and walls all over the city. There are cracks and holes everywhere, and more open every night. Freya knows her way better than anyone."

When they were all ready to leave, Ulla went up to Pendrake and her daughter and silently embraced them in turn. She gave Will and Rowen a look of concern and appeared to be about to say something, when a faint cry from another room drew her attention.

"Thorri often has bad dreams now," she said, hurrying from the room.

"And wakes to find most of them true," Harke muttered under his breath. Will thought about the dreams both he and Jess had had after their mother died. How they would dream she was still alive but had gone away somewhere, and they couldn't find her. And when they woke up, they would remember that she was really gone and cry as if they had just been told for the first time.

Will and the others, with Freya before them, left the house and crossed the courtyard. When they were all through the door, Harke shut it behind them without a word. They heard the bolt grate across and fall heavily into place.

When Freya had lit her lantern, they pulled their cloaks close about them against the night's chill and set off along the deserted street. Dawn was not far off, but a thick pall of fog or smoke sat over the rooftops like a lid. As they hurried along, they heard noises from dark nooks and alleyways: sudden shuffling and skittering, like small animals bolting for cover, that made Shade growl and lunge at the shadows, and sometimes low muttering and other eerier, unidentifiable sounds. Freya's light, however, never picked anything out of the darkness.

The young woman's route through the city seldom went in a straight line for long, and Will guessed that Freya was avoiding the worst-affected areas. Eventually she led them across a half-collapsed bridge over a dried-up canal, and on the far side the companions had their first close sight of the werefire.

On their left was a terrace of houses, the nearest one clearly no longer inhabited. Part of its wall had caved inward, and the gaps showed only blackness inside.

A heap of various objects lay on the street just outside the door, as if they had been carried there and suddenly abandoned by people fleeing the building. Tongues of pale green fire flickered here and there amid the heap: on the leg of a chair, along the rim of an overturned cauldron, across the page of a splayed-open book. The flames darted and danced strangely, in slow, flowing movements and sudden wild

spasms, unlike any fire Will had seen before. At times a spear
of flame would turn pale and transparent and then flare
into brilliance again. And strangest of all, Will could see
shapes forming in the fire . . . shapes that seemed to be
about to become something he could recognize—a sword, a
horse's galloping hooves, a face turning toward him—before
dissolving again.

To his surprise Will discovered he was unwilling to look
away from the werefire. The relentless dance of almost-
shapes held his gaze. He expected Freya to hurry them past,
but she slowed and went toward the fire.

A shape rose from behind the heap, with a clink of glass.

"Get away. I found it. It's mine," rasped a quavering
voice.

"You should be at home, Master Fenric, with your family," Freya said.

The figure moved warily into the light. It was a small,
haggard-looking man, with long matted hair and smoky
spectacles that hid his eyes. He held two large glass bottles
in his gloved hands. Other smaller bottles and vials hung
from his belt.

"Ah, the blacksmith's daughter," the man said, with a
grimace that might have been an attempt at a smile. "Ragnar
has always been a friend. A good friend. He wouldn't drive
me off like the others. They're jealous of me. Always have
been."

"My father would tell you the same thing," Freya said
warningly.

"Ragnar would agree with me," the man babbled on.
"He understands. He knows the sacrifices one must make.
He sends his own child out into the streets at night. I
applaud that. Tell him I'm close to success. So close. Found a
new batch of the stuff, just erupted tonight. Tell him. I'm on

the verge of getting it, you see, getting it bottled safely, so it doesn't eat through the vessel. And when I've done that . . . when I've done—"

He broke off, seized by a cough that doubled him over.

"It can't be kept safely, Master Fenric," Freya said. "It will only destroy you. The nightcrawlers will be here soon, anyway. You're in danger."

Fenric's eyes darted wildly around.

"You . . . you and your friends can hold them off," he rasped. "While I finish. It requires delicate, painstaking work, you see, to induce the base of the flame to move in the direction you wish it to. . . . And the eyes get tired, they start to sting and burn. Difficult to work with these spectacles and gloves on, but there's no other way. I need time. Time. No distractions. Someone watching my back. Yes. Yes. Do this for me and . . . and I'll share the profits with you and your father. Tell Ragnar that. Yes. The profits will be substantial. Beyond any expectation. You'll see. Imagine it. Stories, stories, so many stories to lose oneself in. They'll come flocking from miles around for my bottled werefire."

"We will not help you go down this road," Pendrake said firmly. "Freya says you have a family. They need you to protect them. Go home to them now, before it's too late."

The hands holding the bottle shook violently. Fenric's eyes opened wider as he stared at the toy maker. His cracked lips trembled. For an instant it seemed he might give in and heed Pendrake's advice. Then he shook his head violently and turned away.

"May the shadows take you," he snarled, staggering back to the burning heap, where he crouched, his glassware clinking.

Shade suddenly gave a start and, to Will's surprise, Freya raised her hammer and hurled it in the direction of

the crouching man. It flew over his head and smashed into
the shadows beyond. Something gave a piercing shriek, then
they could hear whimpers and scuffling noises that quickly
faded away. Shade bounded in their direction a short distance, then returned.

Fenric whirled with a choked gasp, then turned and
gaped at Freya, his face white.

"Go home," she said.

With trembling hands Fenric gathered his loose bottles.
Then he fled down the street, with many backward glances,
before vanishing around a corner.

"He was a healer once, a good man," Freya said sadly.
"We've seen many decent folk seduced by the fire. It gives
them visions of greatness, even as it drains their strength
and weakens their minds. I'm afraid he'll be back here as
soon as we leave."

"Let's keep going," Rowen said, and everyone turned to
her. She was gazing into the fire with wide eyes. Pendrake
gently touched her shoulder.

"Rowen?"

She stirred and turned to him with a blank look.

"You're going back to the smithy," the toy maker said
firmly. "Freya, please take her."

"No, Grandfather," Rowen said, and she drew away from
him. "I need to do this. As you did, when you were young.
I need to know who I really am."

Freya retrieved her hammer, and they went on. As they
walked through the silent streets, Will had the eerie feeling that the city had been deserted and that only he and his
friends remained. Then came a sound that stopped everyone
in their tracks. A long, chilling scream of rage and agony that
rose as if out of the last shadows of night and trailed away.

The echo seemed to come from every direction at once. Will and his companions stared at one another with grim faces, then kept on, but more slowly.

After threading their way through the narrow, rising streets, they came out at last into a large, deserted square. Before them lay a wide moat or canal that was almost empty of water, so that the ancient stonework at the bottom was laid bare, except where it was covered by a few stagnant, murky pools.

"Most of the filth hide in the sewers during the day," Freya said. "We've gone down there a few times to rout them out, but the sewers are a maze, and these nightcrawlers are good at hiding."

Rowen leaned forward to look down and pulled back suddenly as Will grabbed her cloak.

"Isn't there a bridge?" she asked.

"The mages used a ferry, but there is another way now."

Freya led them to a short flight of stone steps that descended from the street to the floor of the moat. The companions followed her carefully down the steps, which were crumbling and slick with slime, until they reached the bottom.

"Everyone stay together," Freya said when they were ready to go on, "and watch where you tread."

They set out across the floor of the moat, which was made of huge uneven slabs of stone that sloped down from the walls toward the center. The stench of rot and stagnant water was so strong that Will gagged and had to keep the collar of his cloak over his nose. When they reached the lowest part of the moat, they were forced to walk around a long, narrow pool of still, greenish-brown water.

Shade sniffed the air and made a disgusted face.

"Keep close to me, Will Lightfoot," he said. "There are foul things in this place."

On the far side of the pool, the moat floor, now rising toward the far wall, was heaved and cracked into a jagged ridge, leaving only a slim gap through which they would have to climb in single file.

As Freya reached the top of the ridge, one of the broken slabs of rock beside her moved. To Will's surprise, it shivered like a live thing and began to flow, as if it had suddenly begun melting. Freya gave a shout and stumbled backward. With a grating sound, the rock, or whatever it was, slithered out of sight into a crack in the moat floor.

"Slimestone," Freya said, picking herself up from the ground. "Pretty harmless, compared to most of what we might run into down here."

As they approached the wall, a bright gleam caught at the edge of Will's sight. Turning to find the source, he saw something red and shiny near a small grating over a drain. He bent forward and squinted for a better look. The grating was hoary with encrusted filth, but wedged between two of its bars was an apple.

A big, red, shiny, juicy-looking apple.

After days and days of bannog and thin broth, an apple would be. . . . Will moved away from his companions and crouched down. The apple looked perfectly good, despite being utterly out of place down here in the muck and slime. Someone must have dropped it on the way home from the market, and then it rolled down here. No need for it to go to waste.

His fingers were just touching the cold skin of the apple when he heard Freya shout, "No, Will!"

In the next instant the grating dropped away, and a thick pale arm, like a slab of bloodless meat, shot up and clutched the hem of his cloak. Before he could even cry out, he was pulled down into darkness.

21

Knucklebone, tooth bone,
Bloody bag of meat,
Nibbling on your fingertips,
Gnawing at your feet.

— Troll's song, from an old Skald bedtime story

WILL THRASHED AND FOUGHT, but rough, powerful hands quickly stuffed him into what seemed to be a large canvas sack. He tumbled and kicked in the sudden dark.

"Let me out!" he screamed.

The only result was a blow to his side from an unseen fist that made him gasp with pain.

"Shut your hole, or there's more of that," a deep voice growled.

In the next moment he felt himself picked up and hefted, he thought, over someone or something's shoulder. Then his captor set off at a run that bounced and banged him around like a rag doll.

He was caught. Because of his own carelessness. And now he was being taken away farther from his friends with each step. Panic threatened to take hold of him, but he tried to calm himself, tried to concentrate and pay attention to what was happening, which wasn't easy while being bounced around. He became aware of a rank, sickening stench and realized that they must be in the sewers beneath the city. Where Freya had said the nightcrawlers hid.

Shade will find me, Will thought with a sudden hope, and then remembered the narrowness of the grate he had been pulled through. Would the wolf even be able to fit through it? And what if his captors had sealed the grate behind them? If his friends couldn't follow him through the drain, they would have to find another way down. If there *was* another way.

Thoughts like these went around and around in his head until he was brought back by the sound of a harsh, grating voice, then another.

"Anyone following?"

"Don't think so."

There must be two captors. Will remembered his knife, and although the sack hampered his movements, he was able to reach the hilt. He was about to slide the blade from its sheath, and then he hesitated. Sooner or later, he assumed, they would open the sack to haul him out. Should he come at them then with the knife? Or should he try to cut his way out of the sack while they were still carrying him? If they caught him doing this, he would be almost helpless against them.

Before he could make up his mind which was the better plan, the running stopped. Will curled up just in time and hit the ground painfully on his side.

"I do believe it is your turn to carry this," said the first voice.

"Done in already, are you?" said the second voice, which was softer and yet more menacing than the first.

"Not at all. It's just that I carried the last two, if you remember."

"Very well," the second voice said after a pause, "but let's find out what we've bagged first. See if it's worth the effort."

"Splendid idea," said the first voice, and then hands began to work at the neck of the sack. As it was opened, Will tried to shrink down into a ball, but it was no use. A huge hand groped in the sack and then seized his collar in an iron grip. He was hauled up and out like a kitten and tossed onto a cold stone floor.

Will looked up and had to suppress a cry of horror at the two faces staring back at him—they were hideous with tiny, close-set eyes and turned-up snouts glistening with slime. They belonged to large, fleshy, manlike creatures that looked almost exactly alike, right down to the clothes they were wearing: patched rags that had apparently once been fine suits of dark maroon velvet. There was even some dirty lace still poking out of the cuffs of their sleeves, and tattered white wigs were perched on their massive heads. The only difference Will could see between his captors was that one was slightly less fat than the other and had a long, ugly scar running from his forehead to the corner of his mouth. This one lunged forward and prodded Will in the chest with a dirty finger. His breath reeked like rotting meat. Will's stomach churned.

"Well, look at this, Hodge," the creature said, and the voice was the softer, more menacing one Will had heard from inside the sack. "This is—"

"A most pleasant surprise," the fatter creature interrupted, then licked its lips. "You just don't see many of their young anymore. That stupid slimestone had its eyes open for once."

Will sat up slowly and darted quick looks at the place his captors had brought him. It was a wide, pillared hall with a vaulted ceiling. What little light there was came from a tiny grating far above, like the one that he had been pulled through. Behind him was some sort of underground canal, filled with water that gave off plumes of foul-smelling steam. He was on a wedge-shaped pier that jutted out into the canal, so that he was surrounded on three sides by water, with his captors in front of him. They had trapped him here while they inspected him.

"You'd think they'd have learned to watch their whelps more closely," the fatter of the two said, and Will turned his attention back to his captors.

"All the better for us that they haven't," the scarred one said with a wicked grin. He brought his glistening snout close and took an exploratory sniff. As Will recoiled, he remembered something Rowen had said. In her list of the different kinds of Nightbane, she had mentioned a kind of troll called hogmen. There was no doubt that these two fitted that title perfectly. But what had Rowen told him? They were not very smart, and . . . *they ate people.*

"A trifle on the lean side," the scarred troll said with a frown. "You have to wonder what they're being fed up there."

"I concur, brother," said the one called Hodge. "Shocking neglect. Those abovegrounders have no consideration for us. How are we to get by if they don't fatten up their young? Times are hard, brother. Times are hard."

"Well, never mind," said the other hogman with a nasty chuckle. "We'll just have to watch out for all the little bones."

Will shuddered: it was now absolutely clear what the intentions of these two were. He searched the tunnel for some way of escape but saw nothing. The vaulted hall stretched off in all directions into darkness, without a door or staircase in sight.

"On the other hand, if he's not quite pie-worthy," the scarred hogman went on, "he can be used as bait for something better. But we should be moving on now. We are directly beneath . . ."

He pointed upward significantly. Hodge followed his finger, and then his mouth dropped.

"Dear me," he wheezed. "I had not thought of it in all this excitement. But I do agree—it is time we hurried on."

It must be the keep, Will realized. *They're afraid of whatever's in the keep, like everyone else.*

It occurred to him that this could be his best, if not only, chance to escape. If he could get away from the hogmen here, his friends might still be nearby. Or he could at least find a way up into the keep, and the hogmen would not follow. But how to do it?

Then he remembered Pendrake's tale of Conn the Clever, and he knew what he had to do.

"Right then," said Hodge, rubbing his hands together. "Back into your commodious traveling case, little morsel."

Summoning up all his courage, Will forced himself to smile. He leaped to his feet and clapped his hands.

"This is wonderful," he said, as brightly as he could.

The two hogmen gaped at him, then looked at each other with blank faces.

"If you are really Hodge," Will said, and then turned to the scarred one, "then you must be . . ." He raised his hands in a gesture that said the answer was perfectly obvious.

"You've *heard* of us?" the scarred hogman said, his snout wrinkling.

"Who hasn't?" Will said with a shrug. He swallowed hard, aware that his plan hung by a thread until he had both of their names. "You mean to tell me you don't know how famous the two of you are?"

Hodge, his mouth slack, started to shake his head, but recovered himself and snorted.

"Of course we know it," he spluttered, and then cuffed his companion on the shoulder. "You hear that, Flitch?" he said. "Tuck said we were coming up in the world. He told us things would be different once we got to Skald. 'No more trash heap in a ditch for us,' he said. 'We're going to have a sewer of our own, a whole entire sewer, and then the Marrowbone brothers will get the respect they deserve.' That's what he said, many a time when things looked bleak. You cannot deny that is what he said."

"Tuck was right," Flitch said coldly. "But don't forget that I was the one who finally got us here, when you would have stayed cowering under a pile of abovegrounder trash."

"Oh, now, really, brother—"

"That is how it was, *brother*," Flitch said in a low, menacing tone. "*If* you remember."

"Was it?" Hodge said, backing away. "Was it indeed? I must say I do not recall it quite that way, but I suppose . . . I wouldn't positively assert that my memory is at fault in this matter, but you are of course entitled to your—"

"It doesn't matter," Flitch muttered, and his small, piggy eyes peered coldly at Will. It was clear that he was not as entirely taken in as Hodge. Will knew that he would have to work quickly.

"The Marrowbone brothers at last," he said with a bow. He had no idea who this Tuck was, but he had to proceed with his plan and hope for the best. "Hodge and Flitch, in the . . . flesh. Just when I had given up hope of finding you."

"Finding us for *what*?" Flitch asked.

Will put his hands on his hips.

"To challenge you, of course. To mortal combat."

The trolls turned to look at each other, then broke into snorting, choking fits of laughter.

"I think our friend here is a little cracked," Flitch said, sneering.

"Indubitably, brother," Hodge spluttered. "Or perhaps the poor diet up there has withered his wits."

"Not at all, gentlemen," Will said with a smile. "When I heard that in this city lived the two most feared and respected of . . ." He paused, considering that hogmen might have a more complimentary name for themselves. "Of their kind, well, I simply had to come here and see for myself. And it wasn't easy tracking you down, let me tell you. The mere mention of your names was enough to send most folk running."

He was sure the foul reek coming off the brothers was just as likely to cause such a reaction but kept that thought to himself. Hodge's gaze was stunned and faraway, but Flitch's eyes had not left Will.

"And just who are *you*?" he said slowly.

"Me?" Will said. "Why, my name is . . . Sir William of the . . . Seven Mighty Companions. Tamer of the wolf and . . . friend to the raven. I've crossed the Haunted Forest, the Bog of No Return, and the Lake of . . . Swords to be here today."

The hogmen exchanged dubious glances.

"Tamer of the . . ." Hodge muttered nervously, his eyes darting around.

"Yes, and here I am at last," Will quickly went on, "even though my friends begged me not to come. They warned me that this time I would finally meet my match. They even made bets about which of you would be the bigger challenge. Some said Flitch was the one to worry about, but most said Hodge was the serious contender."

"They said I was—" Hodge burst out, spittle flying from his lips. "They said I was the *what*?"

He didn't wait for an answer but cuffed his brother once more on the arm.

"Did you hear that, my dear Flitch?" he wheezed. "The serious contender."

"I heard it," Flitch said sourly. "That doesn't mean it's true, does it?"

"But what about our brother?" Hodge said, his brow wrinkling and his eyes beginning to glisten with tears. "What did they say about Tuck?"

"Well, of course they said . . . he was . . ." Will began, hoping desperately for inspiration.

"Tuck led us well," Flitch interrupted, "until the garmwolf got him. Let's not forget who led us after, and finished the journey."

Hodge sniffled and wiped his eyes.

"Yes, he led us well. Dear Tuck. So good and brave. He built that house of bricks with his own two hands, but it just wasn't strong enough—"

"Or he wasn't clever enough," Flitch muttered, not seeing the look of hate that flared in Hodge's eyes.

All this time Will had been darting covert glances around the vault, and at last he saw what he had been hoping for. In the wall directly behind the hogmen there was a small round hole that appeared to be the mouth of a drainpipe. An escape route. The hole would have been too high in the wall for him to reach, but below it was a heap of stones from a projecting buttress that had partly collapsed. If he could climb it and get into the drain, the hogmen might be too big to follow him. But first he had to distract them long enough to make a run for it.

"As for myself," he said quickly, "I had my own opinions about which of you was the one to beat, of course."

"Did you," Flitch said icily. "And which of us would that be, in your opinion?"

"Really, it wouldn't be polite of me to—"

Flitch's scarred face came to within an inch of Will's. "Which of us?" he growled.

Will knew the true answer to that question. The watchful, calculating look in Flitch's eyes told him.

"Hodge, of course," Will said, as casually as he could.

Flitch's eyes went cold and deadly, and for one dreadful instant Will thought he had made a fatal mistake. But then Hodge gave a squealing laugh, and Flitch turned to him with a look of loathing.

"I knew it," Hodge crowed, breaking into a clumsy, bobbing dance. "I always knew it. Oh, if only Mother could hear this."

Flitch had regained control of his features, and now he gave a careless shrug.

"You think this scrap's opinion is worth anything?" he snorted.

"He's Sir William of the Seven Mighty Companions," Hodge said, still capering with delight. "If you've never heard of them, brother, then may I say there are clearly a few things you're not cognizant of. He came here to challenge us to mortal combat, and he thinks I'm the one to beat. He considers me the real challenge. At last, at last. Someone who appreciates finesse over brute force. Someone who values brains in an opponent."

"Brains?" Flitch retorted. "If you had any, you would be using them now, instead of bouncing around like a demented dumpling."

"Envy does not become you, brother." Hodge chortled.

"You think I'm envious?" Flitch snarled. "Of *you*? Do you remember what Mother said when she drove us out of the wallow? Do you remember that day?"

The gloating joy in Hodge's eyes dimmed. His smile sagged.

"You do remember, don't you?" Flitch said with a fang-baring grin.

"She told us to go away and never come back," Hodge muttered. "She told us we were big enough to find our own food."

"Yes, she did. And what else did dear Mother say?"

"She told me I . . ." Hodge mumbled brokenly, the corners of his mouth drooping.

"She said that you were a fool," Flitch snapped. "Surely you haven't forgotten that."

Hodge's lower lip began to quiver.

"'Watch over those fool brothers of yours,' she said to me," Flitch went on, his voice rising to a grating creak that was apparently an imitation of Mother Marrowbone. "'But especially Hodge. He doesn't have a runt's chance. There's nothing but gristle between those ears.' That's what she said, and that's what I promised to do. And that's what I have been doing, all these years. Are you cognizant of *that*? Watching over you, keeping you out of harm's way. Squandering my chance to really make something of myself because I was shackled to a useless mound of tallow that wouldn't even make decent candle fat if melted down."

Hodge's eyes blinked repeatedly. His breath was coming in short gusts.

"Forced to listen to you blather," Flitch went on, "with your 'Yes indeed, dear brother,' and your 'I feel it incumbent upon me to inform you, dear brother,' fancying yourself my equal, when if it hadn't been for me thinking, actually *thinking* instead of pretending to think, you wouldn't have had the brains to feed yourself."

As Flitch's rant went on, Hodge's face had been

darkening like a thundercloud, and then, with a speed Will would never have suspected in him, his great lump of a fist lashed out and struck Flitch full in the face. The scarred hog-man staggered back, grunting and wheezing.

No one was more shocked at this outcome than Hodge. He gaped in amazement at his own fist.

"I did it." He giggled deliriously. "I finally did it."

As a moment of triumph it was short-lived. In the next instant, with a snarl of rage, Flitch threw himself at his brother.

Will's chance had come. As the hogmen toppled into a grunting, squealing mass of porcine fury, he slipped past them, dashed across the vault, and leaped onto the heap of fallen stones. Frantically he scrambled up, clutching for hand-holds and banging his knees painfully against the edges of the uneven stones. He had not gotten very far when there was a cry of alarm from behind him, and then a furious howl. Will did not look back. He reached the top of the heap, jumped, and caught the edge of the hole with his fingers. With a desperate effort he hauled himself up and into the drain.

It was too small for him to stand up in, and so he shuffled at a crouch away from the entrance with his head down. Then he saw a glimmer of light and looked up. Ahead of him, only a few feet away, burned a ring of pale green flames.

The werefire.

22

"To the door of darkness I come, and none shall withstand me.
The enemy in his numberless hordes will cower before my wrath.
My flashing blade will sing as it cleaves. Fear? Hah! I set my boot
upon Fear and stamp on its ugly head."

— The Adventures of Sir Boron the Boastful

WILL COULD HEAR HODGE AND FLITCH grunting and
cursing as they scrambled up the heap of stones. "Carrion . . .
bladderbrain . . . bucket of tripe," Flitch growled, and Will
was not sure whether the words were intended for him or for
Hodge. If they were able to squeeze themselves into the drain,
they would be on him in an instant. He had to get farther
from the entrance, but instead of moving, he stayed where
he was, riveted by the trembling ring of flames. It looked to
him like a round, gaping mouth filled with green fangs.

He heard a sound and turned. Flitch's hideous face filled
the hole.

"Now listen, friend," the hogman said with a ghastly
attempt at a smile, "let's just forget everything that's gone
before, and start again. You can't go that way, obviously, so
you might as well come back out. And you mustn't believe

we were serious about"—he gave a simpering laugh—
"about *eating* you."

"Of course we weren't serious, Sir William," Hodge
chimed in from over his brother's shoulder. "We ate some-
body three days ago, and we've got plenty left in the pot."

Flitch jerked violently, and a sharp gasp came from
Hodge.

"My brother is quite the joker," Flitch said, rolling his
eyes. "What he means is that we'd be happy to accept your
challenge and meet you in combat. One at a time, or both of
us together, whichever you prefer. Or if you'd rather just call
the whole thing off and go home, that's fine, too. We could
be your guides out of the sewers. Don't you agree, Hodge?"

"Indubitably, brother, we should be overjoyed to be of
assistance in any way we can. All you have to do, Sir William,
is come out of there—"

"He knows what he has to do, dungflap," Flitch snarled
at his brother, and then caught himself and turned to Will
with a sheepish grin. "Or rather, what he *may* do, when he's
ready. No hurry at all. At your earliest convenience. We can
wait. Happy to wait. Honored, in fact. The thing is, of course,
you don't want to stay in there *too* long. The green fire
attracts . . . nasty company."

As Flitch was delivering this speech, Will noticed, he had
squeezed a little farther into the drain. Only a few feet separated them.

Will turned away and began to inch toward the flames.

"What are you doing?" Flitch growled. "You can't go that
way."

Will reached the ring of fire and then drew back. To his
surprise it gave off no heat. The flames did not even seem to
rise from the floor of the drain or touch it in any way. They
just appeared out of the air and vanished again, sometimes

silently and other times accompanied by faint sounds like whispers or muted, cut-off cries. Though they looked pale green from a distance, Will could see now that the fire was made of many colors. As in the street earlier, he could see shapes in the flames, forming and fading away. They caught his gaze and held it just long enough that he wasn't quite sure what he had seen and wished to see it longer.

And now he saw that the werefire wasn't really fire at all. The shifting shapes were not rising out of the flames, they *were* the flames. The werefire was nothing other than this beautiful, feverish dance of images. He wondered why everyone seemed to fear it so much. If this was the only way to escape the hogmen, he would take it.

He drew a deep breath, held it, and plunged forward.

He was sitting on a horse. He was outside, in the rain, sitting on a dappled gray-and-white horse. He was dressed in armor, and a long sword hung at his side. His head was bare and the cold rain was running down his neck. He shivered, vaguely remembering that he had been somewhere else just a moment before. But now he was here. Wherever *here* was.

Before him stood another horse, bearing a rider in black armor, his face concealed by a tall, gargoyle-faced helmet. Beyond the rider a dark, sinister castle loomed like a giant bat with its wings outspread.

I've been here before, Will thought, although he couldn't say how he knew. The gloomy landscape, the castle, even the black knight, all were familiar. He had come to this place not once but many times. There was something he had to do here. Someone he had to find.

"Where is she?" Will shouted, and then realized he was asking about Jess. She was in danger. If he hadn't left her, this would never have happened. But he was here now. That was all that mattered. He had come to save her.

"Let me pass!" Will shouted.

Without answering the black knight drew his sword, spurred his mount, and charged.

Will had never ridden a horse, but somehow he knew what to do. Gripping the reins with one hand, he dug in his heels, and the horse sprang forward. The black knight thundered toward him, his mount's hooves flinging up clods of mud. As the riders met, the black knight's blade flashed down, but Will met it with his own. There was a clang of steel, and then the black knight was past him and turning to strike again. Will expertly wheeled his horse, and with a deft, accurate stroke, sliced through the other rider's saddle strap.

The black knight slid off his mount and crashed to the wet ground.

Will reined in his horse and leaped from the saddle. The black knight was still down, groping for his fallen sword in the muck. Will reached it before he did and took it in his other hand. The black knight held up his arms in supplication or fear, but Will ignored him and kept on. He crossed the drawbridge and went in under the portcullis of the castle. Seven armored goblins appeared in his path, brandishing jagged-tipped pikes. He knew they were goblins because he had come this way before. He had fought with them, many times, and each time he had lost.

Not this time.

With a wild cry, Will charged. His two blades seemed to take on a life of their own, whirling, darting, slashing. Pikestaffs splintered. Armor rang and split. In a matter of moments, all seven opponents were weaponless and on the ground, groaning and pleading for mercy. Will ignored them as well and ran on.

He came to a door, hacked his way past the three mace-wielding ogres guarding it, and entered. A narrow, winding flight of steps led down to a torch-lit corridor lined with cells. From all directions came shrieks and moans and other ghastly sounds. Then a high, terrified cry that pierced his heart. Jess! Will rushed from one door to the next, looking through each barred window for his sister. To his shock, the cells were all empty.

There was another, larger door at the end of the corridor. That was where the terrible sounds were coming from. Cautiously he approached, with the odd feeling that this was not going the way it was supposed to. He was a hero. He wasn't meant to hesitate. He had battled his way into this castle; he had never come this far before; he was about to *win*. But now . . . now there was something nagging at the back of his mind. Something he was forgetting.

As Will reached for the door handle, he felt a tap on his shoulder, and turned. There stood Rowen, frowning at him.

"Idiot," she muttered.

"What?"

"Numbskull. Blubberbrain. Dolt."

She gave him a shove, and he staggered back, startled. He'd *felt* that. The pikes and maces of his enemies had been like caresses in comparison.

"What's the matter with you?" Will shouted. "I have to find Jess. She's here somewhere."

"Look behind you, stupid," Rowen said. "*Behind* you."

Will turned his head. He was crouched once again in the drainpipe, still within the ring of werefire.

Behind him came Flitch's voice, ragged with rage.

"You can't go that way, idiot. Didn't you hear me? Half-wit. We're not going to lay a finger on you, we swear. . . ."

The hogman had squeezed himself farther into the hole. His fat, grasping hand was only inches from Will's foot.

"We promise!" Hodge shouted from behind him. "Please come back, Sir William. It's not safe in there."

Will scuttled quickly to the other side of the werefire.

"We'll find you, you little vermin," Flitch shrieked, all pretense of friendliness abandoned at last. "We know these sewers inside and out. Every nook and cranny. We can smell your blood like warm broth. We'll find you, and when we do, we'll boil you in a pot and make a stew out of you—"

"Oh, it will be a lovely stew, Sir William," Hodge called. "You'll be amazed what a fine chef my brother is. . . ."

Will crawled away, dazed. Now he understood the true danger of the fire. If Rowen had not appeared, he might have stayed in that story, believing himself a hero, until the hogmen had him back in their clutches.

The drain sloped up around a curve, and the hogmen's shouts quickly faded. Soon Will noticed that the tunnel was widening, and he was able to rise to a stoop instead of crawling on his hands and knees. He went on like this for what seemed a very long time, his way lit by more outbreaks of the werefire, which he passed by quickly without daring even a glance.

Finally he rounded another curve and came to a space where the drain he was in joined two other, larger tunnels. Where they met, there was another shaft running upward at a steep slant into deep shadow. Ragged pennants of werefire fluttered along the walls of the shaft, but Will breathed a sigh of relief at the sight of a row of iron rungs like a ladder. Surely this would take him up into the keep.

He jumped, caught the lowest rung, hauled himself up, and began to climb.

The rungs were farther apart than they had appeared from

below, and the going was harder than Will had expected. After climbing for a long time, he stopped to catch his breath where a smaller drainpipe opened into the shaft. As he clung there, panting, he saw a pair of slitted red eyes watching him from the opening of the drain.

"Get lost!" he roared. Something he could not see hissed and skittered away.

He pressed on, and now when he looked up, he could see a faint green glow above, seeping through the seams of what looked like some sort of circular trapdoor. Will climbed on, and soon he reached the trapdoor, breathing hard. Planting himself as firmly as he could against the sides of the shaft, he reached up and pushed against the door with all of his remaining strength. After a terrible moment in which it seemed the door would not budge, it suddenly came unstuck and lifted with a rusty creak.

Grunting with the effort, Will shoved the door out of his way and hauled himself up out of the shaft. Once he was out, he heaved the trapdoor shut and lay panting, too exhausted to do anything more than look around.

He was in a large, windowless room with damp stone walls and a high ceiling crossed by thick wooden beams. From them, suspended by chains, hung several empty cages whose doors appeared to have been wrenched open. On the opposite wall, a flight of steps climbed steeply to a small door made of iron. All around him the floor was strewn with shards of glass and the splintered remains of shelves, tables, and chairs. A few shelves still stood against the walls, and upon them sat glass bottles and flasks filled with various sorts of liquids, powders, and in some cases, what appeared to be small creatures suspended in thick, murky fluid. Hanging from a hook in one corner was a skeleton that was human-shaped but had curling horns and a long tailbone.

The light in the room came from many small eruptions of werefire, silently burning in corners, along the walls, and on the stairs. There were even flames clinging to the beams and burning down into the room, like ghostly bats stirring in their sleep. The largest and brightest of the fires filled one of the open cages hanging from the beams and seemed to crouch there within the bars like an animal waiting to spring.

It was as if he had found the very source of the fire.

As Will lay there, he heard a faint fluttering, like the wings of countless moths, and sensed the dizzy swarming of a thousand stories trembling to take shape.

He rose unsteadily and made for the stairs. He hoped that he was in a lower room or dungeon of the keep, and that beyond that small iron door he might find a way out. In any event, he had to get out of this room.

As Will set foot on the bottom step, he felt the air in the room grow colder. The hair rose on the back of his neck, and he turned slowly. To his horror he saw that the werefire in the cage was moving, flowing out and dripping like melting wax onto the floor, where it grew stronger and brighter and began to take shape. Before his eyes the fire grew into a humanlike figure, with arms and legs and a head crowned with flames.

The head turned toward him, and in the depths of the flames a face began to form. Its mouth opened wide, and it howled with the sound of a hundred voices.

Will dashed up the steps to the iron door, grabbed the latch, and pulled. The door did not budge. He tugged again and again. The door was stuck fast.

He was trapped.

23

To serve and stand guard,
To illuminate and preserve.
To bring light to the shadows
And hope to those who fear.

— The Charter of the League of Four

FINN AND FREYA CAME TO A PLACE where the tunnel they had been searching branched into three. Three tunnels that were alike in every way: dark, cold, and foul-smelling. They had split up from Pendrake, Rowen, and Shade in order to search more of the sewers in a shorter time.

"We could use Shade's nose at the moment," Finn said, peering into the gloom ahead. "Do these tunnels go on forever?"

"We have lived in Skald for a very long time," Freya said. "Our people built deep into the rock. It's where the very young and the old take refuge when invaders come. And they've come many times. This time, they're already inside."

"If the Errantry had known about this, we would have helped."

"A band of knights-errant did come to Skald once, not long after the League took power. They came as friends, but the mages told us that you Wayfarers were like everyone else. You really wanted the city for yourselves. And many people believed them."

"Did you?"

"I'd met Father Nicholas. I knew what a friend was."

"I've heard your people built Skald after your homeland in the north was lost to the Night King. I don't know the whole story."

Freya smiled bitterly.

"The story is no longer *whole*. We are all that's left. And that is why we find it hard to trust strangers. And also maybe why we were so easily fooled by those who promised to make us strong. But I'd rather not speak of these things, not in this place. Once we've found your friend, there will be time for tales."

Finn nodded. He was about to suggest they take the middle tunnel and hope for the best, when they heard voices. Someone was coming up the tunnel behind them. Finn and Freya quickly moved into the shadow of a recess in the wall beside them and waited. The voices grew louder.

"I really think we should go back and get that apple," one was whining. "It was so juicy-looking."

"I'll shove that apple in your gob and roast you on a spit if you don't keep quiet," hissed another, nastier voice. "The slimestone said there were others with the boy. Do you want them to find us?"

Finn and Freya exchanged a quick, decisive look. They stepped out of the shadows and into the path of the two hog-men, who stumbled to a halt and stared at them with fearful, blinking eyes.

"Too late," Finn said, drawing his sword.

"Where is the boy?" Freya said, brandishing her hammer.

Hodge's lip began to twitch. Flitch stepped back slowly, his eyes narrow and hard.

"What boy?" he said. "We know nothing about any boy. We're just passing through this city on our way to—"

"Where is he?" Finn shouted, as Freya slipped behind the hogmen to cut off their escape.

"We didn't hurt Sir William, honestly," Hodge blubbered. "We took him, yes, we did, we won't deny it, but it was because we knew he was a great champion looking to challenge us, you see, and we—we—we thought we'd make it interesting for him, sort of surprise him, don't you see. He said I was the one to beat. He really did. Are you the Seven Mighty Companions? I mean, two of them?"

"What in the Thunderer's name is he blathering about?" Freya growled.

Finn grinned. "I think Will has learned a few tricks from Master Pendrake."

He thrust the tip of his sword under Hodge's glistening snout.

"Where is he?"

"He went up one of the drains," Flitch snarled, casting a murderous look at his brother. "One that leads to the keep. That's probably where he is. We haven't seen him since. Try the keep, if you have the courage."

"How do we get there from here?"

"There's a staircase down one of those tunnels," Flitch said, pointing.

"Show us."

"Oh, please, mighty friends of Sir William," Hodge whimpered. "We hogmen don't do well at all in places like that.

Show a little pity, for pity's sake. We're just two starving, homeless, harmless fellows. We don't want any trouble."

"Will's not the first person to go missing in these tunnels," Freya said. "There are plenty of folk up above who would like to ask you about that. If you'd rather we took you to see them . . ."

"We'll show you how to get to the keep," Flitch muttered.

The creature of fire was climbing the steps now. Will threw himself against the door and hammered on it. There was nowhere else to go.

At the top of the stairs the creature of fire halted. Its face dissolved and became another, an entirely different face, and then another, as if a multitude of beings were struggling to take form, to persist against the ever-changing ripple and weave of the flames. Finally one face appeared and did not melt away, that of a gaunt, bearded man. There was a look of pain or struggle in his eyes, as though he were fighting to keep himself from vanishing into the fire like all the other faces. He gazed at Will with a beseeching expression. His mouth opened soundlessly.

"What is it?" Will whispered. "Who are you?"

The creature of fire moved closer and held out its arms toward Will.

"From the Untold . . ." It gasped in a voice like dry twigs catching flame. "The emissary seeks you—"

Just then there was a clang of metal, and with a shriek of rusty hinges the door crashed open. Freya rushed in, wielding her hammer, with Finn close behind, his sword drawn.

"Look out!" Will shouted. Before they could react, the creature of fire collapsed in on itself like a burning cloak that had been dropped, then flowed swiftly over and down the sheer side of the stairs. Once it touched the floor, it split once again into many separate flames, which slithered into the farthest corners of the room.

"What is that thing?" Freya whispered.

Before Will could answer, there was a shout from below. They looked down to see Shade climbing out of the shaft, with Rowen and her grandfather close behind him. The wolf bounded up the stairs, and Will threw his arms around him.

"Are you hurt, Will Lightfoot?" Shade asked.

"No," Will said shakily. "I don't think so. Thank you for finding me. I thought I was finished."

They quickly descended the steps to where Pendrake and Rowen stood. Will saw with alarm that Rowen's face was paler than he had ever seen it. She was leaning on her grand-father's arm. When she saw Will looking at her, she gave him a brave smile.

"The creature is still in the room, I think," Finn said. "Is it the dweller in the keep?"

"Perhaps," Pendrake said. "I think we can find out for certain. Everyone stand back."

Freya gently guided Rowen away from the toy maker. He stepped forward and in a loud, commanding voice spoke a few words that Will did not understand. After a few moments, rivulets of werefire flowed together from several corners of the room, brightening as they merged. The fiery figure rose again, this time larger and roaring even louder than it had before. From its outstretched hands dripped gouts of green flame. Will and the others drew back, but the toy maker did not move as the fire blazed around him.

In the next instant the werefire creature had diminished again to its former size and made a dash for the trapdoor.

Pendrake spoke again, and the creature stopped dead and began to tremble and seethe like a flame caught in a gust of wind. The toy maker took a step closer to it and held out his hand. At the same time he struck the floor with his staff. There was a thunderous crack, and the room shook under Will's feet. The werefire whirled up into the air in a frenzied spiral, leaving behind a dark figure that sank down, reaching out a trembling hand to the loremaster. Pendrake took it and eased the dark figure to the floor. At the same time a seething, crackling wreath of flames rose to the roof beams. The other, smaller fires raced and leaped from every corner of the room to join it.

Pendrake straightened and held out his staff. Like a bolt of lightning, the werefire stabbed toward it. For an instant the room blazed with light as a roaring emerald column plunged through the staff and vanished into the floor.

Silence descended. The fire was gone and the room was dark, save for a dim ghostly afterglow that seemed to come from the places where the flames had been. Pendrake leaned wearily on his staff, passed a hand over his brow, then gazed with the others at what lay huddled on the floor before them.

It was a man with a grizzled beard and long, unkempt hair, shivering in the torn and filthy remains of a belted robe. He was pale and gaunt, little more than skin and bone. His eyes stared vacantly past Will and his friends, as if he could not see them.

"Who is he, Grandfather?" Rowen asked. She was still very pale, but some of her old energy had returned to her voice.

"I have no idea."

"I do," Freya said, her face clouding with anger. "This is the mage Strigon, of the League of Four. Has he been hiding here all this time?"

"He was your dweller in the keep," Pendrake said. "And the source of the werefire."

"How can that be?" Freya said. "It should have destroyed him."

"The fathomless fire does not kill. Its source is a power that sustains life. It was keeping Strigon alive, even as it was surely driving him into madness."

Pendrake crouched before the mage and gently put a hand on his shoulder.

"Can you hear me?" he asked. "Do you know where you are?" After a long moment the mage stirred, looked up at Pendrake, and nodded slowly. He opened his mouth and seemed to be struggling to speak.

"We . . ." he said at last, in a voice that was little more than a breathless gasp. "We . . . have done a terrible thing."

"What have you done?"

"We were searching for one of the lost farholds. The wishing portals. It was not there, and then it was there . . . a gateless gate. It began to close. We summoned the werefire to keep it open, but we could not control it. The fire leaped out like a wild beast. It came for me. . . . It . . ."

The mage's eyes widened, and he raised his hand as if to ward off something only he could see.

"Where is this gate?" Pendrake asked.

Strigon shook his head.

"I won't go back there," he whispered feverishly. "Not even if the emissary commands it. . . . I won't."

"Who was this emissary?"

"He did not say, but we knew. . . . We knew who sent him, but we met him anyway. . . . He wanted us to search for . . . a new thread in the Kantar. A disturbance. Something his master was seeking. He said the city would be spared if we aided him, and we would be given much power. . . ." The mage began to tremble violently again, and his head sank. "Now all is lost—"

"Listen to me, Master Strigon," Pendrake said. "It is not too late to undo some of what you have done. This city can still be saved, and many others besides, if we do not give in to despair. Tell me, where did you find the wishing portal?"

The mage shuddered and clutched Pendrake's arm like a drowning swimmer.

"High in the mountains . . . The Needle's Eye . . . We found a secret path leading up . . . to a hidden vale. . . . When the fire took me, the others fled back to the city. . . . I followed, but they did not know me. I could not speak, could not tell them. . . . They drove me into the dungeons. They left me to burn."

The mage looked away from Pendrake, and for the first time he seemed to be aware of the others gathered around him. His gaze darted wildly from face to face and then settled on Will. His eyes stared in fear and he tried to rise, but Pendrake held him back.

"You are from the Untold," he rasped at Will. "It must be you. He will be coming for you. . . ."

His eyes rolled up in his head, and he fell forward into Pendrake's arms.

"Is he dead?" Freya asked.

"No, but he is exhausted, and he may yet die," Pendrake said. "The fire unnaturally sustained his life, but I doubt he has eaten or slept since this all began. He must be cared for and nursed back to health."

"Why should we do that for him?" Freya muttered angrily, her eyes narrowing.

"If he recovers, he can help you restore this city to what it once was. He has power and knowledge that can be used for good."

Freya glared down at the mage, then sighed and nodded.

"You're right, Father Nicholas. He should be given the chance to make amends. It is what Mother and Father often say. If all we have in our hearts is hate, then what are we fighting to save?"

Finn and Freya picked up the insensible mage, and together the companions climbed from the dungeon to the upper floors of the keep. As they made their way through a series of lightless, winding corridors, Will told the story of what had happened to him and how he had escaped the Marrowbone brothers by challenging them to mortal combat. He didn't mention what he had seen when he crawled through the werefire. The fantasy his mind had cooked up seemed too embarrassing to admit.

"Clever," Pendrake said with a wink, when Will told how he'd tricked the hogmen.

"We met the brothers, Will," Finn said. "It turned out they weren't interested in mortal combat after all."

"They will soon have no choice," Freya said.

Now that the werefire was dying down, Shade's senses were keen again, and he led them quickly to a long, high-ceilinged chamber that Freya said was the main hall. There were narrow windows here, letting in thin shafts of daylight, by which Will could make out humped shapes upon the floor. A closer look revealed them to be tapestries that had apparently hung from the walls and were now torn down. There were fragments of glass and masonry scattered every-where, and gouges in the stone floor, as if something very large had clawed its way across the room in a rage.

"What kind of creature could make marks like this?" Finn asked, crouching to run his hand along one of the gouges.

"Master Strigon made them," Pendrake said, "when the

werefire was upon him. It gave him terrible strength, even as it took his wits."

Will swallowed hard, remembering how the fiery creature had reached for him before his friends had arrived. The torment that the mage must have gone through . . .

He felt a hand on his shoulder and turned. It was Rowen.

"Are you all right?" she asked.

He nodded. "How about you?"

"I'm not sure. The visions aren't as bad anymore." She looked at him with concern. "But you went *through* the werefire. What happened?"

Quickly he told Rowen the story, his face reddening when he got to the part where he'd single-handedly defeated the goblins and ogres.

"I was looking for Jess," he said. "I really believed she was there—"

He broke off, struck by a sudden realization. The batwing castle, the black knight, the goblins: they had been familiar to him because they were in Goblin Fortress, the video game he'd been playing in the camper on the way to their new home. The things he had seen in the werefire had come from his own memory.

"What is it?" Rowen said.

"Nothing," he said, and then something even stranger occurred to him. "While I was in the werefire, I forgot all about the hogmen. I would've stayed there, in that imaginary story, but then you appeared. You saved me."

"What did I do?"

"You called me . . . names."

"Names?"

"It doesn't matter. But it was strange, like I was in a dream and you were trying to wake me up. Like you were more real than anything I was imagining."

"But I wasn't really there," she protested, then gazed at him with a troubled look. "Was I?"

Outside, it was morning, and some sunlight had managed to pierce through the gray shroud over the city. When they reached the far side of the moat, Freya left them briefly, and returned with a donkey cart lined with straw, as well as a small parade of onlookers.

"Who is that?" one of the townsfolk said as Finn and Freya lifted the mage into the cart. "Is that one of the mages?"

"It's Strigon," someone else cried. "They've found one of the Four!"

"Come to my father's house at noon, Eikin," Freya said to a tall man in a butcher's apron. "Bring the other sheriffs of the Watch."

"If that's one of the mages, Freya Ragnarsdaughter, you'd better let us have him," an angry voice shouted, and there were a few murmurs of agreement.

"Who are these strangers?" a woman shouted. "Are they going to slip out of the city with that traitor?"

The man named Eikin stepped forward.

"We will get our answers in good time, friends," he said in a loud but calm voice that stilled most of the muttering. "Ragnar and his family have always served this city faithfully. Let them go now."

There were a few more angry remarks and dark looks, but the crowd began to disperse. The companions hurried on again, and without any further encounters they reached the smithy and carried the mage inside the house. Harke met them, and Ulla hurried to make a bed ready. Then she came back down to the kitchen, where Will and his friends had gathered with Freya and her father.

"I will make some broth for him, and something for all of

you," she said, and then she caught sight of Will in his filthy clothes. He hoped that she hadn't caught scent of him, too.

"My dear, what on earth. . . ?" she began, and then thought better of it.

"If it's not too much trouble," Will said, "I'd really like to take a bath."

24

Be courteous to all you meet,
but keep one foot in the stirrup.

— *The Book of Errantry*

THE OTHER SHERIFFS OF THE WATCH arrived at the blacksmith's house sooner than expected. Will and his friends stayed in the upstairs room. They had already been seen by too many townsfolk, Pendrake said, and rumors about a band of strangers were no doubt flying thick and fast. He and Ulla tended to the mage, who had not wakened again since collapsing in the keep. Rowen was very tired and lay down to rest.

When the meeting was over, Harke came upstairs to tell them how things had gone.

"There are reports of the werefire vanishing all over the city," he said. "And the nightcrawlers have started fleeing. The Watch already drove a pack of blood-hobs out of the city. There is still much anger at the mage, but folk have had a weight lifted from their shoulders. They want to celebrate, not hold a trial. Better that than pounding at my gate, I say."

"We will gladly leave you to it, then, my friend, and be on our way. Strigon spoke of the Needle's Eye—"

"The high pass in the mountains," Harke said. "A two-day journey from here, up the valley of the Whitewing."

"The mages found something there," Pendrake went on, with a glance at Will. "Something we must find. We need to leave now, all of us except Rowen. She is in no condition for such a journey. Will you look after her, Ragnar, until I return?"

Will was surprised, but said nothing.

"Of course, old friend," Harke said. "But you can't set out now. The young folk need rest. And we're going to hold a samming."

"What's that?" Will asked.

"Something left undone for far too long," the blacksmith said, clapping his hands together and beaming from ear to ear.

Reluctantly Pendrake agreed to go to the samming. They stayed in the blacksmith's house until evening, when Rowen woke up, insisting that she felt much better, although she still looked pale. Pendrake said nothing about his decision to leave her in Skald, so Will did not mention it either.

Ulla cleaned and mended their clothes, and Freya took Rowen to her room to find her something more "fit for a samming," as she said. When it was time to go, Rowen was still not ready, and so Will and the others set off, agreeing that she and Freya would join them later.

Harke led them to an open square ringed by trees hung with strings of lanterns. The brightly lit space was filled with people, young and old. Children were perched up in the limbs of the trees, and older folk sat on benches, but most of the Skaldings were seated on a carpet of thick, soft furs that had been laid down on the stones. Many curious looks were directed at Will and his friends as they arrived.

"Someone asked me whether you and your companions are the new League," Harke said to Pendrake. "By the Stormrider's helmet, some folk never learn."

Will and his friends found places to sit on the furs. Large platters of bread and meat and fruit were passed around, and cups were filled with a sweet ruby-colored juice. They accepted the meal eagerly. As they ate, no one spoke, and Will was beginning to wonder if this was as lively as the gathering would be. Then a group of people began to gather on a raised wooden platform, carrying pipes and drums and small, rounded instruments that looked like plump fiddles.

The musicians began to play, slowly and softly at first, but soon the music was running along at a lively pace, and some of the Skaldings got up and began to dance. Some danced alone, stepping lively and clapping their hands, while others linked arms and danced in a ring, whirling faster or slower as the music changed pace.

Someone sat down beside Will, and he turned to see that it was Rowen. Her red hair, which she'd worn tied back for much of the journey, now hung thick and full over her shoulders. She was wearing a long green dress studded with tiny, gleaming stones at the collar and wrists. Freya was with her, and she, too, had changed, into a white gown with red embroidery. Will gaped at them, then recovered and turned his attention back to the dancing.

After a while the musicians took a rest and refreshed themselves with food and drink. Some of the children now grew bold enough to approach Will and the others. They were curious about Shade and took turns stroking his fur, patting him, and even pulling his ears, a mauling that he bore with admirable patience. When the music began again, the lanterns were dimmed, and the tune was now slow, and sad.

"First we dance," Harke said. "Then we remember."

An ancient-looking old man with a white beard stood up and began to sing in a language Will could not understand.

"He's telling the story of our lost home," Freya said. "Long ago we Skaldings lived in a far northern land by the sea. A land of foaming rivers, vast pine forests, and snowy mountains where dragons and frost giants dwelled. On winter nights we would look up and see, gleaming among the stars, the citadel of the High Ones, across a shimmering rainbow. The home of the Stormrider, the Thunderer, the Snow Maiden, and their kin. Their story was our story. We thought ourselves powerful like them, and we became proud, and arrogant. Although we already had all we could need, we demanded tribute from weaker folk, in return for our protection. Those who resisted, we conquered. We celebrated our victories in song, and thought ourselves the masters of the world.

"Then a shadow of fever and fear fell upon the land. The rivers dried up; the ice on the mountains melted away; the animals sickened and died. One night there was a mighty storm in the heavens, and after that the citadel of the High Ones was gone. The sky was empty. Our towns and villages fell silent. Tales and songs were forgotten. And then *his* armies came, and with them came those we had conquered, eager for vengeance. They swept our strongest warriors aside like straw. And then we were told there was a new story, and a new power to kneel before."

The old man bowed his head, as if gathering his strength, and then went on with his song.

"He sings of the few who refused to kneel," Freya said.

"How they escaped and set out in search of a new home, wandering for years through dangerous lands. And how they came at last to these mountains, and they looked up at the moonlit peaks, and it seemed to them that they saw the citadel of the High Ones there, once again. And once more they heard the roar of dragons among the clouds and felt the chill of the frost giants on dark winter evenings."

"You built Skald to be like the citadel of the High Ones," Rowen said eagerly. "A city across a bridge of light."

Freya nodded.

"We built the city to remember," she said sadly. "We remember all that we had, and lost. By joining hands, we remember what true strength is."

As the singer reached the end and fell silent, there were tears in many eyes.

"First we dance. Then we remember," Harke said again, and grinned. "Then we celebrate some more."

After a few moments the music began again, and now it was louder than ever, and many voices joined in song, until Will's ears began to throb with the noise.

"We will make a noise this night!" Harke shouted over the din. "A noise that will tell the nightcrawlers their time is over!"

Dancing was the furthest thing from Will's mind, but then a girl came hurrying toward him from among the dancers and pulled him to his feet. Before he could protest, she was whirling him around and around, laughing as he blushed and tried to keep up. As he spun, he glanced at his friends and saw their amused faces, especially that of Rowen, whose look went from wide-eyed disbelief to delight at the spectacle before her. Then a young man crossed the carpet of furs and tugged her out among the dancers, too.

The music began to go faster, and the dancers along with

it, until they were whirling at dizzying speed. Then they began letting go of their partners. Folk tumbled onto the furs amid a chorus of laughter. Before Will could prepare himself, the girl let go of his hands, and he went sprawling, too, his head spinning. He picked himself up, and there was Rowen, also sitting on the furs with a stunned look. They grinned at each other sheepishly, then resumed their seats to endure the applause and laughter of their friends.

"You dance well, Will Lightfoot," Shade said. "Now I see how you got your name." Will looked warily at him, unsure if he was being made fun of.

Ulla danced with the toy maker, and Finn with Freya. Will was surprised to see that Finn was a good dancer. That must be something else the Errantry taught you, he supposed. He also couldn't help noticing that Finn and Freya looked into each other's eyes throughout the dance. When they returned to their places, they sat close together and talked in quiet voices.

All at once there was a shout, and hands pointed skyward. Everyone looked up as the music broke off. Will saw Morrigan spiraling toward them out of the blackness beyond the lanterns, turning end over end. As she neared the ground, she appeared to gain more control of her flight and made straight for Pendrake, who caught her in his arms.

She lay there, her wings beating feebly.

The Skaldings began to back away and mutter among themselves.

"The Stormrider's bird," someone cried. "A messenger of doom."

"She is a friend," the toy maker said loudly. "She did not come from the Stormrider."

He bent his head close to the raven's beak. The crowd had fallen silent, and Will was able to hear Morrigan's whispered clicks and croaks.

"Is she hurt?" Rowen asked anxiously.

"She was keeping watch above," Pendrake said. "The shrowde attacked her. She's injured, but I do not think it is severe. She managed to drive her attacker off."

He looked up at the blacksmith.

"We must leave your city now, my friend," he said.

"We will protect you," Harke said, "as you did us."

Pendrake shook his head.

"This is something far worse than the nightcrawlers," he said, and then he turned to Rowen. "You will stay here, Rowen. And this time there will be no argument."

Rowen gaped at him with shock. Then her eyes blazed.

"No, Grandfather, you can't—"

"I said there would be no argument. I see now how foolish it was to bring you with us. You weren't ready for the Weaving yet, for all of this. And there is no time to teach you how to use your gift, not when we are hunted and on the run."

"I made it this far," she shot back.

"From here the road gets much harder, and you need to recover your strength. If this hope fails, there may be a longer road ahead for all of us. We will take Will to the Needle's Eye and return as soon as we can."

Will expected Rowen to continue to protest, but she went silent and did not say a word on the way back to the smithy. By now Morrigan had recovered enough to fly off in search of Moth. Will and the others hurriedly packed their belongings. The blacksmith's family gathered in the courtyard to see them off. Ulla gave them all warmer fur cloaks for the mountains and had made small, needed repairs to their packs and other gear. Freya had sharpened their weapons.

Will thanked her and Ulla for all they had done. He was sorry to leave them. Despite all that had happened, Skald now seemed a safer place to him than the world beyond its walls.

Ulla leaned close and kissed him on the forehead.

"Find your way home, child," she said.

Harke said a gruff good-bye to everyone and saw them off at the gate of the smithy. Rowen had refused to leave her room, but at the last moment she appeared, came up to Will, and gave him a quick hug.

"Good-bye, Will," she whispered. "Good luck."

Will swallowed hard.

"I don't know where I'd be now if it wasn't for you," he said thickly. "Get home safely. Someday maybe I can come back. We can see each other again. . . ."

Rowen nodded, her eyes filling with tears. She hugged Finn and Shade and clung to her grandfather for a long time before turning away suddenly and running back to the house. Ulla followed her.

Freya led them through the quiet streets to the western wall of the city. Here there was no gate, only a short flight of steps that descended to a low, cramped tunnel, at the end of which was a door guarded by three armored men. It was quickly unlocked, and the companions passed through in single file, into another narrow tunnel and down another staircase, at the bottom of which they found their way blocked by a thick hedge with thorny, intertwining branches. Freya came down the stairs last. She reached a hand in among the branches and tugged at something unseen, and a part of the hedge swung outward like a door.

"Clever," Finn said.

"The League was good for a few things," Freya said.

The companions filed out into a shadowy thicket beyond the hedge. Freya walked with them a short way down a steep path lined with standing stones, to a swiftly running stream bordered by willows. The sun was rising already, and a pale rosy light streamed through the trees and lit the city wall, like the flush on the face of someone who has been ill for a long time and is now recovering. Here Freya gave them some final directions for their road west, and then they said their farewells.

Freya wished them all good fortune on their journey, then she turned to Finn.

"The Errantry will be welcome here now," she said with a shy smile.

"And your people will be welcome in Fable," Finn said, with a blush that surprised Will. "Our cities need no longer be strangers."

When she had gone, Pendrake gazed up into the treetops.

"Now all we have to do is find —" he began, but a gruff bark from Shade cut him off. Before anyone could speak a word, Moth stepped out of the shadows with Morrigan on his shoulder.

"You people make far too much noise," said the archer with a shake of his head.

Moth listened attentively while they told the tale of all that had happened in Skald. He congratulated Will on his clever escape from the hogmen, which made Will grin with pleasure. Then Moth gave his own report.

"There has been no sign of Lotan himself," he said. "But if the shrowde is here, he cannot be far away. And I have overheard frightened talk from folk on the roads. Talk of people who were thought dead but have been seen walking."

"Fetches," Will whispered.

"They may be inhabiting the dead, or simply taking their shape," Moth said. "This is not a good place for us to linger, even if the darkness in Skald is lifting. I found a cave not far

from here, near where this stream flows out into the River
Whitewing. We can rest there for a while before setting out
again. There was another occupant, but Morrigan and I per-
suaded him to leave."

"Who was it?" Will asked.

"It wasn't really a *who* so much as a *what*," Moth said. "It
left in a hurry, having so many legs to run with. At any rate,
we should assume our pursuers have found our trail again,
and we must travel with stealth."

Moth led them along the stream. They came out into a
more open space where the snowy mountains rose up before
them, lit by the morning sun and much closer than Will had
imagined they were. The bank grew steeper and rockier as
they went along, so that when they reached the cave, they
had to scramble up a slope of sand and shale to reach it. The
cave was not warm, but it was dry and out of the wind that
had risen as they walked.

Will listened as Pendrake, Moth, and Finn discussed
the road ahead, but said nothing. His thoughts were on the
portal Strigon had spoken of. If four powerful mages couldn't
keep it open, what hope was there that he could?

25

By most reports the Shining Mountains are pleasant to travel through. They can be crossed without much effort or danger, and at most one should bring a warm cloak, as it can get rather chilly in the high passes.

— The Spindlefog Misguidebook to the Realms of Story

AFTER A FEW HOURS' REST, they set out, Pendrake taking the lead. He walked quickly and said very little. Will had the feeling his thoughts were as much on Rowen as they were on what lay ahead. Ever since he had met the old man, Will had been surprised at his nimbleness and energy. Now that they were traveling over rocky, rising ground, he was even more astonished at the pace Pendrake kept. Even Will's dad, who was many years younger than the toy maker, would have been huffing and puffing by now.

They followed the course of the River Whitewing westward, and the air quickly grew colder. The valley walls grew steeper, sweeping up from vast tree-blanketed slopes to cliffs of bare rock and ridges capped with snow. Each peak, Will discovered, had its own character. One in particular resembled the profile of a face gazing up at the sky. Will remembered the giant in the forest and wondered if this was another such sleeper. He hoped very much that it wasn't.

There was a narrow road of sorts beside the river, but for the most part the companions stayed away from it. With Shade's keen nose and Morrigan's eyes, they managed to avoid whatever Nightbane may have been prowling the region near Skald.

That afternoon they entered a narrower valley where two great slab-shaped peaks, like immense castle keeps, soared into the sky, one on either side of the river. Pendrake called them the Sentinels and said that long ago there had been dwelling places high upon their flanks, where the Fair Folk kept watch on the pass during the great war against the Shadow Realm. As they passed beneath the towering cliffs, Pendrake spoke about the long-ago war against the Night King. His tale of the ancient battle fought here was so vivid that Will began to wonder if he had seen it with his own eyes.

Beyond the Sentinels the river widened to a shallow, slender lake. Throughout the afternoon they walked along the lake's southern shore, which began as a rocky shingle that gave way to low dunes of sand like dull pewter, littered with twisted stumps and limbs of dry driftwood. A wind from the west streamed incessantly through the valley, riffling the surface of the water and forming whitecaps on the waves farther out.

At the western end of the lake, they made camp in the shelter of one of the dunes. They lit no fire, even though there was plenty of dry wood lying all around that looked as if it would burst into a fine flame with little encouragement. The sun disappeared quickly behind the western ranges. The valley filled with shadows, and only the tops of the two sentinel peaks still glowed with a rosy light. Will was grateful for his fur cloak, which kept out the cutting wind.

The waning moon was dimmed by a thin veil of cloud, and shed a hazy light over the waters. As they sat together on the beach, listening to the waves lap, they saw tiny lights on the eastern shore, bobbing and flickering in the darkness. Moth watched intently for a moment and then guessed that they were probably Nightbane with torches.

"Are they following us?" Will asked. "Do they know we're here?"

"I doubt it," Pendrake said. "If they did, it's unlikely they'd announce themselves like this with lights. My guess is they're on the way back to their mountain lair from a raid somewhere in the foothills."

"They are not afraid to use torches because they roam these lands unchallenged," said Moth. "For too long they have had to fear nothing and no one."

"I could change that for them," Shade muttered.

Morrigan flapped off for a closer look and vanished swiftly into the dark. The others all watched for a while as the lights moved slowly along the lake and then climbed the hills along the northern shore, where they grew less distinct, until finally they winked out completely. Not long after, Morrigan returned, bringing confirmation that the torch-bearers were indeed mordog, although there were other Nightbane with them.

"Creech, by the sound of it," said Moth when he'd listened to all of Morrigan's tale. "That is worrisome. These creatures seldom join forces, unless compelled by something they fear even more than they hate each other."

"Should we look for better concealment?" Finn asked.

"I think we should stay here," Pendrake said, "and keep

watch through the night. The wind has shifted and is in our favor, for the moment, and we can count on Shade's ears and Morrigan's eyes."

Shade lifted his muzzle to the wind, sniffed, and then sprang to his feet.

"There is a garm-wolf with them," he growled, his voice so cold and threatening it made Will shiver. "Or more than one."

"That's what Hodge and Flitch said killed their brother," Will said.

"I have met such beasts before," said Moth. "They are large and very powerful. They fear nothing."

"We should return to Skald," said Finn bitterly. "This was folly. They'll soon know we're here, if they don't already."

"It's too late to turn back," Pendrake said. "But the mountains are a hindrance to our enemies, too. If it comes to it, we can find refuge on the heights."

They spent the night huddled together on the dune, and Will's attempt to fall asleep on the cold, hard ground did not go well. He kept thinking about Rowen, left behind in Skald. He already missed her lively presence among them. Was she all right? And he wondered if he was getting any closer to Dad and Jess, or even farther away? His thoughts went around and around the same track. When he finally slipped into sleep, the sound of the wind on the water took shape in his dreams as something rushing toward him, a vast shadow with great gray wings beating like thunder. Several times he started awake, heart pounding. Each time he saw only the forms of his companions around him, and Finn's black silhouette against the starlight on the water, unmoving as a statue. The knight-in-training's calm stillness had always given Will some comfort, but now his feeling of dread was too great. The third time he awoke, he lay there restlessly for a while and then got up and sat down beside Finn. He wanted to speak, but he was afraid his voice would give away how frightened he was.

"Dawn's not far off," Finn said. "Sit and keep watch with me, if you like."

"Is there any point?"

"What do you mean?"

"They're coming for us. They'll never stop coming. I'm . . . not like you. I'm not brave."

Finn laughed softly.

"You think I've never been afraid of anything? You and I, Will, are more alike than you know."

"I doubt it. You've been trained to stand your ground. To fight. All I want to do is run."

"That was me, at your age. After my brother left. He never trained with the Errantry, though he could have been a great knight. He chose to stay and help my mother with the farm after my father died, rather than going to Appleyard. Then a horde of Nightbane raided the farmlands, and many people were killed before the Errantry drove the invaders away. After that my brother grew to hate the Errantry. He said that they only protected Fable and cared nothing for the rest of the Bourne. So he gathered a band of those who thought like him and set out after the Nightbane, to make them pay for what they'd done. Before he left he gave me his ring, and told me never to trust the Errantry."

"And he never came back?"

"No. That was ten years ago. I was a boy, full of anger and fear. I ran away from home, just like you. I came to Fable with nothing and lived on the streets, stealing for my supper.

I'd see knights-errant ride past in their bright armor, and I'd curse them under my breath and steal some more, just to prove I could get away with it right under their noses."

"I didn't know," Will said, greatly surprised. "How did you ever become one of them?"

"One winter I fell ill, and Master Pendrake found me and took me in. At the time, I had no idea why he'd bothered. I didn't see anything in me that was worth saving. In fact, I stole from him. A beautiful chess set that he'd made. The pieces were carved like great figures of Story. Heroes, villains. None of it meant anything to me. I took the chess set and ran. I was going to sell it in the market."

"So what happened?"

"Master Pendrake found me again. He had one of the chess pieces with him. A knight. I'd dropped it when I fled. All he said was 'You'll get a better price if you have the complete set.'"

Will smiled, and then he thought about the motorbike. He heard his father's voice in his head: *You should've taken the helmet.* That's probably what he would say when Will got home. If he got home. Suddenly Will wanted more than anything to hear him say it.

"A few days later, I brought the chess set back to him," Finn went on. "And then he gave me something else: the book I carry with me wherever I go."

"Is that why you joined the Errantry? Because of the book?"

A rare smile lit Finn's face.

"I joined because I thought they would teach me how to be brave."

"Did they?"

"They taught me something far more useful. They taught me how to be afraid and still keep on."

Will gazed across the lake to the dim outline of the far shore.

"How do you do that?" he asked.

"You're doing it, Will," Finn said. "And you're not alone."

Will nodded but said nothing. He found it hard to believe that this serious young man had once been a thief. Despite his coldness, Finn had inspired trust in Will from the beginning, but the story he'd just heard had not changed that. In fact Will realized that he now trusted Finn all the more. And for the first time, he felt he could understand him. In a tangle of mixed emotions, the thought came that if he never found his way home, perhaps he, too, might join the Errantry someday, and learn from Finn how to fight and master his fear.

From somewhere in the darkness rose low, eerie calls that echoed across the lake. The others were instantly on their feet and alert.

"Nightbane! There must be several bands," Finn whispered. "They're calling to each other from a distance, like a pack of—" He broke off and glanced at Shade. "They must know we're here."

"I do not believe so," Moth said. "Morrigan says they are still far off, and upwind. No, I think there must be someone or something else in the valley that has set them off in pursuit. Still, if they are on the move, we had better be as well."

Swiftly they gathered their gear and set out as the sky lightened and the sun rose behind them. Their progress along the narrowing Whitewing was difficult, as the shore was tangled with thick bushes. The mountain slopes around them grew steeper and closer.

As the morning passed, Pendrake led them up through a forest of fragrant spruce and pine. The ground was mostly bare of undergrowth and was crisscrossed with tiers of

snaky roots that they could use at times like steps. Beside
them the river's course narrowed, and soon the water was
rushing through a deep canyon. When they rested briefly,
Will peered over the edge. He saw white water churning and
seething far below.

At midday they left the cool, sweet-smelling forest behind and climbed into fierce sunlight. Pendrake urged them
on even higher, to a steep slope of broken shale, where they
halted at last. Anyone who approached would have to do so
over loose, clattering rocks. Pendrake let them stay here only
long enough to refresh themselves. Carrying on up the slope,
they finally reached the summit and stood upon a narrow
ridge of broken stone.

There, across a dizzying gulf of space, was the Whitewing
Glacier. Its snow-mantled upper reaches gleamed a dazzling
white in the sunshine, while the bare ice farther down was
rent by great crevasses that held a pale blue light.

The valley came to an end here, in a vast bowl of stone
that reminded Will of some mighty amphitheater fallen
into ruin. The sides of the bowl were formed by a curving
mountain wall over which the glacier spilled, tumbling down
to the valley floor, where the newborn river meandered out
in glittering braids from the edge of the ice. Besides the
river valley, the only other outlet from the bowl was to the
southwest, a narrow ravine between the southern flank of
the wall and the three snow-mantled peaks known as the
Sisters.

"That way lies the Pass of the Needle's Eye," Pendrake
said. "It leads over the spine of the Shining Mountains to the
western ranges and the Great Rampart."

As Will's eyes roamed over the dizzying expanse, they
caught a bright glint, midway down the long slope of the
glacier. High upon a horn of iron-gray rock that jutted out

like an island from the ice rose the white spires and battlements of a fortress. They gleamed wetly as though they had
been carved of ice instead of stone.

"That is Aran Tir," Moth said, when Will had pointed out
what he had seen. "It was used by my people as a refuge
against the armies of the Night King, but it was not built by
the Shee. I have never seen it with my own eyes. It was abandoned long ago."

"They say Aran Tir was shaped by the Stewards,"
Pendrake said. "In a time that was already ancient when
the Fair Folk built Eleel-upon-the-Sea. On my last journey
through these mountains, many years ago now, I found a
stone stair that climbs the cliff wall above the northern edge
of the glacier. The steps were partly blocked by fallen debris,
but they took me to a spot where I could safely cross the ice
to the base of Aran Tir. I say we still make for the pass, but
by a more roundabout route that will take us nearer to the
glacier. If our enemies close in on us before we reach the pass,
then we will have a chance to reach the stair."

"Where are these steps?" Finn asked, shading his eyes with
a hand. "There's nothing but sheer rock as far as I can see."

"The stairs were carved with concealment in mind,"
Pendrake answered. "I only found them because the Kantar
speaks of them." He pointed out a waterfall spilling down
the rock face just to the right of the ice. Where the cataract
touched the valley floor, he explained, was the place they
had to reach.

"That is the surest way to Aran Tir. It may be we can
use the citadel as it was once used by your folk, Moth. As a
refuge."

"We won't last long on a rock in the middle of ice," muttered Finn.

"Yet it may give us enough time to think of some other

means of escape," Pendrake said. "As things stand, I do not see any other choice."

"What if we reach Aran Tir and find Nightbane waiting for us?" Will said.

"Such creatures would likely stay away from Aran Tir because it was crafted by the power of the Stewards," Pendrake replied, "and still retains something of their presence. And because of the ice itself. It creaks and shudders like a living thing."

"I remember it rumored among my people that the river of ice is alive," said Moth. "That it will not suffer Nightbane to tread upon it."

"I have seen such things," Shade said. "Where the Stewards walked, the trees and the stones spoke. When we went to war, the earth itself rose against our enemies."

"If you know how to recruit your former allies, Shade, please don't hesitate," the loremaster said.

"I do not, Master Pendrake."

"Then we'll have to do the best we can. Let us hurry now."

The companions set out along the ridge until it became too narrow and steep to climb. At this point they turned and began to descend the western flank of the ridge, into the great bowl itself. Their route took them down a long slope of scree that was tricky to walk on, until they found a goat path and followed it. Below them lay a barren plain of mud and boulders crossed by immense, snaking ridges of heaped stones that Pendrake said had been deposited there as the ice receded over the ages. The few evergreen trees that managed to grow in this inhospitable landscape were stunted, their spindly limbs all growing on one side, away from the knife-sharp wind that streamed down from the ice. From time to time the travelers heard a distant crack and rumble and looked up to see that a chunk of the upper glacier had given way and was tumbling down into the valley in a cloud of snow, the echoes rolling back and forth across the valley like distant thunder. Morrigan circled far above them, keeping watch.

"Ice once filled this entire valley," Pendrake said. "Much of it melted during the Broken Years, when even the sun left its path and grew swollen in the sky."

They kept along the gradually descending path, until the glacier's wide meltwater tarn lay directly below them, its waters a bright blue-green. In the tarn floated chunks of ice that had fallen from the glacier, weirdly shaped by sun and wind and drifting in the water like aimless specters. The midday heat had also released many slender cataracts of white water that spilled down the face of the rock wall, the roar of their fall muted by distance to a faint rumble in the air.

Morrigan gave a cry and swooped down past them. They followed the path of her flight and saw many dark, manlike figures toiling across the valley floor.

"Nightbane!" Moth cried.

"We must forget the stair and make straight for the ice!" Pendrake shouted. "It's our only chance now."

Morrigan gave another, even more piercing cry. She was circling a boulder-strewn area beside the tarn. Will shielded his eyes with his hand and saw two smaller figures darting in and out of the concealment of the boulders. They were wearing heavy cloaks and fur caps that concealed their features, but Will knew at once who they were.

26

It is not hard to understand why wolves are generally feared and even hated. They howl eerily at the moon, their eyes shine in the dark, and they frequent haunted places. This misunderstanding of their character is unfortunate, however, for the wolf is a noble and personable beast, not at all the bloodthirsty monster that so many stories make him out to be.

— Balthazar Budd's *Flora and Fauna of Wildernesse*

"ROWEN AND FREYA ARE DOWN THERE!" Will shouted.

"No," Pendrake said in a choked whisper. He leaned heavily on his staff as if the will and strength that had brought him this far had suddenly deserted him. Then he gave a cry and plunged down the slope. The others quickly followed, Shade soon bounding past the toy maker.

By now Rowen and Freya had seen them and were racing toward the slope. Several hundred yards behind them, a horde of Nightbane had crested the last of the stone ridges and was descending in leaps and bounds toward the tarn. Despite his fear and the slippery slope beneath him, Will couldn't take his eyes from what he was seeing.

Some of the Nightbane were like tall and powerfully built men. They wore bloodred plates of armor and bristled with weapons. The mordog, Will guessed. They were larger than he had imagined. Among them were other creatures, smaller but far stranger. They were thin and bony and moved with an insectlike scuttling of their limbs.

In a few moments Will's party had reached Rowen and Freya. Pendrake clasped his granddaughter in his arms. Freya was limping, and her right leg was bound with a bloody cloth.

"After you left Skald, our lookouts reported a horde of Nightbane heading west along the Whitewing," Freya panted as they gathered around her.

"I had to warn you," Rowen said with a gasp. "I'm sorry. . . ."

"They picked up our trail last night," Freya said. "There's at least five score of them. I tried to stop her, Father Nicholas—"

"No time now," the toy maker said. "Run for the waterfall, all of you, and don't look back."

He took the lead. Shade ran beside Will and Rowen, and behind them came Finn with Freya, and finally Moth. Morrigan flew on ahead, her wings rippling like ragged black pennants as she beat against the streaming wind.

As he raced on Will heard the scuff of feet on rock and the dull clatter of armor, growing louder and louder. It was all he could do not to turn around, expecting at any moment to feel a heavy claw clutch his shoulder.

A hoarse shout came from Moth. Although Will thought he was almost out of strength, he ran faster, leaping over larger stones and miraculously keeping his footing on the uneven ground. The plain began to rise steeply as they neared the rock wall. Will struggled up this last slope, his boots sinking in the soft gravel, his eyes fixed only on the ground before him. Shade stayed beside him, and when Will began to slip and stumble, he gripped the shaggy ruff at the back of the wolf's neck. As they toiled on together, Will heard the swish of a blade behind him and a scream, but he did not turn his head. He clambered on, his breath coming in gasps, and when he next dared to look up, he saw that the rock wall now loomed over them. Pendrake had reached the waterfall and was already vanishing into its billowing cloud of spray, with Rowen close behind him.

"Go on!" Shade shouted to Will. "Do not stop."

The wolf fell back with a snarl. Will lowered his head again for one last burst of speed, feeling the spray upon his face as he ran. The next thing he knew, he had passed through the wall of slashing water and found himself in a dark, shuddering space on the other side, soaked and stunned by the cold. Pendrake was here, with Rowen. At the back of this hidden chamber in the rock was the stone stair, rising steeply in a deep crevice.

Rowen screamed, "Will! Watch out!"

He whirled around just as a huge shape came crashing through the fall into the rock chamber. Will had a brief, terrifying glimpse of cold inhuman eyes, teeth bared in a hideous grimace, a jagged blade raised high. The creature jerked to a halt and stood, teetering like a tree about to fall. Then its weapon hit the floor with a clang, and the mordog toppled headfirst, an arrow in its back.

Finn, Freya, and Moth came bursting through the fall with Shade at their heels. The swords of both men were streaked with black blood, and Finn had a cut above one eye.

"We dealt with the front-runners," Moth said. "The rest of the horde is farther back, but they will be here soon enough."

Pendrake was leaning with a hand against the rock, breathing hard. For a moment Will feared for him, but then the old man took a deep breath, straightened, and picked up his staff. It was as if he had been drawing strength from the stone itself.

"Up the steps, everyone," he said.

Pendrake herded Will and Rowen ahead of him, and the others followed. Shade took his place at Will's side without a word, and Will saw the dark stains on his muzzle.

As they climbed the steps out of the cavern, the outer wall of the stair dropped away, leaving no barrier between them and a sheer drop to the valley floor. Will edged his way along, trying to look only at his feet and not at the terrifying void just beyond them.

After a long, toiling climb, they rounded a bend in the rock face and found their path blocked by a mound of huge fallen stones. Moth leaped without pausing onto the mound and helped the others up. They scrambled as quickly as they could over the wet rocks to the other side. Here they found themselves on the edge of a precipice, with the long lower slope of the glacier revealed beneath them, hundreds of feet below. They were at the top of the stair. Ahead of them it descended steeply to a spur of rock that jutted out onto the ice, like a spearhead aimed at the horn of Aran Tir.

They halted to catch their breath. The wind shrieked in their ears, and all they could see in any direction was ice and rock. Will shivered. He felt as though they had come to the very top of the world.

"There used to be a guard post here," said Pendrake, gazing back at the mound of fallen stones. "And a rope bridge that ran from this height to the base of Aran Tir."

Morrigan swooped down, bringing the news that there were many mordog coming up the stair, but also that the other Nightbane, the smaller, scuttling ones called creech, were scaling the rock wall, as well as climbing the glacier itself.

"I thought they were afraid of the ice," Rowen cried.

"They are being driven," Moth said, "and it is not hard to guess by what."

"They mean to cut us off before we can reach Aran Tir!" Pendrake shouted. "We cannot linger here."

Moth spoke to the raven, who hopped to the edge of the stair and dived into empty space. A moment later Will saw her, already far below, a ragged black arrow speeding across the gulf of air toward the rock island, a small swift ripple of shadow following her upon the ice.

"She has gone ahead to find out if Aran Tir is already taken," Moth said.

"And if it is?" Finn asked.

"Then we look for some other position that can be defended. Perhaps higher up on the glacier," Moth replied.

"The steps down to the ice look open at least," said Pendrake. "Let us hurry."

"Wait—I have some rope!" Finn shouted, digging in his pack. "Not a lot, but enough, I think. We should be roped together on the ice."

There was a clatter of stones from above. As one they looked up and saw a beaked, skull-like face with huge bulging eyes. The creature came scuttling down the rock wall directly at Will, its body squat and carapaced like a crab's, its bonelike limbs strung together with naked red sinews. With an ear-splitting shriek, the thing leaped through the air and landed in the midst of the company, swiftly followed by many more of its kind.

"Creech!" Moth shouted as he blocked a blow from a slashing claw.

"Stay with Shade," Pendrake cried to Will and Rowen as he charged forward with his staff on high. They unsheathed their knives and drew close together with the wall at their backs. Shade planted himself in front of Will with his teeth bared.

The battle was fierce but brief. The creech gabbled and

screamed as they fought, talons and fangs their only weapons. They were smaller and more wiry than the mordog, moving with a speed that amazed Will, but they were reckless and outmatched. The swords of Finn and Moth lopped limbs and split carapaces. Freya's hammer sent her foes tumbling end over end. Pendrake's staff landed with a terrible crack on several skulls. One of the creech jumped on Finn's back and clawed at his face before he managed to fling it over his head and off the edge of the stair.

At Will's side, Rowen gave a sharp gasp. He looked up. A creech had climbed facedown like a huge insect from the wall above. It was clutching Rowen's hair and dragging her head back, its jaws slavering at her neck. Before he could think Will slashed at the creech's bony claw with his knife. The thing hissed and turned its attention to Will, giving Rowen the chance to pull away. The creech lost its grip on the wet rock and tumbled to the stones at their feet. It was up again in an instant, lunging at Will and Rowen before they could move, but now Shade was in front of them, snarling.

The creech froze, then retreated with a guttural sound like bones clattering together as Shade advanced. Another few steps and the creech was at the brink. It bared its fangs at Shade, spat, then flung itself over the edge.

In another moment the fight was over. Those creech that had not fallen to the ice below lay lifeless on the stones.

"They are good climbers," Finn said, gingerly touching the livid scratches on his neck. "They must have scrambled up here ahead of us and lain in wait."

"Which means there may be more of them soon," Pendrake said.

Will tried to keep his hands from shaking as he sheathed his knife.

"You're hurt," Rowen said with concern in her voice. Will

felt a burning on his neck. He touched the spot and his fingers came away bloody. There was no time to do anything about it. They still had to climb down to the ice and then cross it to reach Aran Tir.

Will was already following Rowen down the steps when Shade made a sound unlike anything he had heard before. It was a growl so low and seething with fury that it froze him to the spot.

Will turned. Shade stood among the fallen creech, gazing at the heap of fallen stones, his hackles raised, his ears back.

"Run now, Will Lightfoot," he growled.

There at the top of the heap of stones stood another wolf.

Or something that might once have been a wolf. It was much larger than Shade, its fur black and matted into thick spines, its hulking frame like something that had been twisted into shape by a mind mad with hate. Its ears were torn scraps of raw flesh, and its eyes were not amber like Shade's, but a dead, cold black rimmed with red fire. From its huge jaws thick slaver dripped.

"Run!" Shade barked at Will, and in the next instant he bounded up the heap of stones and met the garm-wolf as it hurtled itself down.

The combatants collided in a writhing, churning mass of fur and snapping jaws, like a single monstrous creature tearing itself apart. Will stumbled backward, his gaze fixed on the terrible sight before him. The sounds coming from the throats of the two wolves he knew he would never forget. In the next moment the desperate frenzy of the struggle had carried the combatants to the brink of the precipice, and they were gone.

27

Some say that the land itself is a living thing.
That does not mean it is friendly.

— *The Book of Errantry*

WILL STARED AT THE PLACE where Shade had been only a moment before. Finn ran back and took him by the arm.

"We have to go, now!"

Numb with shock and sick at heart, Will fell into line with the others. As quickly as they dared, they descended the steps, which were wet and eroded by exposure to the ice. In places they had to leap across a gap from one intact step to another farther down. When they were halfway to the spear-shaped spur, they heard a clatter from above and saw that a band of mordog had reached the heap of fallen stones at the top of the stair and were on their way down. There were many of them, forty at least, and even more were out on the ice, along with a great number of creech, toiling upward in an effort to reach Aran Tir first.

At last the steps ended in a hollow between two standing

stones, and then Will and the others were upon the rock spur, which stretched before them like a flat, wide stage. Desperately Will scanned the surface of the glacier below the cliff from which Shade and the garm-wolf had fallen. Tears stung his eyes.

The companions dashed across the spur, splashing through the shallow meltwater pools that dotted its surface. They reached the end, where another, shorter flight of stone steps led down in a half spiral onto the ice. The Nightbane behind them were still descending the long straight stair, and most of those on the glacier were still a good distance away, except for a vanguard of mordog and creech who had drawn ahead of the rest.

As they stepped out onto the ice, Morrigan returned.

"As far as she can tell, the citadel is empty," Moth said. "The rock is almost completely surrounded by a deep crevasse, but there is a snow bridge we might be able to cross."

"That is how I reached Aran Tir the last time," said Pendrake. "If we can get across the snow bridge to the citadel, there is a stairway that leads up to the great hall. From there we should be able to reach the upper towers, if the way is not blocked. "

The companions set out across the glacier. Despite the cold wind shearing snow off the heights above, the heat of the sun had brought the ice to life: from all around came the sound of water trickling, gushing, spilling, as if the glacier was turning into a river beneath them. Will and the others had to temper their need for haste with the dangers of this unfamiliar and dangerous terrain. Their progress was difficult and uneven, as they were sometimes struggling through drifts of snow, or running across bare ice, and now and then even leaping over narrow meltwater streams.

On they struggled, and as they neared the great jutting

horn of dark stone, they could hear a rushing that grew louder by the moment. The ice beneath them trembled.

Finally they neared the base of Aran Tir and came to a wide crevasse that yawned between them and the rock. The thunderous noise and shaking came from a meltwater stream that poured into the crevasse at its upper end, the water plunging with a roar to unseen depths. As Morrigan had said, there was only one way across this final obstruction: a slender span of snow and ice that arched over the gap to a narrow ledge that ran along the base of the great horn of rock.

Moth took one end of the rope from Finn and led the way. He walked slowly up the arch of the bridge, paying out the rope as he went. At the highest point of the span, he paused and crouched down, placing a hand on the snow at his feet. Then he kept on to the far side, jumping at last onto the ledge at the base of the rock.

"The bridge is strong enough to hold your weight," he called. "Go carefully, and keep some distance between you. Do not run."

Will grasped the rope, followed by Rowen and her grandfather, and then Freya. Finn waited at the start of the bridge, his sword at the ready. When Will was almost halfway across the slender arch, he stopped. A low rumbling, deeper and louder than the roar of the nearby waterfall, sounded from the depths of the crevasse.

The bridge shuddered and Will crouched, gripping the rope. He dared a look down and for an instant had a dizzying vision of glassy aquamarine walls dropping away into an inky well of blue-black shadow. Swiftly the tremor stopped and the sound faded, but Will stayed motionless, his heart pounding. Finally, at a shout from Moth, he forced himself on.

At last he reached the rock ledge and stumbled forward.

"What was that?" he gasped.

"Perhaps the old tales are true," Moth said, clutching Will's arm to steady him. "The ice is alive and does not care for trespassers."

After Freya, Rowen, and her grandfather joined them on the ledge, Finn started across the snow bridge, coiling up the rope as he went. The toy maker turned from watching him and strode up to a pair of thick, slab-sided pillars of grayish stone at one end of the ledge. One of the pillars had collapsed in pieces against the other like a tumbled tower of children's blocks. Both were covered with a layer of ice.

"The stair to the great hall was here, between these pillars," Pendrake said, and Will heard the weariness in his voice. "We can't get through this way."

"You've been here before, Grandfather," Rowen said. "There must be another way. It can't end like this, not after Shade . . ."

The toy maker turned to her with a stricken look, as if he had forgotten she was here with him, in danger, and had just remembered. Will hoped he would say something comforting to her, to all of them, but the old man shook his head.

"We cannot climb sheer rock," he said. "We're trapped on this ledge."

"Then we will make our stand here," Moth said, nocking an arrow in his bowstring. "The Nightbane will pay dearly for crossing the bridge."

Finn was now at the halfway point of the span, and the pursuing Nightbane had drawn up at the far end. They crowded together at the brink, those in front leaning forward hesitantly to inspect the chasm at their feet. It looked as though none would dare the bridge, until at last a huge mordog went among them, snarling and cracking an evil-looking whip. Then the throng began to order itself and move in single file onto the span. Those mordog that carried crossbows took up positions on the edge of the crevasse and began to load their weapons. Moth shouted a warning and Will, Freya, Rowen, and the toy maker took what shelter they could behind a low pile of tumbled stones. Moth let fly one arrow and then another, dropping two of the archers to the ice before the others had a chance to fire.

Finn ran now for the ledge, the black bolts of the enemy whizzing around him. As he did, Freya cried out, rose from where she was crouching beside Will, and charged back onto the bridge. One of the mordog arrows struck the ice directly in front of Finn, and he stumbled. At the same moment, Freya reached him and took his arm. They hurried for the ledge together, but the gap between him and the Nightbane advancing across the bridge had narrowed.

An arrow sped past Will's head, and Rowen screamed. The arrow had struck her in the shoulder. She collapsed, her face contorted with pain. Will and the toy maker knelt beside her.

Rowen's eyes were closed, and she was gasping for breath.

"What can we do?" Will said desperately.

"Do not touch the arrow!" Moth shouted. He shot another arrow of his own and hurried to their side. As he reached them a strange cry went up. Will turned to see something advancing through the ranks of the Nightbane on the bridge.

It was twice the height of the tallest mordog and appeared to be a humped, spiny boulder with arms and legs. Will could see two tiny eyes and a gaping crevice of a mouth in the hump where its head should have been.

"What is *that*?" Will gasped.

"That is an unthunk," Moth said, and even he sounded defeated now. "One of the giant ones."

Finn and Freya had almost reached the end of the bridge. At the unthunk's roar, Finn turned. Freya gripped his shoulder, but he pulled away from her and charged back the way he had come. By now the creature had shouldered its way through the file of mordog on the bridge. With astonishing swiftness for something that seemed to be made of solid rock, it swung a huge fist that Finn barely dodged in time. He dived forward past the gigantic creature, rolled to his feet, and instead of striking at the unthunk from behind, engaged a snarling mordog with an ax. Blade rang against iron, and again Finn dropped, so that the mordog's next swing struck the unthunk's leg as the monster turned in search of Finn. The mordog tugged its weapon free and scrambled to get away. With a howl the enraged unthunk batted it off the bridge and came charging at Finn and the rest of the Nightbane.

Finn dived again and slid between the unthunk's legs. The unthunk whirled and struck Finn as he was scrambling to his feet, sending him sprawling. But the monster's furious swing had thrown it off balance. It did a kind of slow, flailing pirouette, batting several shrieking mordog off the bridge, until at last it stood teetering on the brink. Then, with a groan like a falling tree, it toppled into the abyss.

Finn staggered to his feet as the mordog, only briefly cowed, advanced again in a rush. It looked as if Finn would be overwhelmed, but in the next instant Freya and Moth had joined him on the bridge. Two mordog fell, and the rest drew back. The defenders stood their ground. The grizzled mordog at the rear of the file cracked its spike-tipped whip, and the Nightbane surged forward once more.

As Finn, Freya, and Moth braced to meet the onslaught, the low rumbling began again from below, now much louder. The entire citadel of Aran Tir seemed to shake, and splinters of ice cracked and fell from the bridge. The charging mordog stopped short in fear, piling into one another, and then turned and tried to shove their way back into the horde still filing onto the trembling span. In the scuffle that followed, several more were knocked screaming into the crevasse. Moth shouted something that Will could not hear, and then he, Freya, and Finn turned and ran for the ledge.

Before they could reach it, the bridge began to change beneath them. Sharp spikes of ice jutted from its surface, so quickly that the three had to dart between or leap over them. To his bewilderment Will saw movement within the bridge. A pulse like deep veins of blue water now coursed through the ice. Then the bridge shivered from one end to the other, shards of ice and snow falling from it like glittering scales. The rock under Will's feet shook violently, and he staggered back from the brink of the ledge, but not before he glimpsed horns, an immense scaled body, an icy blue eye.

The bridge was no longer a bridge. Whatever it had become, it was alive.

With a sound like sheets of glass shattering, the creature broke free and plunged downward, sending the shrieking Nightbane on both sides hurtling into the crevasse. Finn and Moth came flying through the air and tumbled onto the rock ledge at Will's feet. At the same instant Finn's hand shot out behind him and grasped Freya's arm. She had fallen short and was clinging to the edge of the rock. As Moth helped him haul her to safety, a huge cloud of snow and ice shards billowed up and out, blinding Will and his friends.

When the cloud had settled, the bridge and the enemy upon it were no more. But the creature was still there. Will and the others watched in stunned silence as it heaved itself out of the crevasse on the far side, its diamond claws digging into the bare ice. As it moved, the creature's white scales gleamed with a faint blue tinge where they overlapped one another. The very air around it was hazy with frost.

A dragon, Will realized, gaping in wonder. A dragon of ice.

The Nightbane that had not ventured onto the bridge were flinging away their weapons in terror and fleeing in all directions, some even heedlessly hurtling themselves into the crevasse. When the dragon's entire form was out on the ice, it lifted its head and gave a roar that made Will clap his hands to his ears. A pair of wings unfolded with a creak and billowed out like massive sails, sending ice crystals glittering through the air. Then the dragon was among the fleeing mordog and creech like an ice storm, its great head sweeping from side to side and its mighty tail lashing.

There was a sound like the huffing and hissing of a steam locomotive, and from the dragon's mouth came not fire but a blast of white air thick with frost. As it swept its immense head around, any Nightbane caught by the blast turned hoary and icicled in an instant. After a few slowing steps, they ceased moving and stood frozen in grotesque poses of terrified flight.

It looked as if many of the Nightbane not directly in its path would still escape, until the dragon did something even more astonishing. Its great head reared and then plunged into the ice, as if it were made of the same element and were merging with it. Moments later its head appeared again, like an upthrust pillar of ice, and to Will's amazement another head rose near it, exactly like the first, and then another farther away, each one in the path of a knot of fleeing Nightbane, who were quickly halted by a blast of frosty breath. As it moved in pursuit of its prey, the dragon's body undulated over and through the ice as though the glacier itself was rippling in waves.

In a short time there were no moving Nightbane on the glacier but only nightmarish white statues. Some of the very few who had escaped were scrambling over the rocky rubble alongside the glacier. Two of the dragon's three heads plunged under the surface and did not reappear. The third stretched high on its scaly neck above the ice, and its body followed.

The dragon opened its mouth wide and gave a thunderous bellow, like the crack and roar of an avalanche.

Now that there were no unfrozen Nightbane within reach, the creature's fury seemed to subside as quickly as it had itself appeared. It snorted a few times for good measure and shook itself briskly from its horns to the tip of its tail. Then, as if as an afterthought, it slowly turned its massive head to look at Will and his companions. The steely blue eyes that regarded them gave no hint of the creature's thoughts.

"What will it do now?" Will whispered.

"Whatever it wants," said Freya.

The dragon heaved its massive body around, folded its wings, and poured itself into the chasm, as if its long, lithe body had melted instantly into rushing water. Moments later it reappeared, crawling up onto the ledge a few feet from Will and his friends. They backed away quickly against the rock wall, Will and Pendrake helping Rowen, who had come to but was still breathing in gasps and looked deathly pale.

The dragon hunkered down on its forelegs and seemed to solidify before their eyes. It studied the small mortals before it as if there were no hurry in the world to decide what should be done about them.

Moth stepped forward, bowed, and spoke a few words in another language. The dragon's eyes narrowed to blue slits, and it gave a deep, frosty huff. Whether this was a sound of approval or scorn or something else entirely, Will had no idea. The dragon rose suddenly and with heavy tread, started forward. Its long blue talons clicked on the stone.

"Keep out of its way," Moth cautioned in an undertone, and they all quickly obeyed, crowding together against the rock face. The dragon went past them without a glance, as if it had forgotten they were there. As its huge ponderous bulk brushed by, like a slowly moving train, its shadow fell over the companions, and the air seemed to grow even colder. Will had the uncanny sense that before him was passing both a living creature and a force of nature, like a storm or lightning or the ice itself, a power that was aware of him and his friends yet apart from them, involved with deep, remote things that he could not fathom.

The ice dragon reached the spot where the steps were blocked by the jumbled remains of the pillars. With one immense claw it began digging at the fallen rock. In a short time it had dislodged one of the huge chunks of stone, and then another. The dragon did not cast away the broken pieces of the pillar but instead nudged them almost tenderly to one side as it continued its work.

Soon the staircase was free of all but a few small fragments of rubble. Briefly the dragon seemed to regard what it had done with a critical eye, and then it turned slowly to Will and his friends again. It now seemed to take particular notice of Rowen, who was doubled over and shaking in Freya's arms.

The dragon bent toward her, and at this, Finn moved to block its way.

"No, wait," Moth said, raising his hand.

Finn drew back. The dragon studied him briefly, then stretched out one of its forelimbs to Rowen. She raised her head and stared in wide-eyed shock at the creature towering over her. The dragon's huge claw reached down toward the black mordog arrow in her shoulder. From this close Will saw that the dragon's scales were translucent, like the ice itself. A bluish fluid pulsed beneath the surface. The claw touched Rowen's shoulder and spread out as if melting like snow on her skin. She winced and gave a cry, and a moment later the claw was moving away from her and the arrow was gone. Will thought he glimpsed it for an instant, a dark sliver vanishing into the liquid depths of the dragon's limb.

Rowen breathed out, the grimace of pain gone from her face, replaced by a look of astonishment.

The dragon turned away, and the now familiar ominous rumble sounded from its throat. It stared out across the ice, as if daring the Nightbane to come near again. Rowen touched her shoulder. She was still breathing heavily but already some of the color had returned to her face.

"It was burning," she said with a shiver.

"The arrowhead must have been poisoned," Pendrake said.

"Now there's no pain," Rowen said. "Just cold."

She gazed up at the dragon.

"Thank you," she said, through chattering teeth.

Moth stepped forward, bowed again, and spoke once more to the dragon. This time it startled them all by answering, in a deep, booming voice that pounded in Will's ears. It gave a long, slow utterance, punctuated with several snorts and rumblings, and then concluded with another mighty huff, so that jets of frost puffed from its nostrils and billowed over its head. Then the dragon turned to face the rim of the ledge and began to crawl headfirst down into the crevasse, its long, lithe body shivering into liquid again as it disappeared. The tail slithered out of sight last.

As suddenly as it had appeared, the dragon was gone.

No one spoke for a long time. Morrigan swooped down

and alighted on one of the nearby fallen stones. She shook herself and gave a wheezy squawk that sounded like a stunned comment on everything they had just witnessed.

"I agree," Finn said.

"There are verses in the Kantar about glaciers," the toy maker said. "It calls them mighty dragons, slow to rouse but swift and deadly when the mood takes them. I should have paid more attention to those lines."

Finn asked Moth what he and the dragon had said to each other.

"I thanked him with all the ceremony I could muster at short notice," the archer said. "For saving us, and for his hospitality. The rock of Aran Tir is his home. He has been here as long as the ice has, if not longer, I would say. When the Stewards came and built their citadel, he befriended them. Now he guards the rock in their memory. I believe that last roar was his name, but I did not quite catch it. Too loud."

With anguish in his heart, Will looked back across the ice the way they had come. The dragon had not saved all of them.

"Why did he help us?" he asked bitterly. "Why didn't he get rid of us like the Nightbane, if we're trespassing?"

"He said we would find that out if we climbed the stairs. Unlike most dragons, he is not given to long conversations. When Rowen is ready, we should do as he said. There will be more shelter from the cold, at any rate. We may be here a long while before it is safe to leave."

"I'm ready now," Rowen said, rising to her feet with Freya's help. "I feel fine."

At the top of the steps, they came out into an open, roof-less space rimmed by tall columns. At the far end of this circular court rose a sheer wall, hundreds of feet high, topped by white towers that gleamed in the late afternoon sunlight, like a vision of a palace in some other world that was far-off and out of reach. At the base of the wall stood a wide archway, partially blocked by rubble and chunks of stone.

"The forecourt of Aran Tir," Pendrake said. "Through that archway is the main staircase up into the citadel. Even though our pursuers have been beaten back, we should probably climb as high as we can in the towers. It will give us a better view of where our enemies are and what they may be doing."

Just then they heard a sound from the archway, a clattering of fallen stones. Moth and Finn drew their swords. Everyone waited without speaking, and then, through the archway, limping and bedraggled, came Shade.

28

Where once armor clashed and swords rang there is now only the keen of the wind, the whisper of water upon stone.

— Redquill's *Atlas and Gazetteer of the Perilous Realm*

WILL SHOUTED AND RAN FORWARD. He knelt and wrapped his arms around the wolf.

"I thought I'd never see you again," he said through his tears. "I thought you were dead."

"I am not dead, Will Lightfoot," Shade said huskily. "I am here. I will not leave you again."

"You found a swifter route across the ice than we did," the toy maker said, laughing. "I know you're fast, my friend, but that is still quite a feat."

"I did not travel across the ice, Master Pendrake," the wolf said. "I went under it."

They all welcomed him with glad smiles and pats. Then, in his calm, methodical manner, Shade related what had happened after he and the garm-wolf fell from the stair. They had tumbled down the cliff to the surface of the ice, and both of them were hurt, but the garm-wolf recovered first and fled across the glacier. Shade gave chase as best he could and caught up with his enemy at the edge of a crevasse, where they struggled and both fell in.

"I do not remember anything else," the wolf went on, "until I woke up and found myself in a cave under the ice, with Whitewing Stonegrinder."

"With who?" Freya asked.

"The guardian of the ice, Freya Ragnarsdaughter," Shade said. "That is his name. He can be in many places at once. Or he can be . . . many of himself at once. It is hard to understand. When I first saw him, I tried to get away, but he was everywhere. There was no escaping him. He put his foot on me, and I could not move. He was very angry, and I thought he was going to crush me. I asked him not to, and he did not, but he wanted to know who had dared to enter his domain. He spoke in the voice of the First Ones, only much louder. I answered him, and after that he was not so angry, but he still kept his foot on me."

"He must have guessed you were one of the Companions," Pendrake said. "Thank goodness for that."

"I agree," Shade said with a nod. "Whitewing Stonegrinder said he had been woken by the *ghool* crawling around his home, and he was going to do something about that, but first he wanted to know what I was doing here. When I told him the story, he called me brother and took his foot off me. I thanked him, and then he asked me if I had seen any of the First Ones in my travels. When I said I had not, he was sad. He growled as though he were angry again, but I saw tears rolling down and freezing on his face."

Shade related how he had told Whitewing Stonegrinder about his friends, that they were in danger from a host of the Nightbane. That had roused the dragon to his former fury. He roared and rumbled and lashed his tail, and the cave shook and spears of ice came crashing to the floor.

"Then he touched my wounds, and they went cold and did not hurt anymore," Shade said.

"He did the same for Rowen," Will said. "If it's the same dragon."

Whitewing Stonegrinder had led Shade through a series of tunnels under the ice to the rock of Aran Tir. He unblocked a passage up into the citadel and told the wolf to take it.

"I asked him if he would help my friends, and he got angry and said he was already doing that. I thought he might step on me again. I was very glad to get out of there."

"There is no doubt you saved us, Shade," said Moth. "From the Nightbane and the dragon both."

They all echoed the archer's words.

"But we're still stranded here," Finn said.

"Our enemies know where we are," Pendrake said, "and if the Angel is with them, they're not likely to abandon the siege. Somehow we must get down off the ice, and pretty quickly. Though how we're going to go through the pass unnoticed and unchallenged is another question."

"We do not have to go through the pass," Shade said. "Whitewing Stonegrinder told me of another way, after he calmed down again. The Shee found it, he said, when they took refuge here. It is a cave that goes under the ice for many leagues, all the way to the other side of the mountains. He showed me where to find it. He keeps it walled up at this end so that no one can use it to reach the citadel, but he said he would open it for us."

Freya gazed at the wolf in admiration.

"In Skald we sometimes heard the dragon's roar in the wind, and none of us ever dared venture into this place. You have spoken to a serpent of the earth and returned to tell of it. Such a thing will make a great story for our sammings."

She turned to see Moth studying her.

"That is fine mail you are wearing," he said. "I was an armorer once, long ago."

"Thank you," Freya said, eyeing the archer curiously, and Will realized this was the first time they'd spoken to each other since they'd met below the glacier. And like Will when he first met Moth, Freya clearly didn't know what to make of him. "My father taught me the craft."

"Does Ragnar know you followed us, Freya?" Pendrake asked.

"I did not have time to tell him, Father Nicholas."

The toy maker sighed.

"You should go home, my child, but it's far too late for that. For better or worse, we must see this to its end together."

As always, Shade was eager to move on, but it was agreed by the company that a short rest was needed. Rowen still looked pale, and Pendrake was leaning heavily on his staff. There was no wood to make a fire, but they found refuge in a sheltered corner of the forecourt. There the toy maker saw to the company's injuries. The cut on Finn's forehead was not deep. He broke an icicle from the overhang of the archway and held it to the wound.

With all that had happened, Will had forgotten about his own injury. He was startled to discover that the creech's claw had cut an ugly gash under his ear. He hadn't felt it at the time, but as the toy maker covered the wound with a sweet-smelling salve, everything they had been through caught up with him at last. He began to shake uncontrollably and felt as if he might be sick.

Rowen sat next to him and put a hand on his arm.

"I never got a chance to thank you," she said.

Will realized that she was talking about the creech that had attacked her on the high stair.

"It wouldn't have made much difference if Shade hadn't been there," he said.

To his surprise, she smiled and kissed him softly on the cheek. While he sat in startled wonder, she gazed around the vast courtyard, and a troubled look came into her eyes.

"Does this place seem . . . strange to you?" she asked him.

"What do you mean?"

She reached down and put a hand to the ground.

"I don't know. Maybe it's nothing. But it's like the stone . . . *knows* we're here."

Will kept still for a moment, then shook his head.

"It just feels cold to me. The sooner we find somewhere warmer, the better." He had no idea what Rowen was talking about, but after what had happened to her in Skald, he thought it better not to question her too much. Something was taking place within her that he could not understand.

Rowen looked up at her grandfather, who was applying salve to the cut on Finn's forehead. She took a deep breath and nodded.

"I suppose you're right," she said brightly, but her eyes betrayed her.

When they were all ready to go on, the wolf led them under the archway and up the wide, curving staircase. The abandoned fortress was filled with a heavy, brooding silence, broken only by the echo of their own footsteps and the distant moan of the wind in the towers above. It was colder here inside the citadel, Will thought, than it had been on the ice.

Soon they came to a broad landing where a shaft of sunlight filled with swirling dust motes slanted down from an embrasure high on the wall. Three corridors branched off from here, one each to the right and left, and one straight ahead. Following the wolf, they took the left-hand passage, which Pendrake said had been sealed off by stones the last time he had been here. This corridor led, after a short distance, to a descending staircase that took them farther and farther from the light, until at last Will and his friends were feeling their way warily through a low-roofed tunnel in a gloomy twilight that grew thicker by the moment.

The toy maker brought out his lantern and on the company went, descending ever deeper. It was even colder here than in the citadel above, so that soon they had their cloaks wrapped tightly about them. The air was damp and stuffy, and any sound they made seemed to be swallowed up instantly.

They walked on and came eventually to a widening of the tunnel, where the roof rose higher above them. Here the air was not quite so stifling, but the heavy, almost suffocating stillness persisted. From time to time Morrigan sped on ahead into the tunnel and then returned to alight on Moth's shoulder. Each time she reported that there was nothing ahead but further darkness and silence.

After some time they heard the steady dripping of water and saw rivulets of meltwater trickling down the walls. The rough stone floor beneath their feet became more uneven, and in places held small pools of water. At one point Pendrake halted and raised his lantern higher. By its light they saw that the stone roof over their heads was riven by a great fissure, and within the fissure a vein of ice gleamed. The light rippled and darted across its wet surface.

"We're underneath the glacier now," Pendrake said. "There are hundreds of feet of solid ice above our heads."

They went on without speaking. The floor began to slope upward. The trickles of meltwater increased and flowed together into a stream that ran down a kind of trough in the middle of the tunnel floor. After they had struggled uphill for some time, Will noticed that the ice above them was glowing with its own pale radiance. He nudged Rowen, and they gazed in awe at the colors overhead, most often vivid shades of blue and green, but also violet, gold, and burnished silver. As they walked, the colors constantly changed and blended and seemed to flow. Will told Rowen about the northern lights he had watched with his family on winter evenings at home. She had never seen such a thing and had difficulty understanding what he meant.

A short time later they came out of the tunnel into a huge, vaulted cavern, roofed with ice supported by massive columns of stone. Along the walls, carved staircases rose to higher galleries, from which other passageways branched off into blackness and stony silence.

Before them, filling most of the cavern, lay a wide pool, its surface rippled by the innumerable drops of water falling from above. The ever-changing light filtering through the ice played over the cavern so that it glowed and glittered like a palace of gemstones. The light also fell in many shafts on the pool, casting rippling reflections like ghostly dancers upon the walls.

Morrigan soared up high, circled the cavern, and returned to report that there were many smaller chambers and halls branching off this one.

"This wasn't a refuge," said Finn, gazing up in wonder. "It was a city."

"But they abandoned it," Rowen added, and Will was alarmed to see how pale and strained her face looked.

"My people are not fond of enclosed places," Moth said. "It's clear that many lived here, but I would think that over the years more and more of them left to join the Green Court.

Until these halls became so lonely that no one wished to stay."

"Listen," Pendrake said, raising his hand. They all went still and heard faint flutelike sounds ringing in the air, some low and some high, harmonizing with one another.

"Wind in the ice tunnels," Moth said. "This was their music."

A gallery ran around the pool on one side, and Will and his friends followed it until they came to the entrance of another tunnel. Reluctantly they left the music and light of the great chamber and plunged back into darkness.

29

In the darkness, the Spirit awoke and danced.

— Apocryphal first verse of the Kantar

THEY SOON CAME TO ANOTHER CHAMBER, smaller than the first, but lit in the same way from above by light filtering through the ice. Here they found recesses in the stone walls, deep alcoves filled with ice, and with something else. Rowen paused at one of the recesses, leaned forward, then drew back with a sharp intake of breath.

"There's someone in there," she whispered. The rest of the company quickly gathered around. Within the ice stood a figure in scarred and dinted silver armor tarnished almost black, its arms folded across its chest and its hands gripping the hilt of a broken sword. A young man with long raven hair. His eyes were closed, and his head rested slightly to one side, as though he were sleeping.

"Is he dead?" Rowen asked shakily.

"Yes, and has been for a very long time," Moth said. He

raised a hand to touch the glasslike surface of the ice tomb. "He was one of my people. The inscriptions on his armor are from the days before the Great Unweaving."

They turned to inspect the nearby recesses and found other Shee in them as well, men and women. Each of them, like the first ice-entombed figure they had seen, could have been a sleeper who might waken at any moment.

"Let us pass on and disturb them no further," Moth said.

They prepared to move on, but Will turned back to see that Rowen had slumped down beside one of the tombs. At his shout they all gathered around her. She looked up at them with fear in her eyes.

"Is it the wound, Rowen?" Pendrake asked as he helped her to her feet.

"Can't you see them, Grandfather?" she breathed.

"The warriors in the ice? Yes. We've all seen them."

"No, the *others*," she said urgently. "Shadows, all around us."

Pendrake studied her. There was a look of pain in his eyes Will had never seen before.

"You're still feverish from the arrow," the toy maker said to Rowen. "We should leave here, find a better place for you to rest."

"No, that's not it," Rowen cried, pulling away from her grandfather. She reached a hand into empty air and then drew it back as if she had touched a flame.

"I can't touch them," she said. "They don't see me."

She walked slowly about the chamber, her hand still outstretched, like someone without sight. Will looked around and saw nothing but their own shadows cast on the floor by the icy light from above. He watched Rowen, saw her legs trembling. He came closer to her, ready to catch her if she fell. She did not seem to see him.

"They're not really here," she said at last. "Not now. They were here once, a long time ago. It's as if they're . . . echoes."

"Is it the Shee?" Moth asked.

"And others," Rowen answered, her eyes still following the movements of things unseen. "Many others. They sought safety here, with the Hidden Folk. Their stories had been destroyed. There was nowhere else for them to go."

She covered her mouth in horror. It was a long time before she could speak again.

"Some faded and became fetches," she went on. "Right before the eyes of their loved ones. There was so much sadness. So many stories died here."

She bowed her head and choked back a sob. Pendrake put his arm around her.

"This place would give anyone strange thoughts," Freya said. "The sooner we leave it, the better."

Rowen looked up searchingly at the toy maker.

"There's something else here, too. Something even older."

"I know, Rowen," Pendrake said softly. "Come, let's find a place to rest. There's more I have to tell you, but not here."

They made their way from the burial chamber, and after a short march the passage swiftly narrowed, until Will could touch both walls by stretching out his hands. At one point they found the tunnel walls had partly collapsed and a massive slab of stone lay across their path. It proved impossible to climb over and so they were forced to take off their packs and push them along while crawling underneath. The space was so narrow Will felt the stone pressing on him from above, and he had to struggle against the fear that at any moment it would fall and crush him.

When he was through, he turned to help Rowen. He took

her arm and felt her shaking, as if with cold, though he knew that was not the reason. She seemed to be struggling simply to go on, and at times he had to guide her, as if she could not see.

Beyond the slab the passage remained narrow and stifling. After a while Pendrake's waylight began to flicker and show signs that it might fail. With a few whispered words he coaxed the light into brightness, but it soon dimmed again, and then suddenly went out. In an instant they were enveloped in a darkness so total that Will had to suppress a cry of fear. He had not realized how completely his courage had depended on that one small source of illumination.

The toy maker's voice spoke out of the darkness.

"Even Sputter must rest. We will have to wait—"

He broke off, as they all became aware of another faint source of light. It was coming, Will realized, from the *gaal* blade, which Moth had pulled partway from its scabbard.

"It is night in the world outside," Moth said in a strained whisper.

Will wasn't sure how the archer knew the time of day, but he could feel the weariness in his bones that told him sleep was past due. To his relief a rest was agreed upon, and Shade's keen eyes quickly found some shelter not far ahead. It was the entrance to a side chamber that had been partially blocked with rubble. The companions had to squeeze through a narrow opening, but once inside, it was clear that a better refuge would not likely be found at short notice. Here they could fend off just about anything that might try to come at them.

Rowen ran her hand along the back wall of the chamber, then turned to her grandfather.

"It's the Stewards, isn't it?" she said. "They made all of this."

Pendrake was resting on a flat ledge of stone jutting from the wall.

"Tell me what you feel," he said quietly.

Rowen closed her eyes and kept her hand pressed to the wall.

"I can feel the Shee, and the others who were here with them," she said slowly. "But there's something deeper. It's moving, alive. Like a fish darting in a pond, just out of my reach. It's like I can *see* it, not with my eyes but with—"

She broke off and opened her eyes.

"Something is *awake*, in the stone. It's . . . familiar. Like a dream I had a long time ago but forgot until now. It's older than the Shee. Much older. I could feel it in Whitewing Stonegrinder when he touched me. Is he a Steward?"

"He is filled with their power, that much I am sure of. The Stewards shaped these tunnels and chambers. The stone carries their thought, their spark. You can touch it even more deeply than I can. The presence of the Stewards will give you strength, and guide you when you join with it."

"*Join* with it? How could I do that?"

Pendrake rose from his seat and placed a hand on Rowen's shoulder.

"Because it is already in you. It is who you are."

Rowen stared up at him.

"What are you talking about?" she blurted out. "The Stewards were not like us. They were not storyfolk or Wayfarers. My father was from Will's world. And you, and Mother—"

"In ancient time a Steward fell in love with a woman of the storyfolk. For her sake he took mortal shape. I am their descendant, Rowen, as was my father, and his mother, and those who came before us."

Rowen slowly shook her head.

"No, that can't be. . . ." she said, her voice falling to a whisper. "That's not possible."

"During the Broken Years," Pendrake went on, "the truth of it was lost. The loremasters of old knew only that they had a powerful gift, but not where it came from. Some used the gift for evil and became mighty storymages in the service of Malabron. When I was a child, my grandmother went deep into the Weaving to find out the truth. She was almost lost, but she found her way back and gave me as much of the history as she had been able to gather. She gave me my legacy. And now I pass it on to you. You, and I, and all loremasters who have come before us, are children of the First Ones."

Rowen backed away from him, looking around with frightened eyes, as if for some way of escape.

"When we first met, Master Pendrake, I thought you were one of them," Shade said. "I was not wrong."

"You cannot stop it, Rowen. To me, the shapes in the ice tombs were hardly visible at all. Whatever gifts I have, I had to learn and develop over many long years of wandering, gathering threads of the Kantar before they were lost forever. But for you . . . I feared what this journey might lead to, and so it has. The storyshard, your exposure to the werefire—"

"Why didn't you tell me?" Rowen demanded. Her eyes shimmered with tears.

Pendrake took her hands in his.

"When you were very young, your mother and father made me promise that if anything happened to them, I would keep you safe. I couldn't save them, I failed at that, but I could at least try to keep my promise."

He paused and took a deep breath.

"You must know, Rowen . . . their deaths were likely

not by chance, though I told you otherwise and wished to believe it myself. The loremasters have been hunted by Malabron since the Broken Years and before. They carry the power of the Stewards, and in them, in you, is the last hope of the Realm. The only way to keep my promise was to keep you hidden. To hide the truth, even from you, until you were ready to hear it. Or until I had no choice. Forgive me."

Rowen pulled her hands away from her grandfather's. She stood motionless, gazing past them all. Tears slid down her cheeks.

"They died . . . because of me," she said.

"No, child," Pendrake said hoarsely. "This began long before any of us. Blame will solve nothing. What we must do is defend what they lived for, and died for."

She didn't seem to hear him. After a long time she stirred and looked around at Will and the others.

"I want to leave this place," she said, and her voice sounded cold and lost.

Moth took first watch. Will lay down near Rowen, using Shade's flank as a warm pillow. It was so dark he wasn't sure for a moment whether he'd closed his eyes yet or not.

"Will?" Rowen whispered. She was an indistinct shape in the darkness.

"Yes?"

"I can still hear them. The storyfolk who took refuge here. I can hear them passing through the halls. Weeping. There's a child crying for its mother. It won't stop."

He heard her troubled breathing in the dark.

"I'm so tired," she said. "I want to sleep, but I can't."

Will struggled to think of something comforting to say. He remembered the fetch's voice in his head, but he wasn't going to tell Rowen about that.

"Tell me a story," Rowen said. "Tell me about where you come from. About the Untold."

"All right. What do you want to know?"

"Anything. Tell me about your life there."

Haltingly, Will began. He talked about Jess, and his father. And then he told her about his mother, and how she had died.

"I'm sorry, Will," Rowen said.

After a time he went on, and told her about his friends and the things they liked to do.

"What is a *video game*?" Rowen asked.

"Well, there's this special box called a television. With a window that shows you pictures."

"Like the movings you talked about."

"*Movies*. Yes. But in a game you can be one of the characters. You can move him, like a puppet. You can make him do things in the game."

"What things?"

"Well, like . . . fighting. Killing monsters and shooting bad guys."

"Like a story," Rowen said. "I see. Like Jack the Giant-killer. Or Conn the Clever. You have to defeat the monsters to end the story. To win the game."

"That's right."

"What happens if you don't win?"

"You die."

"Oh."

"But you can come back to life and try again."

He thought he should change the subject, so he told her about his other favorite pastime, football. When he ran out of things to say, Rowen was silent for a while.

"Why did you run away?" she said finally.

Will thought about that for a long moment.

"My dad got a new job, in another city," he said at last. "He said it would be good for us. But I was mad at him, and I didn't want to go."

"Why not?"

"I didn't want to leave my friends. And my home. It's where we lived when we were . . . all together."

"I understand," Rowen said. "You felt safe there."

Will waited for her to ask him more questions, but she did not speak. Finally he heard in the dark the steady rhythm of her breathing. Despite his troubled thoughts, he felt exhaustion pulling him into sleep.

What seemed like only moments later, Rowen was shaking him awake.

"We have to go," she whispered.

"Already?" Will mumbled groggily.

Shade had raised an alarm. His keen ears had picked up a sound not made by water or stone. The others listened but could hear nothing.

"It's the sound of many feet," the wolf said. "Many feet shod in metal. Coming up the tunnel the way we came."

Morrigan flew back down the tunnel and returned to tell Moth that she could hear what Shade had heard, although she couldn't see anything in the darkness. Whoever or whatever was approaching was moving very slowly, but without another word the companions left their shelter and carried on, Pendrake taking the lead with the waylight.

For what seemed like hours, they went on, stopping now and then to rest briefly. Shade did not hear the sounds again, but he paced like a caged animal whenever the company halted. The slight draft in the tunnel was blowing against them, so he could pick up no scent from the way they had come.

Eventually Pendrake's light began to dim again to a faint glow. He urged the others on.

"The way out cannot be much farther," he said, and in the gloom his voice seemed to come from far away. "There is fresher air in the tunnel."

"I smell it, too," Shade said. "But it means I can't pick up the scent of what's following us."

They went on quickly, and soon the tunnel began to plunge down at a much steeper angle than before. Sometimes there were steps carved in the floor, and sometimes there was only a slope of smooth, wet rock, so that they had to cling to the walls to descend without slipping. The air grew colder. After some time the floor leveled out again, but the darkness was as absolute as ever. Will trod carefully, his eyes staring into the blackness ahead, his hands never leaving the rock wall beside him. At times he thought he heard faint whisperings and glimpsed brief flickers of light, but he couldn't be sure that this wasn't his mind playing tricks.

Then the thought came to him that they might find the end of the tunnel sealed up, and he halted, seized by a fear that was close to panic.

Rowen, coming up closely behind, bumped into him.

"What is it?" she whispered.

"Nothing," he said shakily, relieved by the sound of her voice. "It's just this place."

"I know," she said.

Just then Shade gave a low growl, and Pendrake called for quiet. Everyone went still, and in the silence they all heard it at last, a faint but unmistakable sound of clinking metal, and the slow tread of feet.

No word of encouragement was needed now, as the companions set off at a near run. To Will's relief, he soon caught a faint glimmer of light on the walls and was glad to discover that everyone else could see it, too. They came around a bend and found themselves in a vaulted, echoing space, like the cavern of the pool but on a smaller scale. This chamber was lit from above not by a roof of ice but by slender embrasures in the stonework high above, letting in thin blades of cold blue light. The walls were ornamented with designs like those Will had seen on the stones of Aran Tir, and even the floor had intricate figures carved into it.

Will and the others gathered under the light, as if drawn to it hungrily after the long darkness. They looked up, blinking, and it quickly became clear to them that one more obstacle barred their way. A huge round stone, like a massive wheel, stood against the far wall, its lower rim sunk in a shallow depression in the floor. Small crystals or gemstones were set around its circumference. In the center was the carved figure of a Shee woman, holding up her right hand as if to warn away any who approached.

From the cold light that glowed dimly around the edges of the stone, the same as that from the window slits above, it was clear that beyond it lay an exit from the chamber and the caves.

Moth was first to reach the stone wheel. He pushed it from one side, but it did not budge. Finn and Freya went to his side, and together they planted their feet, lowered their heads, and pushed again. Nothing happened.

"We might have guessed," Finn said, giving the stone a halfhearted kick. "The last to leave sealed the door behind them."

Will's frightening thought had come true. He looked around frantically for another way out, thankful that at least there was some light in the chamber. If they had come to this dead end in the pitch-dark, with the sound of marching feet behind them, he would probably be frozen with panic.

"I don't see how they could have closed off the exit from outside," Pendrake said after briefly pondering in silence. "There must be some sort of mechanism here in the chamber that moves the stone."

At that they all fanned out to search except Freya, who took up watch at the tunnel entrance. There were many small grooves and crevices in the walls, but no matter how much Will and the others poked and prodded, not a sound was heard, and the stone did not budge. Morrigan flew up to the high places that the others could not reach and tapped with her beak at various protrusions and hollows, but to no avail.

Frustrated and growing more uneasy by the moment, Will found himself turning often to look at the figure carved in the stone. It seemed to be watching them with cold unconcern.

Then he looked again at the figure's hand and slowly raised his own.

With a shout he ran to the stone, reached up, and pressed his fingers and palm against the Shee woman's hand. To his disappointment, nothing happened.

"I thought she might be the key," Will said when Pendrake and the others approached. "I thought it wasn't a warning but a farewell to anyone leaving."

"I think you are right about that, Will," said Moth, joining him in front of the wheel, "but the hand is not the key; it is the lock."

The archer went up to the figure and just as Will had, he placed his hand on its hand. At first nothing happened, and then Rowen cried, "Look!" Will and Moth stood aside and saw that the crystals along the rim of the stone were now faintly glowing from within.

"They're wisps," Rowen exclaimed.

"They must have been left behind to wait for any Hidden

Folk that might return," Pendrake said. "Your touch woke them, Moth."

The crystals shrank to tiny points of brilliant light, and then, one by one, they sprang free of the stone wheel and flew bobbing and spinning like fireflies into the air. Soon a humming, pulsing host of wisps was circling above the heads of the company. Then one of the wisps descended, circled around Moth several times, and alighted on the edge of the stone wheel.

"They're going to move it," Rowen said in amazement. "That's how the door was sealed."

"Whatever's following us is almost here," Freya said urgently. In his surprise about the wisps, Will had ignored the sound of their marching pursuers, which had grown louder. But a new sound brought him back to the stone wheel. It was moving ponderously, rolling over the rough, rock-littered floor of the chamber with a deep rumbling that reminded Will of the noises the dragon had made. The wisps pulsed brightly in many colors as the stone moved under their power, but as it rolled away from the opening, their glow was swiftly dimmed by the flood of sunlight that now poured into the chamber. Will had been in the gloom of the caves for so long that he had to shield his eyes against the glare before he could see anything.

Beyond the opening, a short passage ran slightly upward to an archway filled with blue sky.

Pendrake urged the others forward with a wave of his staff. They all ran through the swiftly widening space between the turning wheel and the edge of the opening—Will and Shade, Rowen, Pendrake, Freya, and Finn. Once they were in the passage, Will turned, sensing that Moth was no longer behind them.

To his dismay, he saw that the archer was still inside the chamber, his sword drawn. The stone was already rolling back into place. There was no sign of Morrigan.

Will shouted the archer's name and the others turned.

"What are you doing?" Finn yelled at Moth. He ran to the stone and tried in vain to hold it back with his hands.

"If it is Lotan coming up the tunnel, he will be able to open this door, too," Moth shouted. "Go on, and don't look back."

"Maybe we can jam the opening shut from out here," Freya said, frantically searching the walls of the passage.

"No time," Moth said, and then he looked at Will. "Remember what I said. I will be there. No matter what."

He vanished from the opening, and the stone sealed it up with a cold, grating crunch.

30

*To provide, upon the accident of your disablement or death,
against the failure of your mission and the subsequent danger
to your party, you are authorized, by spoken command or by
any instrument signed and written in your own hand, to name
the person who shall take up the quest.*

— The Charter of the Errantry

NOTHING COULD BE DONE. The companions turned away
numbly from the sealed door. Then, at Pendrake's bidding,
they hurried together to the end of the passage, through the
archway, and into the open air.

To Will's surprise, the landscape that met his eyes was not
mantled in snow and ice. A rocky slope, dotted with lichen-
crusted boulders, descended steeply before them in rises and
hollows. They had come far enough from the ice field that
even a few hardy wildflowers were growing here and there
in the crevices of the stones. Where the companions stood,
above a dazzling carpet of clouds, the afternoon sun shone
down brightly, and the breeze carried a faint scent of green,
growing things. Will turned and gazed up at the mountain
behind them. A dark rock wall rose sheer to a forbidding
brow of ice. For a moment Will thought he glimpsed the

dragon far above, its wings outspread, but when he rubbed his eyes, dazzled by the glare outside the tunnel, he realized he was looking at a plume of snow streaming off a high ridge. They had left the home of Whitewing Stonegrinder far behind. The dragon would not leave it and come to their aid. They were on their own again, and now Moth was gone.

"We're on the high plateau above the Great Rampart," Pendrake said. "Only a league or two north of the Pass of the Needle's Eye, I would say."

"Then the hidden vale, and the wishing portal, can't be far away," said Finn. "The only question is, which way do we go from here?"

"Straight down, if we're not careful," Freya said. She had descended the farthest from the archway, and when they joined her, they saw that the slope fell away abruptly at her feet. A sheer cliff plummeted hundreds of feet to a deeply shadowed valley floor, where a river wound like a silver chain. Birds wheeled far below and wisps of cloud hung in the air. Beyond lay a wide land of woods and rolling hills that seemed to go on and on to the dusky rim of the world itself.

"The Great Rampart," Pendrake said. "Before us lie the Western Lands, the ancient homeland of the Shee."

"But no hidden vale, it seems," Freya said.

"Where's Rowen?" Will said, suddenly aware that she was not with them. It didn't take Shade long to pick up her trail.

"This way," the wolf called, nosing along the edge of the cliff to their left. Quickly the company followed him over a low rise. On the other side, a short distance ahead, the solid wall of the Rampart was cleaved by a wedge-shaped gorge that gashed deep, like a wound, into the mountainside. Rowen stood on its brink. When she heard the others approaching, she turned and waved them over. The rest of the company joined her at the rim of the gorge and gazed down.

"I think I've found the vale," she said simply.

Directly below them, nestled between the gorge walls, lay a slender patch of green dotted with trees. Thin rivulets of water streaming down the rock on all sides fed a kind of moat that ran almost all the way around a grassy island then poured out in two thundering cataracts at the vale's outer rim. The vale was a few hundred feet below the place where the companions stood, but still high above the base of the Rampart itself. Eagerly Will scanned it for a sign of anything that might be a gateway—the wishing portal that would take him home—but from this distance he could make out very little except the remains of stone walls, half buried in the grass. The walls were arranged in curves, like the paths of an ancient hedge maze. From above they could be seen to form a ring of concentric circles that might have been complete once, except for a jagged gap at the outer edge where it appeared that a part of the vale had broken off or crumbled away. Despite this marring of the design, from where Will stood it resembled a great emerald eye, gazing straight up into the heavens.

"The Needle's Eye," Pendrake said with wonder in his voice. "I had always thought the pass was so named because it was narrow and difficult to cross. I never suspected what was hidden so close by."

"This would have been a perfect refuge, until it began to collapse," Finn said. "The vale could not be seen from the foot of the Rampart, and few would dare climb the cliff."

"Such a fortress would have been worthy of the High Ones," Freya said in awe. "I wonder what happened to it."

"Perhaps the werefire caused much of this destruction," Pendrake said.

"It did," Rowen said, and they all turned to look at her. She was gazing down at the vale as if in a trance. "Not long ago. I see . . . the shadow of it. There was werefire, a lot of it. Like bolts of lightning shooting up. Then the rock split and fell away."

She turned to her grandfather with a bewildered expression.

"It's like someone . . . *tore* the world. Tore the fabric of things."

"The mages cut into the Weaving with spells like swords," Pendrake said gravely. He looked at Will, who read his thought with dismay. If part of the vale now lay at the bottom of the Great Rampart, the wishing portal might be there with it, buried under tons of broken stone.

There was only one way to find out. The companions backtracked along the rim of the gorge until they came to a rough path that appeared to lead, in a series of sharp zigzags, to the floor of the vale. The path was narrow, and Will shuffled along it cautiously, with his back pressed against the cliff face. Halfway down, they came to a flat, wide ledge that had been carved directly out of the cliff. They hurried along this wider, more level walkway, passing several narrow openings in the rock that led off into darkness. Will peered into them as he went past, wondering where they led.

As the companions descended, the sky began to darken as swift clouds moved in from the east. A chill wind swept into the gorge from above, bringing with it the scent of snow.

At last the walkway ended in a long steeply sloping ramp that took them swiftly to the bottom of the gorge. There the companions crossed the encircling moat by way of several large stones that jutted from the water and appeared to have once been part of a collapsed bridge. Once across, they debated what to do.

"The vale will take some time to explore," said Pendrake. "But I don't think we should risk splitting up."

"It happened there," Rowen said, pointing to the far end of the vale. "That's where the mages let out the werefire. That's where we should look."

There was no doubt in her voice, and Will looked at her wonderingly. Pendrake studied her briefly, as well, then took up his staff.

"Very well," he said.

They started off and soon passed between two arms of the ancient ring walls. These were sunk so low in the grass that Will could have easily scrambled over them. By this time the hint that the wind had given proved true: a few scattered flakes of snow began to fall, like white petals that melted as soon as they touched the earth.

"In the dream you told us about, didn't you see snow?" Rowen asked. Will turned in surprise. She was watching him. She had seen the troubled look on his face and must have guessed what he was thinking.

Will nodded.

"The Angel was there, too," he said uneasily. A feeling of dread churned in him like nausea. Reluctantly he hurried beside Shade, and soon they reached the center of the vale, a circular area of stonework ringed by the concentric walls. Here the ground descended slightly in a series of terraces to a great moss-covered stone, which stood at the center of the ring like the pointer of a giant sundial. A few yards beyond the stone lay the edge of the jagged gap they had seen from the rim of the gorge. The snow was quickly growing thicker, so that the enclosing walls of the gorge had already begun to vanish behind billowing white curtains.

A few thin tongues of werefire flickered here and there in the grass.

The companions descended to the base of the stone and gazed up at it. Finn bounded up the least steep side. He looked in all directions, blinking through the flurrying snow, then gave a shout and pointed to the gap.

"There's more werefire that way," he shouted.

The others followed his direction and walked cautiously to the edge of the gap. Their view was obscured at first by the swirling snow, but for a moment the wind swept it away and they had a clear view of what lay below them. The vale did not end in a sheer wall plummeting to the valley floor but tumbled steeply for several hundred yards, narrowing at last to a slender outcrop of rock that jutted out like the prow of a ship. The uttermost pinnacle of the rock was lit by a halo of werefire.

In the next instant the snow had closed in again and the vision was gone.

"I can't see any kind of gateway," Will shouted.

"We're looking for a *gateless* gate," said Pendrake, "whatever that may be. But down there is where the werefire is strongest."

"With this wet snow, the climb down will be treacherous," Freya said.

"I will go first," Shade said. "I can find the safest way down and then Will can follow."

Before anyone could move, Rowen cried out, "Someone's coming!"

31

Between one realm and another, there is but a breath.

— The Kantar

WILL WHIRLED AROUND but saw nothing. He peered through the pelting snow and then glimpsed what Rowen had seen: tall, dim figures advancing slowly from all directions, descending the tiers toward the stone. A score of them, or more, Will thought. Through the snow all that he could see for certain was that they wore dull, battered armor and carried pikes and swords.

"They must've been the ones following us in the caves," Finn said as the companions banded together at the edge of the gap.

"What are they?" cried Freya, gripping her hammer tightly.

"We've seen them before," Pendrake said in a voice shaken with weariness and defeat.

The leader was a man with long dark hair, carrying a

broken blade. His face was expressionless, his eyes as blank and lifeless as the snow that fell all around him. Will remembered the Shee in the ice tombs and a shudder ran through him.

"They are Tain Shee," said Finn, drawing his sword. "Or they were."

"They are the dead, inhabited by fetches," Pendrake said.

"Then Moth must be . . ." Rowen began.

She did not finish. Pendrake turned to Will, his face grim and pale.

"You can climb down to that outcrop, while we bar the way," he said. "Shade, you go with Will. And Rowen, you, too."

Rowen gave the loremaster a stricken look.

"Grandfather, no—" she began.

"If Will finds a farhold, you will go through it with him, into the Untold."

"I won't. I won't leave you here."

"Obey me, child. Your father came from that world. It is yours, too. You will be safe there, with Will."

Rowen's gaze traveled from Finn, to Freya, and back to her grandfather. She shook her head. Will stood beside her, struggling with his own tears.

"What about you?" he said to them.

"We can fight better with the two of you out of the way," Finn said. "If there is a wishing portal down there, you have a chance to keep Rowen out of danger."

Will nodded and gripped Shade's ruff.

"All right," he said, swallowing hard.

"Go with Will, Rowen," Freya said. "We will not let your grandfather fall."

Tears filled Rowen's eyes. Pendrake took her by the shoulders.

"I will find a way to bring you back after this is finished,"
he said to her. "I promise. Go now, before it's too late."

He raised his staff and stood beside Finn and Freya.

Shade moved first. He turned and started down the slope,
and Will and Rowen reluctantly followed. Moments later
they were already out of sight of their friends, and soon after
they heard shouts and the clash of metal. Rowen halted and
looked back. Shade urged her on with a nudge, and after a
long moment during which Will wasn't sure what she would
do, she turned and kept on.

The flying snow meant they could see only a few feet in front
of them, which made each step a frightening tread into the
unknown. Both Will and Rowen slipped on the wet, stony
turf and had to clutch Shade to keep from sliding helplessly
down the slope. And here on the Rampart's face, where there
was little shelter from the elements, the wind was free and
howled in their ears like a wild thing unleashed. The ground
beneath them shuddered, and stony chunks of earth thudded
and clattered past, some of them trailing green flames. It was
clear that the werefire was still at work here.

At last they reached the outcrop and began to step out
warily onto its narrow surface, Shade taking the lead. Once
more Rowen paused and looked back. So did Will, but the
top of the slope was already hidden from view, and the
shriek of the wind was so loud there was no way to know
what was happening to their companions up above.

Will and Rowen looked at each other. What he saw in her
eyes filled him with a fierce protectiveness and resolve: for
the first time, it was she who was looking to him for courage, for a reason to keep going. At that moment he knew he
would do anything for her.

"Come on," he said as he took her hand in his. She gripped his hand tightly in response, and they went on.

The outcrop was slippery with wet snow, and Will kept his eyes on the rock until Shade suddenly grunted, and he looked up. They were nearing the pinnacle, silhouetted with flickering werefire, and now Will noticed that the wind had fallen to a low keening. The snow, still thick and obscuring, fluttered straight down, lit eerily by the glow of the werefire.

If Will took another few steps, he would come to the very edge of the precipice. The only journey he would make from there was a plummet to the bottom of the Great Rampart. Rowen turned in a circle, anguish in her eyes.

"There's nothing here, Will," she shouted. "If there was a farhold, it must have collapsed. We should go back."

Will knew she was right, but he could not bring himself to leave. His friends had risked their lives for him, and to come this far only to fail meant it was all in vain. He struggled to remember what the mage Strigon had said. *It was not there, and then it was there . . . a gateless gate.* In desperation he bowed his head and tried to clear his thoughts, in the way that had guided him to Shade, to the knot-path, to the keep in Skald. Instead, he saw only the lifeless face of the dead Shee warrior in the ice tomb, and his thoughts went out to the toy maker, Finn, and Freya. At this very moment they could be hurt. Dying. Their stories did not deserve an ending like this.

He heard a sharp intake of breath from Rowen and opened his eyes.

Everywhere, as before, the falling snow had turned the world to a wilderness of flurrying gloom, except at the summit of the outcrop. There the halo of werefire had intensified, almost solidified, into an arch that seemed to be holding back the snow, leaving a brighter space of light within, as if invisible hands had drawn aside a curtain.

"A gateless gate," Rowen whispered.

"Did you do that, Will Lightfoot?" Shade asked.

"No, I couldn't have."

"I did it," Rowen said, and there was disbelief and fear in her voice. "The portal was still there. I just didn't see it at first. It's almost *not* there. I don't know what I did, but it's open. For now."

Will took a step closer. Within the open space a warm light, like sunset through a fine mist, had begun to grow. He caught the scent of flowers, heard the whisper of wind among green leaves.

"Hurry, Will," Rowen urged him. "It won't stay open much longer. I can feel it closing. Go."

Will turned to her.

"You're not coming with me," he said, already knowing what she had decided.

"I have to go back," Rowen said, her face pale but determined. "I can't leave my grandfather."

"Rowen, no—"

"I'm going, Will. I'm sorry."

"Shade goes with you, then," Will said.

"Only once you're home, Will Lightfoot," the wolf said. "That was my promise."

"Then I discharge you from your promise," Will said, his voice shaking. "I don't want you here. *Go.*"

Both Rowen and the wolf stared at him. Then Rowen threw her arms around Will. She stepped away, brushing tears from her eyes.

"Good-bye, Will," she said in a trembling voice.

"I'll come back," Will said. "Somehow. I'll find a way."

"I know."

"Farewell, Will Lightfoot," Shade said.

"Good-bye, Shade," Will said, choking back tears. "You're free now."

"I was always free," the wolf said. "I am here because we are friends."

Together Rowen and the wolf turned away and hurried back from the precipice. Will watched them until they had vanished into the snow. Then he turned and stepped up slowly to the farhold, half expecting the gate to waver and vanish before his eyes, like a mirage.

He took another step, and now he was directly before the farhold. He caught the damp, cool scent of the woods where he had abandoned the motorcycle. He knew that all he had to do was pass through this gateway, holding the image of home in his thoughts, and he would be there. Away from this story he wasn't supposed to be in. Back to his own life, to Dad, and Jess.

Just as he was about to step through, he thought he heard a faint cry. He halted and looked back, straining to hear. The cry did not come again, and he could see nothing but snow and rock. He wasn't even sure he had heard anything other than the shriek of the wind.

He turned to the farhold, took another step, and then stopped.

"No," he said under his breath. "This isn't right. Not like this."

He turned into the flying snow and ran back along from the pinnacle. He ran until the veil of snow thinned and there, at the base of the outcrop, stood Rowen, her knife held out before her. Shade lay beside her, struggling to rise.

Standing over both of them like a shape of rising fog was a tall figure robed and hooded in white.

Dread seized Will. He knew who it was. As he watched in horror, Rowen screamed, dropped her knife, and staggered backward. The figure stooped and with one hand lifted her by the collar of her cloak. Its other hand, wrapped in ribbons of white as if bandaged, reached toward her face, for some purpose Will could not guess.

"Get away from her!" he shouted, and without another thought he rushed forward. The figure straightened and looked toward him, its face still unseen within the shadows of the hood. Then its arm swept out like a whip and knocked Will aside. He struck the ground hard and rolled to the edge of the outcrop, just managing to clutch at the rock before he went over. As he crawled back onto the pinnacle, he felt an ice-cold shadow fall over him.

"Will Lightfoot," an all-too-familiar voice said, chilling him to the heart. "This is where the story ends."

32

Armor of earth,
Cloak of air,
Shield of water,
Sword of fire.

— Ancient invocation against evil

WILL CHOKED BACK A CRY as Rowen began to vanish into the folds and shadows of the shrowde.

"What are you doing to her?" he shouted. "Leave her alone!"

The Angel turned to him, the face within the ragged hood still concealed, as if by shadows of its own weaving.

"You and your companions have surprised me, Will Lightfoot," the Angel said. "Even dragons take your side. But in the end you played your role, as my master foresaw."

He raised his hand, and there was a loud crack like thunder. The rock beneath the farhold shuddered and then collapsed. The opening within the snow now hovered in space, out of Will's reach. As he watched in despair, the snow began to obscure the gateway again. It was shrinking, narrowing like curtains slowly falling together.

"One more doorway sealed forever," the Angel intoned, as if he was presiding at some dark ceremony. "The memory of the Stewards fades. Their story becomes legend, rumor, lies, and finally, nothing at all. A meaningless word drifting on the wind."

"Let Rowen go," Will said desperately. "It was me you wanted."

The hood turned again in his direction, and a chilling sound came from it, a sound like stone scraping over stone, that Will realized was laughter.

"I *was* looking for you, Will Lightfoot," the Angel said, "but only because I knew that you could lead me to *her*. She is the new thread in the weave that my master seeks. You thought you were the hero of this tale. But you were only a means to an end. Your part is finished. That should please you."

As he spoke, Rowen vanished into the shrowde.

"You don't have to do this!" Will shouted, and then a sudden understanding shot through him. "You want to be free from *him*, too."

As soon as he said it, he knew it was true. He had heard it in the Angel's voice. For a long moment Lotan did not speak or move. The gray shadows within the hood of the shrowde seemed to churn like storm clouds.

"You do not yet understand," Lotan finally said, and once more his voice was cold and lifeless. "Look upon me. I am the Angel of Despair. This is *my* part to play. It could not have been otherwise."

With that the shrowde billowed into the air, and before Will could think or act, the Angel had soared over the edge of the outcrop and was gone.

Will scrambled to his feet. There was a stabbing pain in his chest where the shrowde had struck him.

Shade still lay unmoving nearby. The farhold was a thin

gap, swiftly closing. Will stood helplessly before it, and then, as in the forest when he found the knot-path, the feeling came over him that there was something only he could do. The story he had tried to deny had gathered itself around him in this moment and now everything depended upon what he chose. Rowen was the last hope of the Realm, Pendrake had said. This was her story. She had to survive.

There was no more time to think. He ran for the edge of the outcrop and jumped toward the farhold.

"Take me to Rowen!" he shouted.

The wind shrieked in his ears. He was falling, plummeting into a roaring, snowy abyss. He screamed and shut his eyes in terror. The next thing he knew, there was a violent lurch, as though he had come to a sudden stop.

Will opened his eyes. He could see nothing but a swirling of whiteness and gray shadows. His body seemed to be floating in empty space. He struggled to gain some kind of hold or solid ground, then felt something constrict around him like the cold sliding grip of a python.

He was inside the shrowde. But it was more than a cloak for the Angel, he realized. The thing was somehow larger or deeper than it seemed from the outside. Something with a mind and will. He felt that if it wished, it could pull him down into a bottomless white nothingness from which he would never return. Rowen must be in here somewhere, too, he thought with a surge of fear. And the Angel, but Will could not see or feel him, and for that small mercy he was grateful.

The shrowde shifted and flowed around him, and for one terrifying moment its folds parted, and Will glimpsed the bone-white claws of the Angel, scuttling over cracks in the rock like horrible eyeless spiders.

The Angel was climbing headfirst down the sheer way of the Rampart.

Will thought of his knife. It had been made to cut creatures no ordinary blade could harm, Finn had told him. Slowly he brought his hand down to his side, but even as he did so, he faltered, remembering that Rowen was in the shrowde with him. If he started slashing blindly, he could hurt her. Or the shrowde might let them go, and they would fall. But he had no choice. Without the knife, he and Rowen had no chance at all.

His fingers never made it to the hilt. As though it sensed what he was about to do, the shrowde tightened its grip. His hand was immobilized as if it had been encased in concrete, and then the shrowde began to squeeze. Pain shot up Will's arm, and he gasped.

There was a rush of wind, and Will felt a dizzying sense of weightlessness. He had a final glimpse of the cliff wall soaring above them and then all was whiteness again.

Without warning Will was thrown roughly from the shrowde, out onto the ground. He was in a clearing ringed by dark trees. Rowen lay near him, still and pale. For a terrible moment he thought she was dead, then he saw the faint rise and fall of her breathing. The Angel stood over both of them, but his attention was not on Will or Rowen. He turned this way and that, his hooded head raised to the air, as if he had caught a sound or scent that troubled him but could not find the source. Finally the hood turned in Will's direction, and Lotan's voice came from the shadows within.

"Since you've chosen to join your friend on her final journey, you can earn your passage," he said. "*Knot-paths.* You found one before and almost escaped me. Now you will find another. One that will take us far from here."

"I won't help you," Will managed to whisper.

"I can still call off the fetches and perhaps save the lives of your friends on the Rampart. *If* they still live. Or I can let the fetches finish their work."

Will clenched his fists, struggling for words of defiance, for some weapon to hurl at his enemy. Then he hung his head and choked back a sob. He had failed. He was lost. Everything his friends had gone through for him had been in vain.

"No," he said, defeated. "I'll do it. I'll find a path."

He rose shakily to his feet and gazed slowly around. The Angel moved closer to him. As he had in the forest of Eldark, Will tried simply to be aware of all that was happening around him, not trying to shut it out or see beyond it. He breathed deeply as he had before, but his thoughts would not settle. The presence of the Angel was like an unending scream in his mind. His thoughts kept returning to his friends, to ways that he might still escape, even though he knew it was hopeless. He remembered the trick he had played on the Marrowbone brothers. There was no chance anything like that would work on the Angel.

He thought of his knife and glanced down. It was still on his hip, in its sheath. The Angel had not taken it from him. But if he hadn't, it must be that he didn't see it, or Will, as any threat. The thought only deepened Will's despair. Then something touched his memory, like a tiny glimmer of light.

What was it Finn had said during sword practice at Appleyard? *In combat you always have two weapons. Yours and your opponent's.*

The only weapon the Angel had used against him so far was . . . fear. But was the Angel himself afraid of anything?

"It's no use," Will said at last. "I can't see anything."

"It is because you still hope," the Angel said. "Do not

distract yourself with such vain thoughts. You and the girl are already characters in the story where hope dies."

Will took a deep breath and tensed himself. He had the knife, and his own hands. It would not be enough, but there was nothing else. He looked at Rowen, who still had not stirred. Maybe he could buy her a few moments. One more small chance. As he reached for the blade, he heard a new note on the wind, a swift beat of wings. He looked up just as a black shape swooped down out of the trees and soared over his head with a piercing shriek. Will whirled in time to see ragged black wings and talons before the shadow shot skyward again and vanished.

Morrigan. Will's heart leaped.

He turned away from the Angel, and there on the far side of the clearing was Moth. He was silhouetted by the light of the setting sun, but there was no doubt it was the archer.

For a long moment neither he nor the Angel moved or made a sound. Will longed to run toward Moth, but the silence itself seemed to keep him rooted where he was, so that all he could do was watch what was about to unfold.

At last the Angel stepped forward. He slowly drew back his ragged white hood, and Will cried out. The face before him was a hideous semblance of the one he had seen in his dream. Lotan's hair was white, as before, but the face was a livid mask of raw flesh. The eyes were black holes, the mouth a wound.

"Nightwanderer," the Angel said. "After so long. I knew this boy had a Shee with him whom I looked forward to killing, but I did not know it would be you. And that is your sister, of course. I remember her well. The frantic beating of her heart, as I held her in my hand. Once she had wanted nothing more than to be by my side. Then she only thought to flee. I let her, because I knew that in the end it would make no difference. One by one, the Shee would fall. This day had to come."

Moth said nothing. From the dragon-bone sheath he slowly drew the sword of *gaal* and held it before him. The Angel shuddered and took a step back.

"I have your freedom in my hand, Lotan," Moth said, untying his cloak and letting it fall. "We both knew this day would come."

"There is no freedom here or in my master's domain," Lotan hissed, and the mask of his face contorted with rage. "You will learn that now, as I learned it long ago. Have you never understood?"

His voice dropped to a rasping whisper.

"I cared only to help my people. I was ready to give my life for them. And so I stood against him, and I stared into the abyss at the end of all stories, and it swallowed me whole. As it will swallow you, and you will know that your story already belongs to my master, to shape, to end, as he wishes. And then you will think no more about freedom."

From the folds of his cloak, he drew forth a bloodred sword. As he moved slowly toward Moth, a slanted bar of sunlight fell across him, and for an instant his face twisted with pain.

The shrowde protects him, Will thought, remembering what Moth had told him. *It hides him from the light.*

"You made this sword for me, so long ago," the Angel said. "It has lost none of its power. While you have become a pale shadow of what you once were."

"But you have not changed, Lotan," Moth said. "You are still an emptiness wrapped in a cloak of lies."

The Angel snarled and launched himself through the air.

Moth braced to meet him and their blades clashed. What followed was so furious and quick, Will could barely follow the moves of the two opponents. The swords crashed and rang in the clearing like flashes of lightning. Back and forth the combatants thrust and parried, and in the red light of sunset it seemed that fire ran along their blades. Then Moth came on with a flurry of blows that put Lotan on the defensive and forced him backward. His arm faltered, and the blade of *gaal* swept down and knocked his sword from his hand.

The Angel staggered and would have fallen, but in the next instant one ragged shred of his cloak shot out with the sound of a whip and wrapped itself like a tentacle around Moth's sword-arm.

The archer struggled to free himself, but the shrowde pulled him off balance, and the sword slipped from his grasp. Another tendril of the cloak caught the blade as it fell and flung it away into the shadows. Then, faster than Will could see, the Angel's sword was somehow back in his hand. With a scream he stabbed at Moth, and his red blade found its mark.

Will's heart went cold.

Moth sank slowly to his knees. The Angel pulled his blade free and stood over the archer.

"Now you see, Nightwanderer," Lotan said almost gently. "This is how all stories end. Die knowing you failed everyone you pledged to save."

He raised his blade for a final stroke, but it did not fall. He had forgotten Will, who had crept close with his knife drawn. As Will sprang forward, Lotan heard him and easily dodged his knife. But it was not meant for him: instead Will plunged the blade through the folds of his white cloak and into the ground.

The shrowde shuddered and writhed like a blazing white fire. But it had been caught by the tip of Will's blade and as Lotan leaped aside, the shrowde was torn away from him.

The Angel stood uncloaked.

Without the shrowde he was a gaunt form of rotting flesh and chain mail that had fused into one hideous mass of corruption. The thing that had once been a man raised its arm against the light of the setting sun, its face twisted with such absolute hatred that Will felt his courage wither as though it had been blasted by a fire. He let go of his knife and fell backward.

The shrowde tore free of Will's blade, rose from the grass, and flowed like a deadly fog over its master.

"You ... will suffer ... *agonies* for this," Lotan snarled. He advanced toward Will with his sword raised.

There was a rush of wings, and from behind the Angel, Morrigan swooped into the clearing, the *gaal* sword clutched in her talons. As she passed over her brother, she let the blade fall. With a terrible cry Moth lurched to his feet, caught the sword as it fell, and lunged.

Lotan whirled to face this new threat, but he was too late. With a sound like the hiss of hot metal plunged into icy water, the blade of *gaal* passed through him.

To Will it seemed as if the world held its breath.

Moth let go of the sword, stumbled away from his enemy, and fell to the earth. Lotan made no sound, but his flesh began to peel and blacken, like paper caught in a fire. He staggered forward, clutching at the blade that transfixed him, but he could not grasp it: already he was crumbling into shreds and pieces, his lifeless flesh cracking and falling away. After groping blindly about him, he gave up struggling at last. His arms fell to his sides. His face turned to Will, and there was no hatred in it now. A pale light flared in the dead sockets of the eyes and then died. The breath fled in a long sigh.

The Angel sank upon his own collapsing form like a pyre of dying coals.

The shrowde itself churned and seethed like boiling water, then tore free of Lotan's remains. It writhed in the air and then caught on the bare limb of a tree, where it went limp and stirred faintly in the wind.

Flecks of ash whirled like funereal snowflakes. In another moment there was nothing left where Lotan had been but the *gaal* sword, lying on the grass amid a scattering of mirror shards. While Will gazed in stunned silence, the blade itself crumbled swiftly into dust.

Will crawled to where Rowen lay, and she groaned, and stirred. She was still alive. Will bent close to her, heard the sound of her breathing. Then he rose and staggered over to Moth. The archer was lying with his head against a mossy stone. He was trembling and his breath came in wrenching gasps.

Will knelt beside him, tears streaming down his face.

"Moth," he said, touching the archer's cold hand. "I'll find Master Pendrake. He'll be able to help. . . ."

Moth's eyes seemed to be searching for Will in shadows, and then they fixed on him. The archer smiled.

"We are both going home, Will."

He shut his eyes and uttered a gasp of pain, his body wracked with tremors. When he opened his eyes again, he looked past Will and tried to rise.

"Is she here?" he asked. For an instant Will's mind was blank, and then he thought of Morrigan. He searched for her, but by now the sun had set and the clearing was falling into deep shadow. There was no sign of the raven up in the trees, and then his eye was caught by a dark shape huddled in the grass nearby. It was too large to be Morrigan, he thought, even though it seemed to be covered in black feathers. And then understanding dawned, and Will remembered the story of the Angel's spell. He rose, went over to the huddled form, and knelt.

"Morrigan?"

The figure stirred and lifted its head. It was a young woman with long black hair, her face as thin and dusky as Moth's. Her eyes burned and gazed past or through Will as if she could not see him. She was wrapped in a ragged cloak of black feathers and although beads of sweat were running down her face, she was shivering with cold.

She's dying, too, Will thought. *She carried the* gaal *sword without the sheath.*

He spoke her name again, as softly as he could, and at last she seemed to recognize him, and smiled. Then fear came into her eyes, and she looked wildly around the glade.

"He's here," Will said. He helped Morrigan rise and walk to her brother. She knelt beside him and touched his forehead, and the tears slid down her face. Moth's eyes opened, and he saw her. He raised a hand to stroke her hair. Then a shudder ran through him, and his hand dropped to his side. His breath came out in a long sigh, and his eyes grew fixed and unseeing.

Morrigan lifted her brother's hand to her face, and tears fell upon it. She laid her head on his chest and wept.

"I'll find the others," Will stammered, choking back tears. "I'll get help."

He looked at Rowen once more, then turned away and ran into the forest, calling the names of the toy maker and Finn. He called and called until his voice cracked and gave out, and then he ran on silently, the tears blinding him so that he crashed into low branches and stumbled over roots. He ran on and on into the night, knowing that he was running from his own fear and grief, and that he was lost in an unknown land and he would never get home.

At last, in the utter blackness, he tripped and fell. When he picked himself up, his head spinning, he heard soft voices and saw dim, drifting lights all around him. He shook his head and his sight cleared. The lights became a ring of tall, pale figures, slowly advancing toward him through the trees.

Will's only thought was that the fetches had found him again. He had run as far as he could, and it was not far enough. There was no place the Lord of Story could not reach. His last hope, his last strength slipped away. Shadows clouded his vision, and he fell headlong into darkness.

33

You will journey to strange storylands and meet folk unlike any you have ever seen. Do not think you can pass through these lands unchanged. They will work upon you like the wind and the rain and the long days of your solitary wandering. You will play a part in these tales, and they will become part of you.

— The Book of Errantry

THERE WAS A GOLDEN LIGHT upon his eyelids and the sound of birds singing.

Will opened his eyes. Above him he saw what looked like wide sheets of patched green cloth, held up by poles of peeled white wood. In the center of all this was a circle of blue sky. He was in some kind of tent with an open roof.

He had been running from something. . . . He was lost.

There had to be more, but the memories lay just beyond his reach.

Will sat up, wincing at the stiffness in his arms and legs. Near the pallet of thick quilts on which he was lying sat a woman in a faded blue robe, tending a small fire. The odd thought came to him that she was neither young nor old, and in fact she seemed somehow difficult to see clearly. All he knew for certain was that he had never seen her before.

When he moved, the woman looked up and smiled.

"Awake at last," she said. "Your friends will be glad." She poured a clear liquid from a jug on a small table and brought it to him. He took the cup and looked into it, caught a faint bitter scent. Someone had given him a drink like this, not long ago. . . .

What he had been trying to remember returned to him like the cold bite of a blade.

"Where is Moth?" he asked.

The woman shook her head.

"He is gone," she said, and there was sadness in her voice. "His hurt was deep and could not be healed. Drink. It will help you regain your strength."

Will took a sip of the liquid and then shook his head and fought back tears. He did not know where he was, but the woman was kind, and by the sound of her voice alone he knew that she was not his enemy. From the look of her robe and the worn tent, he must have been found by a band of homeless, exiled folk, like those they had met on their way to Skald.

Then another terrible memory came to him.

"Your other companions are well and whole," the woman said, as if she had read his thoughts. "Two of them are here with you."

Will looked up through his tears. The woman gestured to the far side of the tent, and Will saw Shade there, curled up on a thick bed of straw, and beside him, on a pallet like his own, lay Rowen.

"Are they—"

"They are sleeping," the woman said, and joy and relief flooded through Will. "The Companion was badly hurt, but he will mend. And the other one, the one who won't listen to reason, is finally getting some rest. She was wounded,

too, but still she insisted on staying awake at your side
all through the night and most of this day. That is how
long you have been asleep. You suffered great harm, more
than you know, and you needed healing. It's fortunate that
you found us when you did."

"Master Pendrake, Finn, and Freya," Will said. "Where
are they?"

"Not far away, I believe. Do you wish to see them?"

Will nodded eagerly. He pulled off his blankets and now
noticed that his clothes were fresh and spotlessly clean. He
looked up at the woman.

"Last night in the forest . . ." he began as he climbed from
the pallet. "I thought you were—" He broke off, unable to
name the horrors that seemed, in the light of day, like a fading nightmare. Then another thought occurred to him.

"The Angel," he said, his voice dropping to a whisper.
"Is he really dead?"

"The one given that name died a long time ago," the
woman said. "But his spirit at last knows rest. You are safe
from his master, at least for a time. Go. I will watch over your
friends."

Will walked across the rush-strewn floor of the tent to
the opening, where he stopped abruptly, struck by a sudden
realization. This woman seemed to know the whole story
of what had happened to them. She had called Shade the
Companion, and she knew who the Angel was. Had the loremaster told her everything? Before he could turn back to her
with these new questions, he spotted Pendrake, Finn, and
Freya through the open flap of the tent, standing together
in conversation with a tall, silver-haired man in a long gray
cloak. Will slipped eagerly outside.

The tent, he saw now, was pitched on a wide grassy lawn,
in the midst of a forest of young, slender trees with bright

leaves. His friends turned at his call. Finn's arm was bound in a sling, and the old man had a cut down the side of his face, but they greeted Will with embraces and laughter. In the toy maker's eyes Will saw both sadness and joy.

"You should have been back at home by now," Freya said, regarding him with a wide smile. "And so should I."

The tall man in gray bowed to Will, then left them and strode away through the trees.

"Welcome back, Will," Pendrake said. "I know you hoped to be safely home by now, but if it wasn't for you, Rowen might not be with us."

"It was Moth who saved us both," Will said. "And these people, whoever they are. If they hadn't been nearby . . ."

Through the trees Will caught a glimpse of other tents, and other figures in gray and green moving about, tending fires, or leading horses.

"We've all been invited to the evening meal," Pendrake said. "There we will say a final farewell to Moth."

"I don't know how he found me," Will said. "Or how he got out of the caves. . . ."

"Moth joined us at the stone and helped us defeat the fetches," said Freya. "He told us what had happened."

"Lotan came up the tunnel with the fetches," Finn said. "He wove a spell of darkness that swept over the wisps and doused their sparks. Then he fled, taking his dead army down through another tunnel that led to the hidden vale. Moth followed, and when we had dealt with the fetches, he went on to find you."

"I wonder how he got down the Rampart," Finn mused.

"I suspect," Pendrake said, stroking his beard, "that over the years he learned something of flight from his sister."

"Is Morrigan here?" Will asked, startled. He had thought she was dead, too.

"She came close to death from the touch of the *gaal* blade. But she was brought back by the arts that healed you, too, Will. She is resting now, in another of the tents, with her friends and kin beside her."

"Her kin . . ." Will said slowly. "You mean there are other Hidden Folk here?"

He looked around eagerly, until Pendrake's soft laughter brought his gaze back to his friends. They were smiling at him.

"Who do you think met you in the forest last night?" Freya said, grinning. "And brought us to you?"

"And just invited us all to dinner," Pendrake added.

Like a ray of sunlight through clouds, the truth broke upon Will.

"But their tents and clothing . . ." he began. "They're just like us."

"Or we are just like them," the old man said, and laughed. "When we're at our best. I believe we see them as they wish to be seen. That is one way they remain hidden from their enemies. And from those who've slept too long and need to clear the cobwebs out of their heads."

"But why are they here?" Will asked. "How did they find us?"

"Did they?" Pendrake replied. "Maybe you found them. But perhaps the Lady can enlighten us on that point at dinner."

The Lady, Will thought. He was really going to meet her, at last. And with that thought came another that took a weight from his heart. There was no longer anything pursuing him. He had not brought danger and disaster to the Green Court. And maybe, at last, he could go home.

The companions talked quietly about their hosts for a while, and then they heard a sound and turned. Rowen and Shade were coming out of the tent toward them. The wolf was limping badly, but his tail started to wag when he saw Will. Then he seemed to become conscious of his canine eagerness, and his tail went still. Will ran to Shade and threw his arms around the wolf's neck.

"I am very glad to see you, too, Will Lightfoot," the wolf said huskily.

Will stood, and he and Rowen looked at each other without speaking. There was so much to say, Will thought, and he knew Rowen felt the same.

"You found me," Rowen said at last. "You saved my life. But you didn't get home."

"You're here," Will said. "That's what matters."

In her face he saw something he had never seen there before, a shadow of lingering pain. She smiled at him, and he saw the effort it took. She was further away from him now, in some way he didn't understand. How could he know what was happening to her? All he felt was sadness, and worry for her.

Then he remembered what the Angel had said to him about Rowen, and he wondered if she knew. He would have to speak with her about it, but he couldn't bring himself to do it. Not yet.

As the sun went down behind the treetops, two young men of the Hidden Folk came to bring the companions to the evening meal.

They were led through the trees and down a slope to the bank of a swiftly flowing river. Here many of the Hidden Folk were gathered, sitting on colorful silk cloths spread upon the grass. Will and his friends were welcomed with smiles and kind words, and sat among them.

Morrigan was there, dressed in dark green now, like the

others. Her face was pale and weary-looking, but in her eyes
Will caught the same quick gleam of fire he had seen in her
brother's. He wanted to tell her how much he admired Moth,
how grateful he was, but the words caught in his throat. If
it hadn't been for him, Moth would still be with them. He
looked away, ashamed, and then she spoke.

"Do not blame yourself, Will," she said, and smiled at
him. "My brother and I chose our road a long time ago."

Food and drink were now passed around—bread and
cheese and fruit on simple wooden platters, with cool water to
wash it down. It was plain food, but just what they needed.

When everyone had eaten their fill, a young woman
stood and sang a slow, mournful song in the language of the
Hidden Folk. Will knew somehow that she was singing of
the vanished city of Eleel, and he also knew when the song
changed and became a lament for Moth the Nightwanderer,
who had at last come home to his people. As the singer fell
silent, the Hidden Folk bowed their heads and many wept.
Will and his friends shed tears with them.

Master Pendrake stood then and recounted the story of
how he had first met Moth, and how they had become good
friends, and all that the archer had done for Will and his companions on the journey. After him others told stories about
their friend. Some remembered him as a child, mischievous
and full of laughter. Others remembered him at his forge in
the time of war and spoke of his bravery in the dark days
that followed, before he and Morrigan went their own way.

As these tales came to an end, Will caught a movement
out of the corner of his eye. He looked toward the river, and
there was a long white boat, low in the water like a barge,
gliding to the bank, with two Shee in gleaming white armor
standing at the bow and another at the stern. Everyone rose,
and as the boat came to rest, Will saw that Moth was lying

in it, his arms folded on his breast. There was a silver jewel on his brow.

Morrigan turned to Will and his friends and bowed. She walked down to the river's edge, climbed into the boat, and sat beside her brother. The boat slid away from the bank and glided slowly away over the water.

"He will travel down the River Bel to the sea," a voice said from somewhere near Will. "He will rest in one of our blessed places."

Will turned, and there was the woman he had met when he awoke in the tent. In the sunset her dark hair was fringed with gold, and her blue robe, Will now saw, was richly embroidered with tiny stars that glowed like warm embers in the fading light. He still could not say that she was young or old, but now, he thought, he could see her very well, and at last he knew who she was. At her side stood the tall silver-haired man Will had met earlier.

"I didn't get to thank him," Will said of Moth. "He saved my life. I wish . . . I wish none of this had happened."

"He would wish you to live your life well," the Lady said. "With courage and joy. That is how each of us can thank him."

Her words brought him both pain and comfort, and his eyes filled with tears.

Will had no idea how long they sat and talked with the Hidden Folk. It seemed hours, but when the company rose at last, the sun was no lower in the west, as far as he could tell, than when they had first sat down.

"Rest here tonight in peace and safety," the Lady said at last to Will and his friends. "Those that hunted you are gone. For a short time at least the shadows will withdraw from these lands."

She turned to Pendrake.

"Loremaster, your road home will be long and danger-ous. We must part now, but in the morning a company of our folk will go with you and see you safely to the borders of your own country."

Pendrake thanked her, and then she turned to Rowen.

"You have traveled far, Rowen of Blue Hill," she said. "But this is only the beginning of a longer and more difficult journey. It will take all that you are, but I see much strength in you, and the light of the First Ones. Do not despair."

As Rowen bowed her head, Will saw both fear and resolve in her eyes.

To Freya and to Finn she gave each a breastpin in the shape of the small white flower they had found growing by the pool on the bower island.

"The Bourne, Skald, and the Shee will have need of one another now more than ever," she said, fixing the pins to their cloaks. "Our stories are being woven together. We may meet again."

"The swords of the Errantry are at your service," Finn said solemnly, and bowed.

"And the hammers of Skald," Freya added.

"Do not forget your tales and songs, as well," the Lady said to them. "They will prove as needed as weapons in the great struggle that is upon us. We have a brief time now to breathe, and heal. But everywhere the enemy's forces are rising, like a dark tide across the storylands. If we hope not to be swept under, we must remember who we are."

The Lady turned to Shade and smiled.

"You have been a faithful friend of the Realm since the rivers first sang. We would be honored if you would join our Court and travel with us."

Shade lowered his shaggy head.

"I am the one who is honored, Lady of the Starlight," he said. "But I still have a promise to keep."

"I understand," the Lady said, and she turned to Will, and he knew that she saw the hope he had been trying to hide. "I know what you would ask of me, Will Lightfoot, but I am not the one who can open this door."

"If you can't do it," Will said, abashed, "who can?"

"You have been seeking the gateless gate," the Lady said. "That is where you will find the way."

"But it's gone now. The Angel closed it."

"He closed one gate, yes. There are many others. And one of them has never been far away."

"But how can I find it?" Will asked, and then he noticed that the Lady held a bright object in her hand. A small triangular piece of glass on a slender silver chain.

"When the city of Eleel fell," the Lady said, "the most pure mirror, Samaya, was shattered and taken. Now some of its fragments are back in our keeping. They have been cleansed of deception, and once more reflect only what is true."

The Lady handed Will the shard. He hesitated for a moment, then looked at his reflection. The face he saw was his own, as he was now, but his hair was longer and wilder than it had been when he first came to the Perilous Realm. His skin was darkly tanned, his mouth set and determined. This was the face of a Will Lightfoot who had seen a little more of the world, who had passed through dangers and beheld wonders. This was someone who had kept on the path he had chosen, a Will Lightfoot who had run far enough to see the way back.

"There is the gateless gate," the Lady said. "There it has always been."

Will slipped the chain around his neck and, bowing his head, thanked the Lady for her gift. He remembered the

talk he'd had with Pendrake before they set out from Fable,
how baffled and angry he'd been at the old man's advice
to set out without knowing where he was going. What had
Pendrake said? *Let the way find you.* He hadn't understood
then. He wasn't sure that he understood now, but on an
impulse he held the mirror shard out before him once more,
this time turning it away from his face.

In the shard he saw reflected the trees and the river and
the deepening blue of the sky, and they were not new or
strange. The mirror changed nothing. In disappointment
he turned the shard to his own face, and it was not there.
He was not in the mirror. He had vanished. But after a
moment this no longer frightened him. The mirror showed
the trees and the river and the sky as if to themselves, as they
were, without his hopes and fears showing him only what
he wished to see. This was the woven world itself. And he
was part of it; he always had been. Now he understood the
Lady's words. He was not lost. The way home was not out
there somewhere, waiting to be found. He had been on the
way all along. He was the way. He was the gateless gate.

"Keep the shard close to you," said the Lord of the Shee.
"The eyes of the Lady have looked into it, and it will ward
you from harm."

The Lady smiled at him, and with the Lord of the Shee she
took her farewell. Will and his friends watched as the Hidden
Folk began to move away slowly through the trees. As their
graceful forms melted into the shadows of evening, they
seemed to be taking the light with them. Through the curtain
of leaves, Will now saw that the faded, patched tents he had
glimpsed in daylight had become tall, splendid pavilions of
white and green, with fluttering banners at their crests.

He watched with the others until the light of the Hidden
Folk dimmed and the vision faded.

Will took a deep breath and looked away. He knew that other farewells were before him, and these would be much harder.

"It's getting dark," said Rowen. "You should stay with us for the night, and go in the morning."

"I think he's ready to go now, Rowen," Pendrake said. "Though none of us wishes it."

Will turned to the loremaster.

"I didn't trust you," he said. "I was wrong."

Pendrake waved a hand.

"I told you we would take this journey together, Will," he said. "We both had to learn to trust each other, and ourselves."

Will nodded and embraced the old man. Then he turned to Rowen. It was time to tell her what he knew.

"When the Angel took you," Will said to her, "he told me I wasn't the one he was really after. It was you. It was you all along. He was trying to find you, through me. He said you were the new thread in the weave."

"I know," Rowen said, and a shadow crossed her face. "He didn't say anything, but I knew. He . . . looked into me, with his master's eyes."

"If I hadn't come here, none of this would have happened. You'd still be safe at home."

"We have never been safe," said Pendrake "no matter how much I wanted to believe otherwise. I was even foolish enough not to see why the mirror shards were set so near Fable. By stumbling into the trap meant for Rowen, Will, you didn't cause all of this. The truth is you prevented disaster. You showed us the danger before it was too late, and bought us precious time. Now Rowen and I have much to speak of, and new paths to walk together."

"Look at it this way, Will," Rowen said, smiling. "You

didn't want this to be your story, and now you know it
isn't."

Will shook his head.

"It is," he said. "It still is." As he said the words he thought
of what the Lady had told him, and he knew that it was true.
This had become his story. His friends were still in danger,
and there would be a part for him to play, though he didn't
know what it would be.

With a lump in his throat, Will thanked everyone. Freya
stood at a distance with an unusually shy smile, until Will
went up to her and held out his hand. She took it solemnly,
then laughed and wrapped him in a tight embrace. To his
surprise, Finn handed him the small leather-bound book he
always carried. Will turned it in his hand. *The Book of Errantry*
was printed on the cover in gold lettering.

"You may find it useful someday," Finn said.

"Thank you," Will said, stunned. He put the book in his
pocket and shook Finn's hand.

"Will you be punished when you get back to Appleyard?"
he asked. "You were supposed to be back a long time ago."

"Finn will have my report to add to his own," said
Pendrake. "The Marshal will hear the tale of one who truly
upheld the oath of a knight-errant."

As Will turned to Rowen, she threw her arms around
him.

"Good-bye, Will," she whispered. "Don't forget us."

Will looked into Rowen's eyes.

"I couldn't forget you," he said to her. "I will come back.
I will find you."

At last, with a heavy heart, he turned to Shade.

"I'll walk with you, Will Lightfoot," the wolf said. "My
task is not quite done."

"I was hoping you'd say that."

They turned away then from their friends and from the shining river and walked on through the forest, their way lit by a sky full of stars. Soon they saw a clearing ahead, and when they came to its edge, they halted. Neither spoke for a long time.

"Is this the place?" Shade finally asked. Will looked around. He couldn't answer, and for now that was all right.

"I wish you could come with me, Shade," he said at last, his voice breaking. He struggled for words and then smiled ruefully. "Where I'm going, I'm in a lot of trouble."

"As much as you were here?"

Will laughed. "Not quite."

"I think you will be all right now, Will Lightfoot."

"What about you, Shade? Will you travel with the Hidden Folk?"

"Yes, for a while. But there must be others like me, somewhere. Other Speaking Creatures. I want to find them, if I can."

"There are no others like you," Will said, and he knelt and sank his arms into the wolf's warm fur one last time.

Reluctantly he rose and walked into the clearing. There was the cloven tree on the hill. And beyond it, through a screen of flickering leaves, red and blue lights pulsed in the gloom. The motorcycle would be there, he knew, as if he had left it just a few moments ago. Dad and Jess were not far away, and at that thought his heart lifted: he would soon see them. He looked back once at the dark forest. He thought he glimpsed Shade slipping away like a faint silver-gray gleam amid the shadows, but he couldn't be sure. Then he turned and set out gladly for home.